iN WOLF'S CLOTHiNG

A MYSTERY NOVEL

ANNE PAOLUCCI

Copyright © 2004 by Anne Paolucci

Library of Congress Cataloging-in-Publication Data

Paolucci, Anne
    In wolf's clothing : a mystery novel / by Anne Paolucci.
        p. cm.
    ISBN 1-932107-07-X (alk. paper)
        1. Police–Ontario–Ottawa–Fiction. 2. Trappers–Crimes
against–Fiction. 3. Taxidermists–Crimes against–Fiction.
4. Antique dealers–Crimes against–Fiction. 5. Endangered
species–Fiction. 6. New York (N.Y.)–Fiction. 7. Ottawa
(Ont.)–Fiction. I. Title.

PS3566.A595159 2003
813'.54—dc22

                                                2003058388

Published for
THE BAGEHOT COUNCIL
by

GRIFFON HOUSE PUBLICATIONS
P. O. Box 468
SMYRNA DELAWARE 19977

griffonhse@aol.com

CONTENTS

AUTHOR'S PREFACE

One evening, about two and a half years ago, I came upon a PBS program featuring a tour of the Canadian Museum of Nature, in Ottawa. The program was already in progress; Dr. Darlene Balkwill, Chief Collections Manager of the museum, was taking viewers through the "Wet Room," where hundreds of containers held specimens of all kinds and sizes, preserved in alcohol. I remember thinking: what if one day a tour group were to find a dead body in one of those containers!

The idea intrigued the writer in me. I had started a murder mystery but soon discovered that what I had already written would not serve the new idea that was nagging at me. I scrapped what I had (it became a short story) and started again, only to realize that the body in the "Wet Room" also had to be abandoned, since an altogether different kind of plot was emerging.

Trying to give shape to it was an Oedipal exercise in discovery: two steps forward, one step back, never quite sure what I would stumble into next.

The museum in Ottawa remained central to the story and is the focus of Part One; the American Museum of Natural History in New York is visited briefly in Part Two. I have been to the second any number of times, but I've never visited the first. What this meant was that I often ended up creating my own descriptions of layout and routines connected with the Canadian Museum of Nature. I even presented it with a full-time taxidermist.

My mix of fiction and reality also included placing in Ottawa the annual Modern Language Association Convention (held right after Christmas), where, to my knowledge, those meetings have never been held.

I hope my readers, especially my Canadian friends and my academic colleagues, will not judge me too harshly for having taken such liberties.

Many thanks to my excellent researcher, Azar Attura, for her expert and ready assistance at all times. I am especially grateful for the information provided by staff members of the Canadian Museum of Nature and by others tapped along the way for answers to my many questions. I am indebted to my dentist and good friend, Dr. Francis Cincotta, who followed the progress of the novel with special interest and first mentioned palladium to me. I owe much also to friends and colleagues who nudged me into finishing this book. They gave me the spur I often needed.

ANNE PAOLUCCI
New York, January 2004

Thy *daemon* (that's thy spirit which keeps thee) is noble, courageous, high, unmatchable.
Antony and Cleopatra, 11, 3

. . . that little voice inside, which tells us what not to do. . . .

PART ONE

(OTTAWA)

Not Quite the Beginning
(December 23, 3 PM)

The trapper sat near the fire and rubbed his hands. He unzipped his anorak and watched with narrowed eyes as the man across from him handed him a large envelope full of bills, then took up his heavy wool coat from the back of his chair and started to put it on. He was a tall man, well-dressed, elegant, out of place in this rough cabin. He settled a plaid scarf inside his coat collar.

The trapper coughed. "About the money —" He hesitated, looked down at the envelope in his hands. The man stopped buttoning his coat and waited. The trapper stood up and, still clasping the envelope, rested both hands on the back of his chair.

"What about it? It's all there. Count it if you like." He waited. When the other did not answer, he said: "What, then?" The voice was still pleasant, but the man's eyes glinted like the sharp steel edge of a knife.

"What about the other one? Is he coming back or will I be dealing with you, from now on?"

"He said you wanted to discuss something. I came for that."

"You're the boss?"

"We're partners."

The trapper met the other's cool stare, but only briefly. Something in the man's eyes made him blink nervously. He looked down at the chair seat in front of him.

"Should have been the museum's, this one," he said, straightening up and crossing his arms over his chest. He avoided the other's eyes. "Everybody knows they've been on the lookout for a fresh specimen. And this one's a beauty. By all rights they should have gotten it." When he looked up he met a glacial stare.

"I thought you were a free agent."

"I am." The trapper stroked his chin and walked to

3

the fireplace, where he stood for a moment gazing into the flames. The other did not speak. The trapper turned where he stood, letting the heat warm up his back. "I've got to be extra careful. If someone finds out I'm giving this kind of specimen to an outsider, I may as well pack up and leave."

"You can learn to be extra careful for what we're paying you."

"My reputation is at stake."

The man stared at him, a curious expression on his face. His eyes were frozen points of ice. "Is that right?" The moment passed; the face took on its usual look. "Most of your business is still with the museum. . . . Nothing has changed, has it?" When the trapper didn't answer, the man dismissed the argument with a casual wave. "You told us right at the start that all of you are free to sell to the highest bidder, whoever gives you the best price. That's always been the case. You don't work only for the museum."

"There's an understanding. . . ."

"There always was. You told my partner all about it when you first accepted our offer. Has anything happened since then for you to bring it up now?" the man asked again. Undisguised irritation gave the words a harsh timbre. "Do you want to pull out? Is that what you want?"

The trapper held up his hand. "No, no."

"You admitted, the museum doesn't pay the kind of money we do." The man sat down again. His face grew ruddy from the fire, but the heavy coat remained buttoned up. The trapper seemed to be struggling within himself. There was a doggedness about him, but also an uncertainty, a suggestion of unpleasantness mingled with fear. "What is it, then?" asked the other.

"There's been some talk out there —"

"What about? That you're doing business with me? You can handle that." The man stood up slowly, a tight smile clipping his words when he spoke again. "You feel you should get more, is that it?" He picked up his beaver

4

hat from the table and put it on. It added three inches to his already tall frame. The trapper was momentarily distracted. It was the most unusual fur hat he had ever seen.

"I'm taking big risks here," he said, watching the man's hands, as he pulled on his fur-lined wool gloves.

There was no hesitation now. The man was clearly impatient to be gone. The meeting was over. "I'll see what I can do," he said, his voice even and pleasant again. He opened the door and walked out, not looking back.

The trapper watched him climb into a Grand Cherokee van. A gust of wind swirled into the small room. Quickly he moved forward to shut the door. He stood listening as the motor started. He could hear the van move down the narrow path that led to the dirt road that fed into the highway.

Alone, the trapper took a slow deep breath, then muttering to himself went to a low cupboard and took out a metal container. It had held English biscuits at one time. This he carried to the table where, still standing, he added the bills he had just received to others folded neatly and stacked almost to the top. He didn't stop to count the bills; he'd done that often enough and knew exactly how much was there. With some of the other money stashed away, he could trade in his old Jeep for a Grand Cherokee van, although a Wrangler would do nicely. The trapper smiled. It would be his Christmas present to himself. Maybe he'd get a new hunting rifle too.

Laughing at some hidden joke, he closed the tin and carried it back to the cupboard. From a nearby shelf he took down a bottle of Scotch and poured himself a generous amount. He took off his anorak, pulled his chair closer to the fire, and rested his feet on a nearby stool. He sipped his drink with evident appreciation.

Slowly he began to relax. He took out of his shirt pocket a business card and chuckled as he studied it.

"Oh, I know who you are, Wise Guy, and what you

5

and your partner come up here for! Figured it out when this other one" — here he held up the card for some invisible audience — "came around. No, . . . don't mess around with me, Mister!" He seemed to enjoy the sound of his voice, steady now that he was alone. He toasted some invisible hero with a large sweep of the glass. "I know how to get what I want!"

Outside the wind had picked up. In the distance an animal howled. Slowly the trapper relaxed. He gazed into the fire for a while. When his glass was almost empty, he settled himself deeper in his chair and closed his eyes. Before long, he was fast asleep.

He might not have allowed himself to relax, certainly would not have indulged in name-calling or said what he'd said had he been able to see the face of the man as he stopped the van at the end of the long dirt road, now slick with ice, and stared thoughtfully into the heavy air, his hands clenched on the steering wheel. The purring of the motor was very loud.

It had started to snow heavily. Soon the man came out of his reverie. He continued down the road, driving with deliberate care, his attention focused on some inner vision as well as on the slippery road. After a while he turned on to the highway, toward the city, picking up speed as he leaned into the steering wheel, his head thrust forward, his mouth pressed together in a grimace, as though holding back some dark secret.

CHAPTER 1
CONVENTION CHECK-IN AT THE ELGIN
(December 26, 12:45 PM)

Even before she boarded the plane for Ottawa, Jill Masterson had strong misgivings about the trip. Her mind was elsewhere. She had brooded all through the waiting at Kennedy, right down to this moment, as she stood on line to register at the Elgin. It would have been easy enough to cancel her reservations; but this year's Modern Language Association conference was especially good; her own paper, "Animal Imagery in Shakespeare's Later Tragedies," had been given a special one-hour slot, instead of the usual fifteen-minutes for panel presentations. It was scheduled for late the next morning, prime time! She couldn't have asked for more. No, she would have been foolish to cancel the trip! But why this feeling of failure? No, not failure exactly, more like depression. Depression without a focus. Like *Rebel Without a Cause*. (Was it Jimmy Dean who had starred in that film and later committed suicide, or was she thinking of the sausage king?)

C'mon lady, snap out of it!

The trouble, she forced herself to admit, as she stood on the long line, waiting to check in, the trouble was Kevin Masterson. Kevin who had not returned her calls since they had separated last summer. Kevin who had made no effort to see her before she left, even though it was Christmas, a time for reconciliation, a drink at least. Kevin, suddenly remote, unpredictable, a stranger. How else could she interpret his behavior? He had turned into someone she didn't know.

"Damn it!" She realized she had spoken out loud. The man in front of her shifted and glanced back in surprise, a hesitant smile on his lips. Jill forced a smile in return and shook her head.

7

"Sorry. I just realized I left something back home that I should have taken with me."

"As long as it's not your paper!"

"How did you know I was reading a paper?"

"Who else comes to these things?"

He had distracted her at least. "Pretty grim picture of our lofty profession. Aren't we supposed to be educating the next generation, providing role models?"

"*Supposed* is the key word. Besides, the next generation can't afford these trips. What we're really doing, coming here, is talking to each other, another kind of captive audience." She stared at him, unnerved for a moment. He went on: "Don't you like to hear yourself talk? I do." He lowered his voice as though imparting an important secret. "Truth is, for me it's an excellent excuse to get away for a few days, read a short paper, meet colleagues from other places. It also gives me time to do some work, between meetings, sometimes even *during* meetings —"

Jill burst out laughing. "You may have lost *this* captive audience, Dr. . . . . .?"

"Sorry. Jack Glasner. Georgetown University. I'm into Italian Renaissance."

"Jill Masterson, New York University. English. Mostly Shakespeare." The line had moved up a little. "At this rate, you can start a new book, right here while you wait!"

"I've been doing just that," he answered easily. "In my head. I like to write in my head first, then put it down on paper later on. It's a great way to fill in time, like now, for instance. It exercises the memory too. Aside from that, it really works. How do you work best?

"Lying down," she answered, flushing even as she uttered the words. Kevin used to laugh and tell her she was a good straight man. Glasner tilted his head to one side and grinned, as though she were a clever little girl who had just recited a difficult line. She pushed her long hair behind her ear in an embarrassed gesture. Impatient with herself, she went on: "Let's not get lost in a maze of double meanings. I meant, that just before falling asleep is a good time to review things, work out my next lecture, whatever."

"Does it work?"

"Over a period of time, yes. First, I read, not heavy stuff, mysteries mostly. When I start to drift off, I put the book down, close my eyes, and think about some piece I'm writing. Sometimes it lasts only five minutes. Sometimes I'm asleep before I even begin, but I don't lose anything. It's all there, waiting for me, next time around. By the time I get to the computer with it, even if it's weeks later, I find I've made considerable headway."

They were distracted by the appearance of two more clerks, who opened new registration lines. A number of people ahead of Glasner rushed over to them. Glasner and Jill stayed were they were; their line was now reduced by ten or eleven.

"At last!" Jill exclaimed, relieved that things would move faster now. "Always the same story. The hotels all know by now that for MLA this is peak check-in time, meetings officially start tomorrow morning before eight, so why don't they plan ahead, get more clerks to register the hordes?" She shook her head in frustration. "If I were re-writing *The Divine Comedy*, I'd have a very special torture, way down in lower hell, for the inefficient."

"What kind of torture do you have in mind?"

"Haven't decided yet. Maybe have them starve to death while waiting for a table at The Four Seasons."

"But they're dead already."

"Let's not push a dumb analogy to its precarious edge."

It was his turn to register. As he stood there, talking with the clerk, taking out his credit card, signing the form, replacing his card in his wallet, she had time to look

9

him over. He wasn't very tall, about her height, muscular, a careless dresser, almost to the point of sloppy, a lined face, as though he spent a good deal of time outdoors. His eyes were an unusual shade of light gray that for some reason made her think of albinos, except for his deeply tanned face and his unruly mop of brown hair streaked with gray. Not exactly what most people would call a handsome man. Interesting-looking, maybe.

Having completed his registration, he stepped aside but didn't walk away. When Jill was done, she turned from the desk, putting away her glasses as she did so. Glasner was still standing there, reading the conference program.

"A whole hour for your paper?" He opened his eyes wide in mock surprise.

"If you sit in the back, you can think up a new chapter for your book."

"Not after I've let the cat out of the bag. How can I sit there, making believe I'm listening to you, when I'm dreaming up my next chapter?"

"How about if I promise not to look your way?" Then, wondering if he might have gotten a wrong signal, she added, with a large wave of her hand: "Believe me, you have better things to do than come to hear me. It's just another paper."

"I didn't say I'd come." He had been leafing through the program book. Now he looked up and gave her a big smile. "But yes, I think I will." They started to move rather aimlessly down the wide concourse. Jill saw several colleagues she knew but didn't stop to greet them. Glasner was studying the brochures inside the folders they each had received. "Look, a special tour just for us."

"Oh?"

"At the Canadian Museum of Nature."

"Don't know it."

"This one specializes in animals of the area.

10

Wolves, North American Short-Faced Bears?" He looked up. "What do you supposed a short-faced bear looks like?" "Short-faced anything else?"

Glasner ignored her and went on reading: "The Woolly Mammoth — that's with two *l*s — The American Mastodon, the Giant Beaver, the Great Auk — ah, that's extinct. Let's see, what else? Sharks, lions," he looked up with raised eyebrows, "dinosaurs?"

"Why not? There are reproductions of dinosaurs in every museum of natural history. It helps argue the case for evolution."

"Really." It was an ironic comment, not a question.

"It makes us humble."

"Some more than others." At the end of the long hotel lobby, they stopped. Glasner went on reading, "Crustaceans, insects of the sea, flying reptiles, dragons, spiders, butterflies and moths. Carnivorous plants, the environment, . . . feathers?" He looked up but Jill simply shrugged. "Okay. Do you know how many distinct groups of Athapaskan Indians there are? Ha! You *don't* know! Let me enlighten you. Kutchin, Han, Tutchone, Inland Tlingit, Kaska, and Tagish. All in the Yukon, the land of the midnight sun. They see the sun for all of three months. During that time, it circles around, never sets. I'd like to see *that*, if it weren't so hard to get to. Here's something else you don't know: Furs are not the largest industry of the Yukon. It's mining. Then comes tourism, then forestry. The fur trade is only three percent of the economy, and it's mostly in the hands of the Aborigines. Let's see, there's some fishing in Dawson City —"

"Dawson City?" Jill peered over his shoulder. "Where does it say that?"

He pointed. "Right here." She consulted her own brochure. "Interested?"

"Not in fishing. Dawson City was a busy place during the gold rush. Also the home of Robert Service. Do

11

you know his 'Rhymes of a Rolling Stone,' any of his ballads?"

"Ah, the poet of the Yukon." He laughed. "You like his work?"

"Is that a crime? I don't understand why people think it's a big joke. He was a damn good poet in his own way!"

"Whoa! What have I said?"

"Shakespeare would have loved his ballads!"

"I'm sure he would have. I like some of them myself. He's not my favorite, but that's okay, isn't it?"

She shook her head, wondering what had gotten into her. "I've had to listen to snotty remarks about his poetry so often, I guess I go on the defensive when anyone criticizes him. Aren't you at least interested that he lived in Dawson City?"

"Should I be?"

"I'd like to visit the place."

"You don't want to go there," he said.

"But I do. I just don't know if I can swing it."

"It's all the way over on the other side, in Western Canada. You don't want to go that far out of your way. And not to the Yukon, this time of year. Why don't we take this tour instead?" He studied the small map on the back of the brochure he'd been reading. "The place isn't very far. We can see everything that's important about the Yukon right here, in the —" he flipped back to the brochure cover "— "The Canadian Museum of Nature. Are you game?"

"Not that kind." When he puckered his lips and frowned, she burst out laughing. "Sorry, I'm very good at bad puns. But yes, I'm game."

"We can buy tickets right at the desk there." They strolled over.

"How many have signed up for this tour?" Glasner asked the Concierge, showing him the brochure.

The man shuffled through some papers. "Nine, so

12

far. There's a bus will pick you up right outside;" he pointed to the entrance, "at five this afternoon."

"Is it far?" Jill asked.

"With the bus, only a few minutes."

They paid for their tickets and moved away.

"Have you had any lunch? I haven't eaten since seven this morning."

Jill looked at her watch. It was after two. "I'd like to unpack and settle in . . . ."

"There's plenty of time."

They found a quick service luncheonette and sat down with coffee and the last of the ready-to-go, saran-wrapped sandwiches. They ate in silence for a while, then Glasner asked:

"What do you read, besides Shakespeare and Robert Service?"

"Dylan Thomas, Ann Taylor, Indian short stories written in English, some Australian authors."

He put down his sandwich and studied her face as he chewed. "What do you like about Indian short stories?"

"The cultural flavoring, the economy of language, a kind of immediacy in getting to the point, not really a point but a view of things. Have you ever read anything by Rao? I think I like him best, refreshingly simple. Clean straightforward story line. Down to earth."

Glasner sipped some coffee. "For down to earth, I like Boccaccio."

"I didn't mean it that way."

"What's the difference?" She sat back as he picked up his sandwich again. He caught her staring at him. "Did I say something I shouldn't have?"

"I'm not sure. Anyway, for your kind of earthy, I like Chaucer even more."

"Do your Indian writers match Chaucer or Boccaccio?"

"Are you always so dogmatic?"

13

He raised his eyebrows in mock surprise. "Me, dogmatic? I've been called a lot of things but not dogmatic. Is it life-threatening?"

She laughed in spite of herself. "Only if your kids are taller than you."

"My eleven-year-old thinks I'm sloppy because I don't wear Armani clothes like my ex-wife's boyfriend does."

"How tall is he?"

He stopped chewing. "The boyfriend?"

"Your son."

"Oh. He's five nine and still growing. He'll be twelve in June." Jill burst out laughing. "What's so funny?"

"Watch out. Pretty soon, he'll be taller than you."

Wiping his mouth, he regarded her as she drank her coffee. "Do you have kids?"

"Soon I won't even be married."

"It's an epidemic, divorce. Nobody really seems to want it, but there it is."

"You didn't want it?"

"No. My wife did. I was boring, she said. Actually what she said was, researching old texts was a waste of time and those who wrote about those texts turned into bores. Am I boring you, Dr. Masterson?"

"Not yet."

"That's a relief. Maybe there's still some hope for me. What about you?"

"I'm told I'm irritating. That could be boring, too."

He laughed. "I mean, did you want a divorce?"

Jill found herself saying: "He's a lawyer, my soon-to-be ex, very successful. . . . No, I didn't want a divorce, but I couldn't resign myself to his preferences . . . disco dancing, high-priced entertainment, that sort of thing."

"And what is it you like to do?"

"Go to poetry readings at Barnes and Nobles. Play piano violin sonatas, go down to the Village to see my

14

friends put on their plays, you know, the kind of plays that never get to Broadway. Kevin won't bat an eye at paying over a hundred bucks for a musical. I can't stand them. All that sound and fury. I like music, but I like words even more, the power in words."

He gave her a long look. "You're full of surprises, Dr. Masterson." For the next few minutes he concentrated on finishing his sandwich. As he wiped his hands on a paper napkin, he asked: "Have you been to Ottawa before?"

"Once, several years ago, for a conference on Isabella Crawford."

"Are you a feminist?" he asked bluntly.

"I don't like labels, but I'll join the shouting for a good reason —"

A strand of hair had come loose. She pushed it back behind her ear. A very attractive woman, Glasner allowed himself to observe. Just about his height, with good bones and a figure that was not likely to blow up after a certain age. She dressed well too, spent money on clothes, one could tell, but they were simple, low-key. Certainly didn't draw attention to herself, except possibly in her academic performance, where, he suspected, she didn't mind hamming it up, showing off her best qualities. Well, why not? Didn't everyone aspire to hold the attention of the public, whoever the public?

"— trouble is, no one wants to take the initiative," she was saying. The perverse satisfaction of a crusader made her face glow. She may not be a feminist, thought Glasner, but she sure as hell can get fired up about it!

"Women themselves are often too lazy or too eager for public attention to work toward realistic results," she went on. "Most feminists simply repeat their ideological agenda, indulge in generalities for the most part. The reality is different. You've got to build on a strong, solid base, not just yell and shout. The media love it, but it doesn't help, after a certain point." Her upraised hand warded off any comments, as she continued.

"So what, if until recently all the textbooks were written by men, if until now only men wrote about women? Is a feminist writing about history more to be trusted than a man? The intellect has no gender I hope! On the other hand, what's wrong with wanting to stay home and raise kids? All the arguments about a woman not realizing herself unless she gets a nine to five job — pardon me, but that's a lot of crappola. She's more of a slave than if she stayed home." Sitting back in the small, upholstered armchair, breathless, suddenly deflated, she seemed dazed, disoriented.

"I should have taken notes!"

"Sorry. I didn't mean to lash out like that."

"Hey, I have no quarrel with anything you've said."

"All I meant was, women shouldn't be distracted from the real issues, they shouldn't support factional intellectualism. You think clearly or you don't. . . . We've built insurmountable walls —"

"*Factional intellectualism,*" he repeated, frowning in mock concentration. He pronounced the phrase in italics, as though the title of a book. He looked back at her and smiled. "I like that."

"Sorry. I didn't mean to rant and rave."

"Well, you get my rave review for ranting!" The mood lightened as they both laughed. To hide an unsettling sensation that was building up in her and brought, she could feel it, a flush to her neck and face, she opened her bulky convention program book and leafed through it.

"You're listed here in American literature and history." She looked up. "I thought you said you were in Renaissance."

"My regular courses focus on Jefferson, Franklin, Adams, the early presidency. But I've grown more and more interested in Renaissance authors. Managed to include a few in a history course last year. They definitely relate."

"On what grid?"

"Excuse me?"

She waved the question aside and asked instead, "What Renaissance authors do you like to read?"

"Machiavelli, Spenser, Thomas Cromwell, Thomas More, Bodin, Boccaccio . . . . Do you know how Ben Franklin learned Italian? He used to play chess with a friend, and they both decided that whoever lost a game had to learn a canto of *The Divine Comedy* by heart and recite it the next time they met. Do you play chess?"

Jill couldn't help laughing. "No, but I know Dante. My mom was Italian and very well-read. One summer, I was about eight or nine, she decided she'd read portions of the *Commedia* to me. One hour every single afternoon. With *explication de texte*, mind you. She was good." For a few seconds her eyes stared out at some far-off private place.

"You must know the *Commedia* by heart!"

Jill rolled her eyes to the ceiling. "Mom wasn't a sadist! I was only eight! No, she just wanted me to hear the language, the power of words. I wish I *did* know it by heart!"

"There's always time."

"No, I'm afraid not."

"Don't tell me you're busier than Ben Franklin!"

"Let me ask *you* something. With all that reading in the Renaissance, you should be more into Shakespeare!"

"That's not a question, but in the bard's own words, 'That's true too.' And please don't ask me what play it's from. I can't remember."

"Easy out."

"Okay, I'll tell you why. Too many Shakespearians out there already. Besides it would take too long to catch up with experts like you."

"There's always time."

"*Touché.*"

The lobby was very crowded now, the registration lines much longer. Jill wondered if she had done the right

17

thing choosing the largest of the hotels recommended. On the surface, it was a plus, especially in this weather, since all the English meetings were scheduled in the Elgin; but in some ways, one of the smaller hotels, would have been better. Here, waiting to be seated for meals, even a simple breakfast, could mean long lines. And if people waited for the rush to be over, there was hardly any food left. All she and Glasner could get at the quick service counter at two o'clock was a cellophane-wrapped soggy egg sandwich. And if the weather grew worse and people didn't venture out, waiting for anything would be an ordeal.

"Machiavelli fascinates me most," Glasner's voice broke through. "*The Prince* is an extraordinary book, everybody should read it. It gives you insights already there inside you but buried under a lot of self-righteous rationalizing, have you noticed?" It wasn't really a question and he went right on.

"For instance, the difference between power and authority. All you have to do is read *Richard II*, an incredible Greek tragedy by the way, but I don't have to tell you that. Here's a king in place, doesn't know who to trust or what to do" — he waved off any comment — "and here's a shrewd, capable man, who we know will make a better king, given the chance. My point is, Bolingbroke has the power and backing, the practical know-how, but he doesn't have the blessing of authority, which is crucial if you want to keep your constituency." He took a quick gulp of coffee.

"The dilemma is," he went on in a rush, "Richard is a lousy king but damn interesting as a person, should have been a poet. Bolingbroke is the efficient interloper who wins but will always be suspect, as he himself knows and admits." A sheepish grin betrayed his casual air. He seemed to be waiting for approval of some kind. Jill had finished eating as he talked. Now she wiped her mouth and hands and gave him an enigmatic smile.

"I suppose you'll be lecturing next on Thomas

18

Cromwell and how good a Machiavellian *he* was!"

"Ah, I see I have my work cut out for me!" he said, making a show of accepting the challenge, then abruptly screwed up his face, as though someone had taken away his favorite toy. "Poor, Cromwell!"

"Scoundrel, is more like it!"

He turned his eyes upward in mock supplication, then back to her. "Really, I love Thomas More like the rest of man and womankind — anyone who has seen *Man for All Seasons* can never do less than love him. . . ."

"Sarcasm is cheap. More was a great man."

"But," he held up a finger to demand attention, "Cromwell succeeded where More failed. Sure, he did all the Machiavellian things everybody talks about, but in the only way they can be excused, if that's the proper word to use. *Justified*. Anyway, in his case, he wanted to make England independent and prosperous."

"By destroying the monasteries?"

He grimaced in disapproval. "God, how many times have I heard that! Yes, he destroyed the monasteries to free England from the influence of the Pope. He succeeded in divorcing the English monarchy from Rome."

"And that was good?"

"I can't answer in absolute terms. But even More would have understood political expediency. He wasn't all God and rosary beads. He was a statesman. . . ."

"And would he have destroyed the most pious monasteries in England?"

To mask her growing irritation, Jill took the occasion to turn at the sound of a familiar voice. She saw standing nearby, chatting with two other people, a colleague from UCLA she had promised to look up. The man hadn't seen her, since his back was toward her. She was about to call out to him, ready to excuse herself from what was becoming, for her, an unpleasant argument. Instead, to her surprise, she found herself turning back to

Glasner.

"Poor Sir Thomas," he was saying, "his fate was sealed from the moment he refused to accept the Preamble. He found legal ways to accept the King's divorce, but he couldn't bring himself to accept the King's spiritual supremacy, taking over the Pope's job in England."

"You haven't answered my question."

He frowned over his coffee. "No, I'm sure he wouldn't have destroyed the monasteries. But I'm just as sure that he understood the need for doing so and Cromwell's strategy in the matter."

"You mean Cromwell's ambition? Let's not go overboard trying to whitewash a criminal!"

He stared at her, his mouth a tight line. Had she offended him? Well, what if she had? An argument was an argument. After a brief pause, he replied, softly:

"Why should I want to do that? More was a great lawyer, talked his way out of a lot of difficulties; but on this one point, he was trapped. Cromwell saw the direction things were going and acted accordingly." He leaned forward. "Who was it said the vectors of history are many; but there's only one resultant? Cromwell read the vectors more accurately than anyone else. It doesn't warrant the English and American prejudice against him."

Stubbornly, she persisted. "He left a bitter legacy."

"It's like saying the surgeon left you hurting after the operation. Maybe he did. But if the end is health, then what he did has to have a positive side."

"Ah yes, the end justifies the means!"

"Another misreading!" Leaning forward, as though to underline his next words, he said with deliberate emphasis on each word: "Only *one, one* end only *justifies the means.*"

"Health?" An ironic smiled lurked on her lips.

"Health, right. The health of the body politic." He peered at her through narrowed eyes. "Ah, I see you can't

20

be convinced in one session. There will have to be a series of treatments, starting with dinner right after the tour."

"I don't think so," she said, rising and picking up her things. "I really do have to unpack and sort things out. Will you excuse me?"

"Do I have a choice?" But as she started to move away, he rose and touched her arm lightly. "I hope I didn't offend you with my views on Cromwell. Mine may not be a popular view, but it *is* a legitimate reading of the historical text. . . . I'm not the only one who —"

"Fine," she interrupted sharply. "Since I'm not an expert in history, I can't really judge the merits of your reading. All I know is, I'm offended by people who do ugly things in the name of a higher good. I'm sure you're right about the facts, and I'll admit there's a consistency in your argument, but I'll never be able to see Cromwell as a martyr to the cause of English prosperity. . . . What's to like about politicians, then or now?"

"Not much. . . . See? We agree on a very important point." He smiled and held out his hand.

Why was she so angry at him? It was just one of those arguments people fall into at cocktail parties, or while lounging around in hotel lobbies, at conventions. . . .

She had to admit, he was pretty sharp. . . .

So, what had gotten into her? What was wrong with her?

Kevin, that's what! Not even a call to wish her a merry Christmas! Not even to thank her for having finally agreed to a divorce! She wondered, as she had many times in the last several months, whether he had found someone else, if that was the real reason for his wanting a divorce. He had made no effort at reconciliation. If he had truly loved her, if —

Her eyes burned. She fumbled with her bag and papers.

At her shift in mood, Glasner had dropped his

21

hand. She found her key card and held it up by way of goodbye.

"I'll see you later, then," he called out, as she started to walk away. She waved vaguely, without turning around.

In her room, she sat wearily on the side of the bed, wondering about her outburst, the hostility bottled up inside her.

Did others going through a divorce have these same feelings?

But I was rude, that's not like me. To a perfect stranger! Just because I didn't agree with him!

An odd sensation gripped her. Embarrassment? Frustration? She thought about turning in her ticket for the museum tour. She wasn't up to it, wasn't up to anything. Certainly not more of Glasner! At some other time, she might actually have enjoyed sparring with him, but right now she was hurting, and not just for herself.

Other recent events crowded in, leaving her breathless, tears in her eyes.

She had promised to call Jenny as soon as she got into Ottawa. . . .

Well, this wasn't the best time, she told herself. She wasn't up to it right now. . . .

Excuses, a little voice inside her scolded. *You know she's all alone in that big house, grieving. The least you could do is call, like you promised.* . . .

She groaned out loud and fell back on the bed, her hand over her eyes, as though to keep the gray world outside from filtering through the blinds and settle inside her, stifle her.

Divorce was one thing, painful enough; but to lose a husband, as Jenny had, less than a month ago, after just three years of marriage! All because of bad timing! A stupid accident. . . !

She sat up with a jolt and shook her head, as

22

though to clear it of the oppressive memories that crowded in on her these days, the terrible event that had left her oldest and dearest friend a widow, at twenty-nine. . . .

Having to witness the inexpressible pain in Jenny's eyes, hearing her own inadequate words of comfort, had exhausted her emotional reserves at the time. Even now, remembering, was like a physical blow. . . .

With an effort, she forced her thoughts away from Jenny and back to Glasner. His little lecture on Cromwell had left her unsettled. Not that his arguments, however logical, could ever move her; but her reaction had been unnecessarily sharp, offensive even.

Well, she could easily avoid him, turn in her ticket for the museum tour. And even if she ran into him in the next few days, a nod or just "hello" would be enough. So, why was she so concerned about the impression she might have made?

She felt as though she had failed some kind of test but, strangely enough, looked forward to taking it again.

CHAPTER 2

UNUSUAL EXHIBITS AT THE
CANADIAN MUSEUM OF NATURE
(December 26, 4:30 PM)

It was dark when John Jenene unlocked his office, entered almost surreptitiously, and quickly eased the door shut behind him. The place, he knew was empty — the museum had been closed to the public all day, and the few staff people who had come in to catch up on work, were long gone. Nonetheless, he went to the window and shut the blinds tight. At his desk, he turned on a small light, loosened his coat, but did not sit down. At one point, he got up and peered out through the vertical blinds into the deserted parking lot. He had barely turned away when the sound of an approaching vehicle reached him. Quickly he looked out again through the drawn blinds.

A Grand Cherokee van had pulled up near the entrance. Jenene hurried down the corridor to open the heavy door. He watched a man get out of the van and start toward him. His footsteps crunched on the packed snow as he walked. When the man reached the door, Jenene opened it wide and motioned him inside. As he started to pull it shut, the newcomer put out his hand and kept the door ajar.

"Press the button so it doesn't lock," he said.

Before doing so, Jenene peered out toward the van. "Someone with you —?"

"Yes," said the other, walking inside. Jenene led the way to his office. Gold letters spelled out his name, and right under it, "Taxidermy."

"That's the second stranger in the last few weeks," said Jenene, leading the way inside. "You told me way back, at the beginning, this was between the two of us!"

"And my partner."

"And your partner. Is that who's out there?"

24

"Don't worry about him," said the other, unruffled. Jenene picked up a sheaf of papers from his desk and held them out to the visitor. "Everything's there." He watched anxiously as the other man scanned the sheets. "A pity the wolf has to be destroyed! This is an extraordinary specimen." "That's what we paid for." Unbuttoning his coat, he asked: "The job went well?" His intonation and the clipped careful wording were those of someone who had learned English as an adult.

"See for yourself," said Jenene, moving out into the hall. He unlocked the workroom and switched on the light. The man paused to turn off the light in the office and shut the door before crossing the hall to the workroom. The gold letters on the opaque glass panel on that door read "Taxidermy," and underneath "Authorized Personnel Only."

Jenene stood just inside the door, waiting. He stepped aside as the visitor entered the workroom. As he passed by Jenene, the man held out a thick envelope. Jenene took it, glanced inside at the stack of bills before tucking it inside his jacket.

Across from them, at the other end of the room, a white wolf looked out at the world from a low platform, his head half turned, as though listening for a sound, perhaps a sign of approaching danger. It was a beautiful specimen. Jenene couldn't hide the pride in his voice. "This one is really special. Two and a half feet high, from feet to shoulders, five feet long, a hundred and ten pounds when we got him." He paused to admire the specimen. "Beautiful fur, no teeth missing. You couldn't ask for a better one."

The other went up close, to examine the animal. Jenene stood watching as the man moved first to one side, then the opposite, then directly in front of the specimen to peer into the golden eyes, running his forefinger inside the open mouth, touching the teeth, the snout, finally stroking the animal's back right down to its bushy tail. He

25

straightened up and with both hands tried to lift the animal off the platform.

Jenene ran up close. "Careful! I've warned you about that! Don't ever try to lift a specimen by yourself. Even a small one. You could easily damage it. . . ." As the other straightened up, he added: "Pity he has to be destroyed. I don't think you realize what a prize Dobie brought us!"

The man was about to reply, when someone else entered the room. The second man was taller than his companion or Jenene. A heavy overcoat added to his already impressive size and an unusual beaver hat created a dramatic effect. He reminded Jenene of a young Orson Welles. Now, he too approached the wolf and, after examining it, nodded his satisfaction. To Jenene, the man's response lacked enthusiasm.

A woman's voice reached them from down the hall, then other voices, a man and a second woman. They were jabbering loudly, as though they knew they were alone in the building. Jenene ran to switch off the light. The tall man slowly closed the door. As they drew nearer, there was a burst of laughter. When they had passed the workroom, carrying on in some strange tongue, Jenene whispered: "Cleaning crew. Kaskas from the Yukon. They stick to themselves. We have quite a few working for us." The voices were fainter now, and seemed to have stopped somewhere near the entrance. Jenene watched as the second man, clearly annoyed, whispered something to his companion. The other gestured helplessly, then turned to Jenene and asked in a low hoarse whisper:

"What are they doing here? You said the place would be empty, that the museum would be closed today."

"As far as I know it's empty. But even if there's a clean-up crew in the building, they start at the top, not here. I've run into them once or twice, very late, when they're getting ready to go home. The small lounge at the end of the

26

hall is theirs."

The second man spoke for the first time. "How did they get in? You told us the doors are code-locked after hours. Only you and the Curator have access."

"And the guard up front. The guard let them in. They leave the same way, through the lobby."

"How long are they in the building?"

"About six hours. They come in around five and start with the top floor. They don't reach the basement until ten-thirty or so. This is their last stop."

"— What are they doing down here at five thirty. then?" asked the first man, impatiently. His companion gestured him aside. He spoke to Jenene as though there had been no interruption.

"What about this room?"

"No, they never come inside my workroom. It's off limits except to my staff. They don't enter labs, storage areas, workrooms. Too much expensive material in them, on-going work that no one but authorized personnel is allowed to touch."

The second man checked his watch. The dial glowed in the dark. "Why are they lingering down here?"

"I don't know. It's very unusual," said Jenene. He started for the door, as though to search for an answer. The second man put out a restraining hand. Jenene instinctively took a step back.

"Maybe we should come back later," said the first man, addressing his companion.

The other did not reply. His presence bothered Jenene. He didn't like surprises, . . . unless. . . . Had they changed their minds? Had the second man come to tell him that they were ready to consider his request for more money?"

In the dark, a tuft of white fur caught his eye. He bent down to pick it up, at the same time making a mental note to find out if the clean-up schedules had changed.

Before he could straighten up something was forced against his mouth and nose. He did not feel the hands easing his limp body on to the floor.

"We'll take him out first, then the wolf, as soon as the coast is clear," said the second man. "Here, give me a hand," he added. Together they dragged Jenene toward the door. The second man put up his hand, a warning to the other not to move. In a moment he was outside and down the corridor. When he returned, a few moments later, he spoke quickly, keeping his voice down to a whisper. Everything about him indicated he was in charge.

"They're nibbling on potato chips. The door is wide open. We can't possibly get past them, carrying anything, without being seen."

"We can't wait here!"

The second man glanced around in the dark, turning this way and that. "You heard what he said. The workroom is off limits." He poked Jenene with his boot, seemed satisfied when there was no response. "But no, we don't wait here; *he* does, ... Just to be on the safe side, let's put him out of sight, right there, behind those cartons. Pick up his feet, I'll take his arms." When they had positioned the body, as best they could, in the narrow space against the wall, the second man took a set of keys from Jenene's pocket. "I better check his office. You never know what he might have left lying around." The other watched him from a crack in the door, stepped aside as his companion came back into the workroom, after having locked the office door. They both stood listening for a few seconds; then the second man started to lead the way out into the corridor. At the door he paused, retraced his steps.

"Forgot something," he said, as he went back to where they had dragged Jenene. For a few seconds he was out of view, crouched down behind the cartons. When he emerged, he was putting the thick envelope into his pocket. "Best not to leave this lying around."

His companion frowned in the dark, nervous about the unexpected changes in their routine. "What about the wolf?"

"What about it? Who's going to look in here? Even if someone does, Jenene is safely back there and the wolf is just another specimen ready for display. Don't worry so much. We'll all be out of here in no time."

They stood in the dark, silently, for a few more minutes. A radio suddenly came on, the volume quickly lowered. The second man edged his way out the door. "Wait here while I take another look." When he returned, he was shaking his head. "They're chattering away, as if they had all night."

"We can't keep him here too long!"

"We'll wait in the van."

"How do we get past them?"

"Follow me and do what I do. Don't lock this door. Don't talk. Move when I give you the signal."

The laughter and voices of the three people added to the festive mood produced by the music coming from their portable radio. The second man motioned the other to follow him and to shut the door. They moved stealthily down the corridor, inching their way toward the brightly lit lounge. The second man flattened himself against the side of the lounge door and, as a spurt of laughter filled the air, glanced in at the two women and the man sitting at a small square table. A glass coffee maker on a shelf nearby was perking. The aroma of freshly-brewed coffee was strong.

The second man held up his hand, signaling the other to wait. With the next burst of laughter, he moved quickly, at a crouch, across the lighted doorway. At the next burst, he signaled the other to bend low and cross over, as he had done. In the room, the man and the two women continued jabbering in some strange language.

Leading the way, the second man paused at the entrance. Very gently he pushed open the door, just enough for him to step through. He held it that way until his companion had done the same, then, after checking the lock to make sure it would not click into place, he eased the door shut.

Bending against the wind, the two men ran to the van.

"Think they heard us?"

"Not with all that jabbering and the radio going." They climbed in. "Close the door gently, just let it catch. I'll turn on the heater for a little while."

There was no sound now, except the wind that was building up. It had begun to snow again. It looked as though they were in for a full-fledged blizzard.

"How long do you think we'll have to wait out here?"

"As long as it takes," said the tall man, as he pulled his beaver hat down close around his ears and adjusted his plaid scarf more tightly inside the collar of his heavy wool coat.

Jill purposely delayed going down to the lobby until almost five-thirty, hoping the bus had left without her. What had made her agree to go on this museum tour, anyway! And if she really didn't want to go, why didn't she just walk over to the Concierge and turn in her ticket?

But the tour bus was there. So was Glasner. Did she really think he might have changed his mind? He was standing near the revolving door, talking to a porter. When he spotted her, he hurried over.

"Slight delay. They had to find another driver at the last minute. The one who was scheduled to take us, had an emergency at home. Everything squared away?" She nodded, not trusting herself to answer immediately. Glasner went on, as though sensing her discomfort and trying to ease the tension: "I made some calls, looked over the place. I would have gone for a long walk, even got myself a map of the city," he held up a brochure that had been refolded to show the map, "but decided there wasn't enough time. Besides, it's *cold* out there! What I don't understand is why MLA holds meetings this time of year in Canada instead of Puerto Rico, or Bermuda. I love Ottawa, but in the dead of winter?"

"There aren't many cities that can take a large group like ours," she offered, hoping the conversation would dry up quickly.

"They could have it in the summer, or late in the spring."

"It wouldn't work. Academics scoot off right after final Spring semester grades are in. They go half-way across the world for research or just plain fun, or settle back in their yards to relax with their barbecues, outings with the kids, the beach, small house repairs, forget everything until after Labor Day. It makes sense."

The driver had arrived and people began to board the bus. Before she could hurry inside and find a seat next to someone else, Glasner had found two places together and now waited for her to join him.

"Five forty–five. Not too bad. The concierge called ahead to say we'd be a bit late."

Eventually everyone was accounted for, and the bus took off. The streets were treacherous; even with a thick layer of fresh sand over the ice, the going was slow. As they drove up the road leading to where the driver had been instructed to park, a Grand Cherokee van started toward them, gaining speed as it approached. The driver in the van made no effort to slow down; instead, he hogged the road, causing the bus to skid, swerve into a mound of snow, and come to a stop.

"Did you see that?" exclaimed the bus driver, turning to his passengers. "If I hadn't moved, he would have hit my front fender!" They continued slowly to the entrance.

As they parked, the heavy metal door was opened

and a woman peered out. She motioned the driver to move in closer to the entrance. When the bus finally came to a stop, one of the convention organizers got out and stumbled across the short distance to speak with the woman. After a few seconds, from where she stood, she waved the group inside. When she was sure no one else was coming, the museum official shut the door. She clasped her hands and smiled.

"Welcome to the Canadian Museum of Nature. My name is Frances Enderby, Head Curator. Normally, we close at five, but today is Boxing Day, a holiday in Canada, as you probably know. The museum has been closed to the public all day. I thought this would be a perfect time for our tour. The whole place is ours," she went on lightly, opening her arms wide. "And since I was here earlier, catching up on some paper work, I thought I'd stay on to take you through the museum myself."

There were murmurs of appreciation as she led the way to a small lounge, just inside the entrance. "I understand you had a slight delay. It shouldn't make much difference. The tour takes a little over an hour. You'll have plenty of time for dinner and whatever plans you have for later in the evening." She waved them inside the room, where three people in denim work clothes sat sipping coffee. She said something to them in a strange language. They nodded. "A skeleton crew today. They usually work their way down from the top floor, but I didn't want them in the way as we move upstairs, so today they'll start down here, keeping well behind us." She pointed to a large clothes rack. "There are plenty of hangers for your coats. Leave anything you like, it will be perfectly safe here." When coats, hats, and totes had been discarded, they all reassembled in the corridor.

"Follow me, please," Miss Enderby said. She walked a few steps further down the wide corridor and stopped in front of an opaque glass door. At first, the lock seemed to give her some trouble, but on the second try the door opened easily enough.

"I thought," she began again, as she pushed the door wide and switched on the light, "we'd start with the taxidermy work area." She stood to one side as the visitors entered. "Dr. Jenene, the museum taxidermist, is not here, but as you'll see he and his staff are kept pretty busy."

Jill drew in her breath at the sight before her. There were more than a dozen animals, some ready for displays, others in various stages of repair. Shelves covering most of the walls held labeled boxes, tools, small casts, a variety of materials. Near the back wall, on one side, were several plastic molds, replicas of animal skeletons. But what dominated the room and attracted all eyes was the animal standing on a low platform at the far end, opposite the door. The body stood firmly on its feet, not quite at rest, the head turned to one side and lifted as though trying to identify a sound, perhaps listening for reassurance that all was well. Frozen in a kind of uncertainty, as though it had caught a whiff of potential danger, it was captured beautifully, at the moment of tension that announces action. It looked out over the room, at the intruders. One of the men in the group moved forward.

"Is that an arctic wolf?" he asked, pointing. As her eyes came to rest on the white wolf, Miss Enderby's hand fluttered to her throat, then moved to her mouth, as though to stifle her cry of surprise. Inadvertently she took a small step backwards. Sensing something was wrong, Glasner, quickly moved around from behind, to face her. What he saw was amazement and incomprehension. The woman could not take her eyes off the animal on the platform.

"Are you all right?" he asked, touching her arm gently.

"Oh, yes, it's definitely an arctic wolf," said Miss Enderby, moving slowly forward. The others made way for her. She paused before reaching the platform, her initial reactions giving way to a puzzled look. All eyes were watching her. "Is everything all right?" Glasner persisted.

With a little nervous laugh, Miss Enderby waved off his concern. "I must confess, I was caught off guard. I had no idea we had a new arctic wolf." She waved them closer. When they were clustered around her, she went on: "A fine specimen. A young adult. The fur is full and undamaged." She leaned forward to examine it more closely. "Please," she said, pulling back quickly, "I must ask you not to touch it. If you have questions, ask away." No one spoke for a few seconds. It was Glasner who broke the silence.

"You seemed shocked to see it. Is there something special or unusual about the animal?"

"Well, yes. They're hard to come by." After a slight pause, she went on. "They live, as the name tells you, in the arctic regions, the coldest places in the world. Very few people have actually seen an arctic wolf because getting close to them is almost impossible. We humans can't take those temperatures. So what we do is, we estimate the number of wolves by the number of animals they prey on. The experts have concluded that there are about 200 on Queen Elizabeth Island, about five times that many on Banks and Victoria Islands, just over 2,000 on Baffin Island and 75 in Greenland."

"You're saying they're an endangered species?"

"Not endangered, no," Miss Enderby said, shaking her head. "But we'll never have a complete count; it's just too hard a job." Slowly, she walked around the platform, examining the animal with exaggerated care, frowning all the while. The others watched her with undisguised curiosity.

"Something wrong with it?" someone asked.

"No. It's perfect. An absolutely superb specimen." A small nervous smile fluttered around her lips. The frown persisted, however, as she pointed out other specimens and answered questions. When everyone was outside in the corridor again, she turned to reenter the room.

"Sorry, forgot my notes."

"She did a double-take when she saw that white wolf," someone whispered.

"The usual bureaucratic red tape," someone else commented.

They waited patiently as the Curator disappeared behind a stack of boxes. The notes were on a trestle table in front of some cartons stacked near the wall. As she started to move away, one of the cards fluttered to the floor. She bent to pick it up. It had come to rest just beyond her reach and she was stretching her arm to get it, resting her other arm on the cartons next to her. The effort caused her to lose her balance momentarily and she stumbled into a crouch to avoid falling. There she remained. Her gasp was inaudible. Curious about the delay, two of the men moved tentatively back into the room. Miss Enderby was sitting on the floor, staring at the narrow space between the cartons and the wall. Her face was ashen.

The body of a man was propped up awkwardly against the wall, his legs twisted under him in the constricted space, his chin touching his chest. When someone raised his head, dead eyes stared out.

Miss Enderby looked around helplessly. Glasner knelt beside the man and felt for a pulse. He rose quickly and placed himself in front of Miss Enderby, obstructing her view of the body. "Who is it?" he asked.

"Our taxidermist, John Jenene," she whispered." Voices rose in a medley of confusion.

"What's happened?"

"Who did she say it was?"

"We need an ambulance!"

"Is he really dead?"

Glasner motioned Jill to his side. "Get everyone

outside," he told her "Don't touch anything." He helped Miss Enderby to her feet and led her into the corridor.

"Is there a phone down the hall, where we left our coats?" She nodded.

Hearing the commotion, the cleaning crew had come out to see what was happening. As Miss Enderby approached, they began to ask questions in a language Glasner could not make out. Miss Enderby spoke to them briefly, even as Glasner led her into the small lounge and insisted she sit down.

"Tell them to stay right where they are until the police come." He was about to dial the operator when she took the receiver from him.

"I'll do that."

By the time she hung up the phone, Miss Enderby had recovered enough to quiet the cleaning crew, who were jabbering excitedly. Whatever their language, she seemed to be at home in it. In the corridor again, she spoke to the small group that clustered around her.

"The police are on their way. I'm sure they won't keep us long.

"Was he. . . ?" Someone asked Glasner.

"Dead, yes. Strangled."

As though catching him in some error, Miss Enderby said: "That's really for the Medical Examiner to say." Some color had returned to her cheeks but her legs were not quite steady as she moved toward the entrance. She opened the heavy door a few inches and looked out into the falling snow, as she had earlier. The wind forced her back inside.

Keeping close to one another, the group had followed and now formed a small circle around her, near the heavy door. When she spoke again, her voice was normal and her face had regained some color.

"I'm sure they'll let me get some food together for you from our cafeteria. . . . You may want to cancel appointments, but we'd better wait until the police arrive."

A short time later, they heard car doors closing. A gust of wind blew snow down the wide corridor as several men, carrying an assortment of cases, came through the door Miss Enderby held open for them. The last one to enter shut the door firmly behind him.

Inspector Luke McCalley was a big man with a full head of rust-colored curls. He unbuttoned his heavy wool coat, nodding occasionally, as Miss Enderby told him what had happened. His boots were high and thick, already covered with fresh snow. He listened, without interrupting, his head bent to her level as Miss Enderby reviewed the movements of the little group. When she was finished, he straightened up, lifted his head and turned first to look behind him, where they had entered, then pointed to the workroom, where light streamed out into the hall.

"Is that where you found him?" Miss Enderby nodded. He waved his people in that direction.

As the others moved away, McCalley studied the expectant faces around him. With an authoritative air that brought a measure of reassurance to the people clustered around him, he introduced himself and nodded toward the young man in uniform, who stood beside him.

"This is Sergeant William Kenney, my assistant. Bill will be taking down your statements in a little while. If later, back at the hotel, or at any time, you remember anything else, please call me or the Sergeant. I'll make sure you have the numbers where you can reach me." With scarcely a pause, he went on: "I'm sure Miss Enderby will make you comfortable while you wait." He turned to the Curator. "Some food, coffee, tea?" Miss Enderby nodded. "Please be patient," he added. "I won't keep you any longer than I have to." The group headed for elevators. "Oh, Miss Enderby," the Inspector caught up with her, "would you mind coming back down here as soon as you can?"

He watched them disappear into the elevators

before returning to the workroom. There the photographer had finished taking pictures of the body and Dr. Springer, the medical examiner, was just beginning his examination. Two men were dusting for fingerprints. Two others were bagging items and labeling them, while two uniformed policemen looked on, waiting for other instructions. McCalley pulled on a pair of rubber gloves and walked around the room examining articles, the animals, the molds, making comments along the way, which Sergeant Kenney, at his side, duly noted. When Miss Enderby appeared in the doorway, McCalley and Kenney joined her in the corridor. The Inspector pointed across the way.

"Is that Dr. Jenene's office?"

"Yes."

He gestured toward the lounge. "Do they speak English?"

"Just a few words. They're Kaskas. I can translate for them, if you like, when you're ready."

"Thank you, yes. . . . I hope to get everyone through this quickly, with as little fuss as possible." Pointing to the rubber gloves he still was wearing, he took the key from her, unlocked the door, and switched on the light. "Everyone all right upstairs?"

"I opened up our conference room, next to my office. It's quite comfortable. Right now, they're in the cafeteria. I told them to take anything they wanted from the freezer and bring trays upstairs. There's a microwave in the small pantry inside the conference room. I've already plugged in the urn for hot water. I also stopped in the lobby to alert the guard, there's only one today, Frank Stanton. I told him what happened and that you very likely would want to talk with him."

"Yes, later. Thank you." He nodded approval as he pulled on a fresh pair of rubber gloves and went through the desk drawers, ledgers, books, and closet.

"This whole area will have to be cordoned off for a

while," he said.

"For how long?"

"Can't tell, at this point."

"What exactly are you looking for?"

"Hard to say." He grinned suddenly. "Some of my colleagues insist it gets easier, as we go along."

She couldn't help a small smile. "You don't think so?"

"Until that last piece of the puzzle drops into place, you can't really be sure of anything."

She watched, not without a measure of curiosity, as he and Sergeant Kenney moved through the room, The two men worked in silence, quickly and efficiently, careful with the things they picked up to examine. It didn't take long. Straightening up and pulling off the rubber gloves, McCalley turned to Miss Enderby.

"I'll need to see his personnel file. . . . And Bill, be sure you get his home address."

"He has no immediate family," Miss Enderby volunteered.

"He lives alone?"

"Yes."

"My men will be going over these rooms in the morning. Now let's hear what the Kaskas have to tell us."

They walked briskly toward the lighted lounge at the end of the hall.

The clean-up crew were nursing their coffee. Kenney pulled up extra chairs.

The Inspector's questions were simple, the answers predictable and straightforward. They had clocked in, as usual, the cards in the cloak room up front would show, just before five, and had come directly down to the basement, where they had followed orders relayed to them by the guard upstairs, to wait in the lounge until the tour bus arrived and the group had moved out of that area. For this one time, they were told, the usual routine was reversed. They were to start in the basement and work their way up. They had been waiting in the lounge since five o'clock. The tour arrived just before six. No, they had seen nothing, heard nothing. No, they hadn't seen Dr. Jenene at any time. Everything was dark when they came through the hall, earlier. . . .

The interview was soon over. McCalley dismissed them with the usual request that they get in touch with him if they remembered anything else. Miss Enderby knew where to find him. When they had left, McCalley turned to the woman:

"Before we go on, Miss Enderby, I'd like you to tell me again, slowly, and as accurately as you can remember, what happened, from the time you came down into the basement."

"Around five minutes after five, I received a call from the hotel Concierge," the woman began. "He told me the tour would be late getting started since the driver had an emergency at home and they were waiting for a replacement. I asked him to call me when they were about to set out. He did so, around five forty-five. Usually it's an easy walk from the Elgin to the museum, a short ride by car; but I knew in this weather it would take them a bit longer, so I didn't come down until close to six. I looked outside when I got down here, then, when I heard the bus approaching, I opened the door again and let them in."

"You didn't hear or see anything out of the ordinary?"

"Nothing. There was no one around."

"Are you sure?"

"Well, the Kaskas, of course, were in here."

"And Dr. Jenene was in the workroom. . . . "

She looked confused for a moment. "Yes, of course. Dr. Jenene was still in the building. . . . He must have been here all day, in fact. I ran into him early this morning, coming in, but I thought he'd left around one, with

40

the others. . . ." Her voice trailed off. "Yes. . . . He must have stayed on. . . . But . . . there was a van parked outside." She seemed puzzled at her own words, as she gestured toward the door at the end of the wide corridor.

McCalley picked up the hesitation in her voice. "You mean the jeep that's parked out front?"

"No. that belongs to the Kaskas. This was a closed van. It was parked just about where the bus pulled in, where your people just parked. Only . . . when I looked out, the second time, it was gone."

"You saw it, close to six, when you first looked out?"

"Yes. But, Inspector, Dr. Jenene drives a car and the van wasn't one of ours."

"Whose was it, then?" Miss Enderby shook her head. McCalley went on: "Perhaps it belonged to one of the trappers?'

"I have no idea." Ms. Enderby frowned, as though struggling with a puzzle of her own "Inspector, it wasn't there."

"Yes, you said it was gone when the tour bus arrived."

"I mean, Dr. Jenene's car. It should be parked somewhere, shouldn't it?"

"Isn't it?"

"When I looked out my window just before coming down to meet the group, there was my car of course, the guard's SUV and the Kaskas' jeep. We all have to check in through the lobby," she added by way of explanation. "Of course, I never gave a thought to Dr. Jenene's' car, until now. I thought he'd left with the others."

A pregnant silence followed as they considered the implications of what she had just said. McCalley glanced at his Sergeant, who all the while was busy writing. He waited until Kenney looked up from his notes, then turned back to the woman.

"Could he have planned to drive home with someone else?" When she shook her head and did not answer, he went on: "Can you describe the van?"

"It was black, I think, or dark gray. One of the bigger ones. A Grand Cherokee, I think."

"Didn't you wonder what it might be doing there?"

"I didn't have any reason to think hard about it. I must have assumed it was for a delivery or a pick-up."

"Would there have been deliveries or pick-ups today?"

"Well, no. . . . I don't think so."

"An unscheduled pick-up, maybe?" Miss Enderby pressed her hand against her forehead. McCalley couldn't quite make out the expression on her face. "You're sure it was not a museum vehicle?"

"I'm sure about that, yes."

"Was anyone inside the van?"

Her words came out hesitantly. "No, but then —?"

"But then?" McCalley shifted in his chair. He didn't want the woman jumping to conclusions, but he had to find out as much as possible, as soon as possible, as many facts as possible while they were still fresh in her mind.

"But then, who drove it away?"

It was the same question that had surfaced in McCalley's mind. Without turning his head, McCalley told his assistant. "Bill, check out Dr. Jenene's car, when you get a chance." To the woman, he said: "Would the guard remember seeing Dr. Jenene drive in this morning?"

"Yes, I'm sure he would. We all have to check in through the lobby. Stanton is there now. He's working a double shift today, has been here since eight this morning."

"What make car does Dr. Jenene drive?"

"A small compact. Maroon, I think. We can check ID parking records."

"Thank you. And what about security down here? These doors?" He waved toward the entrance they had used.

"We've never had a guard stationed here. We have a code-alarm system that is activated as soon as the museum closes. Today, it's been on all day; yesterday, as well. Anyone still inside the building after the codes are in effect, like the few of us who came in this morning to catch up on work, have to alert the guard, who deactivates them long enough to allow whoever is still inside to leave."

"In other words, the guard on duty closes up when the museum clears, and whoever is on duty through the night, opens up in the morning."

"Yes."

"So today, all doors were locked?"

"And all day yesterday. Of course, a few staff members came in today, briefly, myself included, to catch up on work. Stanton would know who was here. We all have to sign in and out on days like today, or after normal hours."

"And the guard has to let you out. . . ."

"That's right."

"Does anyone else have access to the codes?"

"I do, of course. And Dr. Jenene had access."

"Oh?"

"Yes, about three years ago he came to me, said it would make pickup and delivery easier for everyone involved."

"So, he has the codes at all times."

"Yes. It's an excellent system. We test the alarms once a month."

"You said the codes go into effect right after the museum closes?"

"Yes."

"And Dr. Jenene was aware of the routine."

"Yes, of course. Everyone working here knows."

"Can you get me a list of staff who came in today?"

Miss Enderby nodded. "Besides myself and Dr.

43

Jenene, no more than five or six. But they were all gone by one thirty, I understand."

"Except for Dr. Jenene. . . .

"I was sure he had left, too."

McCalley tried a fresh track. "From what you've told me, Miss Enderby, especially about the van, it appears that Dr. Jenene had visitors today. Do you have any idea who they might have been?"

"Not the slightest. Have you checked his log?"

"No, not yet. . . . Was he expecting a delivery, perhaps?" The corners of Miss Enderby's lips twitched as she fixed her gaze at a spot near the ceiling. McCalley wondered if his words had registered. "You see, if Dr. Jenene drove in to work in his car, and we will assume at this point that he did, then the van belonged to someone else; and since you tell me it wasn't a museum vehicle, it had to belong to a visitor. That means someone else was in the building at some point, in addition to Dr. Jenene, yourself, the Kaskas, and the guard. And whoever came in that van may have come to see Dr. Jenene."

She turned to him slowly. "I'm sorry. What were you asking?"

McCalley decided to work his way back to it later. Instead of repeating his question, he asked instead:

"Do you usually take tour groups through the museum?"

"No. This was an exception. The MLA convention organizer had written to me last Spring to ask if we could offer a tour for some of their early arrivals. The convention officially opens today, but mostly for business meetings, I understand. Papers, panels, the regular activities aren't scheduled to begin until tomorrow. Today was a good time for all of us. And since I was coming in to do some work, I decided to stay on and give the tour myself."

"Did you speak to Dr Jenene at all when you saw him this morning?"

"No, I just caught a glimpse of him."

"And you didn't see him again until. . . ." He gestured vaguely.

"In there. . . ."

"Where was he going when you saw him this morning?"

"Down to his office, I imagine."

McCalley shifted in his seat. He leaned forward, his hands clasped between his knees. "When you opened and shut the outside door, that first time, Miss Enderby, when you first looked outside, had you deactivated the code yourself?"

Miss Enderby's face took on a strange expression, her hand fluttered at her throat. "I didn't know what was bothering me at the time," she said, "I must have noticed, but it didn't register because right after that the bus *did* arrive and I was busy getting everybody inside."

"What did you notice?"

"That the doors were not even locked. And the codes obviously had already been deactivated. . . ."

"Could the guard have done it?"

"Not without instructions from me. But, Inspector, even the button that locks the door automatically had been pressed in. . . . "

"Can you get in from the outside with a key, if the button is not pressed in and the door locks automatically?"

"Yes."

"And Security has that key?"

"Yes. So do I."

"And Dr. Jenene?"

"And Dr, Jenene, yes."

"And when a delivery or a pick-up is expected, the codes are turned off and that little button on the side is usually pressed in to keep the doors from locking automatically, is that it?"

"Yes. In fact, on those occasions the doors are

often kept wide open to facilitate movement in and out."

"And so long as the doors are unlocked, security codes are not in effect, is that correct?"

"That's right."

"But the codes should have been in effect when you went into the basement, you tell me. The doors should have been locked. Are you sure you didn't deactivate the codes for the tour group?"

"I did just that, Inspector, when I first went down. At least, I thought I did. But instead of opening the doors, I seem to have locked them. I had to try again."

"Ah! Go back a minute, please. . . . You're saying you didn't actually find the doors open. You're *assuming* they had been opened —?"

"Well, yes. They had to have been! What other explanation could there be? I didn't realize it at the time, but I had actually code-locked the doors on the first try and deactivated the codes the second time. . . . In any case, as I already explained, the little button also had been pressed in. The doors were definitely unlocked."

"Could Dr. Jenene have lifted the codes to let his visitors in? An unscheduled delivery, perhaps? Of course, we know he didn't get a chance to close them again. Might that explain why you found the doors unlocked?" McCalley watched the woman struggling with her own conclusions. He said nothing as she rose from her chair and stood beside it uncertainly. A troubled expression crossed her face. After a few moments, she said:

"Inspector, are you suggesting Dr. Jenene might have . . . ." Instead of finishing the sentence, Miss Enderby slowly walked out into the corridor, and stared down the hall in the direction of the workroom. McCalley and Sergeant Kenney quickly followed her.

"A strange thing, Inspector," she went on; "I had trouble unlocking the workroom as well — just a key needed for that — until I realized it was already unlocked."

46

She turned to him. "I didn't have a chance to brood about it, just made a mental note to mention it to Dr. Jenene."

"But the door would have had to be unlocked, since Dr. Jenene was still in there," McCalley reminded her. He waited as Miss Enderby's confusion turned into a hard frown, then prodded gently, "What happened then?"

"We all entered the room, and there, on the platform —" she seemed to be struggling for words, "— was an arctic wolf." The two men waited, Kenney with his pen poised. "I didn't even know we had one, Inspector! I sign for all major expenses — supplies, equipment, requisitions, payment for trappers, releases of one kind or another —"

"Are you telling me that specimen on the platform, the white wolf, is all ready for display, but you know nothing about it? That no papers for it had crossed your desk? You signed nothing? Is that what you're telling me?"

"Yes! That's exactly what I'm telling you!" she burst out, starting toward the workroom with a determined stride. McCalley overtook her, forcing her to a stop.

"An arctic wolf is an *event*, Inspector! They are not easy to find. And we've been trying to get a new specimen for at least three years." Her face was flushed, the words tumbled out of her, an urgent whisper. McCalley realized she was angry, but not with him.

"You think Dr. Jenene was planning to take the specimen elsewhere? Or someone else was picking it up? Is that why you think the van was waiting outside, the codes deactivated, the doors unlocked?"

"Do you have a better answer?"

"I have no answer at all, at this point. Dr. Jenene might have told us, perhaps, but he's dead." In the silence that followed, McCalley stepped inside the workroom, where several of his men were working the crime scene. Miss Enderby had moved closer to the door but stopped when Kenney warned: "We can't go in there."

Dr. Springer, the Medical Examiner, came forward

to meet McCalley. "We're ready to move him," he said, talking off his gloves. "Want another look?"

"No," said McCalley. "What's your guess?" They both stepped aside as Jenene's body was placed in a plastic bag.

"Chloroformed, then strangled."

"Chloroformed, then strangled?"

"Seems that way."

"When will you have the report for me?"

"A day or two." As Springer closed his bag and prepared to leave, he held up his hand, as if to ward off any comment: "I know, I know, you want it yesterday. If you're lucky, you'll get it tomorrow sometime."

When he was gone, and the body had been taken away, McCalley gave further instructions to his men, turning back to add: "Secure the area around the wolf separately. I don't want anyone near it or touching it. Might turn out to be evidence."

Then, with Miss Enderby and Sergeant Kenney hurrying to keep pace behind him, McCalley strode toward the elevators.

It didn't take long to finish cordoning off the entire area. The younger officer, a new recruit assigned to stand guard outside the door of Dr. Jenene's office, now relaxed in his chair, tilting it back against the wall. The other, a thirty-year veteran of the Ottawa Police had been assigned the same duty outside the door of the workroom.

"My first murder," said the new recruit. It sounded like a boast.

"Thank God it didn't happen yesterday. My son and his family flew in from Montreal to have late Christmas dinner with us. Just around this time."

"Do you think we'll still be here New Year's Eve?"

The other shrugged. "Look at the plus side, Tommy. Overtime. . . . A rest for the feet. Nice and cozy

48

indoor duty for a couple of days at least, maybe more."

The younger man smiled. "Hey Ben, you think we'll get on the telly?"

CHAPTER 3
McCalley's Noodle Doodles
(December 26, 7:25 PM)

"This will do nicely," said McCalley, as he put his briefcase down on the Curator's desk. When Miss Enderby excused herself to check on the tour members next door, McCalley went with her. The aroma of hot food wafted out into the corridor as they approached, and McCalley was reminded that his own dinner had been interrupted to answer the call from the museum. Inside the room, most of the people were already eating and drinking. Two women were in the small pantry, heating frozen food packets. A large urn had been plugged in next to a microwave oven.

McCalley picked up some sandwiches for himself and Sergeant Kenney, but, before returning to Miss Enderby's office, he explained to the assembled group that he would be seeing each of them individually for statements and thanked them for their patience. The two men were just finishing eating, when Miss. Enderby returned. She carried a small tray with three steaming containers of coffee and some sugar and cream.

"I'm glad you picked up something to eat. I thought you might like coffee, but if you prefer tea, it won't take a minute —"

"Coffee is fine," McCalley interrupted. "Thank you for thinking of it."

As he sipped the steaming liquid, standing at the window behind Miss Enderby's desk, McCalley could see two vehicles parked below. The Kaskas had already left in their jeep.

"I think you said earlier your car is down there, the Volkswagon?" he asked, as he turned from the window and sat at the desk — a thick slab of northern maple, mirror smooth. It had been cleared of all papers.

"Yes. The other is Stanton's SUV. So, we were right about Jenene's car being taken away."

"We don't know that for certain," McCalley quickly corrected.

"Well, it's not parked anywhere out there."

"It could be parked somewhere else," McCalley explained patiently. "Or he might have driven off during the day, left the car elsewhere, and come back in the van. Alone or with someone else. Until we know more, we shouldn't jump to conclusions."

Miss Enderby waited until McCalley put down his empty cup, then said: "I hope this won't take too long, Inspector. I have to call home, shift schedules and activities for tomorrow, especially if you want to interview my staff."

"I'll do my best," McCalley replied with a smile. By now, it was clear, Miss Enderby had recovered from her double shock of the unexpected presence of a fully processed arctic wolf in the workroom and the discovery of Dr. Jenene's body. Earlier tensions had given way to efficient purpose. In the confusion of their first few exchanges, just after he arrived on the scene, McCalley had not had time to observe her closely. Now, as she spoke in her soft, modulated voice, he realized that the fair-haired woman sitting opposite him was not only very efficient but also quite attractive. In spite of the straight navy skirt, plain white shirtblouse, navy cardigan, and the absence of any jewelry — perhaps a deliberate effort to keep the gender issue in the background and exert her authority as unobtrusively as possible — her perfectly proportioned face and the subtle curve of her neck rising from the open shirt collar drew his appreciative attention. In a different setting, dressed in more flowing lines and softer fabrics, and with some make-up, she could easily turn eyes in her direction. What struck McCalley most, however, was her quiet confidence. Suspicions surfacing about Dr. Jenene's activities had hit her hard, and she was still struggling with them, would be for some time, but there was strength in her voice, assurance in her manner.

"I know we've been through it twice," he began, his hands clasped on the desk," but I'd appreciate your telling me one more time exactly what happened. Let's start from the time you peered outside to the time you discovered Dr. Jenene's body. Take your time."

"Forgive me, Inspector," she began instead, "I couldn't help hearing back there. Dr. Jenene was chloroformed, *then* killed?"

McCalley hesitated. He knew the dangers of giving out information, even to colleagues; how rumors spread and often compromised a case. But the woman had obviously overheard his brief exchange with the Medical Examiner. He chose his words carefully.

"Until Dr. Springer gets back to me officially, I'm not at liberty to say. There are bound to be all sorts of rumors. . . . All I can tell you is that Dr. Jenene was found dead under suspicious circumstances. I'm surprised Dr. Springer said as much as he did. Usually, he won't give me the slightest satisfaction until he's ready with the official report. 'I can't scratch your itch,' is one of his favorite phrases." Miss Enderby nodded, remembering how she had cautioned the tour group herself, about jumping to conclusions.

Kenney, who had been enjoying this exchange, couldn't help admiring, once again, his superior's seemingly casual manner. As he was fond of repeating to his friends and colleagues, the Inspector had a way of making people "feel easy," giving them his whole attention, and leaving them with the impression that he had shared with them what he knew and was counting on their help. He allowed a certain range, let people explain things their way, caught the pauses, the unexpected and extraneous bits of information, and always found his way back to them, even without the help of Kenney's notes. "Never rush things," he had told Kenney, more than once. "It's like digging for precious stones. A lot of rough ore has to be mined. And you never know what else you're going to find, in the process."

McCalley listened closely as Miss Enderby once again described the events that had taken place, shifting his eyes occasionally to watch Kenney taking it all down. Two years earlier, when McCalley was looking for an assistant, Kenney had been one of the four names submitted to him. After reviewing all the credentials, McCalley had chosen Kenney, in part because, in spite of his short record, the young man had made excellent strides, but in particular (and much more important in McCalley's view) because Kenney was the only one who had gone out of his way to learn shorthand. In time, McCalley also discovered that the young officer had a gift for sifting through details quickly and zeroing in on what was essential. These special talents, coupled with an almost photographic memory, soon earned Kenney the kind of reputation even much older colleagues still yearned for. McCalley had never regretted his choice.

When Miss Enderby had finished her account, McCalley asked:

"You had no idea, then, that Dr. Jenene was in the building all day today?"

"None. Of course, he often stays, often stayed on after hours."

"Even on a holiday?"

She shook her head and spread out her hands in a helpless gesture. "I can't answer that. All I know is, he was here this morning. I assumed, because of the weather, that he had left early."

"How many staff people came in today?"

"I'm not sure. Five or six. The log should tell us."

"Could you call security? Ask the guard to check it out?"

As Miss Enderby spoke into the phone, McCalley

53

continued drawing in his small pad, where he had almost filled a page with curving lines and interwoven curlicues. He paused and looked up when Miss Enderby put down the receiver. Her hand continued to rest on the instrument for a few seconds, as she frowned at some point behind the Inspector's head. McCalley waited until her eyes came to focus again on him.

"There were five of us in the building. I was the only one still here, after one thirty. Except for Stanton."

"And Dr. Jenene. . . ."

"Yes. No. The log shows he checked out around one-fifteen, Inspector."

"Perhaps he went to lunch? Came back later?"

Miss Enderby did not reply at once. When she spoke, it was more in answer to some question of her own.

"The guard saw him leave. We all have to go through the lobby, past the guard, who deactivates the codes to allow the doors to open. Except for me, the place was clear by one-thirty. Dr. Jenene never checked back in."

"I see. And you would have left the same way, only much later."

"Yes. I told the guard I would handle the doors in the basement myself, when the tour arrived."

"Well, we know that Dr. Jenene came back into the building at some point, since he was found here."

"But his car is gone. . . ."

McCalley moved quickly into another track. "Can you tell me how many people got off the tour bus?"

She gave him a questioning look. "They're all next door, I'm sure you counted heads at some point. Eleven. There were eleven. And they're still all here."

McCalley smiled and went on easily, ignoring the edge in her voice. "And they all entered the building?"

"Of course. I was eager to close the door because the wind was picking up and it was quite cold. I wouldn't have done that if anyone was still out there."

"What about the driver." It was more a statement than a question. For a moment Miss Enderby looked puzzled, then replied:

"Naturally, he came in with the rest. Went right into the lounge, when he heard the cleaning crew talking. Apparently he's from the same area, speaks their language." She paused a moment, then went on: "I certainly would not have allowed anyone to be left out there —"

"You would have noticed, then, if the driver had remained in the bus."

"But I told you, he came inside with the others."

"Was he number eleven or number twelve?" There was an embarrassed pause. Sergeant Kenney glanced up from his notes. He knew McCalley had counted heads, even as Kenney had jotted down the number. Without glancing up, the Inspector turned the page in his pad and started doodling.

"Number twelve."

"Thank you. Did you think anyone else might still be in the building around five forty-five?"

Not without a trace of annoyance, Miss Enderby replied: "I've told you a number of times, Inspector. I thought I was the only one left. It was a quiet day. I had brought a sandwich and a thermos of coffee and ate lunch in my office. I was there, working, until I went downstairs to wait for the bus. I didn't see or hear anyone else." McCalley put down his pencil and looked up. As though on cue, remembering their earlier exchange and anticipating his question, she went on: "Well, we know, don't we, that Dr. Jenene was still here, also."

"Do you happen to know what he and his staff were working on?"

Miss Enderby traced a large arc in the air. "Any number of things. Dr. Franklin and the rest of his staff can fill you in. If you like, I can pull out copies of minutes of our recent executive meetings, where projects are introduced, reports are given on work in progress, budgets are discussed. But I can tell you right now, there's nothing in there about an arctic wolf."

A small silence followed. The mention of the wolf had brought an expression to the woman's face that McCalley could not quite identify or name. It reminded him of the transformation he'd witnessed on his daughter Patricia's face, on seeing the graduation present he and Susan had gotten for her. She was seventeen, just entering college. That was three years ago, but he still could call up the moment vividly, her flushed cheeks, the surprise and joy in her eyes, as she stood in the open doorway and stared at the new blue convertible, something for which he and his wife had had to economize for over five years.

The moment passed. Miss Enderby leaned forward and said: "We have an executive meeting once a month, Inspector. Each department head reports on what is going on, carries information back to staff, exchanges ideas with other heads. We keep abreast of things that way. The arrival of a new arctic wolf would have been big news even before such a meeting. Word would have gotten around. I might even have opened a bottle of champagne."

"But Dr. Jenene had nothing to report?"

"Not about an arctic wolf, no."

"Perhaps he wanted to surprise you."

She shook her head violently. "Impossible! That's not the way it works! Surprise, indeed! The surprise was finding the animal processed, ready for exhibit. . . . No, no, Inspector, things could not have gotten to that point without my knowing. There are forms to sign, to approve, quite a bit of paper work is involved."

"And nothing of that kind crossed your desk."

"No, nothing."

McCalley drew an elaborate curled loop on his pad. "I'd like to meet with Dr. Jenene's staff tomorrow morning. Will you arrange that for me?"

56

"Yes, of course."

They both rose. "You've been very helpful. I'm sorry for the inconvenience."

"I'm glad to have been of some help."

"Sergeant Kenney and I should be here around eight, tomorrow. Would you have time to give us a quick tour? Oh, and . . . I'll need a map of the museum, if possible."

When she was gone, McCalley stretched his arms and bent over to touch his toes, something he did a few times every day, a concession to his wife's prodding. Grudgingly he gave her credit for nagging him to exercise more, a moderate amount of course, no sense overdoing it at his age. After that, he tore from his pad several sheets of paper, all filled with lines and curlicues, threw them into the wastepaper basket, and sat down again.

"Who would you like to see next, Sir?" Kenney asked.

"Let's get the guard up here. But before that" — he grinned and held up his now empty cup — "let's try for another coffee, and a sandwich too, if there are any left."

It was after eleven, by the time the tour group was ready to return to the hotel. The questioning had gone smoothly enough, and the statements were brief in almost every case and predictably consistent. Stanton, the Security guard had had little to offer, since he had returned to the lobby after making his rounds at four o'clock and was still there when Miss Enderby had called him from the basement. There had been nothing to report at that time. No, there were no lights on in any of the basement rooms. Yes, he was absolutely sure. He would certainly have noticed if any lights were still on, especially in the workroom.

McCalley had taken the opportunity to ask about the code-lock system. It was as Miss Enderby had described

57

it: the code-lock system worked most effectively; the museum had never had any problem with it. The security company that had installed it came every few months to check it out.

It had taken a while for Kenney to transfer the depositions to the word processor Miss Enderby had made available to him, after McCalley had accepted her suggestion that the statements be witnessed and signed before anyone left the building that night. It would save them all a trip to headquarters the following day.

Kenney had produced the printouts with amazing speed. Jill Masterson, the last one to be interviewed, had been pleasantly surprised at the efficiency with which the process was completed. Now, as she rose to leave, she complimented Kenney for preparing the documents so quickly. The Sergeant blushed and looked down at his shoes. McCalley spoke for him:

"Bill is among the best we have, Miss —" he glanced at some papers in his hand "— Sorry. *Doctor* Masterson."

"I don't suppose you'll solve this before I leave?" she asked, as McCalley placed papers inside his briefcase.

"When are you leaving?" he asked.

"I've booked for a flight on the thirtieth. I may have to reschedule, if the weather gets worse. I don't want to be stranded here or at Kennedy." And when McCalley broke out in a smile, she added: "What have I said?"

"A murder investigation rarely is solved in three or four days, even with a signed confession," McCalley said as she took out a woolen ski cap from her bag and put it on.

"Well, good luck. . . . I'm sorry I didn't get a chance to tour the museum, but at least I can say I was in Ottawa. I had a friend back in New York," she went on easily, as McCalley accompanied her to the door, "an import-export agent who occasionally did business with museums. He'd been to Canada, to Ottawa, any number of times. . . .I remember his telling me I should visit Ottawa. He liked it very much. Of course, this time of year —"

McCalley had opened the door but now positioned himself just outside the threshold, virtually obstructing passage. "Excuse me a moment," he interrupted, nodding to Kenney, who, after a few words from the Inspector, walked briskly toward the conference room. McCalley turned back to Jill Masterson.

"I wonder, Dr. Masterson, could you give me just a few more minutes of your time?" He gestured her to the chair she had been occupying, closed the door, and went to stand by the desk. "The Sergeant and I can drop you off at the hotel, in a few minutes. We don't have to keep the bus waiting." She stood uncertainly. "Do sit down, please."

Abruptly she heard herself say: "But I have a dinner appointment."

McCalley pushed the phone toward her. "Could you reschedule it?" He didn't remind her that it was pretty late for dinner, that they all had, in fact, been fed rather well, thanks to a well-stocked cafeteria. When she hesitated, he went on: "Is it someone in this group?" She nodded. "Well, that's easy enough. Sergeant Kenney can relay a message." Kenney had re-entered the room, with the rest of the depositions.

"That's the lot, all properly witnessed and signed," he said, handing McCalley the papers he had collected from next door.

Still standing, Jill said: "It wasn't really firmed up." She turned to Kenney. "Sergeant, would you please tell Dr. Glasner not to wait for me?"

Kenney was back in a matter of seconds. "He prefers to wait, if it's all right with you," he said. "That is, if we can give him a lift back."

McCalley looked at Jill, "No problem. All right with you if he waits?"

She shrugged. "I just met him, early this afternoon,

59

while we were waiting on line to check into the hotel."
There was an embarrassed pause before she shrugged and
added: "If he wants to wait, let him." McCalley nodded to
Kenney, who went out again to give Glasner the message
and was back in a matter of seconds. McCalley was about
to speak, when there was a knock on the door. Miss
Enderby poked her head inside.

"Excuse me, Inspector, I have the floor plans you
asked for earlier. And minutes of some of our recent
executive meetings." Holding on to the open door with one
hand, she offered a large folded set of blueprints and a
folder to Kenney, who took them from her. "I'd like to
leave, now, if you don't need me for anything else tonight.
It's a bit of a drive and I have a number of calls still to
make." They heard voices outside as the tour group walked
to the elevators.

"Yes, of course." McCalley rose and went to the
door to shake her hand and thank her again. "I'll see you in
the morning." He stood by the door as she walked quickly
to the elevator. He had to give her credit. She had bounced
back in no time at all; but the events of the last few hours
had taken a certain toll: the dark patches under her eyes
betrayed the pressure she was under and contrasted
sharply with her face, which was still very pale. As he
turned back into the office, Glasner came out of the
conference room. McCalley nodded.

"We won't be long."

Inside, he waited for Jill Masterson to sit down
before resuming his own seat behind the desk. Leaning
back in his chair, his hands laced across his breast, he
began:

"You said something, back there about a friend in
New York who might have dealt with this museum?"

"That's not what I said, and, anyway, it was just a
passing remark —."

"Can you tell me his name?"

"Ellis Bantry. He was married to my best friend, Jenny. We've known one another, Jenny and I, since high school."

"You used the past tense —"

"Ellis was killed earlier this month, caught in a gang shootout. They'd been married less than three years and had moved into their first home early in November. Now she has a magnificent house, full of unusual and lovely furnishings . . . but no husband." She took out a tissue and blew her nose.

"When was the accident you mentioned?"

"The first Thursday of December."

"You did say it was an accident?"

"The inquest ruled it an accident, yes." Already troubled by these questions, nervous about possible conclusions the Inspector might reach from her casual remark, Jill was even more disconcerted to see McCalley open a pad and start drawing elaborate doodles.

"You said he visited Canada several times?"

"He was a well-known and highly respected export-import agent, Inspector, as well as an expert in antiques. Lincoln Center came to him once, looking for a rare musical manuscript. He had traveled all over the world. At one time, he went to Australia for a client. That was before he met Jenny, I only heard about it later." McCalley glanced up from his drawing.

"What was he looking for in Australia?"

"An emu, among other things."

"The big chicken that doesn't fly?" She had to laugh, in spite of the irritation that was building up inside her. "Who would want an emu?"

"I think it was for a zoo in Detroit or Chicago." For Jill, the conversation, strange to begin with, was turning sour. She looked down at her long skirt, crossed her legs, and passed her hand over the soft wool, as though ironing it out. "Does all of this have a point, Inspector?"

The last thing he wanted to do was offend her, but his training told McCalley he should probe the casual remark she had made, track down even this most improbable suggestion of a lead. Out loud, he said:

"I don't know."

"But humor you anyway, is that it?"

"For the moment, yes. . . . "

"Do I have a choice?"

McCalley sighed. "Of course. We all do."

They exchanged a long look. When she spoke again, there was an effort to sound casual, to hide the irritation in her voice.

"What reason could you possibly have for wanting to know about Ellis?"

"Dr. Masterson, you do research. You know, I'm sure, how sometimes in the middle of reading one book you suddenly are distracted, pick up another, start leafing through it, not really looking for anything specific, and then suddenly you stumble on to something that turns out to be important? Well, we've stumbled on to something that may turn out to be nothing, or something, but right now there's no way we can be sure. So we have to —"

'The white wolf, is that it?"

McCalley knew he could not avoid talking about it. It had come up in several of the statements made by the tour group. Again, he chose his words carefully. "It probably has absolutely nothing to do with Dr. Jenene's death," he said, "but we do have to look into it. You saw it, of course, in the workroom?"

She nodded. "Miss Enderby seemed surprised to see it there."

"Yes, the others told us more or less the same thing. That's why we have now to consider its role in all this, if any. You see, at first, none of us — myself included — paid any attention to it. Our concern was the dead man. But what we've discovered in the course of our questioning, during the past few hours, is that no one knows anything about that arctic wolf you all saw in Dr. Jenene's workroom — an unusual specimen, I'm told. It seems to have turned up out of nowhere, fully processed for wolf heaven, and ends up in limbo, neither here nor there."

"I don't understand. It's museum property."

"Who told you that?" He put down the pencil with exaggerated emphasis.

"It's pretty obvious. . . ."

"Is it?" He wondered how much he should share with her. What she had told him about her friend in New York intrigued him, might be helpful. If so, he would need her cooperation. He decided to explain. "According to Miss Enderby, there's no record of a new acquisition, no paperwork connected with that wolf."

Dr. Masterson examined her nails in silence. McCalley went on: "Right now, we don't quite know where that wolf came from and where it was meant to go. It was found in Dr. Jenene's workroom, where you all saw it. *He* can't tell us about it, but surely you realize that there are a host of new questions that have settled around those facts, like barnacles on a whale." Her wide smile bothered him. "Did I say something funny?"

"A whale of a case . . . . "

He smiled. "I appreciate being educated by a literary expert like yourself. . . ." Was there a touch of irony there? Jill wondered what the Inspector was like, off the job. "I'm truly sorry about all these questions, but we have a murder on our hands, and the man who was killed seems to have been working on, processing, I believe is the word, an arctic wolf without anyone having any knowledge of it. Doesn't that seem odd?"

"Put that way, yes, I suppose so."

"Put that way, I have to find out as much as I can. I need a lot of rope — oops, another bad image?"

"No comment, unless you mean to hang yourself

with it."

This time, he did not respond. "Just tell me this. Your friend's husband — by the way, what is his full name again?"

"Bantry. Ellis Bantry. The house is in Bronxville. Do you want the address?" Her expression had hardened again, her eyes intractable. Before he could even nod, she had taken out a notebook and wrote something on a blank page. "There," she said, getting up from her chair, at the same time tearing out the sheet of paper. She tossed it at him. They both watched it flutter down to the desk. "Both the office and home. Anything else?" The hostility in her tone, the tension in her body could not be mistaken. Her eyes were bright with restrained anger.

For a few seconds, they stared at one another. McCalley rolled back his chair and looked down at his feet. "Please sit down, Dr. Masterson. Just another minute or two." When he looked up, she was once again in her seat, but her expression had not changed. "I'll tell you what my problem is, Doctor. Miss Enderby knows nothing about an arctic wolf for the museum. We therefore have to consider a new and possibly significant factor: that the wolf may have been waiting there to be taken out, transported elsewhere. We'll know more after we interview Dr. Jenene's staff in the morning, but right now, it's a new piece of information that has to be investigated."

"Far-fetched, if you ask me," was the sharp reply.

"Irrelevant, most likely. Still, I have to look into it."

"And, if I may ask, how does Ellis Bantry come into this?"

"I doubt he comes into it at all. But if he had dealings with the museum, we might find out something that will be useful to us. On the other hand, we may be wasting time. . . ." He shook his head, suddenly tired. "We need as much information as possible. Anything might be relevant at this point. Or, we may be following the wrong track. . . ."

"Barking up the wrong tree?"

He shook a finger at her. "For shame, Doctor. Making fun of a poor, culturally illiterate policeman." She was definitely having fun at his expense. It was also, he realized, her way of declaring a truce.

"Just comic relief."

Ignoring the remark, he rose from the chair, a signal to Kenney, who closed his notebook and opened the door for them. "You've been very helpful. Oh, one more thing." He seemed to be struggling for the right words. "I may have to be in touch with you again. I hope you don't mind."

Glasner came out from the next room. With a guilty start, Jill realized she had forgotten he was still there, waiting for her.

"You really should have gone back with the others."

"I thought an old friendly face might help after a grueling third degree."

Jill laughed. "Hardly an old friendly face." To the Inspector she said: "We met just a few hours ago, at the registration desk."

"Yes, you told me. And in the last few minutes," McCalley went on, addressing Glasner, "she's been indulging her excellent literary marksmanship, shooting down my threadbare metaphors with a vengeance."

Glasner turned to Jill. "Am I next, with 'grueling third degree'?"

"Well, I don't know about you," said McCalley, but I'm ready to admit my deficiency in the literary kitchen."

"I'm not. Give her an inch and — "

"It's never too late to learn," said Jill.

"I don't mind settling for the mile," said the Inspector, grinning.

The others stood by, as he closed his briefcase.

Together, they took the elevator down to the basement, where they retrieved their coats, then waited while McCalley spoke with the two officers on duty. The familiar yellow tapes were stretched across the corridor, from near the elevators right up to the entrance doors. Outside, the area close to the entrance had also been taped off and signs had been placed on the door refusing entry except to authorized police personnel. Similar signs were outside Dr. Jenene's office and the workroom. The older officer held up the tapes, so McCalley and the others could get out. McCalley reminded him to call the lobby, tell Stanton they had left.

The new snow was thick on the ground, covering the ice already there. Kenney settled himself behind the wheel of the unmarked police car and waited for the others to get in. The Inspector sat up front; Jill and Glasner in the back. When they reached the hotel, McCalley insisted on getting out to wish them good night and thanked them again.

On their way once more, the Inspector turned to Kenney. "Pick me up around seven-thirty, tomorrow." He glanced at his watch. It was close to midnight. "Not much time for sleep, I'm afraid. And we've got a big day ahead. . . . Check out Bantry as soon as possible. And, Bill, track down Dr. Jenene's car. I'm sure he drove himself in, this morning. Check it carefully for prints, the whole works."

Kenney nodded. Working with the Inspector, he had learned to anticipate and at times answer some of McCalley's questions even before they were phrased. In spite of his tendency to speculate, Kenney had learned also to be as scrupulous in assembling facts and data as the man he worked for. The early phase of any investigation, he knew, was crucial: days of tiresome routine, patient gathering of information, meticulous sorting out of boxes of accumulated material that could be potential evidence, hundreds of telephone calls, careful labeling of every scrap of paper, every cigarette butt, anything and everything that was found on the murder scene, and repeated checking of statements made in depositions. Kenney accepted and respected this part of the work. He knew McCalley appreciated his careful notes; he himself took pride in the skills he had developed. McCalley, he knew, took few notes, and only when Kenney wasn't with him. But the Inspector did use plenty of pads, Kenney discovered early in their relationship; he filled page after page with intricate line drawings. Spiraling in and out of the day's business, woven like gleaming threads into the solid texture of an investigation, was what Kenney liked to refer to — never in his superior's presence, of course — as "McCalley's noodle doodles." More than once, the young Sergeant, who was still somewhat in awe of his superior, would swear to his wife that McCalley solved cases with his doodling — long strands of twisted lines braided into a network of patterns. Once, during a particularly trying interview, he had filled an entire legal-sized pad with his designs.

"The longer the spaghetti, the harder the case," he had confided earnestly to his wife once.

"You're both daft!" she'd laughed. He'd hugged and kissed her and dropped the subject. But in his heart, he knew he was right. Some day he'd get enough courage to ask McCalley what he saw in those doodles of his, how they helped him solve a case. What difference did it make if no one else believed him? Let them laugh, if they wanted to. He had seen it work. More than once he'd watched McCalley suddenly put down his pencil and stare at the doodles he had traced. He still remembered the very first time it happened: the expression on McCalley's face had been just like Father Jamison's when he raised the Eucharist for the blessing, just before communion. It was that kind of look.

CHAPTER 4

NEW DISCOVERIES
(December 27, 7 AM)

By the time Sergeant Kenney and the Inspector reached the museum, just before eight the next morning, the day's business was already well under way.

Earlier, sitting at the kitchen table after a second cup of coffee, Susan still fast asleep in their bedroom, McCalley had reviewed the typed notes Kenney, as usual, had dropped off for him. The Sergeant had, on his own initiative, made it a habit of transcribing his shorthand notes and, before going to bed, would drive back the twenty miles to deposit them in the sturdy metal container attached to the outside wall of the Inspector's house. By the time Kenney picked him up in the morning, McCalley had usually read the typed sheets several times. He had never asked for such fast service but had accepted it gratefully. Both men knew the importance of on-the-scene statements and interviews, and the even greater importance of recording them accurately, when all the details were still fresh. And although McCalley accepted the typed transcript without fuss, Kenney knew exactly how much the Inspector appreciated them. He had learned, early on, that McCalley would have nothing to do with tape recorders. According to witnesses, the Inspector had repeatedly stated that they were not to be trusted.

This particular morning was no different from all the others. When McCalley went down to make himself breakfast, a large envelope containing Kenney's typed notes of the previous day was in the box by the door.

As he went through the sheaf of papers, he realized that the white wolf had become a crucial part of the investigation and had to be accounted for. Just what role it played, if any, in Jenene's murder, he could not and would not try to guess. But the need to explain its presence, given the circumstances and what the Curator had told him, was pretty obvious.

He washed the breakfast dishes he had used and put on his coat and hat.

Kenney was punctual, as always. In the two years they had worked together, McCalley could not remember a time when Kenney had been late. He was always there, waiting in the car for him. Today was no exception, in spite of the long hours spent at the museum the night before, and the additional time spent typing up his notes.

In the car, McCalley called in for messages. Only three, the desk clerk, told him. The first call logged in was from a witness he had interviewed in another case that was ready for trial. It would be referred to the Prosecutor's office. The second was about a continuance which freed McCalley from appearing in court, on another matter, until the following month. The third was from Spingarn. At McCalley's request, the desk sergeant read it verbatim over the phone:

"Strangled. Chloroform prior to death. Between four and six, closer to six. You've got a case." McCalley chuckled at what he had come to refer to as Spingarn's "hammer-blow" style.

Plows had cleared the area around the museum, the stately Victorian landmark, sometimes referred to as "The Castle." They parked up front this time.

"The tabloids ran stories about this place, a few years back," Kenney remarked, as they approached the main entrance, "all about its being haunted, people hearing strange sounds, crazy things happening —"

"Not as crazy as what happened last night," replied MCalley, then reminded his Sergeant that the old building had enjoyed another kind of prominence years earlier, as temporary headquarters for the Canadian Parliament, when their own building was destroyed by fire.

69

A uniformed policeman stood just inside the open door, watching them approach. "It's Norris," Kenney observed. "He'll probably ask for our IDs." The man was known for doggedly "going by the book." Too late, Kenney remembered that Norris was sometimes referred to as "McCalley Junior" and wished he could take back his words. He cast a quick look at his superior, but the Inspector said nothing.

Norris closed the door after them. He didn't ask for IDs but nurtured a look of "serious business, this!" as he greeted them. A museum guard hurried over. "Good morning, Inspector. Miss Enderby said to tell you she's at your disposal, any time you're ready for the tour."

"Beat us to it, eh?" said McCalley, taking off his coat. "Would you please tell her we'll meet her here, in the lobby, in about half an hour?" To Kenney he said: "Let's check downstairs, first."

The officers on duty, who had relieved the others at midnight and were now waiting for their own replacements, had nothing to report, except that the detectives the Inspector had asked for had arrived and were going through the rooms that had been closed off. Two were in Dr. Jenene's office. Two were in the workroom. Two others were checking out the lobby and other areas. McCalley looked into both rooms and chatted briefly with the men. When they returned to the lobby, Miss Enderby was waiting for them. She had set up an interview with the Press for later that morning, she told them but wasn't allowing them into the building until then. McCalley suggested they make a joint statement. The Curator was visibly relieved.

"When will we be able to reopen the museum, Inspector?" she asked, as they started their tour.

"Ask me a little later. Believe me, we're doing our best to clear the place for you."

Miss Enderby nodded. In spite of the personal

inconvenience she had been subjected to, not to mention the distress she was still experiencing at the death of one of the museum's most important department heads; in spite of loss of staff hours and the possibility that the museum would not re-open to the public until late in the day, perhaps not until the following day — things that she did not suffer gracefully — Miss Enderby admitted a grudging admiration for the Inspector. She recognized in him qualities which she cultivated in herself: dedication, competence, a certain detachment, no words wasted. He was thoroughly professional, direct, unrelenting in his search for details, and yet surprisingly considerate. She knew he was doing his very best.

"— that's why we have to be careful what we give the Press," McCalley was saying. "Cases have been lost, criminals acquitted because facts were compromised. Not deliberately, in most instances. Too often, information is leaked inadvertently, by our own people sometimes. Suspects have been tipped off as a result, cases lost because of technicalities that might have been avoided."

"I leave it all to you," said Miss Enderby. Flanking her, the two men paced their steps to hers. They listened closely as she described the various exhibits, pausing with her from time to time as she pointed out a particular display or described a rare specimen. Now and then, McCalley would consult the blueprints Miss Blackwell had given him the night before, occasionally he would ask to look inside one of the closed rooms or a closet, more often than not just ask questions. They rounded a corner and walked toward the opposite wing of the museum. As they started down the wide aisle, she noted: "The majority of our permanent exhibits are along these corridors, inside temperature controlled glass cases. They cannot be opened without several alarms going off." His men, McCalley knew, would be examining the alarm systems during their own tour of the building.

71

"Have you had any recent incident that might be described as out of the ordinary?"

Miss Enderby shook her head. "Can't think of any." After a few seconds, she added: "There was a malfunction in the thermostats on the third floor about eighteen months ago, but that was quickly adjusted."

"Have there been any thefts in recent months?" McCalley asked.

"No. In all my years as Curator, I don't recall a single theft." She stopped and faced them. "You see, Inspector, it would be difficult to sell anything stolen from the museum. Any museum, not just this one. If something were suddenly missing from one of our exhibits, or our storerooms, anything at all, word would get out. No other museum would touch it."

For some reason, the arctic wolf came to mind. McCalley found himself wondering again why the museum had no record of it, unless —

He was jolted out of his musings by Miss Enderby, who seemed to have read his thoughts.

"About the wolf. . . . I still haven't found anything to suggest that it was logged in, Inspector. Nothing like this has ever happened before, in my recollection."

McCalley made no comment. Continuing their tour, they saw, in recreations of their natural habitat, polar bears, the brown bear, hummingbirds and the flowers they favor, carnivorous plants, the sharks of Canada, reproduction of the Giant Auk that had been hunted to extinction, the American lion, the Canadian sabre-tooth tiger, camels, and dinosaurs of other ages; amphibians and reptiles, the bison, the Giant Beaver, crustaceans, insects of the sea, sea dragons, spiders, moths . . . an entire other world featuring actual specimens, primarily Canadian, of animal and plant life.

In one enclosure there was a group of four caribou, two adults and their two young. Three wolves stared at a white bear, which seemed ready to rush at them.

"Are they always so frightening?" asked the Inspector pointing to the bear.

"Even more so, if you get this close to a live one."

The Inspector smiled. "This one looks frisky."

Miss Enderby smiled back. "Eager to rough you up, would be a better description. They're usually well behaved if you just stand still and wait for them to move on," she said. "As a rule, they charge only if you run or threaten them in some way. They're just protecting themselves."

"But best to keep one's distance?"

"Definitely."

Several more wolves and even larger bears were lined up on the opposite wall. One of the exhibits held an arctic wolf.

Kenney read the legend on the side of the case out loud. "*Canis Lupus Arctos*, Queen Elizabeth Island. Weight: 193 lbs. Height: 2.5 feet; Length: 5.3 feet." He knew for himself that these particular wolves were indeed hard to find. One species, the "*Canis Lupus Bernardi*" was extinct. He'd learned about the wolves from helping his eight-year old niece Louisa with a school assignment. There were only two hundred white wolves reported on Queen Elizabeth Island. Banks and Victoria Islands had just over a thousand, the Greenland count was only seventy-five.

"We've had this specimen," Miss Enderby informed them, "for almost ten years."

McCalley offered: "My grandfather had a friend who'd gone on a safari right after college and shot a lion. He had the head mounted on the wall of his study. It was still there, when my grandfather took me with him to visit the man, thirty years later."

"Theoretically, if put together well, they last a long time. But, if for no other reason, displays have to be changed periodically as new environmental information comes our way. Luckily it doesn't have to be done very often. Still, you'd be surprised how new research, say, oh, on what animals eat, for instance, can change things. We review our exhibits periodically, the background, the trees, flowers, everything. We don't want to be caught napping." They moved on.

"This is a grizzly from the area around the Ogilvie Mountains," she continued, pointing toward the animal nearest her. "It's unusually large, as you can see. If you happen to chance on one of these, the best thing is to run before he sees or smells you." She moved down a few steps to the next group. "These are Dall's Sheep. They're found in that same area."

They had come to the end of the corridor. "You'll want to see our 'Wet Room'," she offered, "and some other things. If you have time, that is." McCalley and Kenney followed her as she started walking again. "We have ten million specimens, Inspector."

"Hard to believe."

Glass panels, from floor to ceiling stretched across almost the entire corner where they now stood. Inside were carefully arranged rows of skins and furs on special hangers. Each row seemed to have three or four racks, right up to the ceiling. "We have the best and most extensive collection of arctic furs and skins anywhere in the world. Researches from all over come for samples." She pointed. "There, in that corner," she stepped aside to make room for the two men, "you'll see our prize possession." It was a huge mastodon. "It's the largest on record."

One of the museum guards came up to her and said something. She nodded, and turned back to McCalley. "Dr. Jenene's assistants are ready for you. Shall I have them come to my office?"

"No, I'd rather see them downstairs. But before we go, I'd like to see the 'Wet Room'?"

She seemed pleased at his request and led them

briskly to it. Inside, hundreds of shelves were lined up, floor to ceiling, in an arrangement resembling library stacks, but instead of books these shelves held jars of all sizes and shapes, with parts of animals, insects, specimens of all kinds floating in some kind of liquid.

"Specimens in all stages of development, as you can tell, preserved in alcohol —" She had waved them inside the room. "No danger of contamination here. The containers are sealed tightly."

"Impressive." McCalley offered. He was genuinely surprised, not having ever seen so many different small animals, parts of animals, larvae, things small, medium, and large, preserved in this way.

"Impressive and useful," she replied. "The best collection of its kind anywhere."

"Was Dr. Jenene in charge of this operation also?"

"No, that would be Dr. Carteret. Did you want to ask him anything?"

"Not now. I may want to, later."

Kenney seemed intrigued with all the reptiles, treefrogs, salamanders, turtles, lizards, birds, preserved in the jars.

Eventually, all three wandered out back into the main corridor. When they were downstairs in the lobby again, McCalley took the opportunity to glance at his watch. It was close to ten. As though trying to help him make up his mind, Miss Enderby said:

"There's a good deal more, of course. I'll be happy to continue later, if you wish."

"You've been very generous with your time. Thank you. Right now, we have to get back to our own habitat."

As they parted, in the lobby, she reminded the Inspector of the Press conference later in the day.

"Just have me paged when they arrive."

"Quite a collection, Sir," Kenney commented, as they walked away.

"Indeed it is." But for McCalley, the brief tour had been necessary for other, less obvious reasons. For one thing, it gave him a chance to study Miss Enderby more closely. She was a true professional, he was convinced; dedicated to the museum and genuinely puzzled by the arctic wolf in Dr. Jenene's workroom. It also strengthened his impression that nothing else in the museum was likely to be connected to the incidents of the day before. And although his men were going through each floor carefully, he now was willing to consider lifting the order that had closed down the entire building to the public. The basement would have to remain off limits, of course; but perhaps the rest of the museum could reopen tomorrow. Miss Enderby would be pleased. . . .

They checked first with the officers who had just come on duty, then went further down the hall to a room Miss Enderby had set aside as a temporary workshop and office for Jenene's staff. It would have to serve until the yellow tapes were officially removed. The door was ajar. They could hear voices inside.

A woman and two men turned to the door when McCalley knocked and entered, Kenney behind him. After introducing himself and his assistant, McCalley waved them back into their chairs. Kenney brought up another chair for McCalley, then went to sit just inside the closed door.

"I'm sorry for what happened yesterday," McCalley began. The others nodded. After they had introduced themselves, Dr. Franklin, Jenene's Deputy, spoke up:

"I don't understand it. When I left at a few minutes after one, he was putting on his coat — "

"Where was that, Doctor?"

"Here. I mean in the workroom. He came in from across the hall, putting on his coat, getting ready to leave."

"Did he say anything to you?"

"Nothing special. We commented on the weather and if more snow would pile up during the night."

"Did he say he was about to leave?"

"No. He buttoned up and wished me luck getting home. I assumed he'd be following me out to his own car."

"But you didn't actually see him leave, get into his car. . . ?"

The man shook his head. "No. I hurried away."

"Did Dr. Jenene ask you to come in on Boxing Day?"

"No. It was my idea. I wanted to finish a report. Get it out of the way."

"Was the arctic wolf there, when you left?"

"No! We were just talking about that. None of us knew anything about an arctic wolf having been received, let alone processed!" McCalley had left instructions that they be allowed to look at the wolf from the doorway. Now, McCalley took advantage of their surprise to press on: How could Jenene keep a specimen like that under wraps? On the practical side, just picking up the animal, carrying it, would require help. Had they seen anyone else around? Could Jenene have worked on the wolf elsewhere?

The second man, whose name was Mercado and who had introduced himself as chief technician, answered. "All our materials are in the workroom. We never saw Dr. Jenene, or anyone else, working on the wolf. I can't imagine how he moved the specimen, once the processing got under way. He must have found some way of hiding it. We have a number of storage areas where he might have put the wolf so that it wouldn't be seen."

"You suggested he might have been hiding it. Do you have any reason for saying that? Do you think Dr. Jenene was working on this animal for some personal reason, some secret purpose?" Realizing the implications of his words, Mercado grew somewhat flustered.

"No, no. You misunderstood, Inspector. I was simply responding to your statement earlier, about how Jenene might have kept the specimen under wraps —"

McCalley nodded, went on. "Could he have worked on the animal after hours, used a roller to move the specimen from one place to another?"

"I suppose he could have managed it," Mercado replied, "but, Inspector, why would he want to do that?"

"None of this makes any sense!" Dr. Franklin volunteered.

McCalley ignored both the question and the comment. Instead, he asked: "Could the wolf have been earmarked for some other museum?"

The others stared at him.

The woman, who had been introduced by Mercado as his assistant and whose name was Amy Hawkins, said, after a few seconds:

"For an exchange, it would have to be in the collection already. But from what we were told, the Curator herself had no idea we had a new specimen. If it *is* ours, I don't think Miss Enderby would let it go anywhere, either on loan or exchange."

"And Dr. Jenene never mentioned having received an arctic wolf?"

"Not to us," replied Mercado, somewhat peevishly, looking at the others, who nodded in confirmation.

McCalley got up and stretched his legs. It was also an excuse to give Sergeant Kenney a short break. There was a knock on the door. Kenney reached out and opened it. One of the homicide crew, the outside cold still clinging to him, whispered something to McCalley, as he held out a thin folder. Out loud he said: "It's okay. Everything's been dusted." McCalley thanked him and opened the folder, leafing through the few sheets quickly. Kenney shut the door again and waited. The others watched as the Inspector looked through the contents of the folder a second time, then went to stand by Sergeant Kenney, where he held the folder open for him to go through. Kenney turned the pages quickly as McCalley continued to hold the open folder for him. What the others saw, when Kenney looked up, was surprise; a worried frown on the Inspector's face.

Whatever was troubling McCalley now riveted his attention. He seemed to have forgotten the others in the room. Then, abruptly, he shut the folder and turned back to the curious stares of the three people he had been interviewing.

"Bad news?" Dr. Franklin ventured.

"Some forms I was looking for," he said, sitting down again. His expression was once again unreadable, as he resumed the questioning. "What were you working on recently?"

They gave an account of their activities, explaining the priorities set for them, and went on to describe Dr. Jenene's recent projects. Listening to them, as they interrupted one another to add a comment or correct something, McCalley was ready to believe that Jenene alone was responsible for the wolf's presence in the workroom and that he alone could have told them how it got there and why it was there.

The papers he had been handed moments earlier suggested just that.

They had been found in a locked safe in Jenene's basement at home and indicated that the wolf was going to the American Museum of Natural History in New York City on a long-term loan agreement. In May and August, two other specimens had gone out on a similar arrangement to a museum in New Jersey. Dr. Jenene's name appeared on all the forms, as having processed the animals. The two earlier shipments had been picked up for or by an agent in New York, and a shop in Soho was down as the initial receiver of the goods. The wolf destined for the American Museum of Natural History was to be delivered to the same agent or his representative on December twenty-eight. The shop in Soho was owned by a Paul Tasselbaum. The agent was listed as Ellis Bantry.

After a few more questions, McCalley dismissed the trio, explaining — in answer to their questions — that they could not go back into the regular workroom for some time. He gave each of them his card, with the usual request to call him or his office should they remember anything at all that might be relevant.

Resigned to the inevitable, they left, whispering to one another as they moved down the corridor.

Kenney knew better than to discuss the contents of the folder with McCalley. It was clear that those papers had driven everything else out of the Inspector's head. He himself was still trying to absorb the information they contained.

"Bill, shut the door, please. I have to make a call." Kenney watched as McCalley took from his wallet a business card, pulled out his cordless phone and punched in a number.

To McCalley's surprise, the gravelly voice answered almost at once:

"Markarian."

Lieutenant Ed Markarian was with the New York City Police Department. The two men had met at a firearms convention in Buffalo. The last night of the meeting, they had relaxed over a glass of beer.

"It's Luke McCalley. We met some months ago at the convention in Buffalo?"

"Big Luke, how are you? Everything OK?"

"Fine, everything's fine with me. Not so fine for those who stopped breathing." Let me say it quickly, he thought. If he doesn't have time, or if he doesn't want to see me, I'll hear that in his voice. His own mind was made up. "I'm planning to come to New York next week, New Year's Day to be exact. A case I'm working on. I wondered if you could give me an hour or so while I'm there, to pick your brain." The response at the other end was effusive. McCalley protested.

80

"No, no. I can't let you pick me up at the airport. It's New Year's Day! I'll settle in and call you from the hotel in the morning."

"No, I insist. Listen, after the big meal, the day just drags out until the big snack in the evening, more beer in between, watching television, listening to my mother-in-law's complaints. . . . Except for the food, a whole day wasted. Believe me, you'll be doing me a favor, getting me out of there!" McCalley couldn't help laughing. Markarian raced on: "What's the flight number? We can talk driving in. Hey! There's guile behind my offer. We call it 'Professional Courtesy.' I can give you as much time as you need, treat you to lunch, dinner, anything in-between, during your stay. For me it's a break. Take my word for it." The man was everything McCalley remembered: open, easy to talk to, no bragging, a real pro. McCalley had done his homework when he returned home. He'd discovered that his new friend had one of the highest arrest and conviction records in the entire police department. A homicide detective who did his job without fuss.

"I'll have to get back to you on the flight number and time of arrival," said McCalley. "I wanted to check with you first."

"So, what's up?"

"Murder, what else?" Quickly, he told Markarian about the discovery of Jenene's body. When he mentioned the name Ellis Bantry and what Jill Masterson had told him, Markarian interrupted him.

"Bantry? I remember. The fellow was killed early this month in Soho. Caught in crossfire. A gang shootout. Got caught in the middle."

"I heard it was ruled an accident."

A slight pause. "Yeah, well . . . . ."

"Who were the shots meant for, did you find out?"

"The guys who had insulted one another, who else? Gang reprisals. Teen-agers with guns. And, get this!

No witnesses! It was still early, sure, just going on ten in the morning, but with the mild weather we've been having, there were plenty of early bird tourists and Christmas shoppers around. . . . Oh, and the guns were all registered to the daddys, and the daddys all had permits. The lawyers insisted the kids were under the influence, not responsible, they didn't really mean to harm anyone. Slate clean. No court appearances. No trial. All of them remanded into their parents' custody."

"Under the influence? At that time of day?"

"It wasn't the 'happy hour' kind, Luke." At the other end, McCalley laughed. "Anyway, that's what the lawyers told us. We did tests. They were right. The kids were high on drugs. Oh, and they were really *really* sorry, when they realized what they'd done. Almost had us crying." This time both men laughed. A picture was taking shape, but McCalley wasn't sure what it meant. Musn't jump to conclusions, he warned himself.

"Was anyone else hurt?"

"No, believe it or not. . . ."

"I know the case is closed, Ed," he went on quickly, "but I'd like to ask you, were you satisfied with the ruling of the inquest?" This time he could hear Markarian drawing in a deep breath.

"It wasn't my case, but from what I know, I don't see what else it could have been. I can tell you this much, there were things I never was able to figure out, but, like you said, the case is closed." Was there a doubt in his voice?

"Did the bullets match the gun?"

"Guns, you mean. All thirty-eights."

McCalley frowned into the phone. "All thirty-eights?"

"Hey! They probably got them wholesale."

"All registered, you said?"

"Yeah. All nice and legal."

McCalley persisted. "And all the bullets matched the guns on the scene?"

"Yep."

"Whose gun actually killed Bantry?"

"Ah, there's the rub. We know what gun fired the bullets that killed him, but nobody remembers who fired what or when. Apparently there was a lot of confusion. They were all too excited, too hopping mad. Guns were dropped, picked up again, not always by the same hands. Eventually, they established that Bantry took three bullets. The one that killed him came from a gun registered to Sonny Del Giudice, Son of the Judge. Nice name for the nephew of a mob boss, eh? Anyway, like I was saying, there were so many different prints on it, the police couldn't have made a clean arrest, even if they had wanted to."

"What does that mean?"

He could sense Markarian's frustration in the long drawn-out breath. "All I can tell you is, there was nothing to go on. It was a tragic accident."

"How many bullets *were* fired?"

"Besides the three in the victim, we found five more."

"No witnesses . . . ." McCalley seemed to be thinking out loud.

"Not even the owner of the antiques shop, where Bantry had just come from."

"Let me guess. Paul Tasselbaum?"

"How did you know?"

"Fill you in later. What did Tasselbaum say?"

"According to the police report, he didn't see the actual shooting. Not even people outside remembered anything. Everybody ran for cover."

"Why was Bantry there?"

"Something about wanting Tasselbaum to find him an old ring he was looking for."

Well, McCalley told himself, Markarian must have

wondered about it, had obviously read the report for himself, even though it wasn't his case. How else would he have gotten to know all the details?

"What *did* Tasselbaum say?"

"Only that he stayed inside when he saw the kids coming. Bad news around those parts."

"Why didn't he call Bantry back inside, when he recognized the possible danger?"

Markarian shrugged. "All we know is, he didn't."

"You think you could let me see his statement when I get there?"

"No *problema*. You'll let me know the flight number?"

"Right."

Still trying to absorb the conversation he had just had, McCalley checked his address book and looked up a travel agent he knew. He booked a flight to New York leaving in the afternoon, New Year's Day. His in-laws were driving over for early dinner; he and Susan had accepted an invitation from friends for drinks, later in the evening, but Susan would apologize for him. . . . He asked for an open return ticket but the man told him he'd better book round trip to be on the safe side. It was holiday time, lots of traffic. He could change to another flight later, if he had to. He also reminded McCalley to allow more time for checking in. Since 9/11, security was much tighter. . . .

He rose from his chair, then sat down again and dialed Markarian's number a second time. A Sergeant Morris told him the Lieutenant had just left for a meeting. McCalley left the flight information on voice-mail.

"Well, we've got plenty of work cut out for us, Bill," he said, as they walked toward the elevators. "But right now," he held up the folder, "we've got to see Miss Enderby again."

CHAPTER 5

THE PAPER TRAIL

The area around the administration offices was teeming with reporters, cameramen, newscasters, men and women holding light poles, technicians, as well as several museum guards and three police officers trying to maintain some kind of order. Two guards stood outside the door of the Curator's office. Two more stood by the elevators, to make sure no one, accidentally or deliberately, wandered beyond that point.

Before any of the reporters realized that the elevator door was opening, one of the guards leaned inside: "Sir, I should warn you, they're been waiting for you." Even before the words were out, the press crowd spotted him and started running down the hall shouting, their cameras and microphones ready for him.

Questions blended into a cacophony of sounds. McCalley held up his hand. "Miss Enderby and I will answer your questions in just a few minutes." As he spoke, he elbowed his way through.

The guards outside the Curator's office let the two men in, struggling to keep the crowd of reporters outside. Kenney quickly closed the door.

Miss Enderby hurried across the room. "Here, let me take that," she said, relieving him of his coat and placing it on a nearby chair. As she crossed back to her desk, she asked nervously: "What do we tell them out there?"

McCalley sat down opposite her. "I wasn't sure before, I'm even less sure now," he replied, handing her the folder. "My men found these papers while searching Dr. Jenene's house." Miss Enderby frowned as she began to read, the frown deepening as she leafed through the folder McCalley had given her.

"I don't understand," she said, looking up a few minutes later. "The wolf was being sent somewhere else?"

"It gets worse, I'm afraid. There were two earlier shipments, back in May and August, ostensibly long-term loans from your museum to another in New Jersey: the first, a caribou; the second, a young short-faced bear, a cub according to the description in there. The third is our arctic wolf. As you can see, it was due for pick-up yesterday, the twenty-sixth, for delivery to New York on the twenty-eighth."

McCalley watched as she leafed through the papers, lingering here and there, shaking her head as she silently turned the sheets, going back to reread something from time to time. Finally, she looked up.

"You said these were found in Dr. Jenene's home?"

"In a locked safe, hidden in his basement."

"What does it mean?" She glanced up at him, then back to the papers in her hand. He had expected and dreaded such a question, so he asked one of his own.

"You don't recognize any of those forms? You didn't know about any of those transactions?"

"Thefts, you mean!!" she blurted out. Then, more cautiously, a puzzled frown on her face. "According to these forms, they were all new acquisitions. . . ." McCalley waited, as she scanned the documents again. Finally, in a different tone altogether, she looked up and whispered, almost as though talking to herself: "What in heaven's name was Jenene up to?"

He straightened up in his chair and cleared his throat. "Let me tell you what I know, what we've been able to determine so far." He proceeded to recount what he had discovered, telling her even about Bantry's accidental death early that month and that he would be flying to New York early the next week to find out more about the Bantry connection and talk to people at the museum, where the specimen was supposed to have been taken. When he was

86

done, he held up his hand in a warning gesture, forestalling any comment: "Don't ask me to speculate on what I've just said. All I can tell you is that the facts we have force me to widen the investigation."

"If this man," she searched for the name on the papers she still held, "if Ellis Bantry was involved, he probably was murdered, too."

"Right now, there's absolutely no connection between Bantry's death and Jenene's, and I have no intention of asking the New York City Police Department to reopen what was officially ruled an accidental death. There are no grounds for that, no new evidence to justify it. I have to warn you about jumping to conclusions. All we know for certain is that Bantry's name is given as the agent acting on behalf of the New York museum and Jenene's signature is there as having processed all three specimens."

"And both men are dead!"

"Both men are dead, that's true. One, we know, was murdered. But why, we don't know. That's all we can say right now. Meanwhile, we're looking into Canadian and American customs records, tracking down those shipments, and any others that may have crossed the border. I've talked with Jenene's staff, and thank you for making them available to us, but they seem to know nothing about the wolf. Never saw it. Jenene never even mentioned it to them. They were surprised to learn that the wolf was not officially logged in."

"I should think so!"

"And yet, those papers suggest it's part of the museum collection. . . . "

"You say Bantry was shot accidentally —"

"*I* don't say it; the *official ruling* of the inquest says it. And that fact cannot be altered, not unless new evidence come to light, as I said. Surely you understand the need for such distinctions."

"Yes, yes," Miss Enderby replied, at the same time

87

dismissing what he had just said with an impatient wave of her hand. "But obviously there's much more to it. Jenene and this other man were involved in smuggling, isn't that it? And my trusted colleague was using this museum to cover his tracks. Using a superb and expensive specimen as the means to transport God knows what."

"We don't know that it was anything like that."

"And what about the wolf? According to these documents it belongs to us."

"According to those documents, it's meant to go to the American Museum of Natural History in New York," McCalley replied, with a touch of asperity. They stared at one another across the desk. Miss Enderby's face grew red with restrained emotion. McCalley went on, trying to bring the conversation back to the main track. "All that will be decided later. Right now, the wolf stays here, as evidence."

"You intend to destroy it?" Her voice had risen. Her eyes blazed with an anger she could barely control.

"Not if we can help it." He moved forward in his chair. "You know, it's just possible that Dr. Jenene might have been protecting the museum. He might have been killed for interrupting something, for butting in."

The woman looked properly deflated. "I'm sorry. Yes, I have no right to judge him. Or to question your methods."

McCalley pointed to the folder and asked: "Would you mind looking through those papers again?"

She picked up the folder, somewhat puzzled at the request, and started to scan each sheet, quickly.

"Excuse me," said McCalley, leaning forward in his chair. "Look carefully. It's important." He watched closely as she started examining each sheet again. When she looked up again she made no effort to hide her anger.

"Someone has forged my signature on —" she held up and waved the stack of papers "— on all but the shipping documents!"

"Is that usual?"

"If you mean is that how the paperwork is handled, the answer is yes. Jenene is responsible for setting up shipping schedules. I have nothing to do with those."

"And you never handled any of those forms?"

"I never even saw them!!"

"And that isn't your signature?"

"Absolutely not!!" She squirmed in her chair, trying to control her emotions.

"But it *looks* like your signature?" the Inspector persisted.

"To a careless eye, maybe. But I never signed any of these papers, I know nothing about these transactions!" Indignation was fueling her anger. "Do you realize how long we've been waiting for a specimen of this kind? Suddenly one appears, fully processed, right under our noses, by our own staff, right here on our premises, all done with Jenene's approval, finished and ready for display, but, no, not for *our* museum but for one in New York —!"

"— Excuse me," interrupted McCalley. "I really would not involve Dr. Jenene's staff at this point. All we can say is that Dr. Jenene may have had knowledge of the wolf, may have signed for it, and may have done the processing himself."

"*May* have! His signature is right there, right there in black and white!" She waved the papers in the air as she spoke. The next moment, recognizing the implications of her words, she leaned back in her chair and closed her eyes, taking in deep breaths. McCalley watched her for a few seconds, then asked:

"Do you recognize his signature?"

"Yes, yes, I do," she answered quickly, visibly relieved by the Inspector's unruffled tone. "It's his."

"A few samples will settle the matter," McCalley said, adding casually, "in your case, as well." He drew his chair closer to the desk and lowered his voice, though no one else could hear them, except Kenney, who continued diligently taking notes. "You see why we must be careful, Miss Enderby. Rumors can spread much too easily and compromise the entire case." He pulled back where he sat. "So: you never saw those forms and your signature is not authentic."

"That's right!"

"Do you have any idea where Dr. Jenene might have worked on the animal without anyone else knowing about it? It must have taken him some time. Where could he have kept it hidden all that time? Provided, of course, that he was the one who processed the wolf."

"Do you seriously doubt it?"

"Can't say, on the basis of what we have so far." Miss Enderby was about to reply, but McCalley went on quickly: "I take it, Dr. Jenene had access at all times to materials, equipment, the workroom?"

"Yes."

"Is there any other place, besides the workroom, he could have used to process or store the wolf?"

Miss Enderby did not answer at once. "I suppose one of the storerooms," she said, without conviction, "but it would have been difficult to move the animal back and forth, . . . unless . . . could one of his people, or more than one, have helped him?"

"Possibly, but I doubt it. They seemed completely confused when I interviewed them a little while ago. Could he have used a roller?"

"Yes! Of course! In fact, he probably worked right on the roller, from the beginning.!"

McCalley nodded. Her next words confirmed what McCalley already had come to recognize as an unusual commitment to the museum, to her profession, a commitment that did not accept mistakes easily, that on one level would not tolerate disloyalty, yet, in fairness, could acknowledge the craftsman, the master, even in someone like Jenene.

"Whatever else he might have been, might have done," she now added, "Dr. Jenene was a real artist in his field. He had an international reputation. I still can't conceive, I can't bring myself to accept the fact that . . . he did what he did."

"As I said earlier, let's not rush to conclusions. There may be quite different explanations for all this, facts may emerge that undermine our first impressions."

She cocked her head to one side. For a moment, she looked like a mischievous youngster. She waved the closed folder in the air. "Come now, Inspector, you don't really believe that?"

"I don't believe anything right now. What I *know* is that we have a murdered man and an unclaimed wolf."

"No, no!" Miss Enderby had shot up from her chair, her face flushed, her expression troubled. "The wolf is ours, Inspector. Jenene works, *worked*, for this museum. Legally, the wolf belongs to us."

McCalley did not bother to explain that it would be difficult, impossible in fact, to prove that. He said, instead:

"All that will be settled in due course. Right now, we have a murder to solve."

She had come around to stand in front of him. "Those forms carry the museum's name right at the top," she persisted, "and Jenene signed them in his official capacity. The wolf is ours, Inspector."

McCalley was about to reply, but the Curator was not done.

"Do you think for a moment that I would allow a newly-acquired arctic wolf to leave these premises? It says here, on extended loan. Impossible. No one in his right mind would consider it! Even if it were an old specimen, and this one was definitely not old, it was brand new, no one in his right mind would do such a thing! An arctic wolf is a rarity, an extremely valuable specimen. No museum would give it away, or lend it out. Not ours, certainly! It would be insane!"

McCalley tried to hide his growing impatience. Miss Enderby picked up one of the forms and commented:

"The official requisition form for the wolf is dated early September. And here's the receipt of delivery to the museum, signed by Jenene, in early November. I can't believe this," she continued, almost to herself. "Less than two months to find this kind of rare specimen!"

"If you're going by those documents," said the Inspector, not without a touch of severity, "remember, please, that your signature is on them, too. According to those papers, both you and Dr. Jenene signed over the wolf to another museum."

"*But I didn't!*" she cried out in utter frustration. "I would never do that!" McCalley said nothing. Miss Enderby slammed the folder on her desk and sat down again. "Do you realize how difficult it is to get good specimens, what we have to do to raise money for what we need? Our sponsor list has grown over the last ten years, but money is still scarce even for routine purchases, not to mention replacements. You'd be shocked at what we have to pay for some of our new acquisitions! . . . . I still can't believe John Jenene could do something like this. For any amount of money!"

Again, McCalley chose to ignore her conclusion. He had said enough on the dangers of speculation. Instead, he picked up the folder from the desk and started to leaf through it.

"Who's Dobie?" he asked, looking up.

"One of the local trappers."

"Do you know him?"

"Only his name. I never met the man. I know Dr. Jenene bought a number of animals from him over the last few years."

"Does he work for the museum?"

"No. He's an independent provider. They all are. But in a way, yes; for the most part, in this area they work for us."

"Still, have you considered the possibility that the wolf may not have been intended either for this museum or the one in New York?" McCalley heard himself say and was immediately sorry. What had come over him? He had already given her far too much information, but her dogged insistence that the wolf belonged to the Canadian Museum had made him impatient. He held up a hand to ward off any comment and continued quickly.

"Those papers say that it was destined for the American Museum of Natural History, but that may not be the case. Something else that needs looking into. That and the two earlier shipments." He went on, before she could say anything. "Tell me, Miss Enderby, how often have you sold or lent specimens to other museums?"

"Never! I told you! We neither sell nor lend!" When McCalley did not respond, she went on, in a steadier voice: "To begin with, the competition is fierce. As I just told you, Inspector, it's hard to get good specimens, even harder to find the money to pay for them! In this particular case, I would probably have had to contact several of our more prominent sponsors, would have explained the difficulty of getting such a specimen, that there are any number of museums out there ready to do battle over an arctic wolf!"

"An arctic wolf would never have been sold or loaned to the American Museum of Natural History, is that what you're telling me?"

"That's exactly what I'm telling you! That wolf is here to stay!"

"Let's say, for the moment, that the wolf is indeed meant for this museum. Isn't it possible that Dr. Jenene may have been trying to stop others from taking it elsewhere?"

She gave him a curious look.

"You mentioned that earlier, but there's nothing to suggest Dr. Jenene in that role, is there? Why would his signature be on those forms, if he wasn't part of some devious scheme?"

"The same reason your signature is on them."

"But I didn't sign anything!"

"And Dr. Jenene did?"

"Yes, as far as I can tell, that's his writing."

McCalley hurried on. "All right, let's accept for the moment the signatures *were* forged, yours, at least! But don't you see? The reason may be altogether different from what you've concluded."

By now professional dignity had replaced anger. Miss Enderby relaxed in her chair and crossed her arms. She gave McCalley a long thoughtful look.

"As I indicated earlier, you may be right, Inspector; but personally, I find it hard to believe Dr. Jenene innocent. Those documents were carefully hidden away for weeks. Why? Why didn't he come to me with information? It doesn't make sense!"

McCalley, watching her intently, decided to move away from what was proving to be a dead-end. "Tell me how purchases are made," he said.

"It takes time and a good deal of paperwork," Miss Enderby began, confidently. "If an addition to the collection is approved, the Executive Board decides whether to act immediately or hold off until later. The important thing, always, is money. Is there money in the budget for such a purchase? If funds normally set aside for such a purchase are depleted, we might consider a shift in budget lines to cover the cost of the special item. If such adjustments can't be made, we would search out a special donor."

When McCalley made no comment, she continued.

"The protocol is quite clear, Inspector. It calls for several important considerations and decisions. Nothing of that happened, in this instance. This purchase was never brought before the Board and therefore never voted on. Had we agreed to it, I would have had to sign requisitions and authorizations, would have seen receipts, bank statements, all kinds of paperwork down the line. All we have, instead, are those few forms, obviously meant to clear customs, with my signature forged. The big question then is: How and where did Dr. Jenene get enough money to pay for and process an arctic wolf?"

"From whoever wanted the specimen?"

"This is beginning to sound like a Le Carré mystery," was the dry retort.

McCalley sighed. "The truth of the matter is, Miss Enderby, finding these documents has forced us to reassess yesterday's events in a new light. For example, if the wolf was meant for the museum in New York, why was it to be delivered first to a shop in Soho?"

"Exactly," said Miss Enderby, as though the question had vindicated her.

"Exactly what?"

"That's the sort of matter you should pursue."

"I intend to, but —"

"Whatever happened," she interrupted, "is no fault of this museum. Dr. Jenene must have had plans of his own for the animal. No doubt some smuggling operation —"

She stopped abruptly, realizing she was repeating things the Inspector didn't want to hear. On his part, to keep from warning her again about unfounded comments and loose speculation, McCalley made a show of studying the folder, recognizing the fact that Miss Enderby had said all the things that had been running through his own head but which he wasn't ready to spell out yet, not even to himself. He snapped the folder shut and stood up.

"Here's what I think, Miss Enderby," he offered, in his low, even voice. Everything so far strongly suggests that Dr. Jenene's staff knew nothing about the wolf. I also believe that these papers carry your signature but that you didn't put it there." He placed the folder inside his briefcase. "Sergeant Kenney will know how to reach me, if you need to talk with me at any time."

In the corridor, the clamor had reached a new peak. "We'd better get out there and give them something, or they'll be knocking down your door," McCalley said, picking up his coat and briefcase.

When the two men finally emerged from the building, the sun was shining on the packed snow.

"Glad that's over with!" said the Sergeant, as he unlocked the car and got behind the wheel.

McCalley checked his watch as he eased himself into the car. "Two-thirty. Let's stop for some lunch at that pub we passed earlier, just before the highway."

Two men were at the bar, nursing beers. McCalley led the way into the empty dining room. They ordered the special of the day, shepherd's pie. McCalley drank water. Kenney had a coke while they waited for the food to come.

"More complicated than we thought, eh Bill?" McCalley drummed his fingers on the table.

"Well, Sir, it does seem strange —"

"How do you mean, strange?"

"All those forms hidden away in Dr. Jenene's basement. . . . You think Miss Enderby is telling the truth?"

"You saw her, heard her. What do you think?"

"She did seem surprised. . . ."

"Surprised and angry. . . . No, I don't think she knew about them."

"But then, Sir. . . ." The Sergeant's voice trailed off

"Go on."

"If those were not her signatures —"

"— someone else put them there, right. And if that's the case, then someone else didn't want her to know about the wolf —"

"— because someone else was selling it to the

96

museum in New York."

"Ah, you have a theory?"

Kenney flushed, Well, he deserved the sarcasm; he knew perfectly well how the Inspector felt about theories, especially this early in the game.

The food arrived and they ate in silence. Kenney finished before McCalley, who seemed distracted. Over coffee, the Inspector picked up the thread.

"What do you make of the body?"

"Chloroform strikes me as odd."

"What I meant was, why was the body where we found it?"

"Somebody put it there?"

"Are you suggesting he was killed elsewhere?"

"Oh, no, Sir. I think the body was meant to be taken out, together with the wolf —" He stopped, expecting to hear the usual warning about idle speculation. To Kenney's surprise, however, McCalley nodded and gestured for him to go on. "— but the tour bus arrived." He paused to finish his coke. He was about to resume, when McCalley leaned back in his chair and said:

"Let's go back for a moment, look at the facts before we go on. Jenene was alive around one o'clock, when Dr. Franklin saw him put on his coat, as though he was about to leave. But Dr. Franklin didn't actually see him go out of the building. So we don't know what Jenene really did after that, whether he made a pretense of leaving or actually drove off and came back, although he didn't log back in; and if he did come back later in the day, whether it was in his own car or in that van Miss Enderby saw parked, when she first looked outside. We don't know what he did between one and six, except that by six o'clock he was dead."

"You realize, Sir, that whoever killed Jenene could easily have been caught trapped inside the building, when the tour arrived."

"But it didn't happen that way, did it. They were outside in the van," was McCalley's curt reply. He tapped nervously on the table. "Jenene's car, Bill, We've got to locate it as soon as possible. It may already be too late."

Kenney nodded. "A smart move, Sir, taking the car away. Without the car in place, it would be assumed that Jenene left for home around one. It means, he didn't want anyone to know that he was expecting visitors."

"You're saying, he drove the car off somewhere and trudged back through the snow and ice?"

Ignoring the implicit criticism, Kenney went on, only slightly flustered:

"I suppose it could have happened that way, but I was thinking more along the lines that whoever came to see him, whoever killed him, might have convinced him they had to take the car away, as a precaution."

"Are you saying, Jenene drove his car elsewhere, with the van following, then came back to the museum in the other vehicle?"

"It's a possibility, isn't it?"

"Yes, but it's inconsistent with what we have."

"How's that, Sir?"

"Well, there was a van parked near the entrance when Miss Enderby first looked out. Obviously whoever drove the van there wasn't worried about taking any precautions. After all, it was Boxing Day. The museum was closed. No one was around. If the van could park there without suspicion, why couldn't Jenene's car have been brought around there, also?"

Kenney debated whether he should continue. To his surprise, McCalley waved him on.

"Well Sir, as you said, they were outside in the van. They were waiting until the coast was clear, to pick up Jenene's body and the wolf, and . . . do whatever they had planned after that."

"You said 'they'. . . ."

"Well, I don't see one person alone handling either the wolf or the body. Yes, Sir, I think there were two people at least. . . . And what about the chloroform?"

"What about it?"

"Why would they have used chloroform if they meant to strangle him right then and there? According to Springer, there was just enough in him to knock him out, not enough to kill him. Why bother with chloroform if you're going to strangle a man and leave him there? Unless they planned to take him elsewhere, wanted to keep him unconscious until he could be taken out of the museum to some other place where they would kill him, or, better yet, stage an accident maybe?"

To Kenney's surprise, McCalley seemed to be considering the possibilities. Kenney plunged ahead.

"It would explain a lot of things, Sir, if they had planned to make it look like an accident. It would explain Jenene's car being taken away but not too far, It would explain the chloroform, just enough to knock him out, keep him alive until later. If they had succeeded, Jenene's body might not have been found for days, weeks even."

"What about the wolf?"

"What do you mean, Sir?"

"All ready and waiting to be exhibited? Jenene's assistants told us they never laid eyes on it. I tend to believe them. I am also prepared to entertain the notion that Miss Enderby did not sign those documents we showed her."

Kenney had grown animated. Was the Inspector really considering his theory? He went on, the words tumbling out.

"Sir, do you think the wolf was really meant for the museum in New York?"

Here McCalley gave him a sharp look. Kenney's voice betrayed the kind of excitement which he, McCalley, as a rule, tried his best to discourage; but Kenney was more observant than most, and McCalley had learned to allow his assistant a certain latitude in his approach to things. He suddenly saw the young Sergeant in the years to come, a disciplined, dedicated officer, well trained, restraining but not entirely resisting these leaps into the unknown. He sighed. Maybe it would work for Kenney.

The bill came and was paid, but McCalley gave no indication he was ready to leave.

Kenney, for his part, hearing McCalley sigh, had thought the Inspector was getting impatient with him. It took him a few seconds to realize he was expected to continue. He began again, tentatively:

"We have Jenene unconscious in the workroom, the arctic wolf mounted and ready for . . . whatever. The cleaning crew is down the hall chattering and drinking coffee. Not knowing what to make of all this — the coast had always been clear when they had come before — Jenene's associates decide to go outside and wait in the van. Somehow, they managed to get out without being seen." His words seemed to give him pause. "Imagine, Sir! If the tour bus had been on time —?" The implications of his words were registered in the look on his face.

"If, if, if," muttered the Inspector. "The 'ifs' are legion, Sergeant, but there's only one fact."

"Yes, Sir," replied the other, properly chastised.

"Well, go on, go on," McCalley gestured vaguely.

"And then the tour bus arrives. Jenene was safely out of sight, chloroformed; but suddenly they had to change plans midstream, had to kill him right there, since they couldn't get him out and couldn't risk leaving him simply unconscious. You see, Sir, I think they were interrupted, waited outside for a while, until they realized they couldn't carry out what they'd planned. So they pulled out in a hurry. But first they had to kill Jenene, he knew too much. They were forced to abandon both the body and the wolf."

He paused, somewhat out of breath. McCalley, his elbow resting on the chair arm, his chin in his hand, was intent on examining the floor tiles. When he straightened up, he said:

"Go back, Bill. . . . You said the tour bus came and they couldn't do whatever it was they had planned to do. So they pulled out, you said, but first they had to kill Jenene."

Kenney drew a large breath. "I see what you're getting at, Sir. They killed Jenene *before* they went outside to wait, before they knew a tour bus was coming. Is that it?"

McCalley didn't drive home the obvious point. On his part, Kenney was too excited by this unusual exchange to be embarrassed. Was it possible? The Inspector wanted him to continue?

"The bus coming soon after Miss Enderby looked out that first time must have really surprised them."

"But she saw no one in the van, remember?"

"You're right, Sir; but they may have caught the movement of the door as it opened, then gotten down low in their seats, so as not to be seen. . . . ?"

McCalley nodded. Kenney went on with what was now a summing up.

"The van was there when Miss Enderby looked out that first time. The presence of the cleaning crew had forced them to wait outside. That's when they first started to suspect something wasn't quite right. Their suspicions were confirmed when they heard the tour bus coming up the road. That's when they had to make a quick decision and hurried away. Which meant, of course, that Jenene was already dead. That the decision to kill him had been made much earlier."

McCalley nodded. Kenney went back, testing the ground for his own satisfaction.

"The clean-up crew was waiting for the tour bus to arrive, but Jenene's visitors — Jenene himself — didn't know a special tour had been scheduled that day. It was the last thing they expected. On Boxing Day? . . . Miss Enderby opening the door and looking out was the first sign that something was up, then the bus came and they were forced to leave both the body and the wolf behind."

McCalley's eyes grew wide. Kenney knew that look. It could mean agreement or caution.

"You think so?" It seemed a straightforward question, but on impulse Kenney tossed it back.

"Don't *you*? Why else would they have pulled out in such a hurry? They almost rammed into the tour bus, according to the statements we have. Jenene was already dead, the wolf was ready to be taken out. All according to schedule. Suddenly, all their plans had to be scrapped."

He paused, somewhat out of breath. McCalley was frowning, his elbow resting on the chair arm, his chin in his hand. He straightened up with a long sigh.

"Your account is consistent, Bill, I'll grant you that. But we still don't know anything for sure, do we? Why that van was there? If the people in it were there for Jenene? If the wolf was really meant for them? If, in fact, they were the ones who killed him?"

"But, Sir, they were the only ones there, the only ones who —"

"I said it was a consistent account, but other things may turn up to change that picture."

McCalley got up and placed some money on the table for the tip.

"Anything else?"

"That's it."

As they headed toward the car, Kenney ventured:

"You have to admit, Sir, they left in a big hurry when they heard the bus coming. Knew they were guilty and didn't want to be found there. . . ."

"Oh, I'm sure they're guilty of something! Just what, it's too early to say. Motive is what we need, Bill. And a lot more answers."

Kenney started the engine, put the car into gear. As they eased out into the road, he asked:

102

"So, where does all this take us?"

"Back to the museum, more questions."

McCalley's phone beeped. It was a brief exchange.

"The museum will have to wait," he told Kenney, as he buckled on his seat belt. "We have another body. A trapper. Found shot about fifteen miles out in the woods. His name is Dobie."

CHAPTER 6

BACK TO NORMAL, ALMOST. . . .
(December 27, 2 PM)

The paper had gone very well. Jill was pleased but knew better than to indulge in self-satisfaction on such occasions. Still, she was always exhilarated after giving a talk that she had enjoyed preparing and had delivered well. It made academic life worth while, she had reminded herself often enough. Riding the crest of her successful presentation, she found she had not resented Glasner's presence for all of the fifty minutes her talk lasted. In fact, she had been ready for any questions he might have raised at the end, only to watch him leave as the applause started.

A small knot of people walked out into the corridor with her, some of them still taking notes.

She excused herself, finally, and hurried away. Just enough time to freshen up and call some friends she'd agreed to meet during the convention. At the desk, she discovered that two of them had already left messages, inviting her to join them and some other colleagues for dinner that evening, around seven. They gave phone numbers. She went through three other messages quickly. An editor from Scribner's wanted to discuss a proposal she had sent him for a new text on political writers of the Renaissance. Was she free for lunch or dinner tomorrow? Could she stop by when she had a free moment? With the note, he had included his business card, on which he had written the aisle and stall number of the Scribner's location in the book exhibit hall of the hotel.

Another message was from Housekeeping. Would she mind changing to another room with a wall bed? Last night's storm had temporarily closed down the airport and a good many people had to reschedule flights for the following day. The hotel could use her room, which had two large beds, to accommodate a family of four in the emergency. They would give her a substantial credit if she could help them out.

Why not?

The last message was from Glasner. "Nice going. I'll bow from the waist if or when I see you again in this life. I don't think we'll run into each other in the next." She read it a second time, smiling in spite of herself, then put it away with the others.

The Manager was most appreciative. They would send up a porter to take her bags to the other room as soon as she was ready.

Upstairs, she called her two colleagues. Jacqueline Toronado was in the Foreign Languages Department, a pleasant attractive woman in her forties. They often met in the tiny lounge where a coffee machine had been set up for staff and faculty of the three Departments who had offices on that floor. Steve Porter was a frail looking man in his late fifties, with whom Jill had shared many battles in committees on which they both served. They had known each other for eight years and had become good friends. Yes, she was free for dinner that evening and would meet them in the lobby at seven. Good, good, said Porter. They were getting a nice little group together, said Jacqueline.

She washed up, packed her clothing, sorted out papers and closed her briefcase. She could grab a late lunch while they prepared the new room for her. At the desk she made arrangements to have her luggage transferred. She would stop by later for the room key.

As she crossed the lobby and glanced outside, she paused to take in the bright sun on the packed snow, which sparkled like thousands of precious crystals. No cars were in sight. Two people were hurrying toward the hotel entrance, anxious to get inside. Any thought she might have had of finding a place nearby for a late snack, dissipated as she watched the new arrivals, their faces red with the cold, go through motions that suggested they had come in from a long trek through Siberia. She thought: later, maybe, a very short walk, down the block and back.

She strolled past the hotel gift shop and came to an abrupt stop at the newspaper rack, where a banner headline in one of the afternoon editions proclaimed. "Museum Taxidermist Murdered! Body Found in Museum Basement!" She picked up a copy and started to read as she moved toward the cashier. She paid, turned to leave. Distracted, she bumped hard into a carry-on. Automatically, she turned back to apologize, but the man it belonged to was already paying for his purchase and seemed not to have noticed. His back looked vaguely familiar; but, somewhat embarrassed, anxious to read the story and not in the mood for small talk, Jill quickly walked away.

She tucked the paper under her arm and went toward the hotel coffee shop. It was late for lunch, no waiting on line. In no time, she was comfortably seated at a spacious table for four, her bag and long heavy coat taking up two of the chairs.

She ordered coffee and a salad and opened up the paper. The account there was brief. Deadlines obviously had precluded anything more than the basic facts. The TV morning news probably had carried much more, but she had not turned on her set, using the time, instead, to review the talk she was scheduled to give later that morning.

The story told about a small group of early convention arrivals who had gone to the museum for a special tour the day after Christmas, Boxing Day in Canada. At the very beginning of their tour, they had found Dr. John Jenene, the museum taxidermist, murdered in his basement workroom.

"Frances Enderby, Curator of the Museum," it read, "had offered a special tour to a group of professors attending the annual convention of the Modern Language Association of America, meeting in Ottawa this year. . . ."

Only the Curator, McCalley, and Jenene were mentioned by name. There was a brief description of the MLA with a boxed "filler" giving the number attending this year's convention, the make-up of the organization and some of its publications. The story went on to describe how, early in the tour, the group had found Jenene's body in his workroom, located in the basement of the museum. In a separate entry in the second column, there was another boxed "filler," this one on taxidermy, followed by a short history of the "Haunted Castle," as the museum was sometimes called, with an old photograph of the Victorian structure. The story ended with Inspector McCalley quoted as saying there were "some significant leads," and that "a thorough investigation was already in progress."

She put the paper aside and picked up the thick convention program. The afternoon threatened to close around her, a claustrophobic sequence of sessions, none of which held particular interest for her. The alternative — a leisurely hour or so of window shopping — was out of the question. It was too damn cold out there. The day before, she had discovered a small hole in one of her boots. This might be a good time to have it mended, she decided. She signed her check and headed for the small cubbyhole in a corner of the hotel concourse, where a wizened little man assured her he could do the job while she waited.

Almost immediately, her mind turned to the events of the previous evening, the tour they never took, the poor man who had been found dead, Jack Glasner waiting protectively to accompany her back to the hotel, after they had all signed depositions. She recalled McCalley's efficient but quiet questioning. At the time, she had not really paid much attention, but she realized now how clever he was, letting her speak, not interrupting, timing his questions carefully. Nothing like "Law and Order," "NYPD" — nothing like that. The only time she caught a glimpse of something else came when she mentioned Ellis having been to Canada

107

and having done business with museums. It was a casual statement, carelessly tossed out as they were leaving, but McCalley had looked up sharply as though she had pressed an alarm button. With an effort she shrugged off a vague premonition. . . . Why had she mentioned Ellis?!? Well, she had . . . and that was that. No, damn it, it wasn't. McCalley had asked for Jenny's address. What could Jenny tell him except what he already knew?

She tried to shake off a mounting concern for her friend. Bringing Ellis's name into the conversation may have been a mistake on her part, but what could be read in that casual remark? Jenny might have to answer some questions, but it would all be over quickly.

With all her rationalizing, the worry persisted. She had definitely made a mistake volunteering that bit of information about Ellis. Now, she tried to remember other things she said that might have aroused the Inspector's curiosity. . . . How easily she had carried on! How relaxed he had made her feel! How sure of herself! And all the while, that other one, Kelsey, Kennedy, Kenney, that was it, Kenney, his assistant, Sergeant Kenney was writing it all down!

When the boot was mended she put it back on and strolled into the lobby area. It was almost five. The shops in the concourse, with their attractive holiday displays, drew her briefly. Then, putting on her coat, she strolled toward the entrance. Her friends all teased her about the five-minute walk she took every day and called exercise. Well, she hadn't missed a day in, oh, ages! . . . . Still no cars out there. She'd just go down to the end of the block and back.

Outside, the cold was fierce, but she set out at a slow, even pace. She reached the end of the block and decided to cross over and come back on the other side. As she started across — not without effort, since her boots were not made for this kind of heavy weather — a large vehicle skidded. Almost too late, she saw that it was rolling

108

in her direction. Rather than go where she had been heading, she turned and retraced the shorter distance to the closer curb, where she had just come from. The ice was slick under her feet. Hurrying, across, she slipped as she reached the curb; but by now she was out of range. That instinctive move to go back, she realized later, had probably saved her from serious injury, for the vehicle had gained speed instead of slowing down and would definitely have hit her if she had continued to the opposite side. As she picked herself up, she saw it speeding off.

Shaken up, her knee a large tender bruise where she had hit the curb when she fell, she limped back to the hotel, her heart still pounding. Annoyance now replaced the earlier instinctive emotions that had saved her from being hit. She could still see the car, no, it was a van, a dark van, backing up and driving off, away from the curb where she would have been, had she continued across the street. Still crouching, she had watched it move away, wondering why the driver hadn't stopped at least to see (common courtesy, after all!) if she was all right. Not that the driver was at fault, but he should have stopped, helped her to her feet — or, did he think she might sue him, if she got his name? Luckily, the heavy coat had protected her as she fell. Only her knee hurt, where it had bumped into the sharp broken edge of the pavement, where it came through the ice.

At the desk, she picked up the key to her new room. It was half the size of the one she had relinquished, but she didn't mind. The knee was throbbing now. She cleaned the ugly red gash with alcohol pads from her emergency kit, then pulled down the wall bed and sat on it to check off the meetings she might like to attend the next day. By the time she had showered and dressed, it was close to seven.

Before leaving the room, she took out the card McCalley had given her and placed it next to the phone. She needed to talk with him, discourage him from seeing Jenny.

Damn it, what was he going to ask her? She would call him, first thing in the morning. . . .

In the lobby, Jacqueline and Steve were chatting, near the entrance, with several other people. Jill counted twelve heads. What it meant was that, even if seated together around a large party table, people could talk comfortably only with their immediate neighbors on the left and right. She hoped she wouldn't get stuck with some eager beaver who liked to talk only about his "work in progress." One good thing: everybody was carrying coats, scarves, gloves, hats, which meant they were going "off campus." Good, thought Jill. Eating in expensive hotel restaurants was, or should be — she firmly believed — only a last resort.

"Ah, there you are!" Jacqueline Toronado detached herself from the others and came toward Jill with outstretched hands. The two women kissed on both cheeks, and Jacqueline led her toward the others. "Phil knows a wonderful place. He won't tell us more except that he knows the owner and we're getting a good deal. He and Don Jameson have vans. Room for all of us." She went on to introduce Jill to some of the others.

"How are you, my dear?" Steve Porter hugged her like a long-lost chum, as though he hadn't seen her less than a week ago at one of the faculty parties.

"Did someone say a 'nice *little* group'?"

"More of a caravan, at this point" he laughed. They seemed to be waiting for still others to join them.

"At this rate, we'll have to put on our badges to see who we're talking to, across the table!" Anyone properly registered for the convention was given an ID badge that gave the wearer access to all meetings, special events, lectures, group parties, and, most important, the enormous area where publishers set up their book stalls.

Jacqueline asked: "How was your paper, cherie? I'm so sorry I missed it. Couldn't get out of my delegates

110

meeting."

Jill waved away the apology. She realized suddenly that going out to dinner with her friends was a welcome relief. Unconsciously perhaps, the murder in the museum and her fall trying to avoid the veering van, earlier, had taken their toll. Her nerves were ragged. Impulsively, she hugged her friend.

"You've heard me talk before. You'll hear me again. Nothing to miss." A tap on her shoulder, from behind, made her whirl around. At first she saw only the top of a head and a mop of brown hair streaked with gray. Glasner was bent down low and now straightened up very slowly. He stood there, a big grin on his face, enjoying her surprise.

"I said I'd bow from the waist in your honor, if we met again in this life. . . ." He turned to Jacqueline. "I promised her that, after hearing·her paper."

"Ah, so you've met."

"The one advantage of long registration lines. You have time to get to know the person standing in front and behind you."

The man called Phil pulled Glasner toward him. "It's about time! We're all been standing here waiting for you." Whatever Glasner replied was lost in the hubbub of instructions. Phil was doing a final count of heads.

"All fourteen accounted for. You five," he turned to a group already assembled on his right, "come in my van. Don takes another four or five. The rest go with Mario."

Coats and scarves, hats and gloves quickly went on. Everyone edged up to the revolving doors but did not venture out until the vans came around. As they walked outside, Jacqueline pointed to Jill's leg.

"You're limping. What happened?"

"Oh, just a bruise. I went out for a short walk. A van skidded. I had to move fast, to avoid getting hit and ended up falling against the curb. Nothing serious."

By now Phil had his five people. Everyone else

seemed to be scrambling for Don's van. Mario drew up in his car and waved Jill inside. He seemed impatient as he stomped his feet to keep warm. Jacqueline had already settled down in Don's van. "I'll see you there!" she called out to Jill, as the vans started to move.

Glasner was coming toward them at a fast pace, trying to keep his balance on the ice.

"About time!" Mario said, somewhat grumpily, as he got behind the wheel and started the engine.

"Sorry. A quick walk to get the circulation going." Jill told him about her near miss, earlier, a kind of warning. "Shouldn't have gone out," was his reply.

Good Lord! Was he always so peremptory? And hadn't he just gone for a "quick walk" himself? Out loud she said:

"I did make it safely to the other side."

"Not so safely —" he countered, pointing to her knee, "And it could have been much worse!"

"Well, it wasn't!"

"And I'm still here in one piece."

The going was slow. Most of the avenues had been sanded down, but in some side streets last night's snow was piled high and had turned to ice. At one point, Mario, an impatient driver, had lost the vans and now was on his own.

"Do you know where this place is?" Glasner asked.

"Hey! I live here!" answered the other, peering right and left.

"Why don't you wait for the vans to catch up?" Glasner suggested.

"Just look for Glouster Street. There's a gas station on the corner, a white brick two-story house across from it. Glouster and 11th."

Jill craned her neck to look out at the street signs. "Was that it?"

Glasner was on one knee, trying to read the signs. "Davies . . . . Ha! wait, slow down. We just passed 10th."

112

Mario seemed relieved. "Yes, here it is. 11th coming up, up, up and . . . right or left for Glouster?"

Both of them watched Mario trying to decide. Finally, he swerved to the right. They skidded into 11th and on to a mound of snow. Mario backed up, straightened out, went on. At the end of the block Jill read off:

"Merrick."

"Ta-ta-rataaaa! End of the next block," said Mario. Sure enough, there was the sign and the tiny Christmas icicle-lights hanging from the canopy of *Il Bel Giardino*. A wide path had been cleared in front of the entrance, right down to the curb. "I'll let you out here in front."

"Wait, I'll come with you, to park," said Glasner. He helped Jill from the car. "Go on inside," he told her. "It's freezing out here." But Mario was already moving off. They watched as he skidded around the corner, then both of them burst out laughing. Glasner took Jill's arm and guided her up the walk to the entrance.

"Go on in. I'll wait for him here."

"Let's both go in," said Jill. "He's annoyed with us, I think."

Friendly shouts greeted them as they entered. "You got what you deserved, trying to ditch us!" Glasner looked behind him, as though they were talking or should be talking to someone else. He pointed behind him several times, with dramatic flourish. "Not us!!!!"

The group was already seated at one long table, the result of three smaller ones pushed together from a corner wall out into the open area. Two empty chairs had been kept free at the very end. Jill and Glasner sat down next to one another. Jacqueline was sitting across from Jill, in the opposite corner. Mario came in to catcalls and jeers. He seemed to enjoy it.

Glasner was introducing himself to the person on his right, a young thin man with a bushy beard.

She began to relax. At least, she wouldn't have to

113

do much talking, with Glasner busy listening to bushy beard and Jacqueline, opposite her, deep in conversation with a French colleague. Small blessings, she thought, suddenly very tired. She closed her eyes. . . .

"Red or white?" someone asked. It was Glasner, ready to pour from one of two bottles he was holding.

She straightened up. "A little red, thanks."

It was a very good California merlot, but she put the glass down after a small sip. Solid food was what she needed. It had been a long day and only a salad for lunch.

Across from her, Jacqueline was chattering away in French. On her right, Glasner seemed to have forgotten she was there. Perfect. She might have ended up sitting next to Mario, who had grown boisterous and at that very moment had his arm around the woman next to him, pulling her toward him as she tried to push him away.

Jill's eyes began to droop again, but she sat up with a start as the first round of dishes was brought in by a small parade of waiters, to the vocal fanfare of Phil and his friends.

"Fettucine alla carbonara, lasagne, rigatoni alla marinara, manicotti, linguini with shrimp;

Roulettes of veal, braciolette ai ferri, chicken francese. stuffed pork, fried calamari;

trecolori salad, mozzarella and tomato with basil; salad greens with house dressing; and coming up —

tiramisù, cheese case, eclairs, creme brulée, fresh fruit;

cappuccino, espresso, café au lait, regular and decaf coffee . . . ."

Don had ordered so that everybody could try as many of Mr. Giannini's delicious specialties as possible. At least two large platters of everything were brought out. The dishes were passed down one side, up the other, back down this row, that row, until they were empty.

Jill had a small portion of *rigatoni al filetto di*

pomodoro, the simplest dish available. She ate slowly, as waiters hovered to replace dishes, napkins. spoons, forks, knives, bread and bread sticks, brought fresh bottles of wine, joining in the laughter from time to time, especially when someone said something in broken Italian. At the other end, one of the men started to sing a Neapolitan song. Others chimed in. From other parts of the room, new voices joined theirs. By the time the dessert carts came around, they had gone through the old classics, including familiar arias from *La Boheme*, and were into *Volare*.

Glasner leaned toward her. "Everything all right? You've been awfully quiet."

"It's been a long day." He was about to answer, but just then the owner, Mr. Giannini himself, appeared, in the wake of complimentary liqueurs. Phil got up and offered a toast. Nodding and smiling, Mr. Giannini accepted the compliment, then waxed eloquent in broken English, which no one really understood but everyone encouraged.

He waz uppy dei had enjeeooed hees cuisine, the squisito legacy of five (here he held up the five fingers of his left hand, spread out as far as possible, touching each finger with his right hand as he spoke) *five generations of master cooks* (someone raised his glass of red wine in silent toast to heaven, where those generations now resided). *My fodder, my grenfodder, his fodder and grenfodder, back to the doge of Venezia, Queen of the Adriatico, down to Gramscì himself, the blood of Gramscì the great Gramscì is in these veins* (big applause from the entire room this time), *RIGHT DOWN TO THIS MOMENT, RIGHT DOWN TO ME, GIORGIO GIANNINI!!*

On the other side of the room, someone began to sing the Italian national anthem. Mr. Giannini held up the glass of wine someone had placed in his hand, raised it in a silent toast, and drank half the glass in one gulp. After that, he went around the table shaking everyone's hand.

Phil got up. "Hate to do this, folks, but it's time to

leave if we're going to put on a good show tomorrow!" The reminder was met with loud groans and moans. It was a signal for everyone to push back chairs. Coats and hats were retrieved and put on, while Don and Phil worked out the tip, added that to the bill, and went around collecting money from everyone. Jill found herself arm in arm with Jacqueline. Outside, they hurried into Don's van. They were the first ones on.

Jill turned to glance back. Don was talking to Mario. Glasner and bushy beard were with them.

"Do you think Mario should drive?" she asked her friend.

"No."

"He had quite a bit to drink . . . ."

"At last five glasses of wine," said Jacqueline, "and a couple of glasses of Limoncello at the end . . . but he shouldn't drive drunk or sober. A car is a lethal weapon with Mario behind the wheel. Or didn't you notice?"

Jill couldn't help laughing. She felt a bit tipsy, even though she had not finished her one glass of merlot.

"His friend should be driving. . . ."

Jacqueline shook her head vigorously. She was a little drunk. "No, no. Mario doesn't let anybody touch his car. His buddy George, the young fellow with the beard, always drives back with him after a party. Once, when Mario wouldn't slow down, George turned off the ignition. On the highway. He leaned right over from the passenger seat and steered the car on to the shoulder as it slowed down. Mario was furious with him. Screamed that his car was ruined."

The two women had sat down in the front seats of the van and were the first ones off when they arrived at the hotel. They hurried into the warm lobby.

"If I find nothing more exciting to do, I'll come to your panel on Baudelaire tomorrow," Jill teased her friend. They hugged.

116

"Never mind that. Let's meet later on. I'll tell you about the replacement we found for Obert." Professor Obert was retiring, and one of Jacqueline's tasks was to interview candidates who had applied for the tenure-track position. "And you'll tell me all about the murder at the museum."

Jackie's reminder hit her like a blast of arctic air. Had she told Jackie about last night, about the tour? She must have. Or had Glasner said something at dinner? But, if he had, the others would have asked a zillion questions. Maybe one of them had been there too? All at once, the warm glow of the evening was drained from her. She felt herself trembling. Delayed shock? Guilt for mentioning Ellis's name to McCalley? With a pang she realized she had not called Jenny, as she had promised she would the minute she arrived.

In her room, the little red light was blinking. There was only one message. She listened to it and opted to have it left in her mailbox as well.

Inspector McCalley needed to talk with her again. Would two o'clock tomorrow be all right? He would come by the hotel, meet her in the lobby.

Good! She wouldn't have to call *him*!

It was almost midnight. She dialed the number he had left for her and spoke briefly into the machine. Two o'clock was fine.

For some reason, knowing she would be talking with McCalley again the next day eased some of the tension that threatened to make her night miserable.

She fell asleep almost immediately.

Chapter 7
Picking Up the Scent
(December 28, 9:15 AM)

When she woke up, after an uninterrupted eight hours of sleep, her body felt sluggish, her head ached, her throat was scratchy. Just her luck to come down with something while away from home! Maybe a lot of Vitamin C would stop whatever it was, before it got very far. Sitting on the edge of her narrow bed, she took three full grams of C with her other supplements and munched on some packaged cheese and crackers she'd saved from the flight (was it only two days ago?). Coffee helped.

No point trying to rush to Jackie's panel. Even if she left right now, she'd get there in time to see the room emptying out. Everyone had to keep rigorously to the scheduled time slots. Within a matter of minutes, another group would be coming into the room for the next session. So, no Jackie. She'd call her later. The big question was: shower or not to shower? She decided to postpone it. Her body simply wouldn't cooperate right now.

Trying to put on her slippers, she almost lost her balance. In the bathroom she brushed her teeth, carefully avoiding the mirror. Two aspirins with a second cup of coffee helped a little. But when she felt her eyes closing and her head droop while watching an interview on TV, she decided to lie down and rest some more. The morning was shot anyway; she wasn't up to attending sessions or doing anything until early afternoon, at best.

The phone woke her. She glanced at her watch. Twelve thirty! At least the headache was gone. The nap had done her some good.

"Are you all right?" It was Jacqueline. "I was worried about you."

"I'm sorry. I missed your panel. I felt awful this

118

morning."

"Don't worry about that. We all miss panels. You're feeling better?"

"Yes. I'll be fine. I'm getting dressed. Maybe I'll take a walk to clear my head before I see that policeman again."

"Don't you dare."

"He's not exactly a menace —"

"Never mind the jokes. Don't go outside on your own sgain. . . . What policeman?"

"Inspector McCalley. He's in charge of the murder investigation." Jill remembered that her friend was still waiting to hear more about what had happened on the museum tour that first day. Now was as good a time as any to fill in some of the details. When Jill was through, Jackie asked bluntly:

"Well, what else does the Inspector want? He has your deposition —?"

"And I have a few questions of my own!"

They talked for a few more minutes, then Jackie had to run. "Are you free later? I want to hear about your meeting with McCalley." They agreed to meet late in the afternoon, in the lounge.

Outside, it was gray and dreary but not as cold as yesterday. She wondered what McCalley wanted to talk to her about. He was something of a puzzle, the Inspector. Were all detectives like that? Did they all have that look that bore into you even as they smiled, were they all as efficient, did they all have that quiet lurking humor that surfaced at the most unexpected moments?

When she had showered and dressed, she sat down on the side of the bed and called Jenny.

In New York, the warm temperatures continued. In turn, Jill described the blizzard that had left them pretty much stranded in the hotel.

"Have you met anyone worth listening to, yet?" It

119

was a variation on a familiar theme, standard fare ever since Jill had told Jenny about finally agreeing to a divorce.

"One at least; but what he has to say brings out all the nastiness in me. I can't stand it."

"Sounds promising."

Jill was surprised to find the subject was making her uncomfortable. Quickly, she went on to describe last night's dinner, talked briefly about Jacqueline and Steve, whom Jenny had met several times.

"How was your paper? Did you have a good audience?"

"About sixty. The questions were pretty sharp."

"That means the presentation was pretty good. You're always minimizing what you do. Remember at Columbia, how you'd badger me every time I forgot to put down a source, or misquoted somebody? You used to drive me crazy." It was good to hear Jenny laugh. They chatted some more. Then, Jill asked:

"Have you had any visitors?" At first she thought her friend wasn't going to answer. When she did, her voice sounded brittle, far away.

"This morning the McCarthys in the gray stone house down the road brought me home-made beef stew. Later, that new young couple — Dickson, I think that's the name — came by to ask if they could take me into town or get me anything for me. Just before you called, Mrs. Lennox, the widow at the end of the road, stopped by to say hello. The whole world is at my doorstep. . . ."

"What about the workmen? Are they still at it?"

"They're coming tomorrow to replace the broken crystals in the chandelier and to check the door hinges in the bedroom. Those paneled doors had to be trimmed, you remember, they weren't closing properly." Jill could hear her friend clearing her throat, holding the phone at a distance while she did so. If only she could find the right words to help lighten Jenny's misery. . . . Suddenly, at the

120

other end, she heard Jenny cry out: "Oh, what's the point! I have to sell this place or I'll go crazy!"

Jill held back a sob. "Plenty of time for that kind of decision. Have you mentioned it to Hart?"

"No, not yet. . . ."

"I'm sure he'll agree. He'll tell you, there's a lot to do still. And we've got to help him. Work together to see things through. . . ." The words sounded hollow. She was having a hard time keeping her own voice steady. "What are you doing with yourself while I'm away?" When her friend didn't answer at once, she went on quickly: "Today? What are you doing later today?"

"The Lowells insisted I have dinner with them tonight."

"You're going, of course?"

"I hate to keep saying no to everybody, but honestly, Jill —"

"Hey! Allow them the privilege of feeding you."

"It's a short walk to their place, but Sam insists on picking me up. I guess he's afraid I might change my mind."

"Well, don't! . . . ." The silence at the other end spurred Jill into going on, although she had promised herself she wouldn't press her friend too hard. Alone in that big beautiful mansion, Jenny had too much time to brood. Jill ached for her. "How's the book coming?" Jenny had signed a contract while in Europe to do a book on Renaissance painters. At the time Ellis was killed, she had completed more than two thirds. Since then, she hadn't even looked at the manuscript.

The silence at the other was eloquent. Jill went on, almost recklessly: "Listen, you can't walk around like a robot for the next twenty years."

"Is that all you give me, twenty years?" She could feel Jenny smiling and immediately felt better.

"We'll add time for good behavior. Maybe. What's on for tomorrow?"

"Oh, Jill, I can only do so much. I'm not ready to meet people over cocktails or at the dinner table. I drift off into my own thoughts. People talk to me and I don't hear them, I don't answer. If I go anywhere, I just make others as miserable as I am."

"Then stop being miserable! You're creating a vacuum that's going to suck all the good things out of your life. And don't tell me there aren't good things left. Ellis would scold you in the same way, and you know it!" Guilt spilled over, blinded her eyes with tears as the silence lengthened at the other end, but she couldn't stop now. "You've got to heal, Jenny, but even your friends can do just so much. The rest is up to you. And don't tell me you don't care. You *should* care. You *do* care!" How she wished she could reach out and hug her friend! How she ached for her!

She took a long breath to steady her voice. "Hey, when I get back, and the weather holds, we'll take a little trip. We'll have almost a week before the new semester begins. We'll drive down to Christiana Mall for the big sales."

"I don't need anything."

"So, we'll just look around. We'll eat."

"Where is this place?"

"In Delaware. Just a couple of hours away. We can stay at the Dupont Hotel in Wilmington, that old many-splendoured thing. I hear it's been restored according to the original design, all the wallpapers, the tapestries, rugs, furniture, all as it was when it first went up. You'll love it. Right up your alley. You might even want to write it up for one of the architecture magazines."

"It's been done. I've read a couple."

Jill drew in a long sigh of relief. "Ah, so you know all about the Dupont Hotel. Well, you can admire it with your own expert eyes! The Winterthur Museum is down there, too, and the Delaware Art Museum — they have a marvelous Rossetti, no, pre-Raphaelite collection, their

pride and joy. You've got to see it! and those gardens —
forgot the name. . . . and on the way back we'll stop in
Philadelphia. . . ." The chuckle at the other end made her
feel better. She stretched out on the bed.

"When *are* you coming back?"

"Monday, the thirtieth, if the schedule holds. And
New Year's Eve, I'm coming over with champagne and your
favorite goodies from Zabar's. You can count on it!"

"You're always welcome, you know that; but I'm
sure you have better places to go New Year's Eve. . . . I'll be
all right."

"Don't tell me Hart has invited himself over!"

"No, he hasn't said a word."

"If he does, just tell him I'll be visiting for a few
days. That'll chase him off."

"Oh, Jill, you really should try harder to get along
with him!"

"Why? I don't like his hanging around you, like he
used to, before you married Ellis. He acts as though he's
family!" The words tumbled out, as they always did, when
she thought of Hart and his long-term campaign to win
Jenny for himself. The three of them had met while at
Columbia, where Quinn was studying law and Jenny and Jill
were in graduate school. He had asked Jenny to marry him
then and, in spite of all that had happened since, he seemed
to be trying again, more certain this time, sure of winning
her in the end. . . .

She heard herself saying "He should get married,
but not to you . . ." and immediately regretted the words,
even as they spilled out. How could she be so callous,
especially at a time like this? But, if she was any judge,
Hartley was still courting her . . . *hovering* was the word
that came to mind.

Jill tried to keep her opinions about Quinn to
herself but had never quite succeeded. She wanted to spare
her friend, who had always insisted Jill was wrong about

123

Hart; but to Jill the man's attentions were suspect, always had been, always would be. And now, it was blatantly obvious, he entertained new hopes. After all, Jenny would not remain alone forever. Eventually, she would remarry. But with Hartley pitching his tent so close, so soon, she'd never get a chance to really choose for herself. Hartley would be right there, the obvious candidate. In the old days, even before she met Ellis, Jenny had shrugged off Jill's comments about Hartley. Even after Hart had proposed and she had turned him down, Jenny refused to see in him anything other than a trustworthy friend. Ellis apparently had come to share that opinion, had trusted the man enough to name him his Executor. Why couldn't Jill go along?

"I've got nothing against him," she had told Jenny on the phone one morning, soon after her friend had returned from Europe. She had called to apologize for cutting short her visit the day before, when she had found Hartley in the motel suite, where Jenny and Ellis were staying until the house was ready for them. "He's always around. I feel I'm going to trip over him and get sued for damages." That afternoon, after her last class, Jill had gone to spend some time with Jenny . . . and there was Hartley, in the living room of the small suite, his feet on the coffee table, reading the *Wall Street Journal*, as though he owned the place. Ellis was in Manhattan on business and wouldn't be home until late that evening. Jill made some ironic remark about special working hours for rich lawyers — Hartley always brought out the nastiness in her — and he had answered, without looking up from the newspaper he was reading: "Professors get paid pretty well too, for six or seven hours of pontificating every week to a captive audience." I deserve that, she was fair enough to admit, although it didn't change her attitude toward him one iota.

To Jenny, Hartley's exchanges with Jill were, in the end, just friendly banter. To Jill, his sarcasm seemed at times a veiled threat. On that particular occasion, when she realized Hartley had settled in for the evening "to keep Jenny company until Ellis gets home," she refused Jenny's invitation to join them for dinner, and left. . . .

Jenny's voice at the other end brought Jill back to the present. "I thought you'd gotten over all that. The poor man has never made a pass, he's the soul of courtesy and discretion."

Jill couldn't help laughing. "Good God! You make him sound like a pompous old ass. I almost feel sorry for him!" At the other end, Jenny laughed with her. The mood lightened. Jill went on to describe her adventure at the museum, told her about the arctic wolf, about the Curator, finally zeroed in on McCalley.

"He asked for your address, Jen. I happened to mention that Ellis dealt with museums occasionally, and he wants to pick your brain."

"He'll be better off talking with Henry." Henry Wentworth was Ellis's manager.

"I'm sure he intends to see him as well. . . . I hope you don't mind if he calls on you."

"No, but what can I possibly tell him that will help?"

"Nothing, probably. But he has to follow every lead. Right now he's stumped. So, he's looking into the arctic wolf and its connection with the museum. Remember the emu?" she went on quickly, to avoid more explanations.

"The Australian Big Bird?"

"Didn't Ellis get one for a museum in New Jersey?"

"A zoo. In Chicago."

"Anyway, he's pleasant enough, good at his job, very efficient," Jill picked up, hoping her casual tone sounded convincing. She still felt guilty about mentioning Ellis's name to the Inspector. Now she felt a rush of anxiety as she remembered the sudden alertness in McCalley's expression when she mentioned Ellis's doing business with museums. Why was it so important for him to pursue that perfectly ordinary remark? More to the point, why couldn't she have kept her mouth shut? She felt her defenses give way to an irrational apprehension. Jenny was saying:

"He really should check with Ellis's people at the office, the warehouse. They can tell him much more than I can."

"As I said, I'm sure he will. By the way, he'll be knocking on my door, too. . . .."

"Ah *ha*!. . . . So he's really coming to see *you*!"

"C'mon, Jen," she laughed into the phone. "He's a happily married man. He wears a wedding ring!"

"So? You were happily married once. And Kevin wore a ring."

Jill laughed. "Hey! He only wants to talk to me, ask me questions, not drag me to his cave!" She went on to describe McCalley's deceptively casual manner. "Before you know it, you're telling him things you wouldn't tell your best friend."

"Oh? What have you told him that you haven't told me?"

"Nothing. I'm on to him." They both laughed.

"Famous last words," was her friend's comment, before they hung up.

Having arrived fifteen minutes early to look over the place and see where they might sit, McCalley spotted Jill first. He rose from the comfortable chair at the entrance to the lobby bar and stood waiting for her to see him. He registered something different about her today, but it wasn't until she had almost reached him that he noticed she was limping.

"Is this all right?" he asked, pointing to the alcove where he had been sitting.

"Fine."

At two in the afternoon, the dark interior of the

126

lounge bar already boasted a few drinkers, hangers-on from lunch, maybe. At a table in the back a small group was carrying on a heated discussion about hockey.

They sat down in facing chairs. McCalley began pleasantly:

"Can professors afford this kind of luxury?"

"Reduced rates. I'm sure you get them too when you go to police conventions. . . ."

The waitress came over. McCalley ordered club soda, Jill asked for bottled water Anxious to say her piece quickly, Jill began:

"I was on the phone with Jenny Bantry a little while ago. I told her you might want to talk to her, but it was hard trying to explain why. *Must* you see her?"

"That was thoughtful of you," he said by way of reply. He took out a small pad and an elegant thin ball point pen, placed them on the low table, then sat back and gave her a long look.

"I couldn't help noticing you were limping just now."

She registered surprise and for a moment her frown disappeared. "Oh, that! I fell yesterday, just down the street. A van skidded, and I stumbled against the curb trying to avoid it. It was nothing." The waitress came with the drinks.

McCalley took a sip from his glass before speaking again.

"When I told you, yesterday, that I was going to New York, I wasn't quite sure what to look for, or what I would find. I'm still not sure. But since we talked, I've learned enough to convince me that the trip is important to this investigation. I have to trust to your discretion, Dr. Masterson, because I want you to know a couple of things that ordinarily I wouldn't share with anyone outside of my team."

Jill nodded, wondering why he would tell her

127

things he only shared with his team. . . .

"First of all, Dr. Jenene was definitely murdered. Since then, my men have found crucial evidence that even the press doesn't know about yet —"

"— I understand."

"Yesterday morning some documents were found, having to do with the acquisition and transfer of certain museum specimens."

"Isn't that routine?"

McCalley held up a hand. "Here me out, please. . . . Dr. Jenene had signed them. The Curator's signature also appears on them, but Miss Enderby swears she never signed such documents, never even saw the specimens involved, had no knowledge of any of them." He let that sink in before continuing. "There were three transactions, two dating back to May and August; the third was the arctic wolf you saw in the workroom. The wolf was scheduled for pick-up on December twenty-sixth. . . ."

"The day of the tour?" "McCalley nodded. "And Miss Enderby knew nothing about it?" Again, McCalley nodded.

"That's right."

"No wonder she was taken aback when she first saw it!"

"We're looking into all of this, of course, but I don't think Miss Enderby was involved in the transactions. She was extremely angry when she saw those papers. The museum is a big part of her life and she expects her staff, especially those on her level of responsibility, like Dr. Jenene, to act in its best interests. As I said, these new developments are being checked out."

A subtle change had come over the young woman's face as McCalley spoke. "That's not really what you've come to tell me, is it?" She searched the Inspector's expression with a focused awareness, a new alertness. Before McCalley could answer, she went on, almost breathlessly: "What exactly has all this to do with me, with Jenny, with Ellis Bantry?"

"I was hoping you could tell more about Mr. Bantry —"

"You haven't answered me, Inspector." There was a stridency in her voice. "How does Ellis come into it?" She was flushed now, her eyes troubled. "The other night I made a simple comment on our way out, but you've latched on to it in a big way. Are you that desperate? Don't you have anything better to do?" Her voice had risen. Someone at the bar turned to look in their direction.

"This is not a pleasant task for me. I understand you're very close to the Bantrys, to your friend Jenny. And what I have to tell you was a shock to me as it will be to you, I'm afraid. But I need your help and for that reason I am trusting you with crucial information that must remain very private."

He had struggled with himself all morning about how to justify sharing this important news with her. He had concluded he had no choice. He would have to trust her if he wanted her cooperation. Jill Masterson was Jenny Bantry's best friend. Jenny Bantry was Ellis Bantry's widow. Ellis Bantry, who was killed in New York earlier in the month, was down as the agent in connection with the delivery of an arctic wolf from the Canadian Museum of Nature in Ottawa to the American Museum of Natural History in New York, and for two other deliveries, all three now suspect. It was imperative that he get as much information as possible about Ellis Bantry, place him in the picture that was emerging, or eliminate him from it. To do so, he needed to talk with Mrs. Bantry and her husband's staff and friends. Jill Masterson could help make the task easier for all of them. Most important, she herself could provide him with vital information. . . .

In his quiet, steady voice, he told her about finding Ellis Bantry's name on the documents they had discovered in Dr. Jenene's basement.

When he had finished, she turned away, her face still flushed, her eyes shining with the suggestion of tears. A deep sob escaped her.

McCalley leaned forward and said in a low voice. "I can come back later, if you like . . . ."

She shrugged, made a helpless gesture. "No, now. Go ahead. What do you want to know?"

McCalley took up his pad and looked through it quickly. "You told me Mr. Bantry dealt with museums —"

"And antiques. Their house is full of precious things. Do you want a list of their furnishings?" He ignored the undisguised sarcasm, recognizing it as the result of frustration and an effort to contain anger. Unruffled by her obvious hostility, McCalley said:

"I would appreciate a general description of the kinds of things he handled." He did not look up from his notes, until she started to speak.

"Inspector, Jenny and Ellis left for Europe shortly after they were married. I had met Ellis several months earlier. Hardly enough time to get to know him well. As to his business, all I can tell you is that it was very successful. I'm sure his manager can tell you what you need to know about the things he handled."

McCalley said nothing. Jill heard herself say:

"At first, it was to be a full year's honeymoon, but they stayed on another two years after that. They were gone almost three years." She pushed back a strand of hair. "That's not what you want to hear, is it?"

McCalley raised his head. "Anything you tell me will be useful."

"At the end of the first year," she went on slowly, stroking her forehead as she spoke, "Ellis decided they might as well stay on a bit longer. It gave him a chance to meet with some of his European clients. On her own, Jenny began to search out things for the house they had

130

purchased in Bronxville, a short drive north of the city, a house they bought just before sailing for Europe. It's a big place, an old house that Jenny visited often as she grew up. She had always dreamed of owning a house like that. When it was put up for sale, a few weeks before they were married, she and Ellis quickly closed the deal." She paused to take a sip of water. "All the time they were away, the house was being renovated. About two years ago, their purchases began to arrive. By the time they moved in, early in November, everything was pretty much in place."

"You said they were in Europe for three years?"

"Yes. France, Italy, Austria, Spain, Portugal, I'm not sure about Holland. Oh, yes, Sweden and Denmark, Hong Kong, Japan, China briefly."

"And they were together all that time?"

"I suppose you're going to bother Jen with the same stupid question?" McCalley. looked up. Her eyes bore into him. "Inspector, if you're trying to find out if and when Ellis came to the States to deal with museum specimens, I can't help you. As far as I know, they were together all the time. I didn't see them again until the end of August, when they both returned home . . . *together.* All you need to do is check their passports." She realized, even before the words were out, how stupid a remark it was: McCalley surely had people already checking Ellis's comings and goings, and much else. . . .

"Thank you. I suppose you saw your friend often after they got back?"

"Yes. Classes didn't start for me until after Labor Day. I'd drive out to the motel three, four times a week, and from there we'd go to the house. Twice I met them in Manhattan for dinner."

"When did they move into the house?"

"*Officially,* that was Ellis's little joke, they would be 'at home' by the middle of December, he kept saying. They were planning a housewarming party just before

Christmas. As it turned out, they did have a small dinner party on Thanksgiving. Just the four of us."

"The four of you?"

"Yes, myself and an old friend of ours, Hartley Quinn."

"So, they were settled in their new home by then, by Thanksgiving?"

"Yes. They moved in around the third or fourth of the month, when the renovations were completed."

Without looking up from his notes, McCalley asked: "Who was doing the renovating while they were abroad?"

"Several companies were involved, I can't give you names. Plumbers and electricians, carpenters, general contractors. Architects redesigned spaces, walls were torn down, new ones built, windows replaced, rooms enlarged, dozens of crews were in and out all the time. Hartley of course was supervising everything."

McCalley glanced up. "Hartley Quinn? The man who came to Thanksgiving dinner?"

"Yes. Jenny and I met him at Columbia, years ago, when we were students there."

"Does Mr. Quinn also deal with antiques and museums?"

Jenny laughed in spite of herself. "Only if they come up in court. He's a lawyer. The only thing he shared with Ellis was a taste for expensive clothes. They both dressed well." She almost smiled. "Ellis liked him a lot. Made him his Executor."

McCalley watched her for a few moments, then asked:

"How do you feel about him?"

"Hart? Oh, he gets on my nerves sometimes. But he's reliable. Very protective of Jenny."

"And Hartley — by the way, can you give me his address?" While she rummaged in her tote, he went on: "So

Hartley Quinn kept his eye on things, while the Bantrys were abroad?" She drew out a small ledger, opened it, and held it out to him before answering.

"Yes. Ellis had left a whole set of instructions with Hartley. Hart made sure they were carried out. He was the one who spoke for Ellis, relayed what Ellis wanted done, made decisions, when necessary. He talked with Ellis at least three times a week by phone, and there were e-mails all the time. Then, as furniture and fixtures began to arrive — tables, chairs, cabinets, beds, glassware, china — Hartley was right there, checking them on his list, making sure nothing was damaged. He made sure every piece went right where Ellis had instructed, kept a log even, with dates of arrival, when this or that was done. By the time Ellis and Jenny got back, there was very little left for them to do." McCalley nodded as he copied the information from her ledger. "A great deal of love . . . *and* money went into that house . . . ."

McCalley handed back the ledger. "Mr. Quinn must have had plenty of free time to do all that," he said.

"It wasn't as though he had to be present every minute of every day. If something was wrong, he corrected it quickly. But, yes, he did have plenty of free time. He could arrange his work pretty much as he wanted, since he doesn't have to answer to anyone."

"How come?"

"He inherited his father's law practice. Owns his own firm, comes and goes as he pleases. Oh, don't get me wrong. He's a first-rate lawyer. No trimming, there! But he knows how to use his time to advantage."

"And found time to supervise renovations at the Bantrys' house."

"Hartley is very efficient."

McCalley grinned at her, when he looked up. "Even though he gets on your nerves?"

She grinned back. "'Sometimes,' I said."

He glanced at his notes. "Bronxville. Is that far from Manhattan?"

"Forty, fifty minutes from mid-town."

"Did you ever go with him, to the house, to see how things were progressing?" And in the same breath: "Is this Mr. Quinn's office address?"

"Yes, on both counts."

"Were the Bantrys pleased with the result? With Mr. Quinn's handling of things?"

"Of course. As I said, Hartley is very efficient. And being a lawyer, he knew how to deal with emergencies, insurance claims, that sort of thing. I think Ellis and Jenny realized how much work had been involved only when they actually saw the house, on their return. Without Hartley, things would not have turned out so well."

"Was Mr. Bantry often away from home?"

"I don't know what you mean by 'often.' A certain amount of travel is dictated by the kind of work he did."

"He took trips from time to time . . . ?"

"I suppose. . . . You're forgetting, Inspector, that I knew Ellis only a short time. I'm sure you'll get much more information from his staff, from his records."

McCalley put down his pad and finished his club soda. "I know this is painful, but it would help me a great deal if you were to tell me about Mr. Bantry's death."

"How could that possibly help?" Then, as though dismissing the question, she gestured vaguely and said: "He was caught in crossfire in Soho. He'd rushed into the city after a call from a dealer—"

"— What time was that?"

"The call? Just before eight. Jenny was annoyed at his rushing off without breakfast. He'd gotten back from the West coast late the night before, was still in bed when the call came." Jenny recognized the hard glitter in McCalley's eyes. What had she said *this* time?

"He'd just gotten back from the West coast, you

134

said. Where exactly had he gone?"

"I don't know. To see a client, I suppose."

"How long was he gone?"

"Five, six days."

"And the morning after he came back, he went into the city in response to a call from a dealer and was killed in Soho." Jill nodded helplessly. "Can you give me the name of the dealer who called him?"

She shook her head, wondered briefly if he really hadn't come upon the name yet. "Mr. Wentworth, Ellis's manager, should be able to tell you."

"He was killed instantly?"

"That's what they told Jenny."

"I know this is hard, Dr. Masterson, but I have to ask. Did your friend Jenny ever express concern or surprise, or anything out of the ordinary in connection with her husband's work?"

She shook her head. "The only thing out of the ordinary was that he was top of the line. Dozens of awards: Man of the Year, community service awards, professional recognition from prestigious groups, three Chamber of Commerce awards in a row. Made good money, too." In the pause that followed, Jenny stroked her forehead. "That's all I can tell you." McCalley did not press the fact that she had not really answered his question.

"Tell me what you know about Mrs. Bantry, your friend Jenny. It must be hard on her these days. What does she do? How does she keep busy?"

Jill opened her eyes wide in disbelief. "Inspector, she buried her husband less than a month ago!"

"You said you talked with her earlier today. How did she sound?"

"She talks, she even laughs a little. . . ." Suddenly she leaned forward, bringing her face close to his, her voice charged with emotion: "My God, Inspector! The woman was devastated!" To McCalley, her distress was all too visible. "I

135

spent an entire week with her, while Hartley made all the necessary arrangements. I took time off and stayed with her until after the funeral. Do you know what it's like to see someone you love, she's like a sister to me, to see someone that close to you suffer and not be able to do anything for her?" Making no effort to hide her tears, she shook out a tissue and wiped her eyes.

Caught unawares by the intensity of the outburst, McCalley instinctively had pulled his head back. "I am truly sorry."

She blew her nose and leaned back in the low armchair. "What else do you want to know."

"Did Mr. Bantry have any close relatives?"

"No."

"Close friends?"

"Hartley, I guess."

"And you."

"I came with Jenny, but, yes, we hit it off pretty well. He was an interesting man, fun to be with."

"Enemies?" The tired eyes suddenly blazed. She slapped her knee hard, then turned away. "I'm sorry. I do have to ask these questions," McCalley added quietly.

"Oh, stop saying you're sorry! What do *you* care!" She turned sideways in her chair and crossed her legs.

"Don't give a damn? A hoot? Neither here nor there?"

She tried to hold it back, but a brief hysterical laugh spilled out. McCalley smiled, waited for it to pass.

"I guess you'll never let me forget our little foray into the forest of imagery . . ." she offered lamely.

"Literary kitchen, I think I called it." He made a point of reviewing his notes, giving her a chance to recover, then went on. "Look, I know it's hard," he said gently, "but I've got to find out as much as possible, as soon as possible. It'll be easier all around. Especially for your friend."

"No, it won't be easy for Jenny."

"In the end, it will be. For her, and for you, too." They sat in silence for a while, then McCalley said in his even, quiet voice: "This is a very complex case. I've told you more than I should have. If I do solve it —"

"Is there any reason to think you won't?"

"Several, I'm afraid. But I'm doing my very best. . . . Let me remind you that there is much else I can't talk about but which is terribly important to the case. To all of us, your friend included. These questions, believe me, have to be asked. You'll understand why they're necessary, once the dust clears."

Jill poured out the rest of the water and drank it before replying. "It's not that I don't trust you. I think you're good at your job. But I'm worried about Jenny. How she'll take all this questioning."

"I give you my word, I'll do my best not to upset her . . . ." McCalley put his little notebook and pen away, then searched through his pockets for one of his cards. Still looking for it, he said: "Please feel free to call me, if anything else occurs to you. I'll be flying down to New York on Wednesday."

"New Year's Day?"

"Probably the best time to travel, everybody's getting ready to sit down to the big family dinner."

"What about *your* family?"

"Just my wife Susan. She's used to my strange ways. My daughter is spending the holidays with her college roommate down in Palm Beach, lucky girl!" Having finally found a card, he wrote something on it and held it out to her. "That's where I'll be staying in New York." "You've been very patient and helpful. I can't thank you enough." He stood up. "I may be out of line saying this, but from what you've told me, Mrs. Bantry seems to be very capable, a woman who has suffered a great loss and yet has kept her emotions under control. At least, that's the picture I get."

Not verging on the hysterical, like me, Jill

137

thought. Out loud, she said: "Oh she *feels* deeply, believe me! The shock just hasn't worn off yet."

"What I really wanted to say was, don't fret too much on her account. I'm sure she'll appreciate what I must do, just as you have. Whatever happens in the course of the next few weeks, I'm sure she's strong enough to take it."

"What do you mean, 'whatever happens'?"

Ignoring her question, McCalley went on. "We may have to return to you, to her, to everybody involved, maybe more than once, before this is over. I need your help, Dr. Masterson. I hope I can count on you." Jill was about to raise a question, but there was an urgency in the Inspector's voice that made her pause.

McCalley stood looking down at her for a few more moments, then, without another word, turned and left. Jill remained seated. The meeting had drained her. Even worse, she felt she had not helped Jenny one bit. Just the opposite. She'd given McCalley a lot of information that he seemed to think important. He'd taken all those notes, damn it! Why couldn't she have kept her mouth shut? Out of sheer frustration, she kicked the table beside her, only to grimace as a bolt of pain shot up from her foot into her leg and to her bruised knee. . . .

When Sergeant Kenney saw McCalley buttoning up and getting ready to walk out of the hotel, he started the car and inched it toward the entrance. From behind the wheel, he watched as Jill Masterson hurried toward the Inspector and tapped his shoulder from behind.

Jill was saying: "I'm sorry, Inspector. I was rude back there. I didn't mean to be. And I forgot to say good-bye." He smiled back at her.

"No need to have troubled yourself." They shook hands.

"Pretty slippery out there. Be careful."

He pointed to the waiting car. "My shadow in that very substantial police car will see to it that I get back to headquarters safe and sound. Goodbye then. And good luck in your work."

"I do apologize."

He waved the words aside.

In the car, McCalley gave Kenney instructions, jotting them down as he spoke. "Bill, my flight gets into Kennedy around seven, on Wednesday. Check in about ten or so, if there's anything urgent. After that, call at least once a day — mornings are best, around seven, or late at night, even if you wake me up. Leave messages, if I'm not in my room. I'll page you if there's anything urgent I need to have checked out." He then went through a list of reminders. From time to time Kenney nodded. "As soon as you can, start tracking down car rentals from around the 22nd. My guess is, he, they, flew up from New York and rented a van. That would have been the normal routine. A van to get the specimens back to New York, in this case, the arctic wolf. I've noted for you to check the motels too, although I suspect whoever it was, stayed at one of the larger hotels."

"We may just get lucky," offered Kenney, then blushed, as he remembered (too late!) that McCalley disliked intensely any suggestion that police work was dependent on "luck."

McCalley glanced at Kenney and shook his head. The Sergeant wondered if he was in for the usual rebuke, but this time all the Inspector said, as he continued to jot down notes, was:

"Hard work, Bill. Hard work is what will solve the puzzle. Finding the vital points is what counts. The lines we draw connecting those points become obvious at some stage. We need facts, evidence, all the solid bedrock details that will help us build a case." He let that sink in before continuing. "The Dobie killing complicates things," he said, in the same soft tone he had used a moment earlier. "Spingarn says it looks like an accident."

"Quite a coincidence, I'd say!" Kenney ventured.

McCalley chose to ignore the remark. "Keep on top of it," was his reply.

He tore off the sheets on which he had written his instructions and put them behind the sunshield, under a rubberband which held in place other slips already stored there.

"We may find," he said, leaning back in his seat and pulling on his gloves, "that there is more than a casual connection between Dobie and Jenene. Dobie's name appears on Jenene's documents as the trapper who brought in the wolf. Jenene, we know, processed the wolf. *His* name in on those forms, too. And, for good measure, Ellis Bantry is down as the agent who was to pick up the wolf from a shop in Soho, once it reached New York."

And all three were murdered, Kenney was about to add, but this time, he held his tongue.

"About the wolf," McCalley went on, half turning toward Kenney. "Have you cleared up the paperwork? We need to get inside it and see what's there, if anything."

"They're giving us a hard time."

"The museum?"

"And the politicians, even a cabinet member Miss Enderby recruited to force us to 'return,' that's her word, to 'return' the wolf to the museum."

McCalley drew a long breath and let it out in one hard push, his frustration obvious. "It's evidence, Bill. That has precedence over everything else."

"Not according to Miss Enderby. She says you can't be sure it's evidence and, if it's not, you will have destroyed a very valuable specimen. The lawyers have been at it all day, I understand."

"Well, we can't know if it's evidence unless we see what's inside."

"Even then, it doesn't follow, they say, that it can *stand* as evidence. And the museum wants the wolf very badly, Sir."

140

"I can understand that. And let's not forget the other museum in New York. Officially, one can argue, they have a claim, too."

"But they haven't made any claim."

"Not yet, anyway. And what about Bantry's estate? His name is down as the agent. His estate can claim the wolf, too."

"Who's the owner, then?"

"The museum people here had no idea there was a wolf available to them, certainly didn't pay for it —"

"Who did, then?"

"Good question."

"The *documents* say the wolf is part of the museum collection." Kenney made no effort to hide his frustration. "Officially —"

McCalley turned again in his seat to look at his assistant. "You should have been a lawyer, Bill," he interrupted, not without genuine appreciation. "I'm tempted to send *you* in to argue our case!"

Sergeant Kenney cleared his throat and said: "I called New York, like you asked me to."

"And?"

"You were right. No one seems to know anything about an arctic wolf there either."

"Who did you talk to?"

"Someone in display. All the VIPs seem to have taken off for the holidays."

"So: no one knows anything about an arctic wolf, no one paid for it, no one knows how it got where they found it, but everybody wants it or will want it, once the word is out. Meantime, *we* are claiming it for a murder investigation. And, let me repeat, *that* has priority over everything else."

"I'm sure we'll get it, Sir."

"And we'll open it, as we must, and Miss Enderby will kill me." They both laughed.

"And stuff you for one of her exhibits," added the Sergeant.

McCalley shot a look at his assistant. So Kenney had a sense of humor, after all! The young man had turned a deep shade of red and almost missed the turn into the police garage.

"Sorry Sir, it just slipped out."

McCalley tapped the young man's arm. "Not to worry, Bill. If she comes after me, she'll have to get to you first. We may end up in the same exhibit case!"

PART TWO

(NEW YORK)

CHAPTER 8
HOME SWEET HOME
(December 29, 4:15 PM)

The foreman came down the curving stairs to where Jenny stood waiting by the massive oak door, one of the many items she and Ellis had bought for the house, this one from an old public building in Chartres. The other workmen had already left.

"Everything in order upstairs," he said. He glanced up at the unusual chandelier as he put on his anorak. "Plenty of spare crystals. I've put them in the basement." From one of the pockets of his anorak, he pulled out a card. "In case you need me for anything else."

"Thank you." She closed the door quickly. It was still unseasonably mild for December, but she wondered if he'd remembered to check the new heating unit. . . .

Did it matter?

Did anything matter?

Ellis was gone. Ellis would never see the house again — this chandelier she had designed after reading half a dozen books and visiting any number of museums; the bedroom doors repositioned just as he had instructed, the laundry appliances finally hooked up, the dark oak beds, where they had slept, made love, for only a month. The dream house she had yearned for was finally hers. But Ellis was dead and the house suddenly was oppressive.

She felt her throat constrict, her eyes burn. Who was is said, 'Be careful what you wish for, you might just get it.'

How she had coveted this house! How grand it had seemed back then, when she had first entered it for the first time, a toddler of three! For over a decade she had visited it regularly, taking everything in, hungering for a place like that for herself and her mother. When the house had finally

145

come on the market, just before she and Ellis were married, they quickly bought it, both the house and the ten acres surrounding it.

"Cora Friedley was the last of the four sisters who lived here," she had rattled on, as she and Ellis stood side by side in the magnificent entry hall, after the closing, shortly before they sailed for Europe on their honeymoon. The lawyers had just left.

"I can't believe it's finally mine, . . . ours," she had corrected herself quickly. Ellis — kind, generous Ellis — had paid for it, but in one way, the house was indeed hers. From that very first time when, still a toddler, she had gone with her mother to the imposing brick mansion of the Friedley sisters on Fairmont Drive, on one of those days when Edna Hawthorne could find no obliging neighbor to care for her little girl, Jenny had dreamed of owning such a place.

Mrs. Carnaby, the cook, would take Jenny into the warm kitchen while Edna went upstairs to measure Miss Helene, the oldest of the four sisters, for a new woolen skirt, or cut a pattern for Miss Debra, the youngest, or take up a hem for Miss Louise, while Miss Cora chattered away.

For Jenny's mother was a first-rate seamstress, and much in demand. The old ladies had been clients of hers from the time she had started out, soon after her husband left her stranded with a two-year old child. At first she could only work at home, since Edna felt that Jenny was too young to be left with a baby-sitter, even if she had been able to afford one; but gradually, with the help of obliging older neighbors who were willing to look after the quiet little girl, she began to venture out for an hour or two, picking up pieces for alterations, returning them, taking measurements, bringing samples of her work to prospective clients.

Edna Hawthorne never spoke of those days. Only much later did Jenny realize how painful and difficult a

146

time it must have been for her mother — a young woman, deserted by her husband after three years of marriage, leaving her with a two-year old and only a small account in the bank. . . . . Not an unusual story, but for Jenny an ever-present and painful reality, as she watched her mother, in those early years, struggle to earn enough to pay for their rent and other basic necessities. At first, Edna worked out of their two small rooms, but after a while she had some steady customers who wanted her to do fittings in their homes. Eventually, the Friedley sisters, four spinster ladies, became her best customers. And because they were always among the best-dressed women at church functions, at the board meetings they attended, and the occasional afternoon tea they served in the big house, Edna came to have a steady flow of work. But by the time she was thirty-two, Edna Hawthorne already had deep lines across her forehead, etched into the still smooth skin of her face. Hard work and worries had taken their toll.

The Friedley sisters were kind, gave Edna clothing they no longer used, little gifts now and then; but it was Mrs. Carnaby who looked after the little girl, when Edna had to bring her along, when she could find no one to sit with her at home. Mrs. Carnaby would take Jenny quickly into the kitchen, as though to forestall any explanations. In later years, remembering those visits, Jenny wondered if the Friedley sisters knew all along that their seamstress often brought her child with her and left her in the kitchen with their cook. Some things are better left unsaid, her mother had said once, in reply to a question Jenny had asked. In any case, Mrs. Carnaby always made a fuss over Jenny. She was so easy to care for. Even as a baby, she seldom cried.

Mrs. Carnaby made it a habit to feed the child well, and would always have a plastic bag with small containers of food for them to take home— stew or broth or chicken salad, whatever was on hand. She must have known that

Edna had to watch every penny to make ends meet; but there was no sign of condescension in Mrs. Carnaby's generosity.

The woman found a good listener in the little girl. She would sit Jenny near her and tell her stories as she peeled potatoes or scraped carrots. The little girl would listen wide-eyed, taking in everything. For Jenny, the warm bright kitchen with its inviting odors, was heaven. If it was late morning, she was treated to a thick soup or mashed vegetables and small pieces of meat. If it was afternoon, she had a cup of broth and cookies; and when Edna came downstairs, cook always insisted that she sit with her for a cup of tea before going. Both mother and daughter got to love the Friedleys' kitchen and Mrs. Carnaby. Years later, Jenny made every effort to locate the old woman, who had retired and gone to live with a daughter in Maine. Jenny had traced her as far as Portland, but her stay there apparently had been brief. Nothing further could be learned about Mrs. Carnaby's whereabouts.

Edna had died suddenly, still a young woman, just before Jenny met Ellis, before Jenny bought the house where her mother had worked as a seamstress, where she had entered by the back door that opened directly into the kitchen.

Only once had Jenny seen the rest of the house. She was twelve at the time. The ladies had gone to a church bazaar and Edna had stopped by to deliver some blouses she had taken home to alter.

Mrs. Carnaby had prepared a small lunch for the three of them, and then took them on a tour of the mansion. Jenny had never seen anything like it. She was breathless all the way home on the bus, chattering about the furnishings, the display cases, especially the paintings on the walls. Her mother finally put up her hands, closed her eyes and sighed.

"You're going to give me a splitting headache, if

148

you go on like that." Then, with a fleeting smile: "Who knows? You might have a big house yourself, some day, when you marry. . . ."

With an effort she pushed herself away from the heavy oak door and made her way down to the small alcove, across from the kitchen. It had been a pantry; but the newly-designed kitchen — three smaller rooms made into one — with its ample storage areas, efficient closets, and hidden cabinets didn't need a pantry. Ellis had suggested they convert it into a work space where, every morning, Jenny could plan the day with Mrs. Harris, their newly-acquired housekeeper.

"You've got to establish a routine so that she'll understand you're not to be interrupted at your work. She has to respect your privacy. . . ."

That was the day several large crates had arrived, the last of their major purchases while abroad. Eager to be there, they had eaten a quick breakfast in a diner near the motel where they were staying, then drove to the house. While the workmen carried pieces to where they were instructed, checked outlets, tested locks and window closures, she and Mrs. Harris had set up the last of the dishes in the hutch that extended over the long wall between the two high windows overlooking the patio and the trim back lawn — still green because of the continuing mild weather. Workmen then brought up the chairs and table from the basement. The patina on the old smooth wood gleamed in the sunlight that streamed in from the windows. Alone, Jenny and Ellis stood admiring the result of that morning's work, pleased with the way their sketched plans were coming to life.

They had left the kitchen for last. In the bright light, the beautiful walnut refectory table and the twelve small armchairs looked even better than they had envisioned and blended beautifully with the huge hutch between the high windows, where the colorful dishes they had bought at an estate sale in Portugal were now resting.

The table and chairs filled the alcove in the upper half of the room. The other half of the kitchen was a large work space, an island in three sections which formed a U, and on the wall opposite the windows, the kitchen appliances had been carefully placed for easy access. It was a huge comfortable area.

"I know what you're thinking," Ellis had gone on, rocking her in his arms as they stood in the new alcove, just outside the kitchen. The idea of a housekeeper, even a part-time one, still bothered her. "But, you can't handle this big house by yourself, Jenny. Mrs. Harris is a godsend. She can get extra help if we need it, she's an excellent cook, she'll take care of laundry and all the other chores you should be spared. You just have to make clear to her, from the very beginning, that your being in the house, working in your study, doesn't mean you can be interrupted any time something comes up. You've got to delegate certain tasks, encourage her to make decisions."

As usual, Ellis had been right. The day they had moved into the house, that first week in November, Mrs. Harris worked with them, long into the evening. She was back before seven the next morning and had breakfast ready for them when they came down at nine. Not used to servants, embarrassed by so much attention, Jenny finally got up enough courage to tell Mrs. Harris that her hours would be nine-thirty to four, Monday to Friday. . . .

How long had the telephone been ringing? At once, she recognized Hartley Quinn's careful diction, the deliberate British tones of his voice.

"I almost hung up, but I knew you'd be there. Have they finished, finally?"

"Yes, a little while ago."

"How does it look? —"

"Fine, just fine."

"Fine? Just *fine*?"

150

She smiled, in spite of herself. "Hart, you know there wasn't much to do. Just a few minor things. "

"Listen, What about dinner? You can give me the grand tour before we go eat."

"But you've been in the house at least a dozen times since we moved in."

"Not since before Christmas."

She stood shaking her head, smiling. She heard herself say, "Yes, all right."

"Pick you up around six thirty."

She was still sitting in the small alcove when the doorbell rang. For a few moments, she was disoriented. The ringing continued, a nervous penetrating sound registering impatience. A courier had a small package for Ellis. She signed for it and went upstairs. Sitting on her bed, she opened the bubble envelope. From the small velvet box she drew out a magnificent oval-shaped aquamarine ring, surrounded by small diamonds. The band was silver filigree, delicate yet strong, the border around the outer stones worked into the same filigree design.

She slipped the ring on top of her wedding band. A gift from Ellis, of course, what else could it be? Bought while on their trip perhaps, left somewhere for sizing, and sent on to the house, when Ellis failed to pick it up. She puzzled over its delivery at this time. Much too late for an engagement ring! Besides, she had never wanted one; Ellis used to tease her about going around with a naked finger, without a ring to tell the world that she belonged to him and keep other suitors at bay. A delayed Christmas present? But she had found her Christmas present, while helping Hart look for papers he needed, soon after the funeral. . . . A housewarming present, of course! They had planned a small dinner party, just around this time. . . .

There was no return address on the brown bubble envelope. The velvet box, beautifully lined in sapphire blue satin, did not carry the name of a dealer or a shop. The ring itself looked old, possibly a Victorian antique. Tomorrow she would look through the catalogs Ellis had in the house. She might find in them a reference, a description. . . .

She put it back on after showering. Sitting on the bed in her bathrobe, she admired it again, wondering where Ellis had found it. After a while, she went to the wardrobe and took out and replaced a number of outfits, choosing, finally, a simple dark green suit, one she had not worn for a long time. A silk patterned shirt, stockings, black pumps and a small handbag completed the preparations. When she was dressed, she dabbed on some lipstick, put on her wristwatch. It was only five fifteen.

Perhaps she had made a mistake accepting Hart's invitation. He was an old dear friend, but would she get through the evening without breaking down? Last night had been difficult enough, even though the Lowells had been kind, letting her sit back and relax while Sam told stories about their recent trip to Kenya. She hadn't relaxed but was grateful, she had realized, to be away from the house, which more and more seemed to be closing in, stifling her. At moments, walking past the silent rooms, she would panic at the thought of living in what had suddenly turned into a mausoleum. She remembered her relief — in spite of initial objections — when Jill insisted on driving to White Plains on Christmas Day, where the two of them had a quiet lunch at a small inn Jill had found on the internet. Now she focused on that day, on all the days when her friends had given up their time to be with her, trying to distract her. Hart had been just as solicitous, just as caring. Even Jill had to admit it.

Selfishly, she wondered how she would get through the next few days without Jill. She kept saying she didn't want company, but the truth was, she desperately needed her closest friends beside her. Jill was still in Ottawa (how she missed her!), but Hart was taking her to dinner. Could she manage a social evening, even with Hart?

Could she get through this year into the next? Into a new life without Ellis?

Back downstairs, she turned on some lights. In the living room, the soft lamps brought out all the lovely nuances of the blended pastel designs of the chair fabrics, in dramatic contrast to the dark solid blues of the sofas, the softly draped valances and drapes at the windows. She sat down, leafed aimlessly through a magazine.

When the bell rang a second time, she was startled out of an uneasy nap. Still groggy, she hurried to open the door. Hartley Quinn stepped inside and closed the door behind him. He nodded appreciatively as he gazed up at the chandelier.

"They replaced the ten broken crystals and stored the ones left over," she volunteered. She went down the list of the other last-minute adjustments the workmen had completed earlier that day.

"I'll check everything in a day or two."

"There's no need. . . . "

"I promised I would, remember? Every step of the way. . . . So, where do I buy a ticket for this tour?" In spite of her somber mood, Jenny couldn't help responding to Hartley's appreciative comments. Her study was last. Jenny watched as Hart walked to her computer and picked up a blank sheet of paper from a pile in a wire tray. He turned to her. "I hope you're back on track with your book, Jenny."

"Oh, Hart! How can I even think of writing at a time like this!"

He replaced the sheet and turned to her. "Listen to me, Jenny. You have to get back into stride, whatever it takes. This project is important. It was important to Ellis, too. I don't have to remind you how proud he was of you, your work, this book you were writing?"

She had walked to the window, impatiently. "I may give it up altogether."

He went to her side and forced her to face him.

153

"No, Jenny, you've got to finish it. . . . Or you'll be sued for breaking your contract!"

A small twitching around his lips gave him away, and she broke out into a nervous little laugh. Hartley hugged her and joined in.

"And you'll represent me, if that happens —" He raised his hands and looked up at the ceiling in mock despair.

"And I'll make sure you don't win!" Then, all seriousness again: "You've got to get back to it, Jenny." She moved away from him by way of reply. "Call it therapy, if you like," he went on. "Peace of mind. A distraction. . . . All joking aside, you *did* sign a contract for a book your publisher expects to have in a matter of weeks. He's already given you several extensions. . . ."

"There's plenty of time —"

"Right. Sooner or later, you'll pick up again, but unless 'sooner,' you'll hurt your chances for the future. You know I'm right." She said nothing. "At least promise me you won't just walk away from it. Ellis would be mighty mad at you." She shook her head and started out of the room.

"Don't push, Hart. I have to find my own good time for it. I can't force anything right now." They left it at that.

Downstairs again, he helped her put on the jacket she carried and nodded appreciatively, standing back to study her. "A good color for you. Is it new?"

"No. I had forgotten I had it."

She waited as Quinn activated the elaborate alarm devices, in place now for almost a year. Ellis had designed the basic system and had left all his notes, charts, and instructions for Quinn to follow. The job was begun when costly items began to arrive from Europe. Wiring and micro sensors were placed deep into the walls. Three experts had been called in to supervise the installation of the delicate state-of-the-arts equipment. It was an elaborate system that covered every possible point of entry, including the several

154

chimneys. Quinn had set up work schedules so that he could be free to supervise the complex installations, during the weeks it took to complete the job.

As they walked out into the mild evening, Jenny handed Quinn the key for locking the door — a formality, since the alarm system was the real protection. Like everything else about the house, the key was unusual: cast in bronze, contoured and rounded, slightly larger than ordinary keys, with the monogram JBE engraved on it, the letters intertwined in an elegant baroque design, the middle letter slightly bigger than the other two.

Jenny and Ellis Bantry.

Joined forever.

Forever one. . . .

In the car, Hart said: "I made reservations at a new Italian place, new ownership that is. I've heard it's pretty good. The chef is from Milan. Always the proper escort, he added quickly: "Unless you have some other place you'd prefer. Just say the word."

Jenny smiled. "No, no. I leave it to you."

She was surprised to find that she was hungry. Hart ordered for both of them. A shrimp cocktail followed by the specialty of the house, *ossobuco* with wild rice. Hart insisted she have a glass of wine. It was an excellent meal, during which Hartley succeeded in distracting her with gossip and stories. By the time they were through, she was almost sleepy, her eyes threatening to close.

"I know I've told you many times already it's too early to make decisions," Hartley's voice broke in, "but there are some things you'll have to start thinking about, soon. The business, for example. Whether you might want to run it yourself, or keep it with Wentworth running it, sell it maybe? Not final decisions, of course, but you will have to tell Wentworth and the rest of the staff something, and soon. Let them know you're considering the possibilities but haven't made up your mind yet."

155

She nodded. "I'm sorry. Yes. I should have done it sooner."

"We could talk about it, and I have some papers for you to sign, too, let's see. . . . " He took out a slim gold-trimmed ledger. "Today's Sunday. I'm busy tomorrow. Tuesday is New Year's Eve. . . . What about Thursday?"

Thankful he hadn't asked about her plans for New Year's, praying that he wouldn't, especially since Jill would be coming, she said quickly: "Thursday's fine."

"Is ten all right?"

She nodded. Then, after some hesitation, her voice betraying a certain anxiety, she told him about wanting to sell the house as soon as possible.

"No, no," he said, shaking his head vigorously. "That's the kind of decision you definitely should not make at this time. We haven't even finished cataloging everything yet. No, Jenny, it's premature."

She waved his words aside. "Well, I can't *live* there. . . . The mosaic tiles on the *terrazza*? We drove three hours to a place we heard was being demolished, near Torre del Greco, outside of Naples. We got there just in time. We bought the whole batch, every single one, more than we could possibly use. Then we celebrated at a small *taverna* in the middle of nowhere. Some people want to remember, cherish their memories. I can't. The house is, . . . I feel I'm being sucked into a huge black hole."

He reached out and took her hand in both of his. "Aside from everything else, it's not a good idea to make important decisions at a time of stress."

"That's what Jill said."

He pulled back with a sigh. "For once, we agree, Jill and I." Then, leaning across the table, he went on: "If you really feel you can't be there alone — but remember it's a risk leaving a house like yours empty, before everything has been removed — but if you feel you've got to get away, take a little trip, visit some friend. . . ." Jenny shook her

156

head. "Go on a shopping spree, take a cruise. . . ."

"That's the last thing I want to do!"

"Something else, then, anything. Take one of those tours the McCarthys told you they take every January. Find a beach, loll in the sun, get a tan, go snorkeling."

She couldn't resist smiling. "I'd be bored after two days in the sun."

"Go with Jill to see Shakespeare. Prove to her you haven't given up the great bard altogether." In graduate school at Columbia, they had both started out in literature, but before long Jenny had opted for art history. Jill finished her degree in literature.

"She'll be back teaching soon."

"Tell her to call in sick."

"*You* tell her."

"She's not speaking to me until I read *Bleak House.*" She heard herself giggle. "Does she really think I'm a greedy lawyer? By the way, where is she, these days?"

"The usual annual conference. Up in Ottawa this year. She left the day after Christmas. Should be back tomorrow, if all goes well. She told me when she called yesterday, they've already had one blizzard, and the roads are all ice."

Hartley ordered more coffee. "And here we are, enjoying late Spring weather in the middle of winter. Why schedule conferences in Ottawa, this time of year? Two big strikes against the profession, if you ask me!"

"Usually it's in Washington, New York, San Diego. Once it was New Orleans."

"She goes every year? Why?"

"You get brownie points if you read a paper. More brownie points if you get it published."

"And what do the brownie points get you?"

Jenny shrugged. "Tenure, promotion, things like that. . . . Besides, it's a good opportunity to see colleagues and friends in the profession, find out about openings, if you're looking for a job, plan meetings for the following year. You get to see the major cities, too."

"You can get to see them on your own. . . ."

"Anyway, she got there just in time. The airports closed soon after her plane landed, didn't reopen until the next day. And from what she told me on the phone, things haven't improved much. But the real excitement came the evening she checked in."

"Oh?"

"She signed up for a museum tour, late in the afternoon, and as they started, at their very first stop, they found a body."

"Someone died in the museum?"

"Murdered. The museum taxidermist."

"And Jill was there when they found him?"

"Yes. They all were interviewed and had to sign statements."

"Have they found who did it?"

"Not yet. For some reason, the Ottawa police officer in charge is coming to New York. He asked for my address. Yours too."

He pulled his head back and stared at her in surprise. "What does he want with us?"

"I don't know. Jill said she happened to mention something about Ellis doing occasional business with museums and the Inspector seemed interested in that. Wants to pick my brain, she said."

Hartley laughed suddenly. "This is better than P. D. James!" Then, reaching across the table, he took her hand. "Promise me you'll think about what I said, about going away for a while, about not putting up the house for sale, not right away." As he stroked her hand, he felt the ring on her finger. His eyebrows arched in surprise.

"It's a gift from Ellis." Hartley remained silent. He let go of her hand and sat back in his chair.

"Looks old," he said.

He watched as Jenny turned the ring slowly, side to side, staring at it with a concentration that was focused on something deep inside her, something she alone could see. When she looked up again, Hartley met her gaze with a lingering strained smile that gave his face a clown-like sadness.

"You musn't brood," he said softly.

"I try not to. But memories crowd in. So many memories. . . ."

On the drive home she said: "You're the best friend I have, Hart. You and Jill. Let me find my own way through all this." She tilted her head to one side, studying him. "And yes, I promise not to make any hasty decisions."

He patted her hand, seemed relieved. At the door, he said: "Call me when that police officer comes around. I want to be there for you. I'm sure he'll want to pick my brain, too."

Alone again, she prepared for bed. She made herself a cup of tea and brought it upstairs.

Go ahead, let it all out, some little voice inside her urged. *Here you are, finally, where you wanted to be all these years. . . . You thought the house would make you the happiest woman alive. But something else happened, something changed your life, brought happiness you could never have imagined, the best thing that ever happened to you.*

Now, that's gone. You're alone, but not like before. And this house is just a reminder of the empty chambers of my stricken soul.

She held out her hand and stared at the ring. Its cold glitter was not unlike the stony look in her eyes.

CHAPTER 9

NEW YORK CONNECTION
(January 1, 7:10 PM)

By the time passengers began to come through the gate, Ed Markarian was in place, waiting for Luke McCalley to appear. He didn't have to wait long. The Inspector was one of the first to emerge, carrying a small bag and a tote over his shoulder. The two men exchanged greetings, as Ed took McCalley's bag. They walked leisurely toward the airport entrance, chatting like old friends.

"We stayed home," said Markarian, in answer to McCalley's question about New Year's Eve. "I hate to travel on holidays. And the kids still enjoy having their friends in — we let them use the family room in the basement, where we can look in on them with some excuse from time to time. The grown-ups stay upstairs. It works out okay. How was yours?"

"We spent it with friends down the street. My daughter is in Florida, with her college roommate. The in-laws came for dinner today; I left right after we ate."

Markarian led the way to the car, a short distance away. He grinned as he took from the dashboard some kind of official tag. "Small perks," he said, as they put McCalley's bag and tote in the trunk.

Traffic was heavy out of the airport, but they made good time once they were on the Grand Central.

"I pulled the Bantry file for you. It's on the back seat." McCalley reached for the brown folder but didn't open it at once.

"I appreciate your picking me up, Ed, but I don't want to take up too much of your time while I'm here. You must have plenty else to do."

"Let me explain, so you don't worry about it. My desk is clear. I can always be reached if there's an emergency. I checked it out with the boss. As of now, I'm officially your driver," he traced a wide arc in the air, "or, whatever. . . ."

"You're sure —?"

"I'm sure." He watched as McCalley opened the file. "From what you've told me, we may be in for some surprises."

McCalley started to read, but his attention was elsewhere. He had brooded on the plane about how much information to share with Markarian, and there were still some doubts in his mind. He suspected the New York detective had already gone beyond professional courtesy in pulling the Bantry file for him. Besides, a NYPD contact could be useful, tap resources that an outsider could not. Working together was a distinct advantage. Still, there were difficulties, not the least of which was that Markarian had not been on the Bantry case officially, and any initiative on his part might be construed as stepping on someone else's toes. There were other, more serious considerations. McCalley's trip to New York was to find out all he could about Bantry's connection with the Canadian museum shipments. Anything having to do with his death was off limits, none of his business. Nor Markarian's, for that matter. Officially, Bantry had been caught in crossfire, the result of a dispute between two rival gangs, the fatal shooting, ruled an "accident." They must both be careful, if they didn't want to be accused, later, of having exceeded their official charge.

Well, he'd be careful. And not just in checking out Bantry. He had to discourage all premature conclusions in connection with the two deaths in Canada, as well, and for the same reason: there was no clear connection at this point, they might never find one, between the death of the trapper and Jenene's murder. The findings of the two separate inquests were on record: Jenene's death had been ruled "an act committed by person or person unknown"

161

some time between four and six o'clock on December 26, and Dobie's a "hunting accident" between late Christmas eve, when the trapper was last seen alive, drinking in a tavern on the outskirts of the city, and the afternoon of December 27, when the body was discovered deep in the woods.

But, in spite of his innate caution against reading too much into facts and evidence, McCalley couldn't resist viewing Dobie's "accident" — in the light of the trapper's connection with Jenene — with suspicion. He realized he was ready to pursue the implications of that connection, even as he steered himself away, with equal determination, from any suggestion that Bantry's death might have been more than an accident.

Perhaps it was this dilemma that made up his mind. He put the folder aside and, as they drove toward Manhattan, reviewed for his colleague what had happened at the museum and everything that followed, a full and detailed account, including the discovery of Dobie's body in the woods. He described the documents retrieved from Jenene's safe, Miss Enderby's indignation when she read them, her anger at seeing her signature on those papers; he described the arctic wolf and its possible connection with Jenene's murder; he told him about the tour, the van, Jenene's missing car; and finally, he explained his own dilemma.

"I try not to indulge in speculation, Ed," he said, by way of conclusion. "I'm still gathering facts, can't afford guesswork. We would be making a big mistake to assume at this point that Bantry's death is connected in any way with Jenene's. The reason I'm here is to find out if the American Museum of Natural History was expecting an arctic wolf and to find some explanation for Bantry's name on the documents we found. Whatever else develops, well, we deal with that if and when it comes up."

Markarian had listened closely, nodding from time

162

to time, but not interrupting. Now he asked: "What about those two other specimens, in May and August? From what you've told me, they disappeared into thin air."

"Seems that way. We're checking."

"Well, if you ask me, I think the wolf was meant to disappear too. Didn't you say our museum here knows nothing about it?"

"My Sergeant called, but he didn't actually talk with the Curator. I'm going to see him myself, tomorrow. Kenney set up an appointment before I left Ottawa."

They drove on in silence for a while, Markarian concentrating on the road but now and then stealing a glance to where McCalley sat, deep in thought. Finally, he turned to his colleague and said, somewhat tentatively: "You realize, Luke, you've stumbled on to something that may put a new light on things at this end. Bantry's name on those documents may force us to look again at what happened to him."

McCalley, now alert, seemed bent on following his own train of thought. "Miss Enderby swears that the signatures are not hers. She was furious. Of course, she could have been putting on a good show, but I doubt it. Jenene's own staff were stunned by the fact that an arctic wolf had been processed, right under their noses, without their knowing anything about it. I don't really think we'll find any reason to doubt what they told us. The big problem is this: the forms we found obviously were important to Jenene. He would not otherwise have taken the trouble to make copies and hide them so carefully for so long. That means that Bantry was an important part of whatever the plan, you're right about that. And the same is true of Miss Enderby. The question, however, is not whether or not they knew what was going on. What's important is, why their names are on those forms. . . .Until we have the answer to that question, we won't be any closer to a solution."

"What you're saying, in effect, is that Bantry's

163

name may also have been put there without his knowledge; although we're pretty sure that both Jenene and that trapper Dobie, whose names also appear on those papers, are definitely guilty."

McCalley, shook his head emphatically. "You're missing the point, Ed! We're not talking guilt or innocence here. In any case, what can we accuse Dobie and Jenene of, at this point? Guilty of what?"

"The way I see it," continued the other, easily, "Jenene and the trapper are clearly involved. It's true, we don't know much about the earlier shipments, but the wolf tells us both men were somehow into that operation. Dobie most certainly trapped the animal and sold it on a kind of black market, pocketing a lot more money than the animal normally sold for. Jenene processed it. We don't know their purpose in doing this, but it's pretty clear they were up to no good. Why else would Jenene have made copies of the transfer forms? Hidden them in his basement? He certainly is involved. Can we start with that as our basic premise?"

McCalley said nothing. Markarian went on:

"Miss Enderby's signature may be a forgery and, for the sake of argument, Bantry's name may also have been placed there without his knowing. And he might never have been the wiser, if things had gone according to plan. On the other hand, he may well have been in on it. You have to check out Bantry's connection with the dealer in Soho. If it turns out Bantry was being used, his death may well turn out to be something other than an accident. . . ."

To his surprise, McCalley made no effort to reject or at least caution against the implications of Markarian's summary. The other went on:

"Seems pretty clear that Jenene kept copies of those documents as personal insurance. Leaving aside for the moment the authenticity of the Curator's signatures and the reason for Bantry's name on those forms, Jenene must have thought the documents were important, potentially

164

damaging to certain parties. The question is: to whom?" Markarian glanced at his colleague, before turning back to the Parkway traffic. "I know you don't like to speculate, but let me indulge for a moment, okay? Since the earlier specimens described in those forms have not turned up anywhere, don't we have to assume that something illegal was going on?" McCalley said nothing. "For what it's worth, I think the wolf was destined for the same fate as the earlier two shipments. Finding those documents was a lucky break for you. Whatever was going on may have started way back and might have continued uninterrupted for months, years even!"

"Not a lucky break, Ed. My men pulled up every brick, every plank, spent hours searching."

"Well, it's pretty clear to me that the wolf came out of nowhere and was going nowhere. From what you've told me, I'd say the museum here in New York wasn't expecting any brand-new recently-processed wolf. Jenene must have known that the specimen would be picked up on the twenty-sixth and taken to New York — but *not* for delivery to any museum!"

"But why Bantry's name?"

"If he wasn't involved, then it must have served the major players in some vital way. My hunch is, they never expected those documents to be found. I'm sure the originals were all destroyed, together with the animals."

"Except for the wolf and Jenene's copies of the documents."

"That was unexpected."

"Yes, but why Bantry?" McCalley repeated. "The shopowner —" he snapped his fingers, trying to call up the name.

"— Tasselbaum?"

"Yes, Tasselbaum. He would have served just as well. Better even. After all, the specimens were being delivered to *his* shop, not to Bantry's warehouse. Why was

165

Bantry brought into it, if he wasn't involved and wasn't there to accept the animals himself . . . besides the obvious fact that he was already three weeks dead and, before that, had been in Europe for three years.. He couldn't have been there for any of the three shipments!"

Markarian offered no reply. When they stopped for a red light, McCalley glanced over at his companion.

"I think you're right about Jenene," he said. "He's got to have been involved. After all, he processed the wolf. We can be pretty certain about that," he added somewhat grudgingly.

"And knew what was inside," Markarian finished for him, then added quickly, ". . . . or at least that something was hidden there."

McCalley shook his head. "No, I can't jump that far ahead. We don't know enough to be sure something is inside the animal."

"There's no other way to explain its presence. It would have to have been smuggling of some kind. Haven't you opened it up yet?"

"*That* is turning out to be a problem. The museum wants it very badly, doesn't want us to destroy it. They're threatening to take the matter to court. We'll probably get it, in the long run, but it may take some time . . . . I don't want to destroy it unless I have to, Ed. It's an unusual specimen, I'm told. But so far, X-rays show nothing. We've gone to experts who are trying other sensitive equipment to see if there's anything hidden inside, but so far, a big zero."

Markarian nodded, then said: "Well, one thing is certain: it was meant to be taken away that afternoon, right?"

"I think we can safely assume that, yes."

"You know what I'm thinking?" McCalley gave him a doubtful look. The other went right on. "I think Jenene's body was meant to be taken out also. You said they chloroformed him, but not enough to kill him. He was

166

strangled, you said. That means killing him at the museum was a last-minute decision; they killed and left him there when they realized they couldn't take him out, neither him nor the wolf. They had to change their plans on the spot because of the unexpected turn of events."

McCalley couldn't help recalling Kenney's theory. "It's far-fetched, and we have no evidence."

"Not yet, but it makes sense, doesn't it, if they had meant to make it look like an accident? Like the other one?"

McCalley shook his head. "Slow down, slow down! We need more to go on, Ed."

"All right, let's try something else. I know you're being very careful to keep Bantry's death out of this, but hear me out, please." McCalley shrugged and closed his eyes. "I personally have other thoughts about it, but let's consider the possibility that what applies to Dobie and Jenene may well apply to Bantry as well."

"And what's that?" asked the other, his eyes still closed.

"Greed?" When McCalley remained silent, he elaborated: "Maybe they all wanted more? Okay, so it's a hunch, but it fits." Had he not had his eyes on the car that suddenly braked in front of them, Markarian would have caught McCalley's grimace at the word *hunch*. As they started to move again, he continued:

"I know it's hard for you to admit and it's not that I don't understand and respect your methods, Luke, I work that way too — long hours collecting evidence, studying the facts, hard work around the clock sometimes, sorting out bits and scraps, all of that — but, let's face it, if hadn't been for that tour, you may never have found the body or the wolf, and Jenene might have disappeared for weeks, months, long enough to make any connection with the wolf virtually impossible. You said the weather was bad? Well," he continued, without waiting for an answer, "they might have put him in his car and staged an accident in some remote area."

"You said 'they,' back there. . ." was McCalley's comment.

"There had to be at least two people to carry the body out, then the wolf."

"That's what my Sergeant said."

They were silent as they came out of the midtown tunnel. Markarian turned up Third Avenue, but before reaching McCalley's hotel in the lower seventies, he parked at a hydrant and pulled out a small notebook.

"What's on for tomorrow?"

McCalley had pulled out his pad and was already writing in it. "I'm going to try to set up an appointment with Mrs. Bantry. Is ten all right?"

"Sure. We should allow about an hour."

"Fine."

"A quick lunch after that and, what's on for the afternoon?"

"If you don't mind Ed, I'd like to skip lunch and go directly to the museum to see the Curator. Kenney set up an appointment for twelve-thirty. I need to get that business squared away." He went on tactfully: "It'll give you a few hours to catch up on things."

At the hotel entrance, Markarian pulled out a card: "Before I forget, I wrote down my home number, my beeper and cell numbers on there. Call me any time." He pointed to the folder McCalley was still holding. "I would appreciate getting it back as soon as possible."

"Right. And thanks for everything."

His room was in the back, the drapes drawn to hide an empty lot, where construction was going on. There were, McCalley was pleased to see, a coffee maker, coffee and tea bags. He was eager to make himself a cup of coffee but remembered he had not called Mrs. Bantry yet. She answered on the third ring.

168

Ten o'clock was fine. . . . "No, wait. I have an appointment with my lawyer at ten."

"Hartley Quinn?"

"You know him?"

"Dr. Masterson mentioned him."

"Well, if you don't mind, he was coming anyway, to go over some business matters with me. It might even save you some time if you want to ask him anything. He'll be glad to talk with you."

"He knew I was coming?"

"Well, he didn't know exactly what day, but yes. And, as I said, he was planning to come over tomorrow, anyway, to take care of some business. I. . . . Is it all right if he's here with me?"

It wasn't. He would have preferred seeing Mrs. Bantry alone; it was always best to interview on a one to one basis, but he had no choice. He agreed to Quinn's being present, wondering how much else she had told him.

"Do you know how to get here?"

"My colleague is driving. He knows the way."

She went over the directions anyway, especially how to reach the house once they were off the Parkway. He hung up and dialed Markarian's number, left a message confirming the appointment for ten the next day.

Following the instructions on the machine, he placed a packet of coffee as directed and, when the water boiled, poured it into the top. The result was altogether too weak. He called room service and ordered a light dinner, with a carafe of freshly-brewed coffee.

Waiting for the food to arrive, he sat on the one comfortable chair in the room and let his mind go over his conversation with Markarian.

What exactly was the connection between Jenene and Bantry? The file they had retrieved seemed clear enough. It told them that Jenene had produced two specimens for a museum in New Jersey, ostensibly a long-term loan from the Ottawa museum, that the wolf was being sent on a similar arrangement to the museum in New York, that Jenene was the taxidermist who had worked on the animals and Miss Enderby had officially approved the transfers. In all the documents, Bantry's name appeared as the agent for the museums, a shop in Soho as the first stop in the delivery of the specimens. Already one signature was suspect (there was little reason to doubt Miss Enderby's' indignant denial that she had ever signed those papers); their early inquiries also suggested that the museums named on those forms had never received the specimens described. How much else in those documents was false and misleading?

He settled back and reviewed what Sergeant Kenney had found out, what he had reported to him early on New Year's Day, before McCalley left for New York.

A careful search of Dobie's belongings, still with the police, had revealed receipts for a number of recent purchases, the most interesting being a Grand Cherokee van and a rifle. This information was of little if any interest to the police, at the time the trapper's body was found, since his death had been ruled an accident and the case quickly closed. Now, of course, everything they could find out about Dobie was important.

Dobie had bought the van, signed for it and paid cash, early on December 24. He was due to pick it up, with new registration papers, right after Christmas. It was a top-of-the-line model and had cost close to $34,000. A new rifle, a Safari Browning Automatic with massive seven-lug bolt, recessed bolt face, rotary lock up, all designed for heavy loads, a hunter's dream, with a magazine capacity of 4, a 24-inch barrel length, a 19½ sight radius, and an overall length of 45 inches, was purchased the same morning. It had cost just under $1,000 and Dobie had taken it with him, again paying cash. When the police returned, with Kenney, to search the cabin again, they found it there with two other rifles, both still in good working condition. Apparently, Dobie had had plenty of cash on hand. He paid for all his purchases with bills of a hundred. The salesman who sold him the van told detectives that his customer was very pleased, said something about finally treating himself to a Christmas gift.

He had bought some new clothes, too. Special hunter's gloves, long thermal underwear, a new fur-lined cap and half a dozen heavy socks. All these and a new anorak with a wolf-trimmed hood came close to nine hundred dollars. These items also were paid for in cash. The police also found a bank book with a balance of $2,700. That sum had not been touched for over eight months. Nothing had been deposited either.

What bothered him, Kenney told McCalley, was that, except for some small bills and change in his pockets, no money was found anywhere. At first, one could conclude that Dobie had spent all the currency on hand on those so-called presents he had bought for himself. But nothing left for even a small deposit in the bank? And where did all that cash come from, in the first place?

"Oh, and another thing," the Sergeant had said. "I checked with the Coroner about the bullet that killed him. It came from a Safari Browning Automatic. Not Dobie's new rifle, according to ballistics."

"Did you find who it belongs to?"

"Not yet. And I double-checked with Customs. Nothing there, yet. Double-checked the museum in New Jersey. They know nothing about those May and August shipments."

They had talked a while longer, and McCalley gave Kenney last minute instructions, reminded him to call New York every day, told him to keep up the good work, and wished him a happy new year. For his part, despite the dead ends he had described to his superior, Kenney was confident that the investigation would soon produce positive results. His optimism was fueled by his conviction that Jenene was trying to blackmail the people who paid him for his work, maybe the very ones who had come to the museum the day after Christmas to collect the white wolf. He was convinced that Jenene had become a threat and had to be killed. Naturally, he didn't dare suggest such a notion to his superior. He knew McCalley's reluctance to assume anything, to speculate with so little to go on. He hoped the trip to New York would provide the kind of clear evidence they needed, some tangible connection between Janene and Bantry. . . .

The soup, sandwich, and coffee McCalley had ordered came and were gratefully consumed. Now, lying back on the bed, his hands behind his head, he closed his eyes and tried to sort out the information that had accumulated so far.

One question kept popping up. What exactly happened the night Jenene was killed? Had the tour just missed the murderer or murderers? The coroner had stipulated the time of Jenene's death no earlier than four but very likely closer to six, just about the time Miss Enderby went downstairs to wait for the tour bus. Kenney and Markarian were probably right about there having been two people involved. He was willing to consider that a real possibility. But why hadn't the cleaning crew seen or heard anything? The radio had been on, they told him. He made a mental note to ask Miss Enderby to quiz them again about that, but he was sure the answer would be the same.

To distract himself and clear his head, he picked up a report he had requested on taxidermy. The only one Kenney was able to dig up on short notice was several years old, but it would give him some basic idea of the process, Kenney had explained by way of apology. It was a complicated and delicate procedure involving building clay armatures, setting metal rods in position to hold up the legs and skull, using side templates and connecting boards to

172

give depth to the body, covering the armature with metal lathe or wire mesh to divide the mold into sections, and each section worked on separately — applying plaster first to the lower half of the animal, including the inside half of the legs, then moving up carefully to the clay divider strips, the whole reinforced with iron rods and built up to about an inch thickness. . . .

He began to understand why Miss Enderby was set against their looking inside the specimen. They would have to break the armature, take out rods, mesh, destroy the mold —

He resumed reading.

After the plaster was set, the clay divider strips were removed and liquid soap applied to the edges of the mold, where the strips had been taken away. Then a light oil was painted over the same surface, making a separator. The process was repeated with each section of the upper half. The number of sections varied (he read) with the size of the animal, as did the weight of the completed specimen. In the process, each section had to be no longer than arm's length, if the entire length of the area was to remain accessible when assembling the cast. For easy removal of a mold, the top half of the head should be divided into two sections.

I'd rather build a new house, he thought.

In the final phase, the clay and the entire armature had to be removed very carefully, so as not to break the mold. The center support was sawed off where it joined the lower part of the animal's body. The mold itself at this point had to be welded to the center post by applying excelsior saturated with thin plaster. The inside of the mold was then washed to remove any particles of clay or other debris. The entire inside surface of the mold was then coated, first with liquid soap then with flour or wheat paste.

The idea of pizza and spaghetti distracted him briefly. He read on.

173

Strips or squares of preshrunk burlap were now pressed in, and a thin coat of plaster painted over the burlap. All pieces of the mold had to be treated in this way. The first layer of burlap had to adhere closely to the mold surface. Burlap squares saturated in a thin layer of plaster were then applied over the first layer —

Like mozzarella on pizza . . . .

— three or four times, depending on the size of the animal. After the cheese, that is, the *plaster* had set, all edges of the cast had to be trimmed to the mold with a sharp knife. . . .

His eyes began to droop. He sat up and turned the page thinking: There must be an easier way!

Reinforced wooden boards were inserted at this point. These were secured to the walls of the cast by means of fine excelsior saturated with plaster. Iron rods also had to be secured in the legs with plaster and burlap. When the cast hardened, the mold could be broken away. (Ah, so the mold had to be broken at the end!)

More, still. . . .

McCalley put down the report. Was stuffing an animal really that involved? All this work before the skin was applied? He picked up the report again to see when it had been published. The Smithsonian Institution had issued it sometime in the seventies, but it had been prepared by a well-known taxidermist, years earlier. Well, perhaps they had better materials to work with today, less complicated procedures. Maybe they could get inside the specimen without too much damage? But the bottom line, the Inspector thought grimly, was that they had to find out if someone had hit on the idea of using this kind of processed animal, all this elaborate expertise to insure . . . what, exactly?

He was by no means prepared to admit that the animal was meant as a container for illegal goods, to be destroyed after it had served its purpose. He had to admit, though, that a carefully prepared specimen, a rare one like the arctic wolf, ostensibly destined for a reputable museum, was a perfect means of transporting . . . whatever. If Markarian was right, whoever had orchestrated this project was very clever indeed. Using museum quality animals for smuggling was a genial touch.

Of course, there wasn't any tangible evidence for such a theory. All he was ready to consider at the moment was that Jenene's body probably was not meant to be found on the premises, that, with the arrival of the tour group, his murderer or murderers were forced to leave it behind, together with the wolf.

Something was nagging at him, had been bothering him since his conversation with Kenney in the pub. Now it surfaced, unexpectedly: Dobie, the trapper, had been killed just hours before or soon after Jenene was killed. Bantry was killed about three weeks earlier, the first week in December. If indeed there was a connection, as Kenney had suggested, that sequence was significant. What had triggered it? To someone like Markarian, the timetable might suggest a deliberate plan to get rid of the three people involved with the preparation and transfer of the specimens described in Jenene's documents. But why? Was the operation, if it *was* smuggling, coming to an end? Were all three deaths, murders? What was the motive?

Markarian had suggested *greed.* Would that explain all three deaths? He ached for an answer to the question.

He shook his head and swung off the bed in one quick movement, annoyed at himself for falling into the kind of temptation he was always warning others against. He needed more facts.

Glancing at his radio clock by the bed, he realized it was after ten. He undressed quickly, got into bed and picked up the folder Markarian had left with him.

175

CHAPTER 10

A DRIVE TO BRONXVILLE
(January 2, 8:15 AM)

It was eight-fifteen when Markarian called from downstairs.

"Give me a couple of minutes. . . . You did say nine?"

"Thought you'd like to see the Christmas tree in Rockefeller Center."

Markarian headed south on Fifth Avenue. When they reached the fifties, he moved to the right and slowed down. McCalley craned his neck for a better look as they drove past the giant tree.

"Susan should be here. She'd love it."

Markarian laughed. "If she's anything like my wife and my sister, she'd spend the rest of the day dragging you through the stores and you'd end up buying things you don't really need or can afford. Why don't you take some time off in the Spring? I'll be glad to show you around." He turned east then north. "You might as well see a bit of the new Third Avenue, too. I don't think you saw it before the elevated train was torn down. I was just a kid, seven or eight, but I remember my dad and mom taking me with them to the second-hand stores. In one of them, we found an old baseball bat for a quarter. It wasn't new, but I'd never had a baseball bat. We didn't have money for those things. This time of year, my sister and I were lucky if we found a scarf or a new sweater on our beds on Christmas morning. Anyway, that stick still had plenty of life in it. My dad bought it for me. I had it for years." For a moment he took his hand off the wheel to gesture vaguely. "They're all antiques shops now. And high-rises. When the El came down, property values soared." He glanced over at McCalley. "Did you get a chance to read the file?"

"Do you mind if I keep it until tomorrow? I'm still taking some notes."

"Sure. . . . If you ask me, the two cases are joined at the hip."

McCalley burst out laughing. He explained quickly: "One of the people I had to interview, she was in the tour group, a professor of English, her name is Jill Masterson, took me to task for using expressions like that. She's a friend of Mrs. Bantry's. By the way, Mrs. Bantry will have that lawyer I mentioned, Hartley Quinn, with her."

"Why?"

"I think I told you, back there, he's also Bantry's Executor. I guess he has business to discuss with her."

"Probably represents her now."

"Very likely. Do you mind?"

"Why should I mind?" He smiled and, without taking his hands off the wheel, gave McCalley a friendly poke in the arm. "Hey, I appreciate your asking, but don't feel you have to pass everything by me. You're in charge. I'm just driving you around, remember?"

"And buying me lunch!"

"Right."

"I would have much preferred seeing her alone. And *him* alone." "They drove in silence for a while, then McCalley turned slightly in his seat and said:

"Correct me if I'm wrong, but I have a feeling you're not altogether satisfied with the verdict that was handed down in the Bantry case."

Markarian shot him a look before answering. "A lot of questions come to mind. Those boys who shot Bantry with identical guns, all of them properly registered, in each case, to an adult in the family. Almost as though it had been carefully planned, the mix-up, all the different prints on the gun that killed Bantry —"

"Pure coincidence?"

Markarian laughed. "Point taken. . . . Seriously,

though, a gang dispute at ten in the morning? And Bantry just coming out of that shop?"

"Let me have a go at it," said McCalley by way of reply. "Bantry gets a call early in the morning, rushes out of the house and is shot coming out of a shop in Soho, where a gang battle is taking place or, rather, about to take place. Because, as I recall, nothing really happened until Bantry came out."

Markarian gave his colleague a curious look. "That's right."

"What else do we know about these boys?"

"Not much. There was no follow-up of any kind."

"What else can you tell me about Tasselbaum, the owner of the shop?"

"All I know is what's in the file. There was no need to go into his background at the time of the shooting. Just a routine check. Came over from Austria, he and his mother, about thirty years ago. She died the next year. He seemed to have some money. . . and contacts. . . . It's all in the file."

"Why do you suppose those teenagers were let go?"

"Ha! Tell me about it. Just kids fooling around. They were slapped on the wrist and sent home with mommy and daddy."

"You never actually saw the crime scene?"

"No, I was assigned elsewhere that morning. When the call came in, they sent Jim Slattery. He's okay. Did what had to be done."

"Was Slattery satisfied?"

"There was nothing to suggest more than an open and shut case."

He glanced over at McCalley. "Do you want me to sniff around?" McCalley sensed both hesitation and restrained interest in the question and decided to discourage any action. It must have been tricky enough to pull out the file without — he was certain — official permission. He didn't want to make difficulties by encouraging Markarian's curiosity, and his own, even if well-founded.

McCalley shook his head. "No, better not."

There was a pause, then Markarian said, almost reluctantly: "From what I heard, Slattery was frustrated as hell!" He shook his head. "What you've told me suggests a link of some sort, you've got to admit." He went on quickly. "Oh, nothing I'd bring to Slattery, goes without saying. Not at this point, anyway. And not unless you give the signal." He glanced over and was relieved to see McCalley nodding approval.

Traffic out of Manhattan at that time of day was light. Soon they exited on to a narrow road. Glancing down once or twice at the directions McCalley had taken down the night before and had handed him when they had started out, Markarian reached the stone archway into the Bantry property without any difficulty. He followed the private tree-lined road until they reached the wide apron in front of what was a mansion rather than a big house. Markarian gave a low whistle of appreciation.

It was a gray stone building, set back far enough to be invisible from the public road. The front lawn, still green because of the unusually mild weather, sloped down to the edge of the property, where a stone wall protected the house and grounds from even a casual view from the road. It was a stately, elegant structure, very different from the fashionable homes they had passed along the way. Even to McCalley's inexperienced eye, this house very likely was one of a kind, architecturally interesting in curious ways. What first drew his attention were the oriel windows of the second floor and a turret on the left, suggesting an entire separate suite from the ground up. On either side of the stone canopy which marked the entrance and recalled the archway at the foot of the roadway, were large windows, indicating high ceilings inside. The effect was that of a small chateau built for some eccentric millionaire, an expensive but carefully designed whim. If any restoration had been done on the exterior, it had been effected with great care to produce an integrated whole.

A Jaguar was already parked in front.

"I guess the lawyer got here first," said Markarian as McCalley rang the bell. Chimes sounded somewhere inside the house.

The woman who greeted them had the kind of face that Botticelli might have wanted to paint. Her large hazel eyes calmly studied them as she acknowledged their greeting with a nod and stepped aside to let them in. She was dressed in a long brown skirt of soft wool and a high-necked sweater in a shade of dark coral that made her thick auburn hair, pulled back casually and held in place with a large barrette, take on a blood-red hue, under the sparkling crystals of a delicate chandelier of tinted mosaic glass, shaped like a basket, depicting all around its side, an uninterrupted scene of gods, nymphs and cupids. Tinted glass fruit spilled from it, the reds, blues, greens, whites, yellows, aquamarines repeated in the long cut crystals that hung from the smaller inner circle at the base of the basket. Even unlit, with the sun streaming into the entrance hall from the rooms on either side, the whole glowed like a casket of precious jewels.

Both men found themselves staring as Mrs. Bantry shut the massive oak door and led them into a room, the likes of which McCalley had never seen, even in the magazines that Susan often brought home. He knew that the Bantrys had spent almost three years abroad and had bought and sent back many unusual pieces; but this room took one's breath away. It was large but inviting, the ceiling higher than most. Three large chairs were upholstered in a pastel fabric, the same colors in each case but different patterns, a subtle blend in dramatic contrast with two deep blue sofas. A lighter blue Chinese rug covered almost the entire floor. Around the main sitting area, a number of tables and display cases had been arranged, their soft patina finish gleaming in the sunlight that streamed through the high windows. But clearly the most dramatic thing in the room was the fireplace that took up the entire wall opposite the majestic front windows. It was made of pinkish gray marble, exquisitely sculpted all around with what appeared to be early renaissance figures. On the two other walls were several paintings and a silk tapestry. McCalley recognized a crucifixion by Giotto (surely, not an original!) and two Fra Angelicos. Several others seemed to be from the same period. Between two of the high windows, resting on a smooth marble column, was a rather chubby Michelangelo angel or "putto," fashioned from the same exquisite white carrara marble as the column on which it rested.

It was by far the most interesting room McCalley had ever seen.

A tall man stood by the window. He turned as they entered. Jenny Bantry introduced her lawyer. He looked more like a Hollywood star.

She sat down, Quinn beside her, and waved the two men to chairs opposite them. McCalley introduced Markarian as his "New York colleague, who was helping him find his way around." Quinn seemed about to speak but changed his mind.

"You're very kind to see us on such short notice," McCalley began. Jenny Bantry looked at him with her steady gaze. Her quiet manner had a strange effect on him. He sensed a vulnerability, but an alertness too. Knowing what she had gone through in the last several weeks, he was prepared for a certain emotional fragility; what he saw was stoic resignation.

"How can I help you, Inspector?"

"I believe your friend Jill Masterson told you there was a murder at the Canadian Museum of Nature, in

181

Ottawa, the day after Christmas, the day she arrived for a conference."

"Yes. She goes every year to that convention. This year it was held in Ottawa."

"On that day, just after she arrived and checked into the hotel, she signed up for a special tour of the museum. They arrived there around six o'clock. The curator, Miss Enderby, was giving the tour herself. They began with the taxidermy workroom, where animals are repaired, processed for display, and so on. As they were leaving, Miss Enderby remembered she had left some notes behind and went back to get them. That's when she discovered the body of the museum's taxidermist, a man called John Jenene."

"That's more or less what she told me, yes."

Quinn spoke for the first time: "How can Mrs. Bantry help you?"

"We're looking for any leads that might throw light on museum transactions — sales, loans, exchanges; that sort of thing."

"You think the man's death had something to do with museum business?"

"We don't know, but at this stage, any lead has to be checked out."

"And Mr. Bantry is a 'lead'?"

"He did business with museums, I understand. Including the one in Ottawa." Jenny Bantry looked puzzled. Quinn was frowning and tapping his knee.

"Do you know anything about that, Jenny?" he turned to ask her.

The woman shook her head. "No. But then, I really don't know much about Ellis's business at this end. It's true, we were together most of the time, while in Europe. Ellis had me meet some of his clients from time to time, taught me a great deal about art and antiques. I learned a lot from him these past three years. But Inspector, I think Henry

182

Wentworth, Ellis's Manager, could help you much more than I can."

"I really don't understand why you have to bother Mrs. Bantry with all this. Henry is the man you want to talk to," Quinn said impatiently.

"I assure you, Mr. Quinn, I won't miss anyone, not even you. I understand you took care of many things here, the renovation of this house, for example, receiving items as they arrived, checking on the work as it progressed, all sorts of things, while your friends were abroad. But we'll save all that for, say, tomorrow perhaps?" He turned back to Mrs. Bantry. "It would help if you would alert Mr. Bantry's staff that we would like to talk with them, in the morning. I'll need access to records . . . ."

"I don't see any difficulty in that."

"Good!" He flashed a quick smile as he pulled out his pad and leafed through it. "Investigations of this sort are often a tedious process of elimination, but questions have to be asked."

"I understand."

McCalley consulted his notes, looked up. "Your husband was an export-import dealer?"

"Yes, mostly in connection with antiques."

"But he handled other items?"

"Yes."

"For museums?"

"I believe he did search out and purchase items for museums, from time to time; but I can't give you any specific details. Mr. Wentworth has all the records."

"You said you worked with your husband, while in Europe?" McCalley went on easily, looking up from his notes as he spoke.

"I don't know what you mean, exactly," said Mrs. Bantry. Quinn leaned forward, about to answer, but Mrs. Bantry laid a restraining hand on his arm and went on. "What I said was that I often went with him when he met

183

clients, checked out orders, that sort of thing. A good portion of the time I went off on my own. You see, Inspector, our major project was a personal one: to find furnishings for this house. We bought it just before leaving for Europe."

"Excuse me, Inspector," Quinn said brusquely, "but are you suggesting that Ellis might have had something to do with the murder of the taxidermist in Canada?"

McCalley looked genuinely surprised. "How could he have had anything to do with that? I understand he was killed early in December, in New York!" For the first time since their arrival, McCalley saw pain in Mrs. Bantry's face. She lowered her eyes and clasped her hands tightly in her lap. He made a show of referring to his notes. When he looked up again, the wide hazel eyes were once again focused on him. He chose his next words with great care. Putting his pad to one side, he addressed the lawyer.

"Mr. Quinn, at the risk of laboring the obvious: I'm in charge of a murder investigation. My job is to find out everything I can about John Jenene, his colleagues, friends, enemies, anyone who had dealings with him. Right now, all we have are loose threads. We don't even know what to look for, but I do know that every bit of information may be useful. Mr. Bantry's connection with museums, the Ottawa one in particular, is something that needs to be checked out. Part of the routine." He turned back to Jenny Bantry, but before he could say anything, Quinn asked:

"Inspector, what makes you so sure Ellis had dealings with the museum in Ottawa?"

"We have our sources," replied the Inspector, unruffled. He had no intention of giving out any more information than he had to. "You said a moment ago, Mrs. Bantry, that you met some of your husband's clients, while in Europe."

"From time to time, yes."

"Did you ever meet John Jenene?"

184

"Is it a list of names you're looking for?" Quinn interjected, somewhat sharply.

"That might be useful, yes," replied the other, serenely. Then to Mrs. Bantry. "Do you think you could give us some names?"

"This is ridiculous!" Quinn cried out, jumping up and walking to the doorway and back as he spoke. "Is she supposed to remember everyone she ate with in the last three years?"

Mrs. Bantry turned to him. "Please, Hart, sit down. The Inspector is simply doing his job." Then to McCalley: "No, I never met John Jenene."

"He never came to see your husband in New York?"

"If he did, I wasn't aware of it."

"And you don't know of any dealings he may have had with the museum in Ottawa?"

"As I said, Inspector, he sometimes found things for museums, but I can't give you any details."

"Did your husband keep any records here at home?"

"No."

"He did have a computer —?"

"Yes."

"Perhaps we could look at it?"

Quinn, who had resumed his seat, answered for her — calmly this time. "I would have to advise my client — Mrs. Bantry *is* my client, Inspector — I would have to advise her against that. People have all kinds of private matters on their computers. And you're not suggesting a court order, I hope!"

"Mr. Quinn, really!" McCalley sat back and folded his arms, his tone giving away a certain measure of exasperation. This seemed to please Quinn, whose reactions, until then, had not produced even a trace of annoyance in the Inspector. "We're not dealing with

185

suspects," McCalley went on. "There are no grounds for drastic measures. We're simply looking for information that might help us." He picked up his pad and turned again to Mrs, Bantry. "But if your lawyer advises against it, perhaps you could go through the computer and let us know if you come across anything that might be relevant."

Mrs. Bantry looked at Quinn, who nodded.

"I could do that, but I really wouldn't know what to look for."

"Anything that suggests business with museums, names that might come up in that connection. Perhaps Mr. Quinn could help you."

"We can try."

"Good. . . . Just a few more questions. . . . Your husband flew to the West coast on business, the end of November. Can you tell us what that was about?"

"He was gone only a few days." McCalley waited for more, pen in hand. "He flew out the Friday after Thanksgiving and came back the following Wednesday."

"Do you know why he went? Where he went? The people he saw?"

"No."

"Who called him the morning he was killed?"

She shifted where she sat, placing her arm on the side rest of the chair. "I honestly don't know."

"You took the call, I understand."

"And hung up the phone when I heard Ellis pick it up in our sitting room. I was in the kitchen. When he came downstairs, he was dressed and ready to leave. He said he had some urgent business to take care of and had no time for breakfast."

"Did he say where he was going, with whom he was meeting?"

"No."

"What time did the call come in?"

"Just before eight. He was out of the house by

eight-thirty."

"You didn't recognize the voice of the caller?"

"No. I don't think I ever heard it before. . . . Ellis would receive calls at all hours while we were in Europe, Inspector. I often took messages for him."

"Didn't you mind?"

She smiled. "I got used to it. Especially since *he* didn't seem to mind. . . ."

"Weren't you at all curious about who might be calling your husband so early that morning?"

"As I explained, Inspector, my husband took calls whenever they came in, even after — or, in this case, before — what most of us would consider normal business hours."

Once again, Quinn interrupted, making no effort this time to hide his irritation. "I resent these questions, Inspector. What possible connection could there be between Ellis's death and your murder case?"

"Connection? There's no connection, Mr. Quinn. Nothing beyond the fact that Mr. Bantry had dealings with the Ottawa museum, and we might be able to find in his files, in his records, some reference to a visit or a meeting, a name perhaps, some information that could help us with this case."

Mrs. Bantry stood up abruptly, hugging herself, and went to stand by the window. The men watched her in silence. After a while she turned and spoke from where she stood.

"Inspector McCalley, I buried my husband less than a month ago. He was caught in crossfire as he left a shop in Soho. His death was ruled an accident. . . ."

Quinn went to stand beside her. McCalley and Markarian both stood up. "But, Mrs. Bantry," McCalley said, "I'm not investigating your husband's death. . . ."

Quinn said: "Whatever the reason, you're out of line, bringing it up."

It was clearly a signal for them to leave. McCalley,

however, stood his ground.

"Mr. Quinn, as Mr. Bantry's Executor, could you tell me if there was anything at all in his will that might help us?"

The tall man led Mrs. Bantry away from the window. Only when they were seated again, did the two officers also sit down.

"Nothing. Except for a few bequests, charities, personal gifts to staff, Mrs. Bantry inherits everything."

"Can you tell me what the estate is worth?"

"No. It's too early for that. But, Inspector, even if I had that information, I wouldn't give it to you. Your asking for it is improper, irrelevant, and insensitive."

Without turning to him, Mrs. Bantry placed a hand on his arm and addressed McCalley. "Inspector, my husband's business was a profitable one, this house alone, restored as you see it, is worth several million, the contents several times that much. Ellis was ten years older than I. He had been in business for more than twelve years, when I met him, and had done extremely well. He was a very wealthy man."

"I see." He noted something in his pad. "Thank you. . . . Mr. Quinn, I understand you were here often while the Bantrys were abroad. That you supervised the work that was going on, checked out purchases as they arrived, all of that."

"All of that, yes."

"How long have you known the Bantrys?"

"I've known Jenny since our Columbia days. I was going to law school. She was in art history. I met Ellis rather recently, a few months before he and Jenny were married. I was his Best Man. He had no family."

"Did anything happen at any time, while the Bantrys were in Europe, that might help our investigation?"

Quinn laughed a deep grating sound. "Like what? Having to return a truckload of pipes that were not what had been ordered?"

Ignoring, the sarcasm, McCalley went on. "You had time for supervising the work on this house? What about your practice?"

"My time is flexible. I have my own law firm."

McCalley looked up and smiled. "At your age? You're very fortunate."

"My father was a lawyer. I inherited the firm when he died. And, yes, I have some money too. And plenty of time to help out my friends, if I wish to do so. But, Inspector," he went on, settling in his seat and putting his hands behind his head. "I thought you were saving me for tomorrow!"

"Indeed, I am. But since we're on the subject — you don't mind, do you?"

"Why should I mind?"

"Then, perhaps you can shed some light on why Mr. Bantry went to the West coast at the end of November. Was it something urgent?"

"I was his friend, not his business associate."

McCalley made a show of putting away his pad and pen. "And his lawyer," he added, standing up. He didn't expect an answer and didn't get one. "You've been very helpful. Both of you. I may have some more questions, later, if you don't mind."

Quinn answered for both of them. "Not at all. But Mrs. Bantry may not be here to answer them. I've urged her to go away for a while."

"A good idea." He smiled at her. "And, Mr. Quinn, could you spare us some time, around eleven tomorrow?"

Quinn said nothing but took out a card and handed it to him. "I have to prepare for a court appearance at two," he said bluntly, "Will you need more than an hour?"

McCalley nodded. "An hour will be fine."

No one shook hands.

As he got into the car, McCalley glanced back.

189

Jenny Bantry, Quinn beside her, stood watching them from one of the tall windows.

Although there was plenty of room on the apron to circle around and point the car straight down toward the public road, Markarian — for whatever reason — chose to move out in reverse and backed down all the way. Markarian was smiling. McCalley laughed.

"What was that all about?"

"A whim. I felt like it. Okay, so I was trying to make a statement."

"For whose benefit?"

"Mine. His. I just felt like doing it."

McCalley shook his head. "He *is* hard to take. If it's any consolation, I don't like him either. A bit of a ham, too."

"Bent on impressing Mrs. Bantry, you mean."

"That too."

"He's a *hoverer*."

McCalley laughed. "Is that a sin?"

"It should be a crime."

"Well, I'm sure Mrs. Bantry knows what she wants and I doubt she'll ever settle for someone like Quinn. She may still be in shock, but she thinks straight and is not afraid to say what she's thinking. She's strong and capable. Take the will, for example. I don't think an experienced businessman like Bantry, who's made a fortune in a relatively short time, would have left his business to her, even if she is his wife . . . unless he was pretty certain she could handle it. Your file describes her as a Ph.D. in art and art history, with almost a dozen articles and a published book, even before she met Bantry . . . . Yes, I'm sure they would have ended up working together . . ." he added, almost to himself.

"What bothers me is Quinn's attitude toward her," said Markarian. "They're old friends, have known one another for some time. So, he must know she can take it.

190

Why play the knight protector? She doesn't need looking after that way."

"He's her lawyer, too," McCalley reminded him.

"And he likes her a lot, wouldn't you say?"

When McCalley answered, there was an edge to his voice. "Too much, I think. . . ." They drove in silence for a while, then McCalley said, as though his thoughts had found their way back to a major highway:

"I keep thinking of roadmaps. The sequence of events. Timetables that mesh together and yet are not connected. Bantry's trip to the West coast, for example."

"What about it?"

"He was gone five days. Comes back, and the very next morning he gets a phone call from person unknown, rushes out of the house around eight-thirty —"

"— I don't know about you," McCalley interjected, "but most people start out for work earlier than that, every morning."

"Yes, but he didn't *have* to. Anyone who can take off for Europe and stay there for three years, who can afford a house like that" — he pointed in the direction they had just come from — "doesn't have ordinary working hours. Besides, from what his wife told us, he wasn't planning to go out that early. She was preparing breakfast, remember? He rushes out and meets with — there's no clear indication or proof, but yes, I suspect the call was from Tasselbaum. It had to be, since that was where he ended up."

"Will we get anything out of him, I wonder?"

"If he's one of the players, he'll be very careful."

"So will we," replied the other, as McCalley, fumbled in his pocket.

"Ah, here it is," said the Inspector, after taking out his little pad and leafing through it. "Something Quinn said back there — something about, ah, yes, here we are. At one point he asked: 'You think the man's death had something

191

to do with museum business?'"

"I don't see anything remarkable in that. You were asking about museum transactions."

"And a few minutes later: he asked: 'Are you suggesting that Ellis might have had something to do with the murder of the taxidermist?'"

"Well, Luke, we *are* looking for connections, aren't we." He laughed. "Hey, neither one of us likes the guy" — he took one hand from the wheel to scratch the other — "but you were trying not to give away too much, and that made the questioning hard. Let's see what else he has to say tomorrow. . . . And we want to find out as soon as possible about that trip of Bantry's."

"My Sergeant is tracking down information at that end — where he stayed, car rental, what kind of mileage he put on it. . . . You could do me a big favor if you'd find out what flight he took out of New York, where he was headed."

"Do you know how many people fly on holidays?"

"He probably went first class. That whittles it down."

"Thanks a lot."

CHAPTER 11
VISIT TO THE AMERICAN MUSEUM
OF NATURAL HISTORY
(January 2, 12:30 PM)

The brisk walk from his hotel to the museum did him good. Inside the lobby, he sought out a guard and asked directions to the Curator's office.

A smiling young woman was waiting for him near the elevator. She came forward, her hand extended. "Dr. McCalley? I'm Alene Trainor, Assistant Curator. They called from the lobby to tell me you were here." She stood aside as he entered her office. "Unfortunately, the Curator can't make it."

Trying not to show his annoyance, McCalley entered the small office. Back at her desk, Miss Trainor invited him to sit down opposite her.

"It's Inspector McCalley," he began, with a smile. "I have no claim to the other title." He placed his coat on the back of his chair and sat down.

"Miss Trainor," he began again, "I interrupted my holiday to fly down from Ottawa yesterday on a very important police matter. I'm on a very tight schedule and had arranged days ago to meet with the Curator today. I don't have any other time for him, and my business is urgent." Sergeant Kenney, following his instructions, had specifically asked for the Curator.

Miss Trainor looked properly distressed. "I'm so very sorry, Inspector. The Curator came down with the flu yesterday and had to leave before the end of the day. . . . I'll do my best to answer all your questions. Would you like some tea? Coffee?"

"No, no thank you."

"It was all explained to me. I'm sure I can be of some help."

193

"What exactly was explained to you?"

"That you're here on urgent business connected with the Canadian Museum of Nature in Ottawa."

"And what we say in this room must be held in strictest confidence. Repeating any of it could compromise our ongoing investigation."

She clasped her hands on the desk. "Yes, of course. But what about the Curator?"

"Naturally, you have to report to him, don't you! I'll leave my card should either of you wish to contact me at any later time." He pulled out two business cards and placed them on the desk. She put one inside the desk drawer. "The man who died was the museum taxidermist. He had just processed an arctic wolf —"

"What luck! We've been trying to get one for the longest time."

"Oh? Who is your provider? Do you use an agency?"

"I'll have to look through our records."

"Could you get that information to me, as soon as possible? I'll be staying here for the next day or two." He tore a blank page from his pad, jotted down the name of his hotel, room and phone number, and handed it to her.

"Forgive me Inspector, but how is your wolf connected with us?"

"I don't know that it is. You see, our records are incomplete." (not really a lie, was it?) "but they indicate that the wolf was being sent to New York. We wondered if it was destined for this museum. As I said, the records don't tell us much. Dr. Jenene died before the paperwork was completed."

She had been studying the card still in her hands. "It says here you're from homicide?"

"Yes."

"The man was murdered?"

"We're not sure, but he may have been." He went

on quickly, to avoid elaborating. "Is there any way you can check your records and tell me if this museum was expecting an arctic wolf from Ottawa? Or, direct me to whoever is able to give me that information?"

"I can check, of course, and it does happen to be my job, or part of it, so you've come to the right person. Offhand though, I can tell you we aren't expecting a wolf of any kind. I certainly would have heard about an arctic wolf!!"

"So you would you know if a specimen was being sent to you?"

"Absolutely."

"Could the Curator himself possibly have known and forgot to tell you?"

"Anything is possible, Inspector, but it's never happened that way in all my fifteen years in this job. Whatever information might reach his desk, anything having to do with new purchases, would automatically be passed on to me. All inquiries as well."

"What about loans?"

"Those too." She took out a piece of paper and made some notes.

He waited for her to look up before resuming. "I was told that it is highly unusual for a museum to sell or lend an item to another museum."

"Well, it's not unheard of, but yes, it is unusual. Museums like to have specimens prepared to their specifications, for their particular displays. An animal has to blend in with whatever else is in the exhibit case: other animals, flora, its habitat, even the way it stands is important. Usually what a museum has on hand is not necessarily what another museum wants or needs."

"What about loans?"

"Same answer. There would still be those special requirements."

"Has this museum ever purchased a specimen

195

from another museum?"

"I don't know of any." She wrote something on the paper in front of her. "But I'll check it out."

"I'd appreciate it. That and transfers of any kind."

When she had finished she put down her pencil and said: "Besides, most museums wouldn't dream of getting rid of items that cost them time and a good deal of money to get in the first place."

"Still it's possible?"

"Yes, but unlikely."

McCalley glanced down at his own notes.

"Do you have an arctic wolf in your collection?"

"Oh, yes, but it's quite old."

"Does it matter that it's old?"

"No, not really. But at some point, museums like to replace specimens. Displays are changed to reflect new information about the environment, about the animals, or just to freshen up things."

"Does the name Jenene ring a bell? Dr. John Jenene?"

"Is he the man who died? No. Sorry."

"Have you had any dealing at all in the past with the Canadian museum?"

"Not that I can recall, except for exchanges of information from time to time. We do get their literature, promotional flyers, things like that."

"Perhaps you can let me see what you have? I'll be sure to return it."

"There won't be much. We don't keep such things very long. I'm sure your wife doesn't keep catalogs indefinitely. It's the same with us."

McCalley pursed his lips to resist smiling. Their night table had two shelves crammed with them: Horchow, Ross and Simon, I. Magnin, and others, a whole carton in the basement. "Leafing through them relaxes me," Susan told him once, in answer to the obvious question.

196

"Now think hard, Miss Trainor. Has anyone in the museum or anyone at all expressed any interest in an arctic wolf recently? Let's say in the last six months or so?"

The woman began to shake her head in answer, but then put a finger at the side of her mouth and took on a look of concentration.

"I had completely forgotten. . . . One of our tour guides, Ed Shaney said something to me some weeks ago. Ed was having a late lunch in the cafeteria and I had gone down for a quick bite and sat at his table." She paused, looked away, fixed her eyes on a point just beyond the Inspector's head, frowning in an effort at concentration. McCalley waited. "He said, someone in the early tour —"

McCalley interrupted. "Man or woman?"

"Man, a man in his morning group —" McCalley was busy taking notes on his pad. Now he interrupted again: "Please try to give me as many details as possible, Miss Trainor. Do you remember what day that was?"

"No, but we can ask him. . . . I do know it was before Thanksgiving, because I was late that morning. I had to stop off to order a turkey. I had promised my mother I'd take care of it. She wasn't feeling well."

"The week *before* Thanksgiving, not the week *after* Thanksgiving?"

"I'm pretty sure. We usually order two weeks ahead, You see, Mom doesn't like the supermarket turkeys and insisted I stop by the butcher's to place our order. My sister and her family were coming to dinner, or we wouldn't have even bothered. Our butcher —"

"Can you remember the exact day?"

"It had to be the Friday just *before* Thanksgiving. Yes, I'm sure, because Mr. Feccino, our butcher, waved a finger at me when I placed the order —" here Miss Trainor demonstrated by waving a finger at the Inspector — "and said, 'You wait too long! You know what day is today? Your mother sick? She always come two weeks before!' I told

197

him I was very sorry, mom *was* in fact sick with the flu, couldn't come, and —" Something in McCalley's face must have encouraged her to hurry on. "Yes, well, it *was* definitely the Friday before Thanksgiving, because when I told Mom she said, 'Good thing you went today; Monday, would have been too late!'"

McCalley repeated out loud, as he wrote down the words: "The Friday *before* Thanksgiving,"

"Yes."

"So, that morning, that Friday morning, on the tour of the museum — by the way, how many tours do you have each day?"

"It varies. On that day we had scheduled two groups. Some of our guides had come down with whatever was going around. Ed agreed to take on both of them."

"He would remember that it was that Friday?"

"I'm sure."

"On the morning tour, . . . you were saying?" Here the Inspector twirled his finger and raised his eyebrows for her to continue.

"Yes, well, we were just chatting over coffee, as I said, I hardly took notice, but I do remember his telling me that a man was asking about arctic wolves."

McCalley held up his hand. "All right. Before you go on, let me ask you, please, to be as accurate and as specific as you can. This is important. I will want Ed's version too, but yours first. . . . . Was Ed talking about wolves when the other fellow asked the question?"

"No, that was the point."

"What was the point?"

"The question came out of nowhere."

"What was the question?"

"First he asked if wolves of that region were hard to get."

"Did the visitor actually use those words? 'wolves of that region,' 'hard to get'?"

"I . . . I don't know. I *think* that's what Ed told me."

"Go on, please."

"Ed said the man came right up to him and asked about wolves from the northern regions, arctic wolves. He didn't pay much attention at first; people ask questions all the time. Among other things, he wanted to know how much they cost."

McCalley interrupted. "How much *do* they cost?"

"Arctic wolves are hard to come by, Inspector. I'm not an expert. Mr. Salisbury, head of acquisitions, can give you an accurate figure. I can ask him, if you like."

"Any other expenses?"

"Processing the animal, of course. And a few other fees and payments."

"So. First there's the price of the wolf itself, then the cost of — processing?" He knew the word by now. It had also appeared a number of times in the taxidermy report he had read the night before. "That *is* the word?"

Miss Trainor nodded. "That's right. Getting it ready for display."

He looked up from his notes. "What else did Ed say about this individual?"

"Not much. Oh, he did ask whether we were expecting a fresh specimen."

"Were those his words?"

"That's how Ed phrased it. He wondered about it, he said, because they weren't anywhere near that display, and, besides, only an experienced eye would notice that our specimen is rather old."

"I don't suppose he gave Ed his name."

"I doubt it." She watched him writing in his pad. "At first, Ed thought he might be from Ottawa."

Miss Trainor was startled by her visitor's reaction. In one swift movement McCalley had put down his pen and pad and leaned almost halfway across Miss Trainor's desk, both hands resting, palms down, on it, as though he were

199

about to leap out of his chair."

"*Ottawa*? He told the tour guide he was from Ottawa?"

"Well, I'm not sure he *said* so in *so many words*! —" The woman stared at McCalley, who started to write again.

"Now, this is important, Miss Trainor. What did he say about Ottawa? How did it come up?"

"Something about a museum there having found a fresh specimen. He thought maybe our museum also had one coming."

"What did Ed tell him?"

"That he knew nothing about it. He referred the gentleman to my office, but no one came to see me."

"Might he have seen the Curator?"

"Well, yes, but the Curator would have sent him to me."

"Could the Curator simply have answered the question without bothering you with it?"

"Not really. One of us would have had to check the records and that's *my* job. He would definitely have referred the matter to me. But, Inspector, I probably would not have given him any information."

"Why not?"

"Well . . . the way Ed described the man, he seemed to have some special reason for asking, not just curiosity, not the usual question one asks on a guided tour. It was just a feeling, but Ed became somewhat suspicious. He thought there was some urgency behind the questions. How did he put it? 'Out of context,' that's it. He said the questions were out of context. I'm not exactly sure what he meant by that. . . ."

"Did Ed describe this person?"

"No, but a curious thing. . . . He said the gentleman left before the tour even began. Ed said he almost called him back, but the rest of the group was standing there

200

waiting, so he carried on."

Miss Trainor watched McCalley scribbling notes. When he was finished, he asked: "Would you call Ed for me now?"

She glanced at her watch. "It's one-twenty. He has the afternoon tour at two. Will you keep him for more than half an hour?"

"No, I don't think so." When she had made the call, McCalley rose.

"Is there another room we can use?" He added tactfully: "I don't want to keep you from your work any longer." She opened a side door that led directly into a conference room. "Is this all right?"

"Fine." He placed his raincoat and cap on an empty chair. "By the way, how do you spell Ed's last name?" He wrote it down, thanked her, and went into the hall to wait. Briefly, he wondered at the circumstances that had forced him to meet with Miss Trainor instead of the Curator himself. He scowled, thinking what Markarian or Kenney would say.

Ed Shaney was more than happy to talk about his work, McCalley discovered, after introducing himself. To put him at ease, the Inspector began by asking about his background and learned that the young man had majored in zoology, but had a degree in biology, also, and had studied taxidermy along the way. In fact, Shaney was more than happy to inform the Inspector that he was working on a combined Ph.D. that would eventually make him eligible for a position in museum administration. McCalley was duly impressed.

"Miss Trainor tells me you had a visitor to the museum a few weeks back, a man, asking about arctic wolves. Do you mind if I ask you some questions about that?"

"Not much to tell. This guy wanted to know if we were getting a new specimen."

201

"What day was that?"

"Friday before Thanksgiving. I remember because the museum was short-handed, on account of some bug that was going around. I took on two tours that day, back to back."

"You're sure it was that particular Friday?"

"Yes. I was off the Friday *after* Thanksgiving."

"And in which of the tours was this visitor?

"The first one. At ten. We were already assembled, ready to start, when he rushed in to join the group. It was ten sharp, didn't expect anyone else. We were ready to move out, when he joined us."

"You said the visitor asked if the museum was getting a new specimen. Can you give me more details? Be more specific?" McCalley listened, made notes, and asked the same questions he had asked Miss Trainor. Ed's answers were consistent with hers. He decided to probe in another direction.

"Can you remember anything else about the man? Can you describe him to me?"

"Oh sure. He was tall, good looking, anywhere between thirty-five and forty. Had that look about him —"

"Excuse me, what kind of look?"

"Experienced, sophisticated. High-level executive type. Spoke well, dressed well. A beautifully tailored blazer, dark tan slacks, canary shirt, blue green tan and red patterned tie. Not a wrinkle in anything. Perfect fit. Everything made to order, I'm sure. Most people were in jeans and sweaters, you know, casual wear, light stuff because of the mild weather we've been having. But this guy not only wore a jacket, he was carrying a cashmere coat, too. They cost a fortune, you know!"

"Go on."

"That's it. Oh, and he had on Gucci boots. The very short ones that come up to the ankles only. They're like fancy shoes. I remembered that, because when someone is wearing expensive clothing, have you noticed? you tend to look at the rest of the outfit."

"Er, no, can't say that I have. But it's very keen of you, very observant."

"I do it automatically. Anyway, when I saw how he was dressed, and that cashmere coat over his arm, I looked down to see what he was wearing on his feet. Not just ordinary boots or heavy shoes like mine, but Gucci boots, high shoes, really, the soft leather kind. Which told me that he could afford more solid boots as well, for the nasty weather, the kind you wear when the snow really piles up! I don't know about you, but I can't afford more than one pair." He held out a foot to show McCalley the heavy, high-laced shoes he was wearing. "Army outlet. I've had them for three years and they'll have to last for at least three more. I wear them all the time, even in this mild weather, have to, until summer. Then I switch to sandals." He shifted in his chair and pulled back his foot.

"You're saying he was probably wealthy."

The other nodded. "And, I thought at the time, out of place in the museum at ten in the morning, dressed like that. He looked as though he should have been catching a plane to London or Rome, on business, a board meeting maybe. . . ."

"Anything else you can tell me?"

"No, except he seemed kind of distracted." He watched McCalley writing in his pad, for a few seconds, then went on: "I remember thinking, why is this guy here? Most of our visitors are school groups and tourists."

"You don't think he was a tourist?" McCalley asked, looking up briefly.

"I don't think so, although he did mention Ottawa. At first, I thought he was from there, but he had no accent, not like you. You're from Canada aren't you? He would have talked more like you if he came from Ottawa. We get quite a few Canadians. And the questions he asked, even

203

before we got started, seemed to come from nowhere. As though he had come there just to find out what he wanted to know."

"What did he say about Ottawa?"

"Something about the museum there. I guess you've been in it. It's supposed to have some really great stuff. I asked about some of their exhibits. He couldn't tell me anything."

"What did he say about the museum?"

"He said he'd heard they were sending us a specimen."

"Can you remember his exact words?"

Ed Shaney looked at the ceiling, his face crinkled up in concentration. "I think his words were: 'I hear the museum in Ottawa is sending you a new specimen very soon.' Yeah, that's it."

"Did you think he was connected with the museum in Ottawa?"

"It did cross my mind, but his answers just didn't fit. He couldn't tell me anything about their holdings. In any case, an arctic wolf is big news. I was surprised, to say the least. Museums don't usually sell or donate or lend specimens. Especially an arctic wolf. It's hard to get."

"Didn't you wonder why he was asking those questions?"

"Of course. I was dying to find out more, but I couldn't get into a private conversation with him, could I, not with twelve other people standing there. By then, it was already past the hour. I figured I'd ask him later."

"Did you?"

"There *was* no later. We had barely started to move out, when he took off. Turned and walked straight for the exit. As though he'd stopped by to ask directions."

"Doesn't make much sense, does it?"

"Like I said. He seemed to have come just to ask those questions. Fishing, if you ask me."

"Maybe he'd heard a rumor you were getting a specimen and was doing a story about arctic wolves?"

Shaney frowned. "A writer? Didn't look like a writer."

"Did you check out the story, the rumor?"

"No need. News like that spreads like wildfire. I would have heard, believe me."

"You didn't ask anyone?"

"I didn't have to. When I ran into Miss Trainor in the cafeteria later, I told her what this fellow had asked and she said, 'We should be so lucky.' . . . No, couldn't have been a writer," Shaney went on, as though anxious to tie up loose ends. "He rushed in, bought a ticket, like I said, dressed for a meeting of the board, didn't even check his coat. Stood there with us, asked his questions, next thing I knew" — with a large wave of his arm — "he was gone!"

"You saw him leave?"

"We all did."

McCalley took out a piece of paper and wrote down the hotel's name and his phone number. His own name he put down simply as L. McCalley. "I appreciate your time, Mr. Shaney. If you remember anything else about our visitor, please call me. I'll be staying here for another day or two." He gave Shaney the paper. At the door, he stopped. "And Mr. Shaney, I would be much obliged if you repeated nothing of this conversation. Don't discuss it even with Miss Trainor. I've said the same thing to her. It's a rather important investigation. Involves insurance claims, among other things. We don't want it compromised."

Shaney held up his hand. "Not to worry."

Outside, carrying his coat, McCalley paused on the steps to enjoy the sight of the park across the street. After Ottawa, this mild January weather was a welcome surprise. He checked his watch. It was after two.

Instead of hailing a cab and returning to the hotel and his notes, he surprised himself by giving in to the sunny day, the lure and pace of the great city, and decided to treat himself to a leisurely lunch. He had reached Columbus Circle when he remembered a colleague telling him he should stop in at the Plaza.

His last trip to New York had been twelve years earlier; the first, three years prior to that. There had never been time for the Plaza or for a show or for anything personal. This time, in spite of the tight schedule, he would not pass up at least this one opportunity to pamper himself just a little. On impulse, he decided to have lunch in the Oak Room. He'd heard so much about it; now, he'd be able to report back that he had actually eaten there.

Having made that decision, he felt not just relaxed but adventurous.

The entrance on the Fifth Avenue side seemed unpretentious, small for such an elegant hotel, but the high-ceilinged courtyard-lounge eating area just beyond the entrance, with its palm trees and light tropical atmosphere, drew his attention and admiration. He walked the corridors around it, gazed into the shops, then found the Oak Room and went inside.

By the time he had ordered lunch and a beer, whatever guilt feelings had threatened to spoil his afternoon had dissipated. A sense of well-being came over him as he ate. For a while Bantry and Jenene, the arctic wolf and the museums, were forgotten. He focused his attention, instead, on his surroundings. He made an effort to etch in his mind the décor, the feel of the place, details that Susan would enjoy hearing about.

He relaxed with a second coffee. While waiting for the check, he called Markarian to confirm arrangements for the evening. A clerk told him the detective was at a meeting. McCalley left his message. They would meet at six in the bar-lounge of his hotel.

He crossed to Fifth Avenue, stopping first to admire the Tiffany displays, then continued leisurely down

206

the street, pausing occasionally to look at the bright Christmas decorations in other shop windows. As he was waiting to cross Fifty-Seventh Street, he surprised himself again by turning and retracing his steps.

For a while he stood outside Tiffany's, staring into the elegant items in the small outside window. Inside the store, he walked slowly around the cases, where necklaces, pins, earrings, rings, were beautifully laid out — all gleaming under the bright lights — and stopped to admire the vases, bowls, sparkling china and crystal that rested on shelves and tables.

The last thing Susan expected — the last thing he had intended — was a "souvenir" from Tiffany's. But now, suddenly, he felt bold and generous. Why not? It didn't have to be very expensive. He smiled, trying to picture Susan's expression, her large smile and wide eyes when he gave her the box. It was worth it, definitely! The fact that it would be a real surprise spurred him on. It was a small gesture they would both remember for a long time.

He walked slowly up and down the aisles, savoring the rich variety, finally stopping at what seemed to be a more modest display. After looking at several pieces, he chose a pin, a dragonfly with blue and pink sapphires and one small diamond. The body was in white gold instead of the platinum of a bigger and much more expensive version he had seen in one of the other cases. That one had at least twenty diamonds and many more sapphires. But the pin he chose suited him and would, he knew, suit Susan, who didn't have much jewelry to begin with and especially disliked the big showy pieces some of the women she knew liked to sport. Not that he could afford them. . . . This was the kind of piece she would appreciate and enjoy wearing. It was no more than an inch and a half at its widest point, the wing span. Well worth the price, McCalley decided, even though it was more than he had intended to spend for a "souvenir." Especially if it also allowed Susan to brag a little about her husband remembering to bring her back something . . . from Tiffany's. She would treasure the box as well, with the Tiffany name stamped on the satin lining.

He had the pin gift-wrapped, folded the miniature blue shopping bag and put it, together with the box, in his briefcase.

There goes the television for the study, he thought with a smile. He didn't regret the purchase.

At Forty-Second Street, he turned back uptown, walking this time on the other side, stopping to admire the holiday decorations and displays. It was four forty-five when he reached the hotel. He took a quick shower, was finished dressing by five ten, when the phone rang. Markarian was early again. But when he picked up the receiver it was Miss Trainor at the other end.

"I don't mean to bother you, Inspector, but you did say I should call if —"

"No, no bother!"

She went on to give him the information he had requested. Did he still want the recent brochures from the Canadian museum? The Inspector had decided he didn't really need them.

"And, Inspector, I remembered something that might be useful. A long distance call came in the day before Christmas, late in the morning. We were on a half-day schedule because of the holiday. My assistant was going over messages with me, I wanted to clear my desk before leaving for the holiday. One of the messages was an inquiry about an arctic wolf. My assistant took the call. I was at a meeting. It all came back to me a little while ago, after our conversation."

"Do you know who called?"

"It was a man, I believe."

"Where was he calling from?"

"I'm not sure."

"What exactly did he ask?"

208

"He asked if the museum was expecting an arctic wolf."

"Was that the phrase he used, 'expecting an arctic wolf'?"

"That's what Sally, my assistant, wrote down."

"Go on."

"That's it. It was just that one question."

"What did your assistant say to him?"

"That we had one and, as far as she knew, weren't expecting a new specimen."

"And you don't know where the call came from?"

"No. It was just another question. We get them all the time. From all over. There had been several messages. I'd totally forgotten about this one. It came back to me after you'd left. I tried to get you earlier. . . ."

"Yes, I'm sorry. I had . . ∴ other business . . . ."

"Well, I'm glad I reached you."

"I'm very grateful. Thanks again for calling."

"One more thing, Inspector, for what it's worth. Sally said the person spoke . . . well, his words were a bit slurred. In fact, she had trouble understanding him."

"How did she come to mention this?"

"She was standing by my desk, leaning down to review the messages as she handed them to me. I didn't take any special notice at the time. But she did remark she thought it was a strange question for pardon me, for a bum to be asking."

"Why a bum?"

"As I said, she mentioned that his words were slurred, he sounded — Sally said — as though he'd been drinking."

"Well, thanks again. If you think of anything else, don't hesitate to let me know. I'll still be at this number for another day or two."

It couldn't have been Jenene. Dobie, more likely. Yes, that would make sense, from the description Miss

Trainor had just given him. But why? What had the trapper found out that made him call the museum in New York? Had Bantry talked to him? Raised suspicions? Why hadn't Dobie called the museum in New York right away, then, if he had met with Bantry late in November? Had he waited, brooded about it, and confronted Jenene for more information? Had Jenene warned his contact about Dobie's snooping around?

He realized he was falling into the very trap he warned others about. All they knew was that Bantry had gone to the West coast on business. But Dobie's calling the museum in New York (if it was indeed Dobie) meant the trapper had heard or learned something that made him curious, made him ask for . . . what? More money? Was that why he was killed? Had someone (Bantry? but how was that possible?) planted suspicions in him?

McCalley stroked the back of his neck nervously as he realized he was straying again from the facts, indulging in the kind of speculation he constantly warned others against. But, if Markarian and Kenney were right and it *was* a smuggling operation, Jenene would have known about it; Dobie, on the other hand, would have been given another story, one that he might have begun to doubt. His call to the museum in New York — from the description given, it *must* have been Dobie — could mean that whatever he had hoped to get from his contact was not forthcoming and he was ready with some other strategy. Threats, perhaps? The call to the museum must have told him what he needed to know: that Jenene and others were using the wolf for some purpose of their own.

McCalley knew he was on dangerous ground. Stick with the facts, he reminded himself. Start again with the facts.

Someone had called the museum, probably from Ottawa, although one couldn't be sure about that. If it was from Ottawa, could it have been Dobie? Or was it Jenene?

210

But what reason would Jenene have had to call? What was there to confirm? He would have known the wolf was not meant for any museum!

Or could it have been someone else, who made that call?

Shaking his head in frustration, he drew an exasperated sigh and wrote down what Miss Trainer had relayed on the phone, writing in, as usual, the time and day the information had reached him.

He read over what he had written, then glanced at his earlier notes.

Museums, as a rule, did not buy or sell or lend out specimens. And yet, according to Jenene's documents, the Ottawa museum had sent two new specimens on extended loan to a museum in New Jersey, one in May, one in August; and, the same documents showed, it was sending an arctic wolf to a museum in New York, right after Christmas.

Jenene must have processed the animal. If so, and Markarian and Kenney were right, he also may have known what was going inside the animal, or may have guessed it was something not to be declared, . . . probably had placed it there himself, not without supervision, with someone else watching. The smuggling theory was certainly a plausible one. A rare specimen going out of the country, with all the proper export forms, would have no difficulty being transported across the border. Was that the answer?

Facts!!

Bantry (it *had* to be Bantry!) had gone to the museum in New York the Friday before Thanksgiving, asking about arctic wolves, about a specimen that reportedly was due to arrive from Ottawa. (They would have to go back to Bronxville tomorrow, borrow some recent photos for identification.) On the day after Thanksgiving, he had flown to the West coast. Where had he gone? With whom did he meet? If only they could establish a connection!

The day he returned to New York, he'd received a call, went into Manhattan and was accidentally shot in Soho as he left the dealer whose shop was listed on Jenene's forms as the receiver of all three specimens. Was Bantry the first victim of a quarrel among thieves?

Connect all the little dots and you get. . .what?

Too much to absorb all at once. Besides, he was doing it again! Exactly what he kept warning Sergeant Kenney and others *not* to do: let his imagination take over. He groaned inwardly.

The phone rang. It was Kenney, reporting startling news.

After replacing the receiver, McCalley remained sitting on the side of the bed, deep in thought. The phone ringing again jarred him out of his reverie.

This time it was Markarian calling from the lobby.

Over drinks in the hotel lounge, McCalley told Markarian about his interview with Miss Trainor and the tour guide.

"I guess the Curator being sick turned out to be a plus," Markarian offered tentatively. McCalley admitted his impatience at the time. He also admitted that in the end, the interview had revealed much more than could have been anticipated.

"Bantry's role in all this is getting murkier and murkier," was Markarian's comment.

"I'm not sure 'murkier' is the right word," said McCalley. "Look at what we have. Bantry's name is on Jenene's documents. But, it's just possible that, like Miss Enderby's signature, it was put there by someone else."

"You don't think he's involved?"

"I can't be sure at this point; but if we assume he's a major player, we're faced with a contradiction."

"What's that?"

"If Bantry was involved in some sort of conspiracy

212

with Jenene and others, why would he have gone to the museum to ask those questions about arctic wolves?"

"Then you *don't* think he's involved."

"It's not that simple. He might have heard a different story from the one he'd signed for, and decided to check things out."

Markarian drew back his head and looked at his colleague from under narrowed eyes. "Who's speculating now!"

"I'm not speculating, Ed. I'm trying to figure out all the possibilities, since we have so little to go on."

"All right," said the other, resuming his normal expression. "But if he *was* checking on the story he'd signed for, why would he go to Ottawa, when the major contacts were in New York? Why not go to Soho? To Tasselbaum?"

"Who says he didn't?"

Markarian pointed a long finger at him, nodded, and said: "Good. I like that."

"What's crucial at this point is to find out exactly where Bantry went on that last trip, the people he talked with."

Before McCalley could go on, tell him the news Kenney had called in, Markarian reached inside his jacket and took out a folded slip of paper. "Well, you'll be happy to know I did my homework." He handed the paper to McCalley who read it quickly then looked up and shook his head in disbelief.

"A Delta flight to Los Angeles and then a connecting flight to Ottawa?"

"Weird, right?"

"So we know now for certain that he went to Ottawa. That's a start."

"But, why would he want to cover his tracks?"

"Remember, it could have been just another business trip."

The other waved the comment aside. "You don't really believe that!"

McCalley took a deep breath. "I believe what you just told me, that he went to Ottawa."

"Via Los Angeles."

"Via Los Angeles."

"Don't you think that's suspicious?"

"Devious, maybe. But there could be a very simple explanation."

"OK, so it's a gut feeling, but like faith, I *know*, Luke, I *know* there's a connection. We just have to find it. Everything happened after Bantry's visit to Ottawa. Why else would the old man who sounded drunk — by the way, it *had* to be Dobie, the trapper; Jenene didn't need that information, he already had it — so, why would Dobie be calling the museum here in New York all the way from Ottawa?"

"Wait, slow down," said McCalley with a warning gesture. "It *could* have been Jenene calling. He might not have known all that much and decided to find out more."

"Blackmail?"

"You mentioned that once before."

"No, I said *greed*, then."

"Same thing. You're talking money. And I'll admit, that *is* a possibility. Still, you're assuming a lot, Ed, and on very flimsy evidence. We could be sidetracked and waste precious time if we're not careful. I'll grant you this: we may be closer to eliminating Bantry as an accomplice; I don't see him on the same side as Jenene. Or, maybe it was meeting Mrs. Bantry. I can't picture a woman like that married to someone involved in shady deals, although, God knows, I've seen more than enough instances of intelligent women being conned, blind to reality, no matter how much evidence to the contrary. But there's something else. If this was an illegal operation, why would Bantry, who's worth millions, want any part of it? What would prompt a man like

214

Bantry, who could afford cashmere coats and Gucci boots, to indulge in what may have been illegal activity, to risk everything if caught?"

"Could he have been heavy into gambling? Have overextended himself in some other ways? Lost on the stock market, maybe?"

"I doubt that was the case. And if money was being taken out from the business surreptitiously, to pay off debts, Quinn or Wentworth would have gotten wind of it."

Markarian leaned forward. "Another thing. Did you consider the possibility that he might have been working alone, one way or the other?"

"How do you mean?"

"Either as the person behind whatever the plan, or the one ready to reveal it to the proper authorities."

"The second is a real possibility. But then we have a problem. How and why did his name get on those forms, if he wasn't involved? Here's a man who's highly-respected in his field, a successful and wealthy export-import agent, also a connoisseur of antiques, with expensive and elegant tastes which he can well afford to indulge without resorting to any payoffs — how would the name of such a man find its way on to suspicious shipping documents found in Jenene's possession? We're missing something here, Ed. I don't know what."

McCalley called for the check. While they waited, he went on. "Well. I do have a bit of news that clears up one point at least." The check came and he signed for it. "Kenney called just before you came around. Said they had taken up floorboards in Dobie's cabin and had struck gold. Literally. Gold pieces. And bills. Over fifty-two thousand dollars in all. Trappers make good money, but that much? Remember, he had just bought the Cherokee and the rifle, and some expensive new clothing. He'd spent close to thirty-seven thousand dollars just before Christmas. But he still had almost fifty-three thousand tucked away in gold pieces and bills."

Markarian took it all in, then leaned back and grinned. "I'll give you back your line, for a change. It doesn't prove anything, except that he saved his money and was clever enough to buy gold pieces and tuck them away safely."

McCalley held up his hand. "Ah, but there's more. There was another plastic bag with notes, almost illegible but decipherable, giving dates of deliveries to Jenene, including the ones we already know about; dates when Dobie received payments from "The Man," together with the amounts. Three entries for the last eight months, a total of almost twenty-eight thousand right there. And others, going back at least three years."

"That *is* news," exclaimed the other. "A real break for you!"

"But I'm not sure what it means for *you*, Ed! Among the other things they found was a business card. It had Bantry's name and address on it."

Chapter 12
Featuring Quinn & Associates
(January 3, 9:10 AM)

Their first stop, just after nine in the morning, was Bantry's office and showroom. The sign high above the entrance to the three-story building between Lexington and Third read "Bantry International, Ltd." Henry Wentworth, the Manager, was waiting for them. He led them past the display area on the street floor and up a flight of stairs to the second floor, where the firm's offices were located. A small conference room had been set aside for the interview. At one end of the long table, ledgers, files and records had been piled in neat stacks. When they were all seated, Wentworth picked up a thick folder of printouts and held it out for McCalley.

"I prepared this file for you. Mrs. Bantry called yesterday afternoon and said we were to cooperate in every way. She gave me some idea of what you might want. I've pulled out lists of clients, transactions going back a year, and dealing with museums for the last three years. These are just summaries. The particulars, should you want them, are in the folders on the table. If there's anything else you need, I'll be happy to provide it. My staff and I will answer any questions you may have."

"Thank you, I appreciate that," said McCalley, He glanced quickly through the folder Wentworth had given him, pulled out a single sheet that had museum transactions with dates. Four were with the Ottawa museum (a request for samples from the "Wet Room," with follow-ups), a dozen or so were queries to museums in the States, several to museums abroad. There were no deliveries of specimens to museums in New Jersey or New York.

McCalley closed the folder, put it aside, and asked: "Do you know anything about a recent transaction with a

217

Canadian museum? An arctic wolf?"

Wentworth shook his head. "Can't recall anything like that, no."

"Are there other records elsewhere?"

"For the years you requested? No."

"Mr. Bantry worked at home?"

"Sometimes."

"Could there be more information on his computer at home?"

"I can't say. He took one or two folders with him from time to time, but they were usually back here the next day. I always thought it strange that he was so scrupulous about logging material out and back in, since he was the only one who took folders home."

"No one else ever took work home? Not even you?"

"I simply carry out instructions. My work begins and ends in this office. Mr. Bantry, on the other hand, occasionally would make calls to clients from his home or would want to check something out after hours. It didn't happen often, as I said."

"Is it possible that Mr. Bantry had dealings with a Canadian museum without telling you?"

"I doubt it. Why would he do that?" Wentworth asked, genuinely puzzled.

"A private deal, maybe?"

"I don't know what you mean by 'a private deal.' Are you asking if he wanted to purchase an arctic wolf for his residence?"

Recalling the room he had sat in just twenty-four hours earlier, McCalley resisted a smile as he tried to picture a processed wolf under the Fra Angelico he had admired, or next to the huge marble fireplace.

Out loud he said: "Just eliminating possibilities." He jotted down something in his little book and went on. "Hartley Quinn had access to all these files?"

Wentworth nodded. "Naturally. Everything in the residence, also. I'm sure you know that he is Mr. Bantry's Executor, Inspector. In that capacity he has had access to everything here and at the house. To the warehouse, as well. I've gone there with him several times, in fact."

"Do you think Mrs. Bantry may take over the business?"

"I've heard nothing about that."

"Do you think she's capable of handling it?"

"I haven't known her long, but she seems capable enough," the other replied carefully. "I believe she's an historian, writes books," he went on after a pause. "She may want to pursue that and sell the business. Or she might downsize the operation for the time being."

"How would you feel about her selling Bantry International?"

"Disappointed, of course. But from her point of view, it might be easier all around. Lots of people out there are ready to buy her out. . . . Ah, thank you, Jeanie." This last was addressed to a young girl who had entered with a tray of steaming coffee, hot water, tea bags and a dish of cookies. "Thought you might like something."

As he sipped the coffee that had been poured for him, McCalley leafed casually through one of the folders. The others watched. After a while, he closed it, poured himself a second cup, and asked:

"What can you tell me about Mr. Bantry's recent trip to the West coast?"

"He said he had to see a client."

"Where exactly did he go?"

"Los Angeles."

"Anywhere else?"

"Not that I know of."

"Did he mention the name of the client?"

"Not to me."

"Did he leave a place, a number where he could be

reached?"

"No, but he never did that. He would call, if there was anything to be done or to be communicated."

"Did he?"

"Call from Los Angeles? No."

"How did you learn about his death?"

"Mr. Quinn came in to tell us. On his way to Bronxville, later that same morning." He shook his head. "I still can't believe he's gone. Snuffed out by a quirk of fate!"

"Where is your warehouse located?"

Wentworth gave him an address in Queens, which McCalley jotted down.

"Do you go there often?"

"Once a month, as a rule. And when a shipment arrives, I go there to check it out."

"When were you there last?"

"Twice in the last month, since Mr, Bantry's death. With Mr. Quinn. I helped him with the inventory."

"Nothing out of the ordinary?"

"I don't know what you mean by 'out of the ordinary.' Most of the items have been there for a while. They're all listed. In there," he nodded toward the piles of folders, "including new arrivals."

"One more question for now. Do you know of any communication between Mr. Bantry and a Mr. Paul Tasselbaum?" He watched as Wentworth probed for an answer. "He owns an antiques shop in Soho." There was some hesitation, then:

"Nooooo. . . . For a moment I thought I recognized the name, . . . Mr. Bantry had many colleagues in the business. . . ." McCalley waited as Wentworth sorted out his thoughts. "No," repeated the other, after a minute or two. "I'm afraid I can't help you there."

"Did Mr. Bantry keep a log of his appointments? He might have noted something in there."

"Let me check."

When Wentworth was out of earshot, Markarian said: "If Bantry was doing business with Jenene and his cohorts, he may have handled other interesting items. Do you want me to pull out some of our police circulars listing stolen goods?"

"Good idea. Thanks."

"You might ask Wentworth if he looks at those circulars." Just then the Manager came back into the room.

"Grace, Mr. Bantry's secretary, doesn't remember Mr. Bantry mentioning that name, and there's nothing about a meeting with the gentleman logged in Mr. Bantry's calendar." He held out the leather-bound ledger he had brought back with him. "Would you like to look?"

Bantry's initials in gold were on the cover. Each page was for a single day of the week. It occurred to McCalley that a book like that must have cost quite a bit — an unnecessary expense, given the fact that it was good for only one year. He quickly scanned the pages from August to December: nothing there about meeting or talking with Tasselbaum. He placed a blank sheet of paper where August began and handed back the ledger.

"Could you make copies of the pages from August through December?" Wentworth nodded. "By the way, do you check inventory against police circulars of stolen goods?"

Wentworth was visibly startled. "Stolen goods?"

"Just routine," McCalley said evenly.

"We get notices of that kind, and I do look them over; but I don't have to check the inventory, Inspector, I can tell you right now, this firm has never handled stolen goods!" The man had turned beet red, his voice had risen a notch. "I resent the suggestion."

"I didn't mean to offend," McCalley replied. "But I do have to ask these questions. I apologize if I phrased it badly."

"It's outrageous!"

"I'm truly sorry," he replied, placing the folder in his briefcase and getting his other things together. He followed Wentworth downstairs, Markarian trailing behind. At the entrance, he handed the Manager his card. "Please call if you think of anything else. You've been a big help.'"

Outside, Markarian blew a low whistle of relief. "He took it as a personal insult."

"I realize that, but it couldn't be helped."

"If you want my opinion. Luke, we're not going to find anything here. Wentworth is clean."

"I would like to think so, too."

It was a short distance to Quinn's place. They decided to walk there and come back later for the car.

The law offices of Quinn & Associates were in a high-rise on Third Avenue, the huge lobby all smoky glass with three banks of elevators. They checked in with the guard at the entrance, who then waved them to the last row of elevators. "Thirty-eighth floor," he informed them.

Hartley Quinn was waiting for them just inside the glass double doors leading from the elevators into the suite of offices. McCalley wondered if the name of the firm appeared only in the lobby directory and the phone book. Obviously, you were supposed to know where you were, when you got off on the thirty-eighth floor.

Dressed in a navy blue suit of light wool, the solid color softened by an almost imperceptible lighter blue stripe, a champagne-colored shirt and a patterned tie in brilliant sapphire with touches of gold and red, the lawyer was elegance personified. For some reason, McCalley thought of what Jill Masterson had said about Quinn having the same expensive taste in clothes as Bantry, and what Ed Shaney at the museum had said about the executive type with the cashmere coat who had asked about arctic wolves.

A young blonde sat at the semi-circular teak reception desk just inside the glass doors. Behind her, two small facing sofas with a square glass top table between them dominated the area in front of the floor-to-ceiling windows, which looked out on midtown and lower Manhattan, right down to where the twin towers used to be. It was a spectacular sight.

Quinn introduced the young woman (a nice touch, thought McCalley), then waited as the two men strolled to the windows to admire the view.

"Makes me dizzy, being this far up," Markarian told McCalley.

"Reminds me of the frenetic pace of the big city. But you have to admit it's impressive."

When they joined Quinn again, McCalley said to the receptionist:

"You should have your desk turned around, so you can enjoy the view." The woman smiled; Quinn laughed.

"Her chair has wheels," he said. "She can turn around and enjoy the view any time." He shrugged. "You get used to it, right Joan?" He didn't wait for an answer, but started down the long corridor, leading the way.

Something about the remark and the way Quinn tossed it out, made McCalley frown, as he and Markarian followed the lawyer down the thick-carpeted corridor. They passed a Picasso. A Matisse. A Klee (originals? McCalley wondered). On one side of the glass door at the very end was an unusual round copper Peruvian mask, a green sun disk about eighteen inches in diameter. On the other side, small gold letters spelled out "Hartley Quinn." Everything spoke understated elegance, taste, status, and money.

They entered a small suite, where a woman in her early forties sat at a computer. Her outfit went well with the surroundings: a simple, beautifully-tailored dark gray suit with a cream-colored silk blouse; her only jewelry, besides a simple gold wedding ring, a gold wristwatch and small diamond studs in her ears.

Two fax machines, a copier, and two telephones

rested on the extended work area. One of the phones was ringing as they entered. Quinn waited for the woman to get off the phone before introducing her as his private secretary, Rita Lo Bianco.

Quinn led them into the main office.

"This is my inner sanctum," he said, waving them to a sitting area. "Make yourselves comfortable." It was a corner room. Against one of the internal walls, directly across from Quinn's desk, was a teak table surrounded by eight armchairs upholstered in the same fabric as the sofa and chairs in the sitting area. The small rug under the table was identical to the one where the three men now took their seats. The mirrored wall where the conference alcove had been set up, reflected the large windows on the opposite side of the room and the imposing view outside.

"Can I offer you something? Coffee? Tea? Water?" When the others declined, he reached for some papers on the table between them. "I've pulled out what you asked for, Inspector. Made some notes of my own for you, also prepared a brief summary of Ellis's estate, with other information and figures you might find interesting but, I suspect, of no relevance in connection with your investigation. By the way, I apologize for yesterday. I was worried about Jenny, Mrs. Bantry. She seems all right, carries on and all that, but it's a bleak time for her. I don't like to see her pressured in any way."

McCalley waved the apology aside. "We saw Mr. Wentworth before coming here. He was very cooperative."

"Good. Did he have the information you wanted?" McCalley had been glancing through the papers Quinn had handed him.

"Yes," he said, without looking up. "He was quite thorough." After a few seconds, he held up the sheaf of papers. "Thanks. I'll read them carefully, later." He put them down and took out his small notebook. Quinn went to his desk for an empty folder. When he sat down again, he placed the papers inside it and said:

"I'm not sure how I can help you, Inspector, but feel free to ask whatever questions you have for me."

McCalley had grown more and more uneasy about Markarian not being able to take part in these interviews. Bantry's name kept cropping up; but they both understood it was a delicate situation that required caution. Markarian could get into trouble asking questions about Bantry without official approval. On his part, it was becoming increasingly difficult for McCalley to draw a clear line between the Bantry killing and Jenene's murder: the arctic wolf seemed to be nudging them closer and closer.

Once again, he introduced Markarian, vaguely, as his "New York contact," then went on:

"As I explained yesterday, I'm down from Ottawa to tie up some loose ends in connection with a murder that took place back there, a few days ago." Quinn leaned slightly forward, his attention focused. "We're investigating the death of the taxidermist of the Canadian Museum of Nature, in Ottawa, as I told you and Mrs. Bantry yesterday. A man by the name of John Jenene. He was found the day after Christmas, late that afternoon, in his workroom. What I didn't tell you before, Mr. Quinn, I didn't want to upset Mrs. Bantry, was that we also found documents that suggest Mr. Bantry may have been involved in transactions between the Ottawa museum and at least two other museums in this area. I wonder if you know anything about that?"

"Why ask me? Surely Wentworth would have that information?"

"Well, yes, we did ask him. But we're also asking you. As Mr. Bantry's Executor, I believe you've handled a great many of his papers lately."

"I fail to see a connection, Inspector. In any case, my job as Executor will soon be coming to an end."

"You are also the sole Trustee, as well?"

225

"Yes."

"By the way, how did you become his Executor and Trustee?"

"He asked me," replied the other, opening his eyes wide and spreading his hands in a gesture that suggested it should be pretty obvious. "He asked me to be his Best Man, too," the lawyer added, with a little smile.

"I ask, Mr. Quinn, because from what I've learned, you knew him only a short time. . . ."

"I guess it was long enough for him to trust me," answered the other, sitting back and crossing his legs. Then, almost as an afterthought: "He had no immediate family. . . . Tell me, Inspector, what can I possibly add to what Mr. Wentworth has already told you?" When McCalley didn't answer right away, he went on: "As a matter of fact, I *do* have something for you. Yesterday you asked about assets? Well, you'll find quite a bit in those papers I've given you. Jenny, Mrs. Bantry, doesn't really know the full extent of the holdings now in her name. I have to go over everything with her soon, help her make decisions. The whole estate is worth around two hundred million. That's a conservative estimate. The house alone, renovated as it has been, is worth at least seven million on today's market. The furnishings and all the other precious things in it would bring between eighty or ninety million. More at auction. One painting alone has been appraised at over three million. Then there's Bantry International — the inventory is easily worth another ninety million. I've broken down the figures in there for you." He pointed to the folder.

"And Mrs. Bantry inherits everything?"

"There are a few small legacies, to Wentworth and his staff, Mrs. Harris, the housekeeper, a few others." When McCalley did not comment, he went on. "There's a lot of money involved here. I've already started to work on a revocable trust in her name. She has to protect what's come down to her. A few major decisions will have to be made quite soon — especially with regard to the business holdings: whether to keep or sell the company, run it herself or keep Wentworth on to manage it alone. She'll have to begin thinking also about where all that money will be going, eventually. It has to be protected. . . ."

McCalley greeted this information with a wide smile. "You're very efficient, Mr. Quinn."

"I'm a lawyer, Inspector. Besides, Mrs. Bantry is my client. And although I don't want her to make hasty decisions, I don't want her to drag things out either, if she can possibly avoid it."

"What about you, Mr. Quinn? Did Mr. Bantry leave you some sort of legacy? After all, you were his Best Man —?" Quinn chose to ignore the barb.

"No. No legacy."

"Nothing at all?"

"Some small gifts. A pair of cuff links I'd admired. His golf clubs. His Rolex watch, although I already have one. A few personal things like that. . . ."

McCalley wondered what it must be like to own two Rolex watches. Out loud, he said: "I understand Mr. Bantry had you supervise the renovations on the house while they were away."

"It was a favor. I was happy to do it."

"It must have been time consuming? How often were you there?"

"My time is flexible, Inspector. Except for court appearances, I set up my own priorities, my own daily agenda. I was able to fit in many visits to the house. I got to know the workmen, they got to know me. They realized I was there for Ellis and spoke for him. It worked out pretty well."

"So for three years you were acting as Mr. Bantry's deputy?"

"Until last August, when they got back. By then, most of the work was done. They took on the last minute changes and adjustments."

"Were they pleased?"

"I believe so."

"What can you tell me about his last trip, when he went to the West coast right after Thanksgiving."

"You asked me yesterday, Inspector. The answer is still the same."

"You have no idea at all why he went?" McCalley persisted. Quinn spread out his hands in a helpless gesture. "Never saw him alive again?"

"That's right."

"When was the last time you saw him?"

Quinn did not hesitate. "Thanksgiving. The four of us had dinner in the new house. But I'm sure you already know that."

"Your wife was with you?"

"Inspector, I'm sure you also have found out by now that I'm not married. The fourth was Jill Masterson."

"What did you talk about?"

"The usual. Gossip about colleagues — that was Jill mostly — about the book Jenny was writing, *is* writing; about some contracts Ellis wanted me to check out for him. After dinner the two of us went into his study I read the papers he had put aside for me, made some suggestions."

"And he never mentioned going to the West coast the next day?"

"No."

"Why do you suppose?"

Quinn drew an exasperated breath. "Why in heaven's name should he tell me that? I certainly never provided him with my court schedule!"

"Friendly conversation over dinner?"

"Well, the answer is no. He didn't mention the trip, whatever the reason."

"Can you tell me anything about the phone call he received the Thursday morning he was killed?"

"No, sorry. As I told you, I didn't see him again —"

"Didn't he call when he got back?"

"No."

"Where did you spend Christmas, Mr. Quinn?"

The lawyer seemed genuinely taken aback. "What sort of question is that?" he asked by way of reply.

McCalley waved vaguely. "Just trying to clear up loose ends." He waited expectantly.

"Why the hell should I answer that?" He got up, went to the bar, and poured himself some bottled water. When he returned, he had regained his composure. "You're asking me some strange questions, Inspector. . . . This is beginning to sound like an interrogation." He seemed to think the answer would serve. McCalley repeated the question and added:

"I do have to know, Mr. Quinn."

I went skiing in Maine. I have a cabin there."

"Alone?"

"Yes, Inspector, alone. I'm lucky. I don't have to sit through a family dinner on holidays."

"You have no family?"

"A brother in Boston. An aunt in Florida. I rarely see them."

Quinn gave him a long look. "Pity."

"I wouldn't say that. We'd bore one another to death after ten minutes. . . ."

McCalley put his notebook away and stood up. "I appreciate your time, Mr. Quinn. I may have some more questions later." He retrieved his belongings and the folder.

Quinn led the way through the secretary's office. The woman was not at her desk. A note on the computer keyboard told them she'd be back in an hour. He did not escort them to the elevator but stood watching as they walked down the corridor and through the glass doors. He stood there a few more seconds then went back to his desk, where he picked up a brief and started to read through it.

CHAPTER 13
ANTICS AND ANTIQUES
(January 3, 12:30 PM)

The small Chinese restaurant Markarian chose for their lunch was within walking distance of Tasselbaum's shop. Markarian ordered for both, but to McCalley's dismay the list of dishes seemed to have no end. He interrupted, shaking his head —

"Wait. Hold it. . . . Most of it is for you, I hope; I can't eat even a fraction of that. Besides, I'm supposed to be watching my weight. Susan warned me that —"

"Trust me," said the other. "It's just a sampling of a lot of different things."

"A small Chinese feast," was the way McCalley later described it to his wife. Never had he tasted, at one time, such a variety of soups, hot and cold dumplings, rice and noodles prepared in so many different ways.

Over tea, they reviewed their morning visits.

They agreed that Wentworth had no surprises for them. He seemed efficient, loyal, prided himself in his competence and his knowledge of the business. Bantry's confidence and trust in him appeared well-founded.

For reasons of his own, or at the urging of Mrs. Bantry, Quinn had decided to be more cooperative.

Many more questions had surfaced during both those interviews, they concluded, but they still had very few answers.

"Bantry becomes more and more a puzzle as we go on," Markarian commented.

McCalley put down his teacup and relaxed in his chair. "It may seem that way. But the more we learn about him, the closer we are to a solution. . . . We now know that he flew to Ottawa by way of Los Angeles, but we don't have a clear reason for his doing that. But with that information we can track him down, find the places he stayed, the people he saw or who remember him. Why he went there will become clear soon enough. We shouldn't speculate any further, not until we've gathered more information."

"Okay, so those are the facts. But let me pass this by you. I know you don't like to indulge in theories, but even the facts we have so far, and they may be meager, cry for some kind of explanation." He cocked his head to one side, the exaggerated thin smile across his face giving him the appearance of a friendly clown. "Pleeeaaase?"

McCalley couldn't help laughing, waved him on. "Might as well. You'll force it on me, sooner or later, whatever it is, this brainstorm of yours. The whole case seems to be inching along on intuition, theories, and lucky breaks!"

"Hey, don't trash them! Scientists use theories all the. That's all they have. They hit on an idea and test it in the lab or through the telescope. It's not too early for us to start testing some of our ideas."

McCalley poured himself more tea. "I'm listening."

"Okay. For starters, Bantry's questions to the museum guide, his going to the West coast soon after that, erasing or trying to erase his tracks —"

"We don't know for certain that was his intention," McCalley interrupted.

"Sure, he could have had clients in both places, but the fact of the matter is, as you well know, he had about forty minutes between flights, hardly enough time for a cup of coffee." He let that sink in before continuing. "My point is, suppose he had somehow learned about the shipment of the arctic wolf? I know, I know," this in answer to his colleague's impatient gesture, "it's a bit far-fetched, but humor me —?"

"Far-fetched? You're free floating in space, with that one!"

"Then why all those questions at the museum? I'm

convinced something made him suspicious. He asked questions at the museum here, then flew to Ottawa to find out what he could. Why go to Ottawa, unless he knew something about the shipments and the museum? I'll swear he went there to talk with Jenene or Dobie. Probably both."

"If he knew that much, why didn't he try to see the Curator, as well? We know he didn't, because I'm sure she would have told me if Bantry had approached her. Would certainly have recognized the name, when it came up. "

"Hey, I don't have all the answers, but, like you said, they'll come to light sooner or later. Just hear me out, for now."

"Ed, his going to Jenene and or Dobie suggests he saw some of those documents we found, or learned about them in some way. We have no grounds for making such an assumption."

"Let's just say, he knew something of what was on them. . . . Let me finish, okay?. . . . Let's say he'd gotten hold of those names, saw and talked with both Jenene and Dobie." He took no notice as McCalley shook his head. "Dobie had Bantry's card tucked safely away, remember? So they must have crossed paths —"

"Not necessarily. He might have found the card. Picked it up somewhere. Bantry may have left it behind someplace and Dobie got curious. I can think of any number of reasons why he had it in his possession."

"Hidden with his valuables, isn't that where they found it? Under the floorboards of the cabin? With all his money? No, Luke, I'm sure the card was given to him by Bantry, and Dobie took great care to hide it safely."

"Your theory is swiss cheese, Ed. Full of holes."

"The card, where it was found," the other went on, not in the least disconcerted, "suggests — to me, at least — that Bantry met with Dobie, that Bantry may have paid him for more information, may have posed as someone who could address his demand for more money. It tells me that he asked his own questions, and these, in turn, made Dobie suspicious. Bantry learned enough about the wolf to confirm what *he* suspected. And if at any time he happened to mention the museum in New York, it would explain why Dobie got up enough nerve to call New York, later, to check on the wolf's destination. Until then, Dobie probably knew nothing beyond his part in delivering the animal to Jenene. Maybe he thought it was an expensive trophy someone had ordered. Bantry made him suspicious."

"So, you believe it was Dobie called the museum?"

"The woman said he sounded drunk."

"Couldn't Jenene have had a few, to get up enough courage up to make the call?"

"I don't think so. Neither do you. . . . Look, bottom line is, Bantry stumbled on to something, we don't know how. Went to the museum just before Thanksgiving asking about arctic wolves. A few days later, he's in Ottawa, to check that end of it. Whatever he found out confirmed his suspicions. Back in New York, he's shot in Soho. I think he went to confront Tasselbaum, threaten him —"

"Threaten him with what? He wasn't out to gain anything for himself. . . . No, I don't see Bantry in that role. Furious, yes, if, as you say, he had discovered they had been using his name. . . . No, if anything, he went there to tell him he was going to the police with what he knew."

"And got killed for it."

"Maybe. I can't jump that far yet. If he got killed for it, accidental death becomes something else — and I'm not ready for that. What interests me at the moment is that something triggered his fishing expeditions. And if I'm to play your game, that suggests he might have been targeted even before he left for Ottawa."

The last remark seemed to give Markarian pause.

McCalley went on. "No, Ed. Something's missing. And if he *was* targeted, it means Tasselbaum and whoever else was in on it knew what Bantry was up to and were

233

ready for him long before he got back from Ottawa."

"You're saying he was a dead man even before he left for the West coast. The gang-war scenario was already in place and played out the minute he left Tasselbaum's shop." McCalley made no comment. "Something else occurs to me," Markarian added, "although I don't believe it happened this way: all three may have been killed because the operation had run dry and those in charge didn't want any loose ends that might cause trouble later."

When McCalley spoke again, it was to pick up where he had left off. "It's been nagging at me, the sequence of events. It suggests careful planning, as far back as the first week in November. Bantry's death may have been the beginning of an effort to close shop, if we accept your idea, or, more likely, in my view — and only in the context of what you have just put forward, of course — an effort to keep things from escalating, from having the police learn of illegal activities — always according to your theory, mind you — and therefore making it necessary to get rid of the three people who had become expendable —"

"Why is it nagging at you? At one end, Bantry stirs things up with all his questions; at the other end, Jenene, or maybe he and Dobie both, wanted more money and turned to him when the others didn't deliver. The rest follows." McCalley frowned, his elbow resting on the arm of his chair, his chin cupped in his hand. Markarian went on:

"Look: Bantry knew something. His questions were rooted in information that he could only have gotten through — I know I'm really stretching it, but listen for a minute — he could only have gotten through Jenene and or Dobie. He went to Ottawa to talk to them, to confirm what he'd learned, see what they wanted, something like that. He knew exactly where to go, Luke. That means he had learned something. Knew the answers to his questions were in Ottawa."

McCalley remained silent.

234

"There had to be some contact between the two, Jenene and Bantry, all three, eventually. How else would Bantry have gotten wind of their using his name on those forms?"

McCalley drew a deep breath. "Ed, we don't know that it happened that way."

"Nothing else makes sense. He must have found out, must have known at some point that they were using his name. Everything else we've said hinges on that."

"That's what's bothering me. The assumptions your conclusions are based on. They're tempting, but we can't be misled by them."

"Admit it. My theories, assumptions, whatever you want to call them, do explain your timetable." McCalley did not answer. "I'm sure you've already worked it out for yourself. . . . Bantry had gummed up the works and so they got rid of him the minute he got back from the West coast. No one questioned his accidental death. And no one would dream of connecting it with later events in Ottawa. No one did. But those events could only take place *after* the wolf was safely out of the museum, and that could only be carried out around Christmas, when they had a block of time to do everything they had planned and all the paperwork and preparations were in place. The holidays were a great cover. Boxing Day was perfect for picking up the wolf: the museum was closed to the public all day. Once the wolf was safely out of the museum, Jenene could disappear, his death eventually listed as an accident, the result of the blizzard and the icy roads. Dobie's would be called a hunting accident, but they couldn't kill him before Jenene went missing. They had to do it just before or after, or else the trapper would get suspicious and run for cover."

McCalley was still frowning, but his eyes were riveted on his colleague. Markarian pressed on with a dramatic flourish, tracing a wide arc with both arms:

"Then 'Poof!' All gone, everything lost, because of

an unscheduled museum tour! Don't tell me you're going to deny that coincidence played a major part in uncovering three murders and a smuggling operation! What an irony!"

McCalley drew himself up, as though coming out of a reverie. "I'm sure there would have been a falling out among them, sooner or later," he said, by way of answer.

"Maybe. But, as you like to remind me, it didn't happen that way."

"It might have. It's still a possibility, in my book."

"For someone who doesn't like to indulge in theories, you're reaching pretty far!"

"Just touching up yours. . . ."

They went back to review their visit with Quinn, concluded he was a shrewd apple and in love with Jenny Bantry.

"Ah, a motive, at last!" laughed McCalley, as his companion signaled for the check.

It was still incredibly warm, a spring-like day. The two men walked leisurely toward their destination, McCalley stopping now and then to look at the exotic oriental displays. As they approached a dark green door with lit sconces resembling torches on either side, the name "Tasselbaum Antiques" in large gold letters on a small round canopy over the entrance, Markarian pointed:

"Here we are."

McCalley stopped and held out a restraining arm. The time had come to broach a subject that had been bothering him for some time: Ed's role in the investigation. Clearly, the NYPD detective could not work officially with McCalley, nor, for that matter, could he take on the Bantry case, if it were to be reopened. Officially, it remained Slattery's case. Still, McCalley felt he should ask the question — he owed Markarian that — since Bantry was emerging as a crucial player in the large scenario, although just how he fit in was still not clear.

"Isn't it time we took a closer look at the Bantry

case, Ed?"

Markarian had stopped. Now he shook his head and said:

"We both know how that works, Luke. It's not my call. Anyway, there's not enough hard evidence to re-open the case, nothing new to suggest anything but a freak accident — even if we can prove he did see those people in Canada and talk to them." Suddenly he threw up his hands in a helpless gesture and burst out laughing. "I can't believe this! You've got me talking like *you!*"

"But how do you feel about it?"

Markarian did not reply at once. "There *has* to be a connection! But until we come up with something definite, it's just a gut feeling. I don't mind telling you, since all this began I've been playing over and over again, in my head, the events of that Thursday. The guns all the same make, as thought to create confusion, diversion if you like, the kids not punished. It reads like a script —"

"— and Bantry there, at that precise moment," McCalley finished for him. "I know it's hard on you, not being able to ask questions —"

Markarian interrupted, with a vigorous shake of his head. "Not my case, remember? But you're forgetting something. . . . You've been briefing me all along. Shared information, picked my brain. You didn't have to do that. It means a lot to me. But we both know that if I took initiative now, we could both find ourselves in big trouble. And trouble is the last thing I want for you. Or for me!"

It was the answer McCalley had expected, but he was glad he had brought up the subject. It cleared the air between them. Markarian, he realized, was as frustrated as he was at not being able to take an active part in the investigation. Still, they both knew the rules.

From the outside, the shop appeared small. The window display held a Queen Anne side table, an unusual yellow Tiffany lamp, a small Victorian desk with a silver writing set on it, a small bronze bust of Dante resting on a marble column, a heavy floor lamp with a silk shade fringed in dark red crystals and, next to it, a low bookshelf that held a number of well-preserved books in red and green leather bindings with gold lettering on the spines. On the floor of the window, against a black velvet cloth, was a delicate oriental fan, artfully placed and fully open to show a Japanese scene in pastel colors. There were no prices on any of the items.

"By the way," said McCalley, as Markarian opened the door and chimes sounded somewhere in the back, "I didn't call ahead."

Inside, the shop was much larger than the width of the display window suggested. It consisted of one large room about thirty feet deep and almost as wide. A heavy velvet drape separated the front from a back area, which was even larger and turned out to be a combination office and receiving/packing space.

The shop boasted a number of period tables and chairs, several Victorian floor lamps, some deco art, three federal-style sideboards, a stone fireplace, several busts on pedestals, and three long trestle tables with fine china and glassware arranged on damask cloths, as though for formal dinner parties about to begin. Although the room was full, everything was arranged to avoid the appearance of clutter.

A young man came out from behind the drape, brushing his hair in place with one hand as he extended the other in greeting. McCalley shook hands.

"May I help you?"

"Mr. Tasselbaum?" McCalley asked.

"No. I'm his assistant, George Leffert."

McCalley identified himself as he handed the young man his card and introduced his "New York contact."

"Could you spare us a few minutes?"

Leffert studied the card. "Inspector?" He looked up. "What's it about?"

"A man was killed in Ottawa a few days ago. Apparently, he did business with a number of places in New York. Yours was one of them." The young man studied the card again. McCalley said: "Can we talk without being interrupted? Perhaps you could close the shop for a few minutes."

They watched as Leffert flipped the "Open" sign to read "Closed" and turned the lock, then followed him into the back. A number of open crates filled one side of the area, several filing cabinets were lined up against one wall, and, under a small high window, was a metal desk and chair. Across from the desk was a small sofa and three cane-back chairs.

McCalley draped his coat over one of the chairs and sat down. "As I was saying, I'm checking out Dr. Jenene's contacts in New York, that's his name, the man who was killed. It's routine business, and somewhat tedious, but it has to be done. By the way, when do you expect Mr. Tasselbaum?"

"He left just a few minutes before you came in. Had to see a client in Stamford. Won't be back today, I'm afraid. I don't believe you had an appointment . . .?"

"No."

"I can set one up for you." He watched as McCalley took out his notepad then, tapping his chin lightly, turning his eyes toward the ceiling, muttered: "Ottawa, Ottawa. . . ." He came back to focus on McCalley with a wide smile. "For a minute I thought it rang a bell." McCalley waited. Leffert shook his head. "Sorry."

"Mr. Leffert —"

The other interrupted: "Call me George."

"George, do you have a client by the name of Bantry? Ellis Bantry?"

George gave him a wide grin. "Now, *there* I can help you. Mr. Bantry came in around the beginning of November, let's see, it was the second Monday —" He took

239

out a small pocket calendar, glanced at it, and held it out for McCalley. "There it is, November eleventh." He waited as the Inspector glanced at the card and handed it back. "He and Paul, Mr. Tasselbaum, had a rather animated discussion." His expression suddenly turned grim. "You *do* know he was killed, don't you? Right outside this shop?"

McCalled nodded. "Yes. I'd like to hear about that in a moment. What did Mr. Bantry want?"

"He asked about a ring, I was told. Mr. Tasselbaum is very well known in the business, we have clients all over the world. Have you visited our website?"

"Not yet," said McCalley.

"The last issue of *Architecture* magazine? Paul helped with the renovation of a renaissance villa near Tivoli. That's in Italy, Beautiful photographs. You should get hold of the article and read it."

McCalley assured him he would. "You said Bantry was a client?"

"I'd never seen him before. And as far as I know, there's no record of any transaction."

"Could you check your files for the last year?"

"That would take days! Besides, there was no sale, Inspector!" Suddenly his face lit up. "I do have a list of current clients!" He started to get up, abruptly changed his mind and sat back again. "Excuse me, Inspector, but what exactly has Mr. Bantry or this shop have to do with the man who was killed in Ottawa?"

"Nothing, probably. But we have to check out all leads that come our way," he replied, with a vague gesture.

Leffert went to one of the cabinets and pulled out a thin folder. He checked it quickly before handing it to McCalley.

"Here we are. Our recent list of current clients. If Mr. Bantry had any dealings with us at any time this past year, his name would be on there. As you see, it's not."

McCalley looked through the sheets quickly and

handed them to Markarian. Leffert went on:

"I didn't even know the gentleman's name until his second visit, after the shooting, when the police questioned us, and Paul, Mr. Tasselbaum, told them who the man was." McCalley wasn't ready or willing to talk about the shooting yet, but he couldn't resist asking:

"What did Mr. Tasselbaum tell the police about Bantry?"

"I don't remember his exact words, but it had to do with a ring Bantry wanted. He had asked Mr. Tasselbaum to locate it for him. . . . You know, I wondered about that, later, when I learned that Mr. Bantry was an antiques dealer himself. Why would he need Mr. Taaselbaum to find an antique ring? He knew where to look, who to contact."

"Did Mr. Tasselbaum log the visit?"

"No. I didn't see any reference to it in the log. I glance at the book every morning when I open up, just to remind myself of Mr. Tasselbaum's appointments for the day. There was nothing about Bantry's visit."

"You mean he just walked in off the street asking about a valuable ring?"

"It's not unusual. People walk in all the time, ask about this or that. . . ."

"And Mr. Tasselbaum said nothing to the police about an 'animated discussion'?"

Suddenly on the defensive, Leffert shifted position in his chair. "You'll have to talk with Mr. Tasselbaum about that," he said, avoiding the Inspector's eyes.

McCalley decided not to pursue the subject for the time being. "I noticed you have no museums on your list."

"That's right."

"How long have you worked for Mr. Tasselbaum, George?"

"Just over eight years."

"When did you say Mr. Bantry first came to you?"

"November eleventh, a Monday."

241

"But there's no record of his visit."

"That's right."

McCalley put down the notepad on which he had been writing. "Did Mr. Tasselbaum ever find the ring Mr. Bantry was looking for?"

"Not that I know of. There would be a receipt of some kind, if he had. But as I told you, there was no record of any transaction."

"Not even for services rendered?"

The young man frowned. "Well, no."

"There should have been?"

"Probably, . . . ordinarily, yes. . . ."

"But not in this case."

"No. . . ."

"What did *you* tell the police, George, when they questioned you after the shooting? Did you tell them Bantry and Mr. Tasselbaum had been arguing?"

"For heaven's sake! I never used that word, I never said they were *arguing*!" the young man cried out, troubled by the Inspector's referring again to what he had said earlier. He hurried to the cooler and poured himself a cup of water, which he drank standing up.

"Come, sit down again, George, sit down," said McCalley. He waited until Leffert had resumed his seat. "All I want to know is what you told them. That shouldn't be too hard. After all, it's a matter of record, isn't it?"

They both knew it was. McCalley, in fact, had read the police report in the file Markarian had left with him. It said pretty much what Leffert had been telling them. For McCalley, Leffert's reactions were of greater interest to him, right now.

Still upset, Leffert said, in a rush of words: "I don't want to get Mr. Tasselbaum in any trouble. . . ."

"What trouble? He gave the police his statement and you gave yours. It's a matter of record," he repeated.

Leffert had taken on a mulish look. "I told them

242

pretty much what Mr. Tasselbaum told them. I described Bantry's coming in, their talking —"

"— talking? not 'animated discussion'?" McCalley interrupted.

Leffert jumped out of his chair and went to stand behind it, his hands resting on the cane back. "Yes. No! *Yes!* I said they were talking. *Talking.* And then Bantry left."

McCalley nodded then said, calmly: "Just want to get the wording straight, George." He decided to return to his earlier questioning, but Leffert was not ready to let go.

"I'm sure they were talking about the cost of the ring. Nothing loud, mind you. And of course it was none of my business —"

"You didn't hear what they were saying?"

"No. Bantry's voice would come through at times, just a word or two, then become inaudible again." He glanced at the card McCalley had given him. "It says here you're from homicide. . . ."

"That's right."

"And the person murdered in Ottawa had dealings with us?"

"The name of this shop appears on some papers we found, yes."

"In regard to what?"

"That's what we're trying to find out, George."

Suddenly, Leffert's face lit up. "That's it! That's it!" he cried, pleased with himself. He struck the arm of the chair with his palm, all excited. "That's when I heard Ottawa mentioned!"

"What did you hear? When, George?" McCalley had stopped writing, his pen suspended in midair.

"I was up front with a client, Mrs. Jensen. We had stopped talking for a moment, seconds really, when we heard Mr. Bantry's voice, actually it was a loud whisper —"

"What did he say?"

"He was asking about a specimen, that was the

243

word, 'specimen,' and mentioned Ottawa."

The reaction his words produced on the two men sitting opposite startled him. McCalley was staring at the young man, his pen still suspended in air. His colleague pushed back his chair in a nervous thrust and leaned forward expectantly. Leffert spread his hands wide and grinned at them uncertainly.

"What? What is it?"

McCalley cleared his throat. "Mrs. Jensen is a client? She can be reached?"

"Yes. She's bought a number of lovely porcelain pieces from us."

Out of the corner of his eye, McCalley saw his colleague pick up the list of clients Leffert had pulled out for them and copy something on a slip of paper he took out of his pocket.

"Now, George. Think back carefully. What exactly did you hear?"

"What I just told you."

"Tell me again, please."

Leffert assumed an air of concentration. "Mrs. Jensen was asking about some figurines she had seen. I went to get some catalogs that might list what she was looking for and in those few seconds we both heard — well, *I* know I did, and how could she have missed it? — Mr. Bantry ask about a specimen from Ottawa. Paul answered, but his voice did not carry. It was only seconds. I came back with the catalogs and we continued our conversation."

"Could you repeat the very words you heard, exactly the way they came to you?"

"I went to get the catalogs — we keep most of them on shelves and drawers up front — when we heard Mr. Bantry in the back, a loud whisper, as I said, sort of excited, angry maybe, . . . say 'a specimen coming from Ottawa' . . . . Wait, wait, I remember, it went like this: 'a specimen coming for me from Ottawa.' Yes, those were his

244

very words."

"You said he sounded angry?"

"Excited."

"And you say there's nothing in your records about a specimen from Ottawa?"

"No. It was all a mistake, Paul told me later, when he asked how I'd fared with Mrs. Jensen and learned that we had overheard something."

"He asked about that?"

"Just talking. I was complaining about people not making up their minds."

"He didn't actually refer to Bantry? Or what he said?"

"No. Well he did take time to tell me the gentleman was looking for a rare Victorian ring and got excited when Paul told him it wasn't on the market."

"But you did tell him what you'd heard?"

"Yes, but as I told you, it was all a mistake."

McCalley decided not to push. "How long was Mr. Bantry in the back with Mr. Tasselbaum?"

"About twenty minutes."

"Was Mrs. Jensen there when he arrived?"

"Yes. She'd been there about half an hour."

"She saw him, then. . . . Was she still there when he left?"

"No."

"But *you* saw him leave, didn't you?"

"Of course. He hurried right past me and out the door."

"You would be able to recognize him?"

"Definitely. You don't easily forget a man like that. Distinguished-looking, elegant."

"Did he seem angry when he hurried past you?"

"Not angry, no. Agitated, maybe." He watched as McCalley continued to write in his notepad.

"And you didn't see Mr. Bantry again until the day

245

of the shootout, that right?" the Inspector asked, looking up.

"Yes."

"Let's go back for a minute, George," McCalley continued. "I want to be sure we've got this right. You never saw Mr. Bantry before November eleventh and, as far as you know, or the records show, he was not a client. He had a conversation with Mr. Tasselbaum about an old ring he was searching for, an antique Victorian ring, and in the course of their conversation you overheard, by accident, Mr. Bantry ask about a specimen that he thought was coming for him from Ottawa. Is that correct?"

"Yes."

"Have you ever received or handled museum specimens?"

"We're talking stuffed animals?

"That's right."

"No. I don't remember any coming our way, ever. At least not in all the years I've worked here."

"But you've had dealings with museums?"

"Inquiries mostly."

"No sales, ever?"

The young man threw up his hands in frustration. "Really, Inspector! You can't expect me to know everything! You really should talk with Mr. Tasselbaum!"

McCalley smiled, waved a calming hand. "A simple question, George. I don't mean to upset you."

"Well, I *am* upset! I don't know what you want me to answer!"

"The truth, George. Only the truth. What you know for certain. That's not hard, is it?. . . . I have just a few more questions for you. . . . Are you all right?"

George took a deep breath. "Go ahead, then. . . . Yes, I'm fine."

"You told me that the next time you saw Mr. Bantry in the shop was the day he was killed. Tell me about that."

"He was starting to cross the street to the other side when he got caught in a gang shootout. What a shame! Just back from his honeymoon! It happened the week after Thanksgiving, December fifth, it was. A Thursday."

"What time did you get in that morning?"

"A little after nine-thirty. I usually come in around nine, make coffee, dust a little, check Mr. Tasselbaum's schedule for the day, that sort of thing. But Paul, Mr. Tasselbaum, had told me the day before that he would open up, since he had an appointment around nine."

"He didn't mention who it was?"

"No."

"Was it in the log for that morning?"

"It wasn't there when I left the day before. I didn't get a chance to check it the next morning. The client was already there."

"And it turned out to be Mr. Bantry."

"That's right."

"What time does Mr. Tasselbaum usually get in?"

"Ten, ten-thirty."

"Does he often come in at nine?"

"No. I was somewhat surprised, in fact. Usually, he sets up appointments to suit his personal routine. He rarely gets in before ten. He's not an early morning person."

McCalley made a show of placing his notepad on the desk and relaxing in his chair, before he spoke again. "Tell me what happened that morning, George. . . ."

"Well, like I said, I usually get in around nine. That Thursday, I arrived at nine-thirty. Mr. Tasselbaum was already in back, with his client. I could hear their voices . . . not loud enough to make out what they were saying, except now and then, when the client got excited. . . . I puttered around a bit, straightened things out, did some dusting. A few minutes before ten, I opened up."

"How long were they in the back?"

247

"After I got there, about half an hour. They came out just before ten."

"Go on. What happened then?"

"I waited for a signal from Paul, Mr. Tasselbaum. If he wants me to help him get rid of someone, he asks me a question or introduces me. That's a clue for me to say something about a call he's got to make, or remind him he has an appointment in a few minutes, that sort of thing. That morning he didn't even glance my way. But there was no need for any of that. Mr. Bantry went straight for the door and out."

"Did anyone come into the shop, after you opened up?"

"I'd barely unlocked the door, Inspector. Exactly at ten."

"What were they saying, when they came out from the back"?"

"I don't know. Mr. Bantry wasn't saying anything, he looked sort of grim, just walked through the shop and out the door. Mr. Tasselbaum was talking softly to him until they reached the door. At the last moment, he took his arm, as though he wanted him to stop and listen to what he had to say, but Bantry shook it off and walked out. We both watched him start across the street. That's when it all happened."

"Tell me exactly what happened."

"You must have read about it. A gang shootout. Mr. Bantry was caught in the middle. He got bullets meant for someone else."

"What did Mr. Tasselbaum do?"

"What could he do?" We could have been shot ourselves!""

"What did *you* do, George?"

"I started to run out, where Mr. Bantry had fallen, but Mr. Tasselbaum grabbed my arm and held me back."

McCalley glanced up from his notes. "Oh?"

"He said to call the police and an ambulance. That's what I did. The paramedics told us later the poor man was already dead when he hit the pavement."

"Was Mr. Tasselbaum upset?"

"Wouldn't you be? It's a good thing we stayed put. Outside, it was pandemonium. Those kids were running all over the place. They had dropped their guns and were fighting when the police got there."

"No onlookers, tourists around?"

"Sure. But they scattered like ants the minute the kids appeared. When the paramedics got there, a crowd gathered, but by then the police were on the scene and pushed everybody back. Traffic was diverted for hours."

"Let's backtrack a bit, George. I'm sorry about all these questions, but they have to be asked. . . . Did Mr. Tasselbaum say anything to you about why Mr. Bantry had come to see him, and so early in the day?"

"No. Why should he? It was none of my business."

"Weren't you curious?"

"Sure, but it wasn't my place to ask questions."

"Well, that will do for now, George." He pointed to the computer on the side of the desk. "One more thing. We need you to sign a statement. You could do it down at headquarters, or we could prepare it here and have you sign it right now."

Half an hour later, they were back in the car with Leffert's signed statement, having also set up, before leaving, an appointment to meet with Tasselbaum the next morning.

"Still not convinced about Bantry?" Markarian ventured.

"That he's innocent? It can still play both ways, Ed. It could just as easily have been a falling out among thieves. Too bad Tasselbaum wasn't there. By tomorrow, he'll be ready for us."

"On the other hand," Markarian reminded him,

249

"George gave us some interesting information we would never have learned if Tasselbaum had been there. Admit it: another fortunate coincidence. . . ."

"I'm getting a strange feeling about all this," was McCalley's reply.

Markarian had his own point to make. "I'm sure it was Tasselbaum who called him that morning and got him to Soho for the early meeting. Made sure he was there for ten o'clock, when the shooting was to take place. When he left, everything outside was ready for him."

They were headed back uptown, to Bronxville again, to pick up some photos of Bantry and to ask a few more questions.

The concentrated look on the Inspector's face kept Markarian from going on. For a while they drove in silence. When McCalley finally did speak, it was almost as though he was thinking out loud.

"First Tasselbaum, then the museum, then Ottawa, then Tasselbaum again."

It took Markarian a few seconds to pick up the thread. "Bantry's timetable?"

McCalley came out of his reverie, nodded. "On November eleventh he visits Tasselbaum, ostensibly about an antique piece of jewelry. On November twenty-second, the Friday before Thanksgiving, he visits the museum to ask about arctic wolves. The Friday after Thanksgiving, he flies to Los Angeles to pick up a flight to Ottawa. The next Wednesday, December fourth, he's back in New York. The morning of the fifth, he gets an urgent call around eight, rushes into the city, to Tasselbaum's shop in Soho, where he remains until ten. He rushes out of the shop at ten, and as he crosses the street, gets caught in a gang shootout and is killed." He turned in his seat to study his partner's reaction. When Markarian did not comment, he went on.

"Bantry seems to have taken on an active role in all this as early as November eleventh. . . ."

250

"It explains a lot of things," said Markarian, picking up where he had left off, earlier, "especially the shootout. Everything carefully timed and orchestrated. Planned well ahead of time. . . . So we're back to: What exactly did Bantry find out, and how and why was he targeted? By the way," he went on, turning to glance at McCalley, "Tasselbaum couldn't have set it up by himself. All those people and all of them 'connected'? He or his partner must have had contacts."

McCalley had missed nothing his colleague had said, even as he debated a conclusion of his own. He turned to Markarian.

"I think it's time to alert your people, Ed. If Leffert really heard what he heard — and we have no reason to doubt him — then Bantry's first visit to Soho must have triggered the events that followed. The wolf, the museum in Ottawa and everything else are meshed together in some way. First thing that has to be done at this end is check Tasselbaum's recent activities and financial records . . . bank accounts, trips, especially around Christmas. We've got to work fast, Ed. By tomorrow morning he will have realized we're on to something. We can't wait. . . ."

"No," his colleague agreed.

"We seem to be stumbling back to some critical point," McCalley added, as though to himself, "without a clue as to what it might be. We've got to get there as soon as possible."

"I'll call the Chief the minute we get back."

"I think you're right about the shootout. Don't see how else to read what happened that Thursday. It's too precise, too well-orchestrated. Even the timing was perfect, as though some one had given orders for the action to start exactly at ten. . . ."

The decision having been made, they spent the rest of the time chatting about other matters, as though a weight had been lifted, some respite granted. By the time

251

they turned into the private road that led to the Bantry residence, McCalley's mood had lightened considerably.

"Happy hour in this part of the world," he said, stretching his arms. "Think we'll be interrupting?"

"Only one way to find out," replied the other, as he came to a stop on the large apron in front of the house.

CHAPTER 14

JACK AND JILL
(January 3, 5:30 PM)

"Good afternoon," said McCalley to the gray-haired woman who opened the door. "I wonder if I might have a word with Mrs. Bantry? Inspector McCalley." The woman disappeared down the hall, came back out almost immediately with Mrs. Bantry.

"Oh, Inspector, I'm glad you were able to come. We were beginning to think my message didn't reach you." McCalley had to wonder briefly what he had missed.

"We?" The housekeeper took the coat he was carrying and hung it in the closet. Mrs. Bantry once again led the way into the lovely room he had admired the day before. To his surprise, he found Jill Masterson sitting there with the man who had waited to see her back to the hotel, in Ottawa, the night of the murder. Glasser? Glasman? Glasner, Jack Glasner.

He shook hands with both of them and introduced his "contact" in New York. They all sat down. "Now, what is it I should know?"

Mrs. Bantry answered. "It was Jill's idea, really. *And* Jack's. I invited them to dinner, since Dr. Glasner is going back to Washington day after tomorrow."

"All good things come to an end," McCalley said pleasantly. To his surprise, Jill Masterson blushed.

"Thought I'd do some research at the New York Public before going back to Washington," Glasner said by way of explanation. "So I flew to New York with Jill."

McCalley doubted he had spent much time in the library.

"We've been sitting here most of the afternoon, talking things over and debating whether to call you," said Mrs. Bantry. "Jill remembered something she thought you should know."

"You did say we should call, if we remembered anything else?" Jill Masterson added.

"I certainly did. And I'm glad you remembered to do so. What exactly do you have for me?"

It was Glasner who answered.

'That night at the museum, while I was waiting for Dr. Masterson — we were the last ones out, you remember; I was waiting in the room next to Miss Enderby's office, everyone else had left —" McCalley nodded, almost absent-mindedly; he wondered where it all was going — "I looked out and saw the guard's van up front. When we left, later, your police car was the only one in the parking area where the bus had driven in. Shouldn't Dr. Jenene's car also have been parked out there somewhere?"

"Ah. Very observant of you, Dr. Glasner."

"Well, don't you see?" Jill Masterson picked up, impatiently. "Someone must have driven Dr. Jenene's car away, before the tour arrived. Before or just after he was killed."

"Before, I would think," Glasner remarked. "That van was waiting to take Jenene's body and the wolf out of the museum. All other business had been cleared. If they planned to take Jenene's body away, as I'm sure they did, they couldn't very well have left his car behind, could they?"

"Well, they could have," Jill Masterson conceded, turning to Glasner, "but that would have raised suspicions right away." Then, to McCalley: "Don't you, see, Inspector? It was all carefully planned. The car had been driven away earlier, why, by whom, that's your job to find out."

McCalley's strained smile seemed not to register. She went on, almost breathlessly.

"They killed Dr. Jenene and waited outside in the van to take him out with the wolf. Jack, Dr. Glasner, thinks they were going to take the body elsewhere and stage an accident with the car. He probably wouldn't have been found for a while."

Damn all amateur detectives! McCalley almost blurted out.

"You see, Inspector," Glasner picked up, "someone besides Jenene and the cleaning crew was still in the basement around the time the Kaskas arrived. He, or more probably, they, couldn't risk remaining inside the building, so they sneaked out and waited in the van, hoping to get back inside, once the coast was clear. So, Jenene must have been dead by then, his car driven away long before, because they never *did* get back in and we *did* find the dead body. I think we can all agree that whoever was in the van left only when they heard the tour bus coming. They had no choice, they left in a hurry, leaving the wolf and Jenene's body behind."

McCalley took a deep breath and tried to remain calm. "I agree they left in a hurry, but everything else is conjecture, Dr. Glasner. You're *guessing*. That could be misleading as well as dangerous."

"How else would you explain it?"

"I don't intend to explain *anything*," was the rather sharp retort "I'm trying very hard to sift through facts that may or may not turn out to be evidence."

"The van was out there," Jill Masterson broke in, heedless of the warning, "and it left when we arrived. Why?"

"I don't have the answer to that, Dr. Masterson. But I will tell you this much: we've gone through at least a dozen possibilities, explanations, if you like, to account for what you have observed and much more, which I have no intention to share with you. Much as I appreciate your interest, I must warn you that your talking publicly about this case, as you seem to have been doing, could easily compromise our investigation."

There was small satisfaction in seeing the young

woman turn beet red. At once he regretted his words; he had not meant to show his irritation. Masterson had turned away; now she rose and walked to the window and stood there, looking out. Glasner went to her, put his arm around her shoulder and leaned close to whisper something. McCalley decided to breach the unpleasant pause.

"I truly appreciate your efforts to help," McCalley said, "and since you've been so good as to let me in on what you thought is important — it *is* important — I will confide to you that we have been looking for Dr. Jenene's car since the night he was murdered. Still, we have to consider every possibility. For instance, Dr. Jenene may have come in yesterday morning with a colleague and may have expected to drive home again with that same person. Or, perhaps at some point, he turned down that person's offer of a lift home because a friend had offered to drive him back in the van." Jill Masterson had recovered by this time and was about to say something. McCalley held up his hand and went on smoothly: "Or, perhaps the van was his, or one he had borrowed for the day, or —" Glasner and Jill Masterson had walked back to their seats as McCalley spoke. Now Glasner interrupted:

"— Friends, Inspector. There were two people in the van. We all saw them."

"That's true. But we don't necessarily know they were the same two people that were there to handle the wolf and the body," he added, in an effort to discourage this particular exchange.

Masterson and Glasner looked at one another but said nothing. McCalley went on:

"There are any number of ways you can explain a fact, when there isn't much to go on. Jenene himself could have left his car behind and made arrangements for his visitors to give him a ride home in their van. We're still checking his movements on the twenty-sixth."

"Oh, I'm sure they planned to give him a ride, but

not home!" was Jill Masterson's retort. Impatience and frustration were evident in her expression. "Inspector, you know as well as I that Jenene's car had been driven away much earlier!"

"No, I don't know that for certain," McCalley countered, not succeeding this time in hiding his annoyance. "And neither do you." He went on, without pausing. "I didn't get your message, Mrs. Bantry, but I was headed this way in any case — and please forgive the intrusion, I meant it to be brief — I came to ask if you could lend us a recent photo of your husband. And, if you don't mind, we'd like to take a look at his wardrobe, if you haven't cleared it out yet. It shouldn't take long."

Initial surprise turned to indignation. "I *do* mind!" she cried. It was more like a sob. Jill Masterson, suddenly calm again, reached over and took her friend's hand and surprised McCalley by saying:

"I'm sure he has good reasons for asking, Jen."

"No, I haven't touched any of his things yet," Jenny Bantry said, her eyes closed, her hands clasped tightly in her lap.

"Let me explain, Mrs. Bantry. Only a small part of what we find in the course of an investigation turns out to be relevant, in the end. But we have to check out everything, no matter how far-fetched it seems. Right now, we need to eliminate certain possibilities. Mistaken identity, for starters. We need to show your husband's photograph to certain people."

"You mean someone resembling my husband is involved in all this?"

"It appears that way." Not exactly a lie, he told himself.

"Let's get it over with then," she said, getting up with nervous determination.

"Wait, Jen. Sit down. There's more we have to tell the Inspector, remember?"

"Oh, yes, the ring."

She sat down again and held out her hand. "Jill thought I should tell you about this." McCalley took her outstretched hand and stared at the large aquamarine she wore with her wedding band. "A courier delivered it," said Mrs. Bantry, withdrawing her hand gently. "It was the day after Jill called me from Ottawa —"

"The twenty-ninth," Dr. Masterson offered. "The day after our talk in the lobby of the Elgin, Inspector. The Sunday after Christmas." McCalley couldn't resist glancing at Markarian, who gave a small shrug. Could this be the ring Leffert had referred to, that Tasselbaum told his assistant Bantry had been searching for? No, that's wasn't possible. According to Leffert, Tasselbaum had not found such a ring and there had been no transaction. Could Bantry have located the ring in some other way? They would ask Tasselbaum about it tomorrow morning.

"It looks expensive," McCalley commented, Jill Masterson leaned forward and said:

"It looks like a museum piece, one of a kind. Early Victorian, I would guess. Jenny is convinced it was a gift from Ellis." As though they had agreed beforehand that she should be the one to relay the incident, Jill Masterson quickly went on to recount what Jenny had told her about receiving the ring. When she was through, Jenny Bantry said, as though on cue:

"It may sound bizarre, Inspector, and Jill doesn't agree, but I'm sure the ring was meant for me. When Ellis failed to pick it up, it was delivered by courier."

"It was addressed to Mr. Bantry?"

"Yes."

"Did he often receive merchandise by courier?" He knew Ed was making a mental note to check it out.

"In Europe, yes. Here, I don't know. We'd just settled in, but I suppose so."

Jill said: "Inspector, this is an expensive ring, but

there was no return address, not a thing inside the box to indicate the shop where it was purchased or the name of the jeweler." He remembered the small Tiffany box with the prestigious name inside.

"No note of any kind?"

"Nothing at all, except the box with the ring inside."

"A delayed Christmas gift, maybe?"

The two women exchanged glances. Again it was Jill Masterson who spoke. "Ellis *did* have a Christmas gift for Jenny, but it wasn't the ring. Jenny found her present in his study, hidden in one of the filing cabinets."

McCaley turned to Mrs. Bantry. "What made you look in there?"

"It was right after the funeral. Hart, Mr. Quinn, had already begun sorting out Ellis's papers. He had started, he and Mr. Wentworth, Ellis's manager, with the office files, even before the inquest. Soon after that, he took on Ellis's study. At one point Hart asked me to pull out the deed to the house and some other things — receipts, purchases, recent bills . . . . I guess he wanted to give me something to do. There was a whole list of things he asked me to look for. So I did. I found them easily enough. I piled the folders on the desk for him, and when I was through, just as I finished straightening out the rest of the folders — you know how they topple forward unless you push the divider close — well I was doing that, I pushed the divider forward, and as it moved, I saw a box behind it. I almost missed it." She picked up a small red box that had been lying on the table beside her, opened it, and offered it to McCalley, together with a small card edged in red and gold. "The box was gift wrapped and the card tucked under the ribbon," she said. The others watched as McCalley examined the brooch in the box, then passed it to his colleague. He did the same with the note, after reading it.

It was a small braided filigree wreath about two

inches across, silver or white gold, with small but very bright diamonds, rubies, emeralds, sapphires and other precious stones set like colorful ornaments inside the wreath. On the bottom right was a tiny gold bow, its ribbons trailing down an inch or so. It was an unusual piece, obviously old, very likely one of a kind, and no doubt very expensive.

The note read: "To my dearest wife, Jenny, more precious to me than all these stones . . . but these will do as a small token, the first of many to come, of my commitment to you, my love, on this, our first Christmas together in our first home."

When finally McCalley looked up, it was Jill Masterson who spoke.

"I told Jenny she would find her Christmas present sooner or later. . . . You see, Inspector," she moved closer to the edge of her seat and clasped her hands in her lap, "Ellis was a careful shopper, the kind of person who would have looked long and hard for just the right gift for his wife and allowed enough time to get it ready. He was meticulous, deliberate, precise in everything he did. It came as no surprise to me that he had purchased and wrapped Jenny's Christmas gift probably weeks before he died. Even the choice of a wreath for this time of year. . . ." She took a long breath and went on.

"But the ring, this ring just doesn't make sense. For starters, no reputable dealer would package and deliver an expensive item so carelessly, with nothing to trace it should it get lost. In any case, I told Jenny to discuss it with Hart. After all, the package was addressed to Ellis, and even if it turns out to be a gift for Jenny, it's part of Ellis's estate. There may even be a bill pending. Quinn, as Executor of Ellis's will, must be told."

"Yes, I agree," said the Inspector. He turned to Mrs. Bantry. "Has he seen the ring?"

"I was still wearing it when he took me to dinner

later in the evening. When he asked about it, I told him it was a gift from Ellis."

"What did he say?"

"That it was lovely." She turned to her friend. "I don't know why you're making such a fuss about it. Hart said nothing about having to log it in, anything like that."

"He must have assumed you'd had it for a long time, if it was — as you told him — a gift from Ellis," her friend replied. Was there a touch of irritation there? Mrs. Bantry looked down at her hand.

"But you did tell Dr. Masterson about it," McCalley observed. "How it arrived, what you thought —?"

"Well, yes. But that was different. It didn't occur to me to go into all that with Hart. Had he wanted more information, he would have asked."

"I guess he was holding your hand when he saw the ring . . . ." her friend commented wryly.

"Jill, I know you don't like Hart, but, please, be reasonable!"

"You're right. I don't like him. But you've known that for a long time. I don't like him hanging around you every chance he gets."

"Well, he's not around now, is he?" replied Mrs. Bantry, somewhat sharply. "I really don't understand your attitude, Jill. The man has taken hours off work, gone out of his way to make things easy for me, the will, the funeral, all the records that had to be sorted out. He's been around for all that, yes. And I'm grateful. I couldn't have handled it all myself, and you know it!"

Spontaneously Jill reached over and took her friend's hands into hers. "I'm sorry, Jill. Sometimes I can't help myself. I feel I have to protect you from . . . everything out there. . . . "

"From Hart, you mean. . . ."

"I never said that."

"Not in so many words."

During this brief exchange, the two women seemed to have forgotten the others in the room, but now they turned back to McCalley, somewhat embarrassed.

Jill spoke. "I'm sorry, Inspector. This is nothing new. Hart is a favorite topic with us." She tried to smile. "He proposed to Jenny, back in our Columbia days. She turned him down, but he never stopped trying. As far as I can tell, he's still courting her."

McCalley tried to redirect the conversation. He addressed Mrs. Bantry. "Like him or not, Dr. Masterson is right about your telling Mr. Quinn about the ring. He'll have to look for the bill, a receipt, might need to have the ring appraised, find out where and when it was bought. You see," he added gently, "it might have been purchased for a client. Mr. Quinn will have to look into all that."

"I'm *sure* it was meant for me." Mrs. Bantry went on, as though she needed desperately to justify her certainty. "You see, Inspector, I don't wear rings as a rule. Jill can tell you, I never wanted an engagement ring, even. So if you think I'm simply greedy for this kind of thing, rest assured I'm not." As McCalley was about to speak, she raised her hand in an authoritative gesture and went on, without pausing: "Ellis was always surprising me with little gifts, Inspector. That's why I'm convinced he meant to give me the ring at the housewarming we were planning, right about Christmas."

"You still have to tell Hartley how you got it, Jen," Jill Masterson said, reaching out to touch her friend's arm.

"I will, I will," replied the other, not hiding her distress. McCalley said:

"Didn't you wonder about there being no name in the box or a return address on the container in which it arrived?"

"Yes, of course I did. But Ellis may have bought the ring in a bazaar, or while we were abroad. The original box may have been lost."

"And no insurance receipt or bill?"

"As you reminded me earlier, we'll have to look for them."

"So. You found one gift, all wrapped and ready for Christmas, and another you also think was meant for you, delivered by courier, but not gift wrapped and with nothing to trace it to a dealer or a store."

"Yes."

"The courier had to be local —" Glasner suggested.

McCalley dismissed the comment brusquely with a wave of the hand. "But the request for a courier can come from anywhere in the world." Turning back to Mrs. Bantry, he went on: "I know I asked you this when I was here yesterday, Mrs. Bantry, but please think hard. Have you any idea where your husband went on that trip he took at the end of November?"

"No. He said he'd call me and he did, several times."

"Were they collect calls?"

"Why? Was he a college freshman calling mom from the dorm?" McCalley had to resist smiling, recognizing something in her that was both unexpected and attractive. He had a glimpse of what she must be like under normal circumstances, what she was like before the shock of her husband's death set in, what she would be like after it passed.

"Tell me again, please. How long was he gone?"

"He left the Friday after Thanksgiving and came back the following Wednesday, the fourth of December."

"Did he ever mention where he was calling from?"

"No. And he didn't leave a list of phone numbers or an itinerary, either. In Europe, he sometimes made several stops in one day. He called me whenever he could."

"How often did he make those trips you just mentioned? While you were in Europe?"

"Sometimes two in one week, sometimes nothing

263

for a month. They were never long trips. Many were local, across town you might say. The longest time he was away was four days. He'd gone to see a client in Amsterdam and the snow and ice closed down the airports. He had to wait a day and a half to get on a flight back to Madrid, where we were at the time. It was during our first winter abroad."

"Can you give me a date?"

"Early December, three years ago, around the tenth or eleventh."

McCalley put away his little pad and stood up. "I'm very grateful to all of you, for what you've told me. . . ." To Mrs. Bantry he said, turning his gaze to the upstairs: "Could we. . .?"

She led the way into the hall. The housekeeper appeared from the back, as though waiting for this break.

"Excuse me, Mrs. Bantry. What time do you want dinner?"

Jenny Bantry glanced back at McCalley. "We'll only be a few minutes," he assured her.

"Around seven," Jenny Bantry told the woman. "I'm sorry I kept you so long today, Mrs. Harris. We'll help ourselves to dinner. Just get things ready."

When the housekeeper had disappeared down the hall and the others had gone upstairs, Jill Masterson muttered:

"Hasn't said a word, that other one."

"The detective? Oh, I'm sure he will," Glasner replied, placing an arm behind her, along the top of the sofa. "There's more to this than they're letting on."

"They seem especially interested in Ellis, all of a sudden. . . ."

Glasner raised a hand in warning. "Watch yourself, young lady. Your big mouth could easily compromise this relationship."

"How so?" she challenged, raising her eyebrows.

"He almost lost his cool back there. You might

drive him to put out an APB. Arrest you for unfounded speculation!" He lowered his chin and furrowed his brows, "'Dangerous amateur sleuth on the loose. Poses as a college professor. Do not approach without a fool-proof argument and plenty of research to back it up.'" Then, resuming his normal look: "I might have to give you up." Here, he pulled her close and kissed her, hard and long. She put her arms around his neck. After a while, she pulled away.

"'Mistaken identity,' he said." True to her promise, she had not shared with Glasner what McCalley had told her in Ottawa.

"Weeellll. . . ." He put his arm across the top of the sofa again, leaning his body into the soft upholstery.

"What? Tell me —"

"There must be some other reason to explain that detective he carries around with him." Jill giggled. Glasner waved a long finger at her. "Bad girl! Laughing at those poor tired officers of law and order."

"Oh, be serious!"

"All right. Here's what I think. I think they're ready to reopen the Bantry case."

"Oh God, I hope not!"

"Markarian probably was in on the Bantry case. Why else would McCalley have him tagging along?"

"You think they're working together?"

"You think he's just driving McCalley around?"

"But he hasn't said a word."

"But our boy made a point of handing his 'driver,' his 'contact,' Ellis's note to read, passed him the brooch, too. . . ."

"Maybe it wasn't an accident, after all, then, Ellis's death. . . ."

"Don't tell me you haven't considered that?"

His words visibly distressed the young woman. She walked to the doorway and glanced up the wide stairway, then slowly came back into the room. Glasner crossed his arms and watched her silently. After a while he said: "Don't tell me the thought hasn't occurred to you."

She sat down again. "Listen Jack. Ellis could never have been involved in a shady deal. He didn't need money and wasn't the type."

"I'm sure you're right," he replied soothingly. "No use worrying. McCalley will work it all out, you'll see."

"Meantime, poor Jenny will be in the spotlight again."

He leaned over and took her hand in his. "We'll have answers very soon, you'll see. He's very competent, our Inspector."

"Unrelenting," was the skeptical answer.

"What's with the wardrobe?" said Glasner, raising his eyes to the ceiling.

"Who knows, . . . I think I'll invite myself over in the morning and get her to clear out the closet, drawers, everything. All his suits, shoes, coats still hanging there, as though he's coming back for dinner!" Impulsively, she put her arms around Glasner's neck again. "It must hurt so much, Jack. I hope I never have to go through something like that!"

"You want to die before I do?"

She laughed, holding back tears. "We'll work out something!"

He drew her close, touched her cheek. After a while, he said softly: "Does she realize how very lucky she is to have you?"

Upstairs, there were no surprises. The cashmere coat and the Gucci ankle boots were there, together with four suits — two charcoal gray, one navy, one black — and a tuxedo; two jackets, one in a subtle dark gray-green stripe, the other a houndstooth; four pairs of slacks hanging separately; four pairs of shoes, each shoe in a wooden tree; a pair of snow boots, and two other coats. The garment bag contained a long coat, not quite black, fully lined in beaver, with the same fur covering the large collar.

"As you can see, my husband didn't believe in a large wardrobe."

But what he had, McCalley thought, must have cost a small fortune. Ed Shaney had been right. The man had expensive taste in clothes. Pointing to each of the items Shaney had mentioned, McCalley asked if her husband had worn or taken it on his trip to the West coast.

"Not the cashmere coat, he carried the fur-lined one. And he packed the snow boots. He wore his Gucci shoes and packed the boots." McCalley nodded. "The photos are across the way," said Mrs. Bantry, leading them through a comfortable sitting room, into her bedroom. She opened a drawer and pulled out some photographs.

"Choose what you need. You'll return them?"

"Of course."

Most of them were studio portraits. Only a few were casual shots, several taken in front of the house, probably early in November, around the time the Bantrys moved in. In one, Bantry was caught looking up from where he was crouched, on the lawn, to pick up something; in another he was standing near the front door, his arms on his hips, smiling at the camera. He was dressed in a long-sleeved shirt, no jacket. Well, it had been warm, still was, though they were into January. Two others showed Bantry with his wife, Quinn, and Jill Masterson. They were raising glasses of champagne, as though making a toast. McCalley chose four, including a studio shot, passed them on to Markarian, who nodded his approval.

"These will do," said McCalley, returning the rest of the photos to Mrs. Bantry.

Downstairs again, they did not leave at once.

Jill Masterson and Jack Glasner were standing by one of the tall windows. They turned back into the room as the others joined them again.

"Just a few more questions," McCalley said affably, sitting down again. He waited for the others to resume their seats, then, leaning forward, as though to punctuate the transition, he said: "Please forgive me if I seemed annoyed back there. This case has many strange twists and turns. It's been a trying time for all of us. I apologize if I seemed harsh and want you to know that I honestly appreciate your help. . . . There is something else you might be able to help me with," we went on, unhurriedly. "The van you saw leaving, as you arrived at the museum. Tell me everything you remember about it." It was Glasner who replied, after a quick look at Jill Masterson.

"Don't know what else we can add, Inspector. As we told you, it was coming pretty fast. Our driver had to swerve to avoid hitting it. You would think with all that ice on the ground, they would be more careful. Whoever was at the wheel was in a heck of a hurry, if you ask me."

"Could one have been a woman? Both, perhaps?"

"Well, I won't swear either way, but they were big and all bundled up. They looked like men to me."

"But you actually did not see their faces?"

"No." Jill Masterson nodded agreement.

"Did you wonder what they were doing there?"

Jill Masterson chimed in: "Not at the time. Later, thinking back on it, we decided they were up to no good. We probably wouldn't have given them a second thought except for the way they hogged the roadway. We thought they were inconsiderate, to say the least. Later, we realized they probably were the ones who murdered Dr. Jenene."

Glasner continued: "Well, now that we know what we know, their lack of consideration may have been due to their hurry to leave the grounds, knowing that soon we would find Dr. Jenene's body."

"Yes, well try to remember exactly what you saw," said McCalley. "You say there were two people inside, probably two men —"

"Big guys," said Glasner. "They filled the whole space up front. I remember thinking that their heads must be touching the roof. One had a cap on, the other a fur hat. You could hardly see their faces."

McCalley saw no need to tell them that, in the light of recent events, he himself had reread the depositions more than once and had found nothing that could be construed as new leads. In those statements, the people who had been looking in the direction of the van, Glasner and Dr. Masterson included, remembered the bus swerving but little else. But these two were sitting mid-way down the aisle, on the side where the bus passed them. They had more time to observe the vehicle as it moved down the roadway. He had hoped they could be prodded into remembering more.

One thing they were sure of: two rather large people had been in the van. Which probably meant they were the very people who were with Jenene earlier, maybe the very people who murdered him.

Still, McCalley felt compelled to review the ground again, in the light of recent information and because of certain doubts forming in his own mind.

Yes, both Glasner and Jill Masterson remembered staring out at the van as it went past.

"Do you remember what time that was?"

"Close to six. I think we were inside the museum just after six. Miss Enderby can help to establish that."

"As I recall, Dr. Glasner," McCalley said, glancing up from his notes, "you were late getting started. The bus was to leave at five?"

"That's right, but the driver had an emergency at home. We had to wait for a substitute to arrive. He got there around five-forty. I remember checking my watch."

"And you arrived around six?"

"Just about. Took twelve, fourteen minutes to get there. Considering the condition of the roads, we made pretty good time."

"Inspector, something has been bothering me," Jill Masterson said. She turned to Gasner. "Remember, what I told you, Jack? About the man in the hotel shop?" Then to McCalley again: "I bought a newspaper in the hotel lobby late the morning after the murder, after I'd given my talk, and as I left the cashier's desk and stepped aside, I almost fell over a carry-on the fellow behind me had left standing in the aisle."

"You *did* fall in the street, later that afternoon. Nearly got yourself killed." Glasner reminded her.

She waved aside his comment. "That had nothing to do with this. . . . I had paid for my newspaper, Inspector, and was leaving. I guess it was my fault I tripped. I had started to read about the murder and wasn't looking. My automatic reaction was to turn and say 'Sorry,' which I started to do, but the fellow was busy paying for whatever he had bought and didn't hear me. I was relieved. His back was to me, and for just a second I thought I recognized him; but I was embarrassed about tripping, you see, so when I realized he hadn't heard me, probably hadn't even noticed my clumsiness, I hurried out."

Watching her, McCalley once again was struck at what could be dredged up in an ordinary conversation. Jill Masterson went on:

"As we were talking just now, about the bus and the van, the incident in the hotel shop came back to me, I don't know why. I suddenly remembered thinking the man in the gift shop looked familiar in the same way."

"The same impression you had of the driver of the van?"

"Yes, but they were both bundled up, Inspector. I still don't understand it, why a connection between the two should have popped into my head." She turned to Glasner. "Odd, isn't it. It never occurred to me until just now."

"I'd like you both to concentrate for a minute,"

said McCalley, easing forward in his chair. The last thing he wanted to do was put his thoughts in their head, his words in their mouth. "Think back to the moment the van passed your bus," he went on softly, his hands clasped between his knees. "Try to visualize it as it moved in the opposite direction." He waited patiently as Jill Masterson closed her eyes. No one spoke. Finally, she opened her eyes and shook her head.

"I'm sorry Inspector."

"But you *did* see something," McCalley persisted. "You must have noticed something or you would not have made the connection."

"I know, I know. Maybe something will come to me later. Right now, I can't imagine why it came to mind."

"It does seem far-fetched," said Glasner. "What could you possibly have noticed that made you connect the two?"

"I don't know," she grimaced and shook her head." They had reached a dead-end, for the moment at least, McCalley decided. "Was that the same day you fell?" he asked.

"It was nothing."

"'Nothing,' was it? You were limping there for a while. And what about the gash and bruises on your knee?" Gasner reminded her.

"What exactly happened?" McCalley asked. She told him about the van almost hitting her and not stopping to see if she had been hurt by the fall.

"Probably had been drinking," Glasner added.

McCalley made a last note in his pad, closed the little book and rose. He thanked them again.

The others followed the two men into the entry hall and watched as Mrs. Harris handed the Inspector his coat. "Enjoy your dinner," said McCalley with a wave, as he and Markarian walked toward their car.

They were back in Manhattan in less than an hour.

271

McCalley declined an invitation to dinner. His mind was racing. He needed space to lay out what they had learned that day, wait for Kenney's call, order his thoughts. He reminded Markarian about getting copies of Bantry's photo to Kenney and to look into Tasselbaum's operation and finances. Markarian would pick him up at nine-thirty the next morning for their appointment with the antiques dealer.

"I'll have a definite answer by morning, I'm pretty sure," said Markarian before driving off. "I hope to catch the Chief tonight, even if I have to call him at home."

Over a small steak and salad in the hotel dining room McCalley let his mind wander over the day's events. Were they really moving ahead? Would they ever know the whole truth, even if the three cases were connected and the murders solved? Markarian was right. Lucky breaks had propelled them forward, from the very beginning. All those wild surmises — who was it said that? — first Kenney's, then Markarian's, continued to plague him.

Later, after a shower, he pulled back the drapes and stood at the window looking out at the empty lot across the way, the huge crane now at rest. His thoughts were still on the personal dilemma he had tried to articulate earlier: Was it all just intuition and coincidences? All his training, his meticulous sorting of data, the countless hours double-checking seemingly irrelevant details — what did it amount to in the light of lucky coincidences? There had to be, he argued, trying to shore up his conviction, there had to be some rational explanation, clear evidence buttressing the three deaths he was investigating, yes, including Bantry's, for he was definitely in the picture now. Only careful and methodical investigation would yield results, reveal the connection with the deaths in Ottawa. And yet, as everyone seemed bent on reminding him, lucky coincidences had certainly played an important part in this case. No use denying it. But experience forced him to suspect hunches and speculation. How often they had led detectives astray! How many precious hours, days, weeks had been lost, cases dismissed, because someone had followed a hunch instead of gathering evidence while it was still fresh and available! Still, it wouldn't be a bad idea to start testing Markarian's theories, and Kenney's; to consider at least what Glasner and Jill Masterson had put forward.

He knew he was right in being cautious, but he had to admire the way Markarian — and Kenney too, for that matter — had jumped a number of fences with ease and conviction. Forced to it, he had to admit that he too entertained some of their outrageous conclusions; he too was grateful for the unexpected turn of events that already had led to a number of important but unanticipated revelations. Hadn't he felt the same excitement Markarian obviously had felt on hearing George Leffert tell about Bantry's meeting with Tasselbaum? The wolf and Ottawa had been mentioned. George Leffert's statement was now part of the record. Markarian was right. They might easily have missed all that if in fact Tasselbaum, not Leffert, had been in the shop that afternoon. Of course, Tasselbaum might have some surprises for them also, tomorrow. . . .

Would coincidences break this case? He was pretty sure they would never have learned about the "animated discussion" between Bantry and Tasselbaum, would not have heard about Bantry's reference to the specimen and the museum in Ottawa, if Tasselbaum had been present when they first visited the shop. And suppose the Curator at the American Museum of Natural History had not come down with the flu; . . . if, the day before, Miss Trainor had not been the one to receive him, talk with him, . . . if Ed Shaney's name had not come up? —

The phone rang. It was Kenney with his report for the day.

They had located Dobie's Jeep in the woods, some distance from where the body had been discovered. The

273

team had been working all day on it. At least four other sets of prints had been checked out. On inquiry, Kenney had learned that other traders often borrowed Dobie's vehicle to make deliveries. That helped identify most of the prints. Only one set remained, a partial palm print ("a lucky break for us, Sir!"), on the steering wheel.

When Kenney paused, McCalley knew the question his Sergeant was trying to hold back.

"Well, it's not likely to be Bantry's, Bill, even if he was in Dobie's Jeep at some point, which I very much doubt. We don't know if he even talked with Dobie."

"What about the card we found in the cabin?"

"It doesn't prove he *talked* with him." Reminded of his own dilemma, McCalley held back more words of caution. "I'll have Markarian send Bantry's prints to check against those in the Jeep."

"We found fibers too. Not Dobie's. And some fur."

"Well, he did use the jeep for animals."

"Yes, but these hairs were processed. Probably from a coat or a fur collar."

"Make sure everything you find is stored away safely."

"Already under lock and key in the fortress." The fortress was their private nickname for a part of the evidence storage area that only top personnel could enter, and then, only if accompanied by a second officer.

He went on to tell Kenney about his visits to Bantry's office, Quinn, the Bantry house, about not seeing the Curator but talking with Miss Trainor instead, about missing Tasselbaum and talking with his assistant instead, about the meeting earlier in the day with Glasner and Jill Masterson. At the other end, he heard a low whistle.

"That is *weird*, Sir!" was the Sergeant's reaction. "You probably wouldn't have learned all that, if Tasselbaum had been there, if you hadn't had the chance to talk with Miss Trainor and the tour guide."

McCalley stared at to the ceiling for a few seconds before answering: "I'll admit that, Bill. But let's not leap ahead of ourselves . . . ."

Kenney didn't have much else to report. He sounded disappointed. McCalley told him recent photos of Bantry were on their way and ended with: "Don't worry. We're definitely moving ahead."

"One last thing," said Kenney. "Bantry stayed at the Elgin while he was in Ottawa. And he rented a jeep. Put some mileage on it. But no one at the museum remembers seeing him, seeing a stranger, or a visitor, with Jenene."

"Double check the hotel, show them the photos you'll be getting tomorrow. Same with the car rental. We want to confirm it was the same man who signed in at the Elgin, rented the car. Ask around again, find out if anyone remembers seeing him. Blow up the photos if you have to. Oh, and remember, he was tall. About six-one or two. Ask what he was wearing. We need a positive ID. But please keep in mind that even with that, even if we place Bantry in the area, even in the museum itself, we can't jump to conclusions about his intentions or motives or actions."

If he had been able to see his Sergeant turning imploring eyes to heaven at the familiar warning, McCalley might have been somewhat disconcerted. Into the phone, Kenney replied: "Will do, Sir."

In the kitchen, where his supper was waiting, Kenney said to his wife: "I can't figure out how he moves ahead, with all the double and triple checking he forces on us. It's two steps forward, one step back, right to the end!"

His wife commented, ruffling his hair: "If you ask me, you're just as hard on others as he is on you."

"Never!" he protested, leaning back, his hands upraised as if to ward off even the mere suggestion. His wife laughed as they sat down to eat. But he knew that a lot of McCalley had rubbed off on him in the two years they had worked together. The thought pleased him.

CHAPTER 15
DEAD MEN TALK
(January 4, 10:15 AM)

"I really don't see why you've come to me about a murder in Ottawa," Paul Tasselbaum said, the minute McCalley took out his badge and introduced himself and his colleague, Lieutenant Ed Markarian, of the New York Police Department. The big news that morning was that the Chief had managed to have the Bantry case reopened and, since Slattery was busy on another assignment and Markarian was familiar with the case, had put Ed in charge. "A real break!" Markarian had said, with undisguised enthusiasm, when McCalley congratulated him. The Inspector was more than pleased that his friend could now take an active part in the investigation. As far as he was concerned, they had been partners all along. His decision to share information with Markarian had proved a distinct advantage. . . .

Tasselbaum was avoiding all eye contact with his visitors. He moved about the shop, shifting a box from here to there, holding a glass up to the light, dusting a book cover with his handkerchief, rearranging a display of music boxes, his mouth pursed in disapproval, all the while. His entire demeanor suggested displeasure and impatience. What might normally have passed for Old World formality had turned into a nervous tightness, a stiffness of manner and posture, which betrayed his show of arrogance.

In a somber dark wool suit, white shirt, and dark tie, he reminded McCalley of old Mr. Bassovitch, who had come with his family from Poland, as a boy, and ran a bookstore for six decades. McCalley still had a vivid memory of the old man, who died at the age of ninety-five. He was one of the first "foreigners" young McCalley had ever met. Tasselbaum had that same foreign look.

George Leffert had made himself inconspicuous,

checking and unpacking merchandise in the back. McCalley wondered how much he had told Tasselbaum, before they arrived: the man clearly was ready for them.

"Could we go into your office to talk for a few minutes?"

"I'm expecting a client soon," answered the other sullenly. His voice was low, his diction precise, as though trying to work the words around a lingering accent.

"We won't keep you long," said McCalley.

As Tasselbaum led the way into the back, Leffert came forward from behind the drape and busied himself arranging a new display from some open cartons.

When they were seated, McCalley said:

"Sorry we missed you yesterday. We came, and are here now, to follow up leads that could help us solve a murder in Ottawa, as well as a second death which recently occurred there and may be connected to the first." He met Tasselbaum's stony look head on. "Mr. Leffert I'm sure informed you about our visit yesterday? The victim was a man called John Jenene, the taxidermist of the Canadian Museum of Nature, in Ottawa. He was killed in his workroom the day after Christmas. There was a processed specimen in the workroom, an arctic wolf, waiting to be brought back to New York, to this shop, in fact. Can you tell us about that?"

Tasselbaum registered no surprise. He replied at once, without any hesitation: "That was a mistake. We have nothing in our records about such a transaction. I'm sure Mr. Leffert told you that when you were here yesterday?"

"He did, as a matter of fact. But we now have to ask you the same question, since you are the one ultimately responsible for all transactions, are you not?" McCalley didn't expect an answer and didn't get one. "You see, there is every indication that the specimen was to arrive here just after Christmas and a client of yours, a Mr. Bantry, was to have received it."

277

"As I said, Inspector, it was a mistake. Mr. Leffert told you yesterday about Mr. Bantry. He came to see me about a ring. That's all I know."

"Tell us about the ring."

"He was looking for a Victorian ring. As he described it, I thought I recognized it as a museum piece, nothing that could possibly be up for sale. I brought out a few museum catalogs and sure enough I found it. There was a fine photograph too."

"It belongs to a museum?"

"Until recently." He opened a desk drawer and took out a folder, leafed through it quickly, and handed McCalley a sheet of paper. As he did so, he addressed Markarian. "That's one of your NYPD circulars, Lieutenant. I see you recognize it." Markarian handed it to McCalley and pointed to an entry half-way down the page.

"It's a current list of stolen goods," Markarian said "Here's the ring." McCalley looked where his colleague was pointing, then returned the sheet to Tasselbaum.

"We'll need a copy of that, if you don't mind. And could we borrow the museum catalog?"

Tasselbaum got up, made the copy and placed it inside the museum catalog, which he then handed McCalley with a look of smug confidence, as though he had scored points. He seemed almost cordial.

McCalley examined the photograph in the catalog. It showed a rather large ring with an oval aquamarine stone in a gold setting, surrounded by small diamonds around the edge. To McCalley's eye it appeared to be the very ring Mrs. Bantry had been wearing the day before. He passed the open book to Markarian, who nodded but said nothing.

"DId Mr. Bantry say this was the very ring he wanted?"

"Yes, indeed. I told him it was impossible to get that very one but offered to have an excellent copy made. That wasn't the answer he wanted."

"Was that what you quarreled about?"

"Quarreled? No quarrel, Inspector. Mr. Bantry got a bit excited, that's all. Apparently, he had seen the ring and wanted it very badly. As I said, I offered to get a copy made for him, but he refused to consider that."

"Why, do you suppose?"

"I have no idea."

"Was he a collector?"

"I think not. A collector would have understood at once the ring was not for sale. And if it was for a gift, a good copy with quality stones — even old stones to match the originals could have been found — would have served the purpose. But he insisted he wanted the very one that was in the catalog. He had seen a copy in Europe, he said, and was tracking down the original. Nothing else would do. I told him I couldn't help him."

"Did you tell him it was on this list?" McCalley asked, holding out the paper Tasselbaum had shown them.

"Oh, but it wasn't. Not when he first came asking about it."

McCalley examined the list again. It had been issued just before Thanksgiving.

"And this is the date it first appeared on such a list?"

"As far as I know." They both watched Markarian writing something on the back of an envelope he took from his pocket.

"I can double check that," he said, putting the envelope away.

"I'd like to get back to your connection with the specimen we found in Dr. Jenene's workroom," said McCalley.

"There is no connection, Inspector, I told you that. Why Mr. Bantry would have thought I'd be receiving an order of his here, when, as I understand it, he has his own warehouse, is beyond me. It was all a mistake."

279

"Yes, I know what you told me, but I still don't understand why your shop should appear on official shipping documents which show the specimen was destined for this location. Have you ever had dealings with museums?"

"Not the kind you're talking about. I think Mr. Leffert told you that yesterday."

"Well, Mr. Bantry apparently did. And so have you. If fact, he came to see you because of that specimen that was coming from the museum in Ottawa. Can you tell us about that?"

For the first time since their arrival, Tasselbaum's eyes betrayed surprise, a touch of fear, but he did not avert his eyes from the Inspector's stare.

"I wonder too," McCalley went on in his easy, even tone, "why anything meant for him should be sent here, rather than his own warehouse, which is much larger than the space you have here. Why would he have anything sent to this shop?"

"I just said that. The answer is that nothing of his was sent or came to this shop," said the other, masking his nervousness in an expression of irritation.

Casually, unhurriedly, McCalley took out from his inside jacket pocket an envelope. He opened the flap and withdrew some papers. He handed them to Tasselbaum and allowed the man some seconds to scan the sheets before he said: "How do you explain these, then?"

Clutching the papers, Tasselbaum jumped up and stood behind his chair, glaring at him. "What exactly are you accusing me of, Inspector?"

"I'm not accusing you of anything," said McCalley. But I do need explanations. Two other specimens came to your shop earlier in the year, did they not? The wolf is now in our custody, as evidence. That one, you understand, will never reach you now." He let the full implications of his words sink in. He had been careful not to say anything to suggest that, since legal actions about ownership of the wolf were pending, the police had still not been able to ascertain what was inside the specimen.

With a show of anger, the dealer threw the papers on his desk and turned his back to the two men. They watched as he hugged himself tightly, as though to stop the twitching in his shoulders. When he sat down again, after a minute or two, he seemed to have regained his composure. He ignored the papers he had been shown and picked up some of his own, instead, browsing through them as though he were alone. The silence grew oppressive. Looking up finally, he said, in his clipped, precise diction:

"I don't think I will continue this conversation without a lawyer. If you'll excuse me, gentlemen —"

For the first time, Markarian spoke to him directly. "Your best bet is to cooperate, Mr. Tasselbaum," he said as he walked toward the drape separating them from the showroom. "The Bantry case has been officially reopened, and I'll be conducting the new investigation. If you're involved in any way, if you helped target Mr. Bantry, you will be charged with first degree murder. We have proof that this shop has been receiving specimens, three at least this year, from the museum in Ottawa. And we know that there is a connection with Bantry."

"They weren't for me!" Tasselbaum exclaimed.

McCalley had also gotten up from his chair. "Who *were* they for, Mr. Tasselbaum?" he asked.

"I never had any specimens in my shop. Mr. Leffert told you yesterday: we don't deal with stuffed animals."

"Those papers say otherwise, even if you didn't see the specimens yourself."

There was a pregnant silence. McCalley later admitted to Markarian that he was hopeful at that moment that Tasselbaum would pick up the bait he'd offered, clearing him of knowledge of the shipments. They could see Tasselbaum struggling with conflicting emotions, but in the end he repeated what he had said earlier: "I never saw any specimens."

Markarian had the last word. "But you did have dealings with Bantry. And Bantry knew all about your dealings with the museum in Ottawa and the wolf that was expected. Sooner or later you'll have to explain all that. If not, well, as I said, we have reopened the Bantry case. You may end up being charged with three murders."

The man had risen where he sat, leaning forward, his two fists resting on the desk, as though to support the rest of his body. His face had grown pale, his confidence and arrogance gone. The others waited for him to say something; when he didn't, they walked slowly through the showroom and out into the street.

George Leffert had obviously heard everything. His eyes followed McCalley and Markarian as they went out the door, closing it behind them. When a few minutes had passed, he took a deep breath and resumed his work, checking a carton of Irish stem glasses and placing them on a small dining table all set for an elegant dinner for six. He had almost forgotten Tasselbaum when, some twenty minutes later, the man emerged from the back and told him he was going out briefly.

Two blocks down the street, well out of sight of the shop, Tasselbaum took out some quarters and dialed a number. The muffled voice at the other end sounded annoyed, then angry.

"Where are you calling from?"

"Don't worry. It's the public phone. The police were just here —" Before he could finish the sentence, the line at the other end went dead. Tasselbaum replaced the receiver slowly. He waited, biting his lip. In a few minutes the phone rang.

"Never do that again."

"Yes, I'm sorry, I wasn't thinking —"

"You said the police were there."

"Yes."

"Well, you know what to say, what to do. I thought I could count on you."

"You can, you certainly can! But I had to tell you, they know a great deal. And they've reopened the Bantry case. That fellow from NYPD is in charge." There was a brief silence at the other end. Tasselbaum cut into it with more information. "And they warned me I could be charged in three murders."

"What did you tell them?"

"Nothing. I said it was all a mistake, that I never saw any specimens. That Bantry came to see me about a ring that I discovered belonged to a museum. Pulled out the catalog for them, the police list, too."

"They mentioned "specimens"?"

"Yes. They have documents showing all three were coming here. The wolf is with the police. They're holding it as evidence. That means they know about —"

"It doesn't mean anything. Put some more quarters in and tell me from the beginning exactly what happened."

Tasselbaum did so and recounted the visit.

The voice at the other end remained steady, calm. "Nothing to worry about. They'll follow up on the ring. Bantry receiving stolen goods. Meanwhile, I'll find you a good lawyer —"

"But I thought —"

"— I said I'll find you a good lawyer," interrupted the other. "And don't call me without signaling first. Stick to instructions."

The line went dead.

As they started back uptown, Markarian's phone beeped. He pulled over to the curb to take the call. "It's Jill Masterson.," he told McCalley, still holding the phone. "She has something for us. Do you want to go by there now? She lives right off Gramercy Park, a few blocks from here."

"Fine with me," said McCalley.

Neither one was surprised to find Glasner with Jill Masterson. An open carry-on stood in the corner of the small living room. The aroma of bacon and coffee lingered, even though the windows were wide open. It was still unseasonably warm for January.

"I'm glad you could swing by," said Jill Masterson.

"We were just a few blocks away."

"I'm sorry if we took you from your work, but both Jack and I thought this was important." She motioned them to chairs. She herself sat down on the small sofa where Glasner made room for her, his arm stretched over the back.

"When you were in Bronxville yesterday and asked to see Ellis's clothing," she began, "I realized I had to help Jenny clear his closet and chest of drawers as soon as possible. I invited myself over this morning to do that. I'm happy to say we sorted out and bagged everything. It's all ready for the local church to pick up for their clothing drive next month."

"Not exactly everything," Glasner interjected. She patted his arm,

"I'm coming to that. We had gone through his personal things in the study and had finished sorting and packaging things in the bedroom drawers. The closet was next. We got all the suits folded and packed, then sorted out the shoes and boots. We were down to jackets and coats. Jenny had taken an armful of jackets and the green anorak, and brought them to the bed, where she was folding them and putting them into large plastic bags. I had packed the cashmere coat and had taken down the fur-lined coat. I did what we had done all along, checked the pockets to make sure nothing valuable was left inside, and I came across this."

She reached for an envelope on the table beside her and held it out for McCalley, who took it but did not open it at once. Jill Masterson continued:

"I started to fold the coat, it was quite heavy and bulky, and to free my hand I put the envelope inside my own pocket, just to get it out of the way as I folded the heavy coat. When we had finished, we dragged the bags to the landing outside the bedroom suite. Jenny wanted to take them down the stairs, have them ready for pick-up, later, but it wasn't a job for us, and I told her that. So we went downstairs and Jenny made fresh coffee and brought out some cookies. We sat and talked for a while. When I was about ready to leave I went to freshen up and saw the edge of the envelope sticking out of my pocket. It had already been opened, of course, so I decided to see what was in it. It gave me a shock, I have to tell you, when I saw copies of the documents you had mentioned, back at the Elgin, the afternoon you asked to see me." Here she turned to Glasner and said, almost apologetically: "I'm sorry, Jack. I couldn't have told you or anyone else about it at the time. I'd promised the Inspector. He'd gone out of his way to tell me what he knew about Ellis, when he saw how angry I was at his poking around."

"No need to explain."

Both men had been listening intently, McCalley still holding the envelope and making no effort to look inside. Now, as Jill brought her brief account to a close, he scrutinized the envelope.

It was addressed to Bantry at "Bantry International Ltd." The words "Personal and Confidential" were printed in one corner. The stamp was Canadian; the postmark Ottawa. The date was November fifth.

He drew out the four sheets of paper. Three he recognized at once as copies of the shipping releases for the wolf, signed by Jenene, whose name, as well as the shop in Soho and Bantry's name, was highlighted with a yellow marker.

The top sheet was an unsigned note: "We need to

285

talk!"

McCalley's brows arched as he went through the four sheets. Markarian had leaned to one side so that he could read with him. When he was finished, McCalley held out the papers to him.

"You should know," he said, addressing both Glasner and Jill Masterson, "that Lieutenant Markarian will accompany me from now on in an official capacity. As of this morning, the Bantry case has been reopened and the Lieutenant has been placed in charge of the new investigation." Jill Masterson's hand went to her mouth, as though to cover any sound that might come from it. Her eyes narrowed and filmed over. Glasner put his arm around her shoulder. "I'm sorry, Doctor," McCalley continued. "We have no choice."

"Poor Jenny!"

"I do believe," McCalley said trying to hide a certain impatience, "that Mrs. Bantry can take it, as the saying goes. You may be short-changing her thinking she's going to collapse on us. She's a strong person, fully aware of the responsibilities she's inherited, and not just the tangible, obvious ones. She can handle whatever comes her way, I've noticed."

"I've been telling her the same thing, Inspector," said Glasner, taking his arm away and resting it on the back of the sofa.

Jill shook her head. "I didn't want Jenny to see those papers, not right away. In any case, we would have had to get them to you. I saved you another trip out to Bronxville!" she ended with a sad smile.

"The coat was left for the clothing drive?"

"Oh no, I should have explained. At first I didn't know what to do, but by the time I went downstairs and was ready to drive off, I realized you would want the coat also. I asked Jenny if I could take it for our doorman. It's in my trunk."

McCalley was visibly pleased. "Yes, we'll need to hold on to it for a while, as evidence."

He picked up the papers again and the envelope. "What did you think when you saw these?"

"As I told you, I was shocked at first. Of course I recognized these must be some of the documents you referred to back at the Elgin, when we met that afternoon, when you explained your interest in Ellis. When I realized the implications, all I could think of was keeping Jenny from finding out, not that way, not another jolt. She's had too many! I decided it would be best for you to get the papers as soon as possible and let you explain it all to her, in your own way. I just can't do it, Inspector. . . ."

"You did the right thing," said McCalley.

She went on, in her clear, strong voice, pointing to the papers in McCalley's hand: "But, Inspector, I will never believe Ellis was involved in all that!!"

"We don't know that he was —"

Ignoring the remark, Jill. Masterson interrupted, as though an irresistible force was pulling the words out of her: "My first reaction, back then, when you began asking questions about Ellis was disbelief, indignation. Now, I'm frightened . . . . You don't really believe that Ellis was part of a smuggling operation?"

McCalley shook his head. "I've warned you about jumping to conclusions," he said kindly. "First of all: we have nothing at all pointing to a smuggling operation, just speculation. To assume it as fact, at this point, could prove counterproductive. What I *will* say is that we can't be sure that Bantry knew what was going on, just as we can't be sure that the Curator, Miss Enderby, actually signed some of the forms we found."

Relief momentarily flooded the young woman's face. "But what about that top sheet? Who would send Ellis those three shipment releases, with that message? Was it Jenene, the man who was killed?"

"We don't know," said McCalley, carefully. He had confided in her that one time, out of necessity, to get her to tell him about the Bantrys. But he could not and would not tell her, knowing all that he now knew, that he was pretty sure the sender had to be either Jenene or Dobie — he was ready to exclude Miss Enderby as a real suspect. To share any more information with her would only complicate things.

He examined the envelope again. Whoever sent the forms had done a bit of research, had found Bantry's business address — easy enough on the internet, where "Bantry International, Ltd." had an impressive website — and sent the documents there.

The few words on the cover note — "We need to talk!" — were printed in a neat hand in capital letters and made comparison with Jenene's handwriting impossible. Jenene's name, highlighted on the forms, might have been an awkward effort to avoid a second signature that could be scrutinized against those already on the forms.

It didn't really matter, McCalley reminded himself. By process of elimination, the sender had to be Jenene. The important thing was, they now had proof that Bantry had been contacted with crucial information, and that the note and shipping forms had triggered a search that began with the visit to Tasselbaum on November eleventh, then, just before Thanksgiving, the visit to the American Museum of Natural History, and, on the twenty-ninth of November, the trip to Los Angeles and Ottawa. Then back to Tasselbaum on December fifth. Had the call that drew Bantry to Soho on that fateful day been a ploy to lure him to his death? What had Tasselbaum (it *had* to be Tasselbaum!) said to him on the phone to get him into the city that morning?

Bantry's role, McCalley reminded himself, was still not clear. But surely one could now assume that he went to Ottawa expressly to contact Jenene, the only other name on those documents he had received, besides the shop in Soho as the ultimate destination of the shipments. Why else had the name been highlighted, if not to draw attention to the sender? Once in Ottawa, it would not have been difficult to track down Dobie as well (or for Dobie to approach the stranger who was asking questions about an arctic wolf).

If I'm right, McCalley thought, it could mean that Jenene wanted a bigger piece of the pie, and when it was denied or if he was put off with excuses, he may have decided to go elsewhere, beyond his contact, the man who came to take away the specimens and paid him for his work and his silence. If it was more money he wanted, Jenene may have decided that Bantry, as the agent listed, was the obvious person to tap next. Once in Ottawa, Bantry must have realized what was going on, tracked down Dobie (or Dobie found *him*) and learned more, no doubt paying the trapper handsomely for whatever information he provided, maybe even promising to look into his demands for a bigger "take." Back in New York, Bantry was then prepared to confront Tasselbaum a second time with what he had learned. But by then, the wheels had been set in motion, the stage had been set. . . .

Or could Bantry's death really have been an accident?

Everything in him now repudiated that possibility, although it was still the official ruling in the case; but McCalley also knew that there was no proof yet to sustain what his instincts, honed by long experience, told him was the truth.

He and Markarian rose to leave. Jill Masterson and Glasner remained seated.

"One more thing, Inspector," Jill said. She waited until the two men had sat down again before continuing. "The van that skidded and almost hit me in the street? Jack thinks it was coming for me, that it didn't skid."

"From the way Jill described it, Inspector, the van backed up and took off without any difficulty," Glasner said, eager to explain. "If it had skidded, it would have turned slightly, then straightened itself before moving on. From what Jill told me, it came at her directly, hit the curb where she was first headed, then backed up and drove off."

"Is that true, Doctor?" McCalley asked.

"Accurate enough, yes. The van was moving in a straight line —"

"— in a diagonal, across the road, you told me," Glasner interrupted.

"Yes, a diagonal, headed straight for me. That's when I turned and stumbled back to the other side. I could see the van would hit me if I continued in the same direction. But don't tell me it was deliberate! That's crazy, Jack, and you know it!"

"Listen Inspector, I've been thinking about this all morning," Glasner said, with new earnestness, inching forward on his seat and clasping his hands between his knees. "Who would want to do something like that? It does sound far-fetched. But suppose Jill saw something —"

"What? What did I see that you didn't see! We've been all through this, for goodness' sake! We were together most of the time! You saw the same things I saw. No one came after you?!"

Glasner turned to her. "You're wrong, Jill. I wasn't with you most of the time, and I didn't see everything you saw. Think back. It happened just after you bumped into the tall fellow in the gift shop. I wasn't there, remember?" He turned to McCalley. "That's right, Inspector. She won't admit it, but I think she recognized who it was both times. Unconsciously. At the museum and in the gift shop."

"I *didn't!*" Then, turning to the Inspector: "I told you about the gift shop, remember?" McCalley nodded. "I had bought a paper and moved away. The carry-on was behind me slightly to one side, and I tripped over it. That's all it was. I didn't get hurt, and the fellow seemed not to have taken any notice of it, so I hurried out. To tell you the truth, I was embarrassed. I was relieved he hadn't taken notice."

"She unconsciously recognized who it was."

"Are you a psychoanalyst, all of a sudden?"

"Be reasonable, Jill. What I'm saying makes sense." Then, to McCalley: "More to the point, whoever it was may have recognized *her*! . . . . You see, don't you, what I'm getting at Inspector?" McCalley didn't dare answer; what Glasner had said came dangerously close to certain notions he had been trying to hold back for some time. It was Markarian who answered for him.

"You're saying that Jill subconsciously recognized the man in the hotel shop but that the man saw her clearly and avoided her."

"Why would he do that, if he knew me?"

"Because he didn't want to be seen, my darling," her friend replied, turning to clasp her hand. "Because he wasn't supposed to be there."

Markarian said: "You said, Doctor, he was tall, had a carry-on. What else do you remember about him?" Jill described the man as best she could.

"Wore dark clothes. Wide shoulders. All bundled up for the weather outside."

"And you didn't see his face."

"If I had, I'd know who it was!" she cried, jumping up and pacing around them before sitting down again. "All this fuss! Sometimes I really don't understand you, Jack!" Glasner watched her but said nothing. McCalley, startled into a new awareness by what was emerging, resisted any comment. They could feel the tension growing in the small room. "You might as well finish what you started," she said at last, breaking the uneasy silence that had fallen over them like a pall.

Glasner glanced at the two men opposite him. "I don't know if I should, it's just a hunch." He scratched his head, then, in a nervous gesture, wiped his hand on his trousers. He turned to look at the girl sitting beside him. "I'm truly sorry I brought it up, Jill. I didn't mean to upset you. I was worried . . . ." She waved his words aside, but not impatiently. "You see, Inspector, I think the man recognized Jill and that it was the same man who tried to run her down, a little while later."

Jill Masterson sighed. "You see how absurd it is!" she exclaimed.

McCalley asked, although he was sure he knew the answer: "Why do you suppose he wanted to run her down, Dr. Glasner?"

"Because in time he knew she would remember seeing him not only in the hotel shop, but earlier, in the van, the van that drove off when we arrived at the museum."

"And do you think it was the same man, on all three occasions, Dr. Masterson?" McCalley asked.

She shook her head back and forth several times. "I don't know, I don't know."

Glasner said: "You won't admit it, not consciously at least."

Markarian said: "Your friend thinks the man you saw in the van, at the museum, realized that sooner or later you would recognize him as the man you saw in the gift shop. That means it was someone you know, someone you could in due course identify."

"How could I do that? I never got to see his face!"

"But something about him, about them, the one in the hotel shop, let's stay with him, something about him struck you," Markarian persisted. "And without really being aware of it, you may have come around to connecting him with one or both of the two drivers."

"Don't you think I'd tell you, if I had?"

"All right," said Glasner, holding up both hands as though to ward off any more speculation. "I've said what I had to say. We're wasting the Inspector's time. I owe him an apology." Markarian was surprised to hear McCalley reply:

"Nonsense. There's always room for speculation, once we have our facts straight. I think, Dr. Glasner, what you told us is worth considering. The van driving off like that, when Dr. Masterson was still crouching at the curb, with a gash in her knee — is that correct? You stumbled and fell against the curb —?" and when Jill nodded, went on, "might suggest a certain intention. In any case, the driver never stopped to see if you were hurt. That needs some explaining. That, and the fact that, as you just described it, Dr. Glasner, and you have confirmed, Dr. Masterson, the van didn't seem to skid in her direction, it seemed to be aiming for her." When he saw that Jill Masterson was about to speak, he added quickly. "Of course, whether or not the episode is significant in terms of our case remains to be seen." In the silence that followed, McCalley walked slowly to the open window, gazed out briefly, came back, but remained standing.

"Could you spare a few minutes to come with us? It won't take long. Just a few blocks from here. There's someone I want you to see. . . . You can come along, if you like, Dr. Glasner."

Before they reached their destination, he warned their passengers in the back seat: "Don't say anything out of the ordinary. Just follow whatever cue I give you. You probably won't have to speak at all. It won't take long. I'll explain later."

This time Markarian parked at a nearby hydrant, his police sticker on the windshield.

Tasselbaum waited for the phone to ring. When it did, he closed the door to the booth.

"Well? What is it now?"

"They were here again, a few minutes ago. With the woman."

"What woman?"

"Bantry's friend."

293

"What did they want?"

"The Inspector asked about Ottawa."

"What did he say?"

"'We want to clear up a misunderstanding,' he said, and then, right out of the blue, 'Were you in Ottawa just after Christmas?'"

"What did you tell him?"

"What I told him earlier, I was skiing in Vermont."

"That's it, then."

"I thought you should know."

"Nothing to worry about." The line went dead.

Back in the shop, George Leffert expressed his indignation at the Inspector's impromptu visit. "Doesn't know when to let go, that one."

Mr. Tasselbaum made no comment.

Going back in the car, Jill Masterson was saying, "No, Inspector, I didn't recognize him. I'm certain I never saw him before."

Driving uptown, after they had left the other two in front of Masterson's building, Markarian commented:

"She didn't know this one from Adam, she didn't hesitate a second when you asked her; but the other one she saw in the van, at the museum, seemed familiar. Why is that? They were both bundled up. She never saw their faces at any time. . . ."

"Yes, it's curious, isn't it?"

"She saw both in passing only; hardly enough time to be able to identify either one."

"But she saw one of them twice, remember? In the van, that first time at the museum, and the next day in the hotel gift shop."

"Three times, if the same person was driving the van that almost ran her down."

"Can't be sure about the last one," said McCalley. "She caught only a glimpse of the driver."

"But she never really saw the one in the shop, either. He had his back to her, as he paid the cashier. She didn't see his face, she said. All bundled up in a heavy black coat. But *him* she thought she recognized. . . . How come?"

"She saw what seemed a familiar build, a certain posture maybe, the way he stood —?"

" — a certain shape, height —" Markarian added. "Broad shoulders? The shape of the neck. . . . The head, maybe. . . ."

"No. She couldn't have seen his head. He was wearing a hat, remember? Both times, in the shop and in the van they saw leaving the museum, he was wearing a hat." McCalley paused, his mind racing. An all-too-familiar sensation coursed through him, his reasoning dimmed by it. It made no sense at all, but he knew he couldn't ignore it.

CHAPTER 16

CLOSING IN
(January 4, 12:30 PM – January 5, 10 AM)

Over a quick lunch at a nearby Greek diner, the two men reviewed recent events and planned the rest of their day.

McCalley was eager to check in with Kenney and give him new instructions. He would also call the museum about the authenticity of the ring and make arrangements for them to identify it — more properly Markarian's task, but McCalley had offered to do it to give his colleague more time for the crucial interviews with gang members and their parents, all of whom would be subjected to intense scrutiny this time. One, or several of the teenagers would certainly be held accountable if the ruling of accidental death was reversed, as it was very likely to be. The first to come forward with information might be able to make a deal with the DA. Meanwhile, the photos borrowed from Mrs. Bantry were already in Kenney's hands; they had been sent out the evening before, when Markarian had stopped off briefly at the precinct.

Both men knew they had to work fast. Every piece in the complex network of three deaths had to be firmly connected before they could make an arrest.

Before driving to the hotel to pick up McCalley that morning, Markarian had checked out Tasselbaum's website. No surprises there. His business was exclusively with antiques, everything from furniture to jewelry, even *incunabula*. All, very expensive. . . . Detectives assigned to check Tasselbaum's finances were still at it. So far, nothing suspicious had turned up.

Predictably, as an importer-exporter as well as an antiques dealer, Bantry had worked a broader, more varied spectrum of possibilities. His clients included zoos, cultural groups and organizations, schools, architects, dealers, libraries, museums, just about any institution or individual who wanted to find and purchase . . . whatever.

Nothing had turned up about an arctic wolf . . . except for the shipping documents Jill Masterson had found in Bantry's coat.

They were on their second cups of coffee when McCalley's beeper went off. It was Kenney. The noise from a nearby table, where a cake had just been brought out and everyone was singing 'happy birthday," forced McCalley to take the call outside.

They still had not been able to identify the palm prints on the steering wheel of Dobie's Jeep, Kenney told him, but they definitely were not Bantry's. The photos had yielded better results.

"Bantry was here, all right. Checked in very late on the Friday and left the following Tuesday. Probably spent the night in LA before starting back the next day for New York. Do you want me to check the hotels in Los Angeles?"

"Not now. He probably did stay over; we know his flight to New York was on Wednesday morning. We'll check it later, if we need to."

"Right. The clerk at the airport, who rented a Jeep to an Ellis Bantry the Friday night, thought he recognized him as the man in the photo I showed him, but he couldn't be sure. The Jeep was turned in on the Tuesday, which fits in with his leaving that day for LA. He put around eighty miles on it. Dobie's cabin, Sir, is twenty-six miles out of the city. The rest, give or take, might account for the trip to and from the airport."

"But no positive ID at the airport rental. . . ."

"No, Sir. The clerk said, he was all bundled up."

"Go back, ask what he was wearing. In detail."

There was a pause, then "Yes, Sir."

"Go back to the Elgin, too. Show the photos again to anyone who might have had contact with him — the

297

hotel clerk and maids, the bartender, the Concierge, ask the same questions again. Be sure you do that. And the hotel gift shop. Show the pictures to the person who was at the cashier's desk."

"But, Sir, that was the twenty-seventh! It couldn't have been Bantry. He was dead by then!"

"Bill, just do as I ask. I'll explain later. Get to me as soon as you have information."

"Yes, Sir."

McCalley went on to give him other instructions. Top on the list: he was to check out three other sets of prints Markarian would be sending him. "Check them against the prints in Dobie's Jeep and other things of his we're holding in the Fortress. Do the same for Jenene. Check them against prints in his workroom and office. . . ."

"Yes, Sir."

"Good work, Bill."

"Thank you, Sir."

Back inside, Markarian was paying their bill. As they walked toward the garage where they had left the car, McCalley told him what he had learned. They had cleared the ramp on to the street, when Markarian's phone beeped.

"That was Wentworth. Quinn is with him. They found something they want us to see. It's about the ring."

They drove through midtown traffic in silence. As they neared Bantry's showroom and office, Markarian said: "I can't make it out, that business of the ring. The piece was stolen some time before November. We saw the report, read the description. And suddenly, just after Christmas, a courier turns up at Bantry's door with it."

McCalley shook his head. "We don't know for sure yet, if it's the same ring."

Markarian gave him a quizzical look.

When they arrived at the showroom, Wentworth was again waiting to take them upstairs. The ledgers and folders were still piled on the conference table. Quinn rose to greet them.

"Ah, Inspector, Lieutenant, I'm glad to see you," he said affably. "Henry and I were sorting out some papers this morning . . . I'm amazed how much still remains to be done . . . and we came across this." He handed McCalley a printed sheet. As McCalley read it, Wentworth said:

"Yesterday, when you were here, just before you left, you asked about stolen goods." McCalley looked up, nodded. "Well, of course I don't know of any, as I told you yesterday, and I don't know anything about this ring. But a little while ago, I came across this page. It's been torn from a museum catalog, as you can see. I was handing it to Mr. Quinn for him to look at before throwing it away."

"At first it didn't register," said Quinn, but then I remembered Jenny was wearing something like this when I took her to dinner, just after Christmas."

McCalley showed surprise. "You think it's the same ring? This one belongs to a museum."

"It does, and it was stolen at some point. We found that out when I told Henry about seeing a ring just like it recently, and he pulled out the NYPD circular to show me. But it can't be the same ring. . . . Ellis must have had a copy made for Jenny."

The Inspector didn't mention what Tasselbaum had told them. He asked, instead: "Have you found a receipt for Mrs. Bantry's ring?"

"No. But I'm sure it will turn up."

"May I borrow these for a few days?"

"Of course," Quinn said, handing him a folder with the papers.

Wentworth seemed distracted as McCalley asked if statements could be typed up and signed before they left. Quinn went to find Grace, Bantry's secretary. In the lull, Wentworth turned to McCalley and said: "Excuse me, Inspector, . . . you mentioned a name, yesterday, you asked if I knew a Mr. . . . what was it again? . . . some sort of

'Baum' was it?"

"Tasselbaum?"

"That's it! Yes."

"Paul Tasselbaum."

"Yes. And it came back to me just now, that I heard Mr. Bantry making a call, as I was entering my office one morning, about a month before he was killed. He had left the connecting door ajar and I could hear him asking for a Mr. Paul Tasselbaum."

"What was the conversation about?"

"I don't know. I had to check something with my assistant. When I came back, Mr. Bantry was off the phone, working at his desk."

"Can you remember exactly when that was?"

"Early in November. They had just moved into the house. That was on the fifth or sixth, I think."

"What brought the name back to you just now?"

"I'm not sure. It just clicked into place. That and his reference to Ottawa."

"You heard him mention 'Ottawa'?"

"Yes."

"Try to remember exactly what you heard."

"He asked for Mr. Tasselbaum, then identified himself and asked for information about a specimen from Ottawa."

"Were those his very words?"

"I think so. Let's see. What he said was, "Tell me about this specimen I'm supposed to receive from Ottawa."

Quinn had returned with Grace. Wentworth first, then Quinn repeated their stories, as the secretary took them down. McCalley had Wentworth add the conversation he had overheard. When the statements had been typed up, signed and witnessed, McCalley added them to the folder he was holding.

As they hurried to the elevators, Markarian asked:

"You're not thinking that Bantry actually —?"

300

"It still could play both ways, Ed. Let's not be hasty. Right now, we have to put pressure on Tasselbaum."

"He'll deny he ever had that call. Did you notice how he's pushing the business about the ring?"

"A decoy, I'm sure. We'll know soon enough. Right now, we have to follow up what we've learned. We have two witnesses, Leffert and Wentworth, each of whom signed statements that they overheard exchanges between Tasselbaum and Bantry, exchanges having to do with specimens from Ottawa."

"But, in your mind, that doesn't take Bantry off the hook —"

"Nobody's on or off the hook, in my mind. But we're definitely closing in on something that will clear things up."

"Tasselbaum can deny everything, of course. Or simply repeat he knew nothing about Ottawa and specimens for Bantry."

"Sure. But we have the statements *and* those forms."

"He'll claim he never saw them."

"Who then, Leffert?" They both laughed. After a while, McCalley said: "We've got to find out more about the morning of the fifth, Ed."

"I'm working on it," said Markarian, as he pulled up in front of the hotel to drop off McCalley. They each agreed to check back later in the evening.

In his room, McCalley spent a long time looking out his window, at the crane moving up and down in the empty lot across the way. Then he sat at the small desk nearby and filled a page of hotel stationery with doodles, concentrating on the intricate designs as though nothing else mattered. Rousing himself at last, he checked his watch. Close to four. He folded the sheet of paper and tucked it inside his notebook, then picked up the phone and made three quick calls. The first was to Jill Masterson, whom he tracked down at Mrs. Bantry's. The second was to a certain museum. It was almost closing time, but he got through to the Curator, who, hearing what McCalley had to say, assured him he would stop by the hotel later in the day, right after the museum closed. The third call was to Markarian, who had still not returned to the precinct. McCalley left a message: instead of phoning in, could he come over?

He was rinsing his face when the phone rang. It was Kenney, with a detailed report.

When he put down the phone, the lines in his face seemed to have deepened, his eyes had a clouded look. He changed his tie, pausing thoughtfully now and then at the image reflected in the bathroom mirror. Finally, he put on his jacket and went down to an early dinner in the hotel dining room, stopping first at the desk to ask that he be paged, should anyone come looking for him or should any calls come in.

Markarian announced his presence a little after nine. The Inspector found him at a small table in the bar, just finishing a roast beef sandwich and a beer.

"Catching up on essentials," he said, as McCalley sat down. When he had finished eating, Markarian ordered a second beer. McCalley also asked for a beer before they moved into the lounge and settled down in a comfortable corner. The place was empty.

"Everybody's out on the town. You can't go back home without having seen at least one Broadway play," Markarian commented, as the drinks arrived. "The last play *I* saw was *Oklahoma.*"

"You could do worse. I've never seen *any* play in New York!"

They both drank in silence for a minute or two, then Markarian said:

"Well, we've got our own script to work on! Might

as well get started." After a long sip of beer, he sat back. "Me, first, okay?" McCalley waved him on.

"As we guessed, there's nothing on Leffert. He was simply a spectator. Tasselbaum has some money in tax-free bonds, no stocks, nothing 'iffy,' straight as they come. If he's got money stashed away it's in Switzerland or in the Caymans. We're looking into that. . . . Next: I got to three of the kids, and their mommies and daddies. They were, shall we say, uneasy? Especially when I told them the Bantry case had been reopened and reminded them that one of them was bound to spill the beans and get some sort of immunity. I told each of them the same thing: whoever got there first would score. I left them thinking about it, especially the parents. They don't want to see Junior behind bars, with all the bad guys . . . . Tomorrow, bright and early, I'll get to the others. By the end of the day, one of them will have talked. Meanwhile, I've got two officers reviewing the evidence and the statements made that day. We've already found some discrepancies, inconsistencies. This time, we're putting the screws on."

"Ed, if that was really premeditated, if Bantry was deliberately lured into the city to be killed, Tasselbaum couldn't have staged it on his own —"

"We've agreed, haven't we, that there was an accomplice? Had to be. Masterson and the others on the tour confirmed there were two men in the van coming from the museum." He held up his hand to ward off any caution McCalley might express. "I know, I know. We haven't actually placed Tasselbaum in Ottawa, but —"

To his surprise, McCalley stopped him short. "Actually, we *have*. When Kenney called earlier, he reported that on the twenty-seventh Tasselbaum booked two tickets for a flight to New York from Ottawa, that very evening."

Markarian slapped his thigh, a broad grin lighting up his face. "So! We've got him on the scene!"

But McCalley only frowned. "Not so fast. We'll

need to place him with Jenene or Dobie, or at the museum."

Markarian leaned forward and peered across at his colleague, still grinning. "Why that look? We're zooming in on him, Luke. We've put him right smack in Ottawa, the day after the murder, not skiing in Vermont. And we know he was right here, in New York, right on the scene, on the fifth, when Bantry was killed."

"Still, it's all circumstantial. I wish we could nail him down!?"

"Okay, so we can't connect him directly with Bantry's death right now, but he'll talk, you'll see. He knows we're on to something. You saw how he reacted yesterday!"

"That's just it! He's getting nervous. And there's a very cool killer out there, with friends to help, who's already targeted three people. . . ."

"Mob involvement, for sure. But, so far, we've found no connection with Tasselbaum. If we find the accomplice —"

"We may have," McCalley cut in. "But first: I got through to the museum about the ring. The Curator was pretty anxious to pick it up. I told him it was still part of an ongoing investigation, but when I showed it to them a little while ago — he came with his Deputy and one of their experts — they all agreed it was the missing ring. I drew up a preliminary statement and had them sign it. And gave them a receipt for the ring. I have it in the safe for now."

"How did you get it here?"

"I called Masterson, tracked her down at Jenny Bantry's. I asked Mrs. Bantry if she would lend us the ring. Jill Masterson and Glasner brought it here around six. The museum people came soon after that."

"What did they say about its disappearance?"

"They had a jewelry exhibit late in August. It lasted about six weeks. The original wasn't missed until the exhibit closed around mid-October. That and several other items had been cleverly replaced by copies."

"You mean, more things were stolen?"

"Yes, including a rare necklace of black diamonds worth at least three million dollars.. None of them has been retrieved. Except the ring. The Curator and the police too believe it was an inside job."

"Whoever stole it had to have access, or plenty of money for security to look the other way," Markarian commented. "Anyway, I'm convinced Bantry was not involved in the theft, even if we believe Tasselbaum's story about Bantry's asking about that particular ring and insisting that only the original would do."

"I'm sure Bantry never asked about any ring. . . ."

McCalley's answer drew a long silence, during which Markarian studied his colleague, as the Inspector steepled his hands over is face, closed his eyes, and contemplated some inner scene.

"You think he was set up," Markarian offered, at last, "somebody was out to frame him, somebody wants us to think Bantry was dealing in stolen goods all along. First the ring, then the wolf. . . ."

"It means, someone may have wanted to distract us. . . ."

". . . make us think Bantry was the bad guy, Planted evidence, hoping we'd follow that lead and connect the ring with the wolf. It might have worked, too, if Jenene had been found in his car, another accidental death, completely unconnected with anything that happened here; meanwhile Bantry already dead, an innocent victim in a gang shootout, conveniently unavailable for questioning. . . . Everything nicely wrapped up. . . . You were right about Bantry probably being targeted from way back. . . . Things are getting more and more complicated, if you ask me!"

"But simpler, in a way," replied the other.

"Let me get this straight. You're saying the ring was planted and —"

"— I'm saying, we have no proof that Bantry ever

305

asked about a ring. We do know for certain that he asked about arctic wolves and went twice to Tasselbaum to find out about specimens ostensibly coming to him from Ottawa."

McCalley's subtle shift away from the notion that the ring had been used to prove Bantry a thief did not seem to register with Markarian, who added, bluntly:

"You can't deny they used the ring to frame him!"

"Who's 'they'? . . . . The theft appears to have been carefully planned weeks, months ahead of time, with help from the inside. It was carried out by professionals, who knew and took the risks as a matter of course. The job itself appears to have no connection with our case."

"How do you explain Bantry and the ring, then?"

"Right now, I can't," McCalley replied.

"But we can say, can't we, that at some point someone had the brilliant idea of using the ring from that loot to suggest that Bantry was into stolen goods. . . ."

"Possibly. . . ."

"Which means the thieves are the same people *we're* trying to nail, right?"

"Maybe. . . ."

To avoid lingering on that particular subject, McCalley quickly went on to tell his colleague about Kenney's inquiries at the Elgin and the car rental.

"Why trace all that again? We know Bantry was there. We have the dates. Their ledger shows clearly he signed in on the Friday and checked out on Tuesday. Rented a Jeep when he arrived on the Friday, we even have the mileage he put on it. And we know what he brought with him, in the way of outerwear. We checked all that with Mrs. Bantry."

McCalley smiled and waved a long finger at him. "Remember our conversation about the man in the gift shop? What Jill Masterson saw or didn't see?" He told him what Kenney had found out. Markarian gaped. "So, we'll need search warrants, first thing in the morning, Ed. The sooner the better." For a while, Markarian said nothing. The initial surprise at what McCalley had revealed was soon replaced by a grim bleak look. He sat forward in his chair, his hands steepled over his mouth, as if in prayer, his gaze on some point at the back of the room. He seemed to be struggling with some deep emotion held at bay. McCalley watched the shifting expressions on the other's face. When he spoke, Markarian seemed startled, as though the sound of his own voice had roused him roughly from sleep.

"If that's true, then —?"

"— we could be in for some more surprises," the Inspector finished for him and went on. "Kenney scanned Tasselbaum's picture on the website and showed it around, with the photographs we sent him. All three men have been identified. We've got to move fast."

"I'll knock on some doors and try to get through for warrants tonight, pick them up in the morning. . . ."

"Remember, it's still all circumstantial . . . . "

"You never know what else we'll dredge up," said the other, reassuringly, "or who will decide to talk. Besides, circumstantial, the way we've got it right now, would work fine in court."

They agreed Tasselbaum's shop would be their first stop in the morning, with search warrants in hand."

Tasselbaum exploded with anger when he walked into his shop, a little after ten the next morning, and saw a team of NYPD detectives going through his files. He examined the warrants, spluttering indignation all the while, threatened law suits. . . . They wouldn't get away with this kind of harassment; he had contacts, "powerful friends" in the right places! . . . . George Leffert hovered uneasily in the background, went into the showroom when Tasselbaum waved him off.

Several times the chimes sounded, and clients

came and went.

After his initial outburst, Tasselbaum settled behind his desk and watched in glum silence as detectives methodically pulled out ledgers, papers, account books, file folders, piling everything on a table that had been cleared for the purpose. Markarian and McCalley had pulled up chairs and were examining folders as they were brought out. They didn't really expect to find in them anything relevant to the case; the search was a strategic ploy, meant to erode whatever confidence Tasselbaum might still have, put pressure on him. . . .

An hour had gone by before McCalley put aside a ledger he had been examining, pushed back his chair so it faced Tasselbaum, and said:

"I don't mind telling you, Mr. Tasselbaum, that a report from Ottawa, early this morning, has put an entirely new light on this case. You should consider cooperating, before it's too late." Tasselbaum gave him a stony look.

Markarian picked up the cue: "We know you have been lying to us. For starters, you weren't skiing in Vermont during the holidays . . . . "

Something flickered in the man's eyes. He looked away. McCalley turned on the floodlights:

"Yesterday, you denied having received specimens from the museum in Ottawa. You should consider changing your story, Mr. Tasselbaum, since, in addition to the documents we showed you yesterday, that prove at least two specimens were received by this shop, by you, within the last few months, Customs has now verified those shipments. They were destined eventually for a museum in New Jersey, but they never got there, it seems."

Tasselbaum said nothing. The Inspector went on.

"But *you* know about them. And you also know about a third specimen, an arctic wolf, allegedly destined for the American Museum of Natural History here in New York. Of course, you never got to take that one with you,

308

back to New York. We have it. It's part of our investigation into the murder of Dr. Jenene, the museum taxidermist." He paused to let his words register, then resumed: "Ask yourself, Mr. Tasselbaum, why would I have come to New York to investigate Dr. Jenene's murder, a murder that took place in Ottawa? And why has Lieutenant Markarian been assigned to reopen the Bantry case?"

A nervous flutter of the hand as it moved over the desk betrayed Tasselbaum's nervousness. He cleared his throat and clasped his hands tightly in his lap, to keep them from shaking. McCalley went on:

"And now that the case has been officially reopened, Lieutenant Markarian is looking again into the circumstances of Mr. Bantry's death, interviewing those teenagers again. The ground is beginning to shift. We have three new statements already." There was enough truth in what he said.

Again he paused, allowing the implications of his words to sink in. Then, a quick stab in the dark, why not? The interviews Markarian had reported had more than suggested mob involvement. "Do you know someone called —" here he named a well-known underworld figure, often in the news. Tasselbaum shifted in his seat behind the desk. "Let me rephrase that. Do you know anyone who has been talking with him? Leaving aside all the rest for the moment, are you aware that there is a law against consorting with known criminals? But of course you know, we all do!"

Tasselbaum kept his gaze averted. He appeared calm, but his hands, now resting on the desk, were again moving restlessly over the items arranged there — pens, a pad, a bowl with clips, some figurines — flitting over the empty spaces in between, until he clenched them tightly in an effort to hold them still. As the two men spoke in turn, his face had undergone a number of quick changes. Caught off guard, at first he blanched, then took a few deep breaths, pushed back his chair and crossed his legs. For a while he studied the ceiling. Finally, he stood up, went to stand behind his chair, and asked in a hoarse voice:

"What the hell is this all about?"

McCalley studied him calmly. "Why don't you tell *us*?"

"Look. I don't know what Leffert said to you, but he doesn't know anything about my clients, my business —"

"Oh, he was the soul of discretion! He told us you were the one we should talk to."

"That's right. And I have nothing to tell you."

"Aren't you at all curious how we know what we know? Where the information came from? Why I am here in New York working with the Lieutenant?"

"Should I be? Whatever you learned, it doesn't concern me. I can't answer your questions."

"Not a wise decision, Mr. Tasselbaum. You would do well to consider our questions and answer them. Later, well, later may be too late. But let me tell you straight on that the documents we found were in Dr. Jenene's safe, tucked away in his home. You would do yourself a favor by telling us what you know."

"Fine! You have so-called documents, you don't need anything from me!" He came around and sat down again at his desk. McCalley wondered if he had moved in too soon. He decided to continue with the narrative, give Tasselbaum time to consider what might be in store for him.

"The wolf was supposed to come here and then delivered to the American Museum of Natural History," he went on. "Trouble is, the museum people know nothing about such a delivery coming their way. Are you sure you can't tell us something about that shipment? It was supposed to arrive, oh, about the twenty-seventh or eighth. You were back here by then, weren't you? Flew back on the twenty-seventh, . . . *flew* back, since you had no wolf and no need of a van."

310

"I told you, Inspector, I was skiing in Vermont over Christmas!"

Markarian's detectives had in fact confirmed Tasselbaum's statement that he had been skiing in Vermont over the holidays — that is, someone with his name had checked in at the lodge where Tasselbaum claimed he had stayed, but no clear identification had been possible. With sudden confidence, Tasselbaum added:

"Nice try, Inspector. But we both know, don't we, that I was in Vermont through January second." Ignoring the remark, McCalley picked up his narrative.

"Mr. Leffert must have told you that he reported overhearing a heated discussion between you and Mr. Bantry. But it wasn't about the ring. That was clever, but I'm afraid it won't work, Mr. Tasselbaum. The two of you were arguing about the specimen, about the arctic wolf. Mr. Bantry wanted to know how his name got on those documents, wasn't that it?"

"I don't know what you're talking about."

"We have a signed statement from your assistant. He referred to it as an 'animated discussion'. And he told us Bantry was angry when he stormed out of your shop."

"He didn't storm out, Inspector. George has a talent for inconsequential talk. At times, it's useful. Some clients like to chat. He also tends to exaggerate."

"What was the urgent business you called Bantry about, the Thursday morning he was killed?"

"I never said it was urgent business."

"He seemed to think so. He rushed out of the house without breakfast to come here."

"I don't know anything about that."

"What did you tell him?"

"Probably something about the ring he wanted. I don't remember."

"I think you wanted him here at a certain time, to step through that door at a certain moment, that all was ready and in place for him to be shot as he left your shop that morning."

With a violent thrust, Tasselbaum pushed his chair backward and rose, fists resting on the desk. He glared across at the two men, who sat watching him. "That's a lie! It's slander!"

"You called him that morning, got him out of his house just after eight. He arrived about an hour later and was with you until he left, just before ten. Walked out the door and was shot. What did you talk about for almost an hour?"

"I gave my statement to the police at the time."

"Well, here's your chance to tell us what really happened. For your own sake." Tasselbaum busied himself picking up the chair, which had toppled when he jumped out of it. When he had done so, he stood beside it, his hands behind his back. McCalkey repeated the question. "What was the urgent business that brought Bantry to your door so early that morning?"

"Nothing urgent, I told you. If he chose to rush out, that was his business."

"And now it's yours, Mr. Tasselbaum. Very much so." Tasselbaum stared at him, said nothing. "There's something else you might be able to explain," McCalley went on, glancing at his notes. "Why would you call him urgently that morning about a ring you still could not get for him and which you had already explained, three weeks earlier, would never be available for purchase. . . .? But, of course, there was no ring, was there?" McCalley barely paused.

"Or did you have some fresh information for him? *Was* there a ring? Had that ring you told us he wanted so badly come into your possession after all? Did you tell him you had it for a certain price? Is that what got him here? Is that what you were quarreling about? Was that the urgent message?"

312

"I had nothing to do with the ring!" cried the other, turning away abruptly in confusion, when he realized his words might have given away more than he intended.

"According to the statement you gave the police, you told him on the eleventh of November that the ring was not for sale, something he must have known perfectly well, since he too was an experienced dealer," McCalley went on doggedly. "Whatever you told him on the phone the morning of December fifth had to be something else, news of a different kind."

"I don't know what you're talking about."

"What did you call him about?"

"You have the statement I gave the police at the time," the other repeated.

"But there was no ring, Mr. Tasselbaum. Not in that context. . . ." Tasselbaum said nothing. Almost reluctantly, McCalley decided to push ahead.

"Where were you over Christmas?"

"Skiing in Vermont. We went through all that, Inspector! Do you really think you'll trip me up by repeating things?"

"Where did you go?" McCalley persisted.

With exaggerated emphasis, he gave the name and address of the lodge. "I believe the place is still there. But I'm sure you've checked it out."

"Yes, we have. And your name appears on their register. But you were seen in Ottawa during that same time, Mr. Tasselbaum. How do you explain that?"

The dealer dropped back into his chair. His face had turned pale, a small twitch had started around his mouth.

"I don't have to answer any more questions about my personal business! Next time you come, if you decide to harass me still, I'll have my lawyer with me!" He rose again, as though about to leave the room but didn't move very far. McCalley also rose and took a few steps toward him.

313

"You see, Mr. Tasselbaum, we think you knew all along about the wolf, about the other two specimens, about Jenene's murder. We know you were very much involved. That means you're in big trouble." He knew he had nothing solid to go on, that he was doing precisely what he always warned others not to do — follow a hunch — but, watching Tasselbaum take in what he had said, convinced him he had touched a very sore nerve. The man seemed to cave in. The twitch around his mouth was quite noticeable now. He tried to cover it, but his hand was trembling.

Markarian had gone to stand by the heavy drape. In the showroom a woman laughed. They could hear George Leffert say something to her. A few seconds later, they heard the chimes, as the shop door opened and closed.

"I don't know why you're asking me all these questions," Tasselbaum said, "trying to trick me into saying things." He walked back to his desk and sat down again. The others remained standing. "I don't have to listen to you, or answer any more questions. Please leave now."

"We've checked your movements from the twenty-second to the twenty-eighth of December," said Markarian bluntly. "You could save us a lot of time and trouble, and save *yourself*, if you cooperate now."

"What do you mean, 'save myself'! You're charging me with something? Are you arresting me??"

"No."

"Then, I have nothing more to say to you, without my lawyer present."

A muffled ring interrupted the uncomfortable exchange. Markarian checked his beeper, rose, pulled back the drape and walked through, into the showroom, to dial. The conversation was brief. The others watched as he put the phone away and said something to George, who went to the door and flipped the "Open" sign to "Closed." Before resuming his seat, he gave McCalley an imperceptible nod and continued, as though there had been no interruption.

314

"As I said, you'll save everybody a lot of trouble if you help us in this, Mr. Tasselbaum. We're pretty sure about what happened, but you can help us corroborate what we have. It would certainly be to your advantage. For example, who made the arrangements for the shootout? I'm sure it wasn't you, but we are just as sure that you know the person who did. Someone with mob connections? Just tell us who took the initiative." When Tasselbaum said nothing, McCalley picked it up:

"What I don't understand is why the shipments had to come here first. I'm sure they weren't taken apart in this shop."

"What the hell are you talking about!"

"The animals weren't destroyed? Taken apart, relieved of whatever they were carrying, then thrown away, burned perhaps?"

"Look, I'm not answering any more questions. From either of you." His voice had risen. "Especially you!" He pointed to Markarian. "Who are you, anyway?"

"I thought we explained. As of yesterday, I'm officially in charge of the Bantry case, which, as you were told, has been reopened. And that investigation is now intimately connected with the two murders in Ottawa."

When he saw the expression on Tasselbaum's face, McCalley said: "You didn't know about Dobie? The trapper who got the wolf for you? He was found dead. Ruled an accident, at first. Like Bantry's death." He waited a few seconds before continuing.

"You may not have known about it, but, if nothing else, you can be held as an accessory after the fact, Mr. Tasselbaum. And that's just the beginning. You will have to answer for Bantry's death as well as Jenene's. And those deaths can definitely be linked to you. Perhaps only to you. Whoever else was in on them knows how to save his skin."

They could see Tasselbaum struggling with the doubts they had raised in him, trying to keep his emotions

315

under control.

"Now is the time to cooperate," Markarian said, in turn. "It's beginning to look as if Mr. Bantry triggered events by making certain inquiries. And we have documents that have this address and your shop as the recipient of illegal shipments, the transfer of at least two other specimens, besides the arctic wolf. Bantry knew too much, he was the first to go. Then Jenene, who prepared the specimens for you; then the trapper, Dobie, who also seems to have grown suspicious and greedy. There are lots of questions that need answers Mr. Tasselbaum. You would do yourself a big favor if you helped us now, before we take formal action."

"Why are you harassing me like this? I had nothing to do with any of that!"

"You do have information; tell us what you know."

"I don't know a thing!"

"Be reasonable, Mr. Tasselbaum. Your connection with Bantry is already on record; other things are surfacing . . . . We have documents, we have new statements from George Leffert and three of the teenagers who did the shooting, as well depositions from their parents; we have reports from Ottawa placing you on the scene of the two murders that took place there, just before and after Christmas, you and a second man. You could also help yourself by telling us why Bantry's name was listed as the receiver, although at this point it's easy enough to figure out. You could tell us where the specimens were taken, what was inside them."

"I have nothing more to say."

Outside, Leffert was opening the door to let in several police officers and plainclothesmen. Tasselbaum said nothing as Markarian went out to greet them, took some papers from one of the officers, then led them into the back.

"Mr. Tasselbaum, we have been to your home as well. All legal, rest assured. We've going through your cars,

316

also, the Mercedes and your van. The van is of special interest to us. We're sure to find fibers, fur, that will prove that animals were transported in it, over the past several months, although you insist you never dealt with specimens. Oh, not brought in from Ottawa, you rented a van for that, we're convinced, but you must have used your own van to take the specimens to where they were finally destroyed. I'm sure it wasn't done here!" Tasselbaum was taking it all in, his face flushed. "We've checked the license number and know the van is registered to you, which means you're responsible for what we find in it."

Tasselbaum moved forward in his chair and pointed a shaky finger at him.

"I'll sue you for this!"

"You'd do better to answer our questions," replied Markarian from where he had remained standing, just inside the drape.

"I want to call my lawyer!"

"Go ahead. You're under no constraint!" They watched as Tasselbaum reached for the phone, then abruptly changed his mind and seemed to collapse where he sat. For a while the only sounds were drawers opening and closing, the ruffling of papers as Markarian's men continued going through the filing cabinets.

"You see, Mr. Tasselbaum," McCalley picked up, as though carrying on a casual conversation with a friendly neighbor, "we have a great many answers already. Your lies won't stand up. In the eyes of the law, you're an accomplice before, during, and after the fact. On three counts of murder. Oh, yes, you can be charged in all three murders. And there are other charges as well: illegal trafficking, stolen goods, perjury . . . . Once the legal machinery starts to turn, there's no stopping it. Eventually, you'll be forced to answer. If you cooperate now, it will be easier for you. But I'm sure you understand all that." Tasselbaum turned away, as though dismissing his visitors.

"The documents in our possession offer eloquent testimony to your lying," McCalley went on. He paused briefly. Tasselbaum continued sitting with his back to them.

"There are witnesses who saw the van, with two men in it, coming from the museum, just after Jenene was killed. And customs is checking on all museum transfers from Canada to New York for the last three years. It won't be long before we track down every single thing we need for an air-tight case. Every hour, new information reaches us. Pretty soon we'll have the whole picture. If you have anything to tell us, now is the time. . . .

"Why don't you start by telling us about Bantry? We know how he stumbled on your operation. Who else knew about it?"

When the man didn't answer, Markarian chimed in: "Do you really want to go down alone? Answer for three murders?"

Tasselbaum rose and walked slowly to the drawn drape. He stood there for a few seconds, looking out. Leffert took a hesitant step toward him, then stopped.

After a while, he returned to his desk and sat down. He watched silently as Markarian's men, at a signal from the Lieutenant, moved out, to wait up front. McCalley slowly pulled the drape closed behind them. Several minutes passed. No one spoke.

At last, sitting back in his chair, his arms folded across his chest, Tasselbaum turned to meet the Inspector's cool gaze and gave him a name.

CHAPTER 17
SIGHTING THE QUARRY
(January 5, 6 PM)

It was almost six by the time they pulled into the driveway of the Bantry house. They recognized Quinn's Jaguar. Three other vehicles were parked in the large tarmac apron in front.

Markarian brought the car around, so it faced in the opposite direction, pointing toward the street. "Guess they're all here." He turned off the ignition. "My people will be pulling in right about now. I told them to park at the end of the street and come up on foot. They'll bring the cars up later." The two men reviewed briefly the strategy they had worked out for the meeting, earlier, after Tasselbaum had signed a lengthy statement and had been given directions to the Bantry residence. He had also been given instructions of another kind. "Ready?"

"Any time you are."

The weather continued to be unseasonably warm, but McCalley still carried his coat, "just in case." He also brought into the house a heavy black plastic bag.

In the now familiar living room they found, in addition to their hostess, Jill Masterson, Glasner, and Quinn, Henry Wentworth as well, and, already in place, Paul Tasselbaum and his assistant, George Leffert.

"What's this about, Inspector?" Quinn asked affably "Are you playing Poirot, today?" Someone laughed.

"Bad casting," answered the Inspector, tapping with a finger his mop of red hair.

After greeting the new arrivals, Jenny Bantry had sat down next to Quinn. The others had already found seats. Only Glasner chose to remain standing. He had taken his place behind Jill Masterson's chair.

All eyes watched McCalley, as he rested the bag

319

between his chair and Markarian's, who sat next to him.

"You said it was urgent, Inspector," said Jenny Bantry.

He nodded to her then turned to the others. "Lieutenant Markarian and I have news we want to share with you. First, and I'm sorry about it, but we have no choice, the first thing we want you all to know is that the New York police have reopened the investigation into Mr. Bantry's death."

Jenny Bantry had grown very pale.

"Why?" she whispered, "what are you saying?"

"There is strong evidence that your husband may have been targeted."

"Someone wanted him killed?"

"We can't be sure, but it's a very real possibility."

"But that's ridiculous! Ellis didn't have an enemy in the world!" Jill Masterson exclaimed. She started to rise, as though to go to her friend's side, but from behind, where he was standing, Glasner put out a restraining hand on her shoulder. She turned to look up at him, momentarily disoriented, then sat back in her chair. Glasner whispered something in her ear.

"We discovered yesterday, in Mr. Bantry's papers, a page torn from a museum catalog, showing the ring, the aquamarine ring that came to you by courier, Mrs. Bantry," the Inspector went on. "Mr. Wentworth also found a recent police circular listing stolen goods. The ring was on it. The description matched the description in the catalog. You knew about that circular, about the ring, is that correct, Mr. Tasselbaum? You mentioned showing it to Mr. Bantry, when he came to see you on November eleventh and asked you to get it for him."

"And I told him it was not for sale, that it was museum property."

"And you showed him that very page in the museum catalog, you said. At the time you had no idea the ring had been stolen. Then, on the twentieth-ninth of December, that very ring was delivered to Mr. Bantry by courier. And Mrs. Bantry, of course, accepted the package."

"Are you saying my husband stole the ring?" Jenny Bantry cried, jumping out of her chair and glaring down at the Inspector. "Ellis was not a thief! You have a case to solve, I understand that. But surely not at the expense of Ellis's reputation!"

This time Jill did reach out to her friend. "I'm sure there's an explanation, Jen." She turned to the Inspector, tried to read the expression on his face. It remained calm, inscrutable.

With an impatient gesture, Jenny Bantry shook off her friend's arm, and went on, in a rush of words, her voice threatening to break:

"My husband may have been asking about that ring, although God knows why — he knew I don't care for rings, don't wear much jewelry — but if it did come into his possession, rest assured it was by perfectly honest means! Hart? Say something. How can you sit there and listen to this! You too Jenny" — she looked from one to the other — "you both knew him, trusted him. Would he ever have done such a thing?"

"Please, sit down, Mrs. Bantry," McCalley broke in, "Allow me to go on, please." Jill helped her friend back to her seat then turned to McCalley, her arms crossed over her breast, her body rigidly defiant:

"I'm sorry, Inspector, but you're absolutely wrong about this. Ellis would never have handled stolen goods. Never!"

"There, you see!? Jenny Bantry cried out. She turned where she sat, to face Quinn. "You too, Hart!" Then back to McCalley: "Hart can tell you, Hart got to know my husband well, worked with him, was his lawyer, served as his Best Man when we were married, became his Executor. He knows everything about Ellis. Hart can tell you how

321

scrupulous my husband was! Tell them, Hart!"

"I'm sure the Inspector has more to say, Jenny. Why don't we let him finish?" Then, to McCalley: "There is more, isn't there, Inspector?"

The words had an unexpected effect on Mrs. Bantry, who turned to Quinn and burst out: "I don't want to hear any more! I want them out, Hart! I want them out of this house. This minute!"

"Calm down, Jenny," Quinn said, reaching for her hand. She brushed it off impatiently. Wentworth, who had been fidgeting nervously, now spoke up.

"I tell you, Inspector, your accusation is totally unfounded. I've never known a more honest, kind, generous human being than Ellis Bantry."

"But I haven't accused Mr Bantry of anything." McCalley said, in his even-tempered voice. They all looked at him as though they had been caught in some awful gaffe.

Jenny Bantry said: "You just accused my husband of being a thief!"

"I simply reported certain facts. May I go on?"

The room grew still. Jenny Bantry, flustered, brushed back her hair and closed her eyes, her face still flushed. Glasner remained standing behind Jill Masterson's chair.

At McCalley's request, Quinn repeated how Henry Wentworth had found the torn page from the catalog and had handed it to him, for him to glance at it before it was thrown out; how he, Quinn, had recognized or thought he recognized the ring he'd seen on Jenny's hand the night he took her to dinner; how he and Henry had grown suspicious and had pulled out the list of stolen goods and found in it the description of the ring — ending with: "I'm sure Jenny's is a copy, Inspector."

Jill Masterson rose and walked a few steps as though to release the tension inside her, then came back and stopped in front of Quinn and said, in a voice she could barely control: "It *has* to be a copy! Ellis would never have accepted stolen goods! Never! There has to be some other explanation."

"I'm not an expert on rings," replied the lawyer, spreading his hands in a gesture that said, 'Spare me!' Then, nodding toward McCalley: "Let's hear what else the Inspector has to say."

"You seem to have a great deal of papers and ledgers to go through still," McCalley began again, turning to Quinn. "How much longer will it take?"

"I don't know. We're doing the best we can."

"Have you found anything else that might seem, well, suspicious?"

"No, nothing. Just that one page. We were about to throw it away, as I told you, except that I remembered seeing the ring, or one very much like it, on Jenny's finger."

"Did she tell you how it had come to her?"

"I didn't ask."

It was Jenny Bantry who explained. "He admired it. I told him it was a gift from Ellis . . . . "

"But you didn't tell him about the courier delivering it? That there was no receipt, no return address?"

"Should I have?"

He turned again to Quinn: "Weren't you at all curious about how it had come to her, almost a month after her husband's death?"

"No. I assumed she'd had it for a while. Jenny doesn't wear much jewelry."

"You made no comment about it?"

"As Jenny just explained, Inspector, I admired it and she told me it was a gift from Ellis."

"Well, I can tell you, the ring is genuine. It's the original all right. And it is definitely museum property. The Curator" — here he gave a well-known name — "claimed it last night. Experts have examined it, others will be back in the morning to look at it again, but there seems to be little

323

doubt about its authenticity."

"It may have been stolen, but not by Ellis!" Jenny Bantry shot out. Quinn whispered something to her. McCalley went on.

"What else did you and Mrs. Bantry talk about at dinner that night, Mr. Quinn" — here he consulted his notes — "the night of the twenty-ninth?"

Hartley rose, his hands in his pockets, moved a short distance away, then came back to stand in front of the Inspector, as the rest watched. His lips twitched as he tried to suppress a smile. "Chit-chat, Inspector. This and that. What does one talk about over dinner? And, in any case, what business is it of yours?"

McCalley studied his nails. Jenny looked from Quinn back to the Inspector, then volunteered:

"I told him about talking with Jill, Inspector. About the murder at the museum. I told him about wanting to sell the house."

"And what did he say to that?"

"He said I should wait a while before making that kind of decision."

"And what did he say about the murder?"

"He said it was better than P. D. James."

McCalley turned back to the lawyer. "Whatever prompted you to say that, Mr. Quinn?"

"Oh, are you a mystery fan?" replied the other, with a toss of his handsome head. He sat down again and crossed his legs. "From what Jenny told me Jill had told her, you seemed bent on finding a connection between a murder in Ottawa and the accidental shooting of my friend, here in New York. You were even coming down to pursue that crazy notion. You have a fondness for intricate scenarios."

"I suppose in a way I do deal in mysteries," replied the other. "But I did not come to New York to pursue any connection of the kind you mentioned. That connection

324

surfaced very recently, as a result of an investigation into certain shipments coming out of Ottawa, destined for New York."

As though responding to some internal cue, Jenny Bantry asked:

"You said the case had been reopened, Inspector. My husband's case. I need to know why."

The painful uncertainty in those hazel eyes spurred McCalley to say: "I want to dispel even the slightest suggestion that your husband is guilty of anything, Mrs. Bantry. Except, curiosity maybe."

His words brought everyone's attention to focus again on him with renewed interest.

"You said he was targeted — "

"— *May* have been targeted. . . ." He gave her a reassuring smile. "Yes, well, I'm coming to that." They all watched as he consulted his notes. When he straightened up, there was a grim determination in his craggy face. His eyes took in his audience. With a small nod, he began:

"I'm glad you could all be here this afternoon," he said, shifting in his chair, as though alerting them to the major event. "First, I will tell you that Mr. Bantry was never interested in a Victorian ring. He knew nothing about the ring we have been talking about, the ring delivered to you by courier, Mrs. Bantry. That was not the reason for his visits to you, Mr. Tasselbaum."

The dealer looked properly indignant. ""Oh, you're sure about that, are you?"

"Yes, yes I am." In the stunned silence that followed, the Inspector crossed his arms and stared back at Tasselbaum. "Mr. Bantry came to you about something entirely different. But we'll get back to that in a moment. First, I'd like to clear up something you brought up, Dr. Masterson, in one of our earlier conversations. You seemed to have made some kind of connection, not a clear one, I'll admit, but something about the driver of the van that almost ran into the tour bus at the museum came back to you the next day, when you saw a man in the museum gift shop. He seemed familiar, you told me, but you couldn't explain why. That was the same day you took a short walk and was almost hit by a van that skidded in your direction as you crossed the street in front of the hotel. Is that correct, so far?"

"That's about it, Inspector," said Jill Masterson. "I still can't help you any more than that."

"Perhaps you can. But let's leave that for the moment."

"Mr. Tasselbaum, you said you spent the holidays skiing in Vermont? Are you sure about that?"

"What do you mean? Of course, I'm sure!"

"We have a problem, then. You see, you were positively identified as having been in Ottawa during that same time."

Impulsively, too late to restrain himself — or so it seemed — Paul Tasselbaum glanced at Hartley Quinn. McCalley took no notice, went right on. "You told us, when we stopped by this morning, that you never met Mr. Quinn. Is that true?"

"That's what I said, yes."

"But is it true?"

Quinn leaped out of his chair and pointed an accusing finger at McCalley. "This is harassment, Inspector! I'm not Mr. Tasselbaum's lawyer, but I would strongly urge him not to answer any more of your provocative and leading questions!"

During this exchange, as though at some signal, Markarian had picked up the plastic bag McCalley had brought with them into the house and quietly left the room. Nobody seemed to miss him.

McCalley turned to Quinn: "Do you know this gentleman, Mr. Quinn? It's a simple question and will dispel some confusion that has arisen."

"I don't know him, no. That's not to say I haven't run into him, at some place or other."

"Parties, you mean? Social occasions?"

"Whatever."

"And you yourself, are you sure you also were skiing over the holidays?"

Turning his back to the others, Quinn heaved a huge sigh and gazed at the ceiling. From where she sat, Jenny Bantry edged forward and reached out to touch him. "You said yourself, Hart, the Inspector has to ask these questions."

He turned to her, his face an angry mask. "He's fishing. I don't have to listen or answer!"

He made as though to leave, stopped abruptly when Markarian re-entered the room. No one had noticed his brief absence, but now all eyes fixed on him. He had put on a beautifully tailored coat and a most unusual beaver hat. It had a high crown and a slender wired brim.

Mrs. Bantry stood transfixed. Jill Masterson gave a small gasp. Quinn said, in a raspy voice: "Where did you get those?"

"From your closet, Mr. Quinn. We went to your apartment this morning, You had already left for the office."

"You broke into my apartment?!"

"Come, come, Mr. Quinn, we both know how it works. All perfectly legal."

"We'll see about that!"

Jenny Bantry had walked the few steps to where Markarian was still standing, just inside the room. She stared in fascination at the hat. She put out a hand and touched it gently. "Ellis had it made to his specifications." She turned where she stood, frowning. "What are you trying to prove, Inspector?"

"You recognize your husband's beaver hat?"

"Of course I recognize it. There isn't another like it anywhere."

"Are you sure?"

"Yes, I'm sure."

"Then how did it get into Mr. Quinn's closet?"

"I gave it to Hart, soon after the funeral. He had always admired it."

"I see."

"Why did you bring these things here?"

McCalley didn't answer. They all watched as Markarian moved into the room and went to stand by the tall elegant windows, his back to the others. McCalley's eyes were on Jill Masterson. When he spoke, it was not in answer to Mrs. Bantry's question.

"You told us, Dr. Masterson, that the two vehicles were very close at one point, that your bus had to swerve to avoid impact with the van. Is that right?" He knew the answer, having reread that very morning, before leaving the hotel, the depositions and statements any number of times.

Not taking her eyes off Markarian's back, she replied, in a small voice. "Yes."

"Something nagged at you later, something about the driver, although, as you said, he was all bundled up, even his face partly covered by a scarf." When the other remained silent, he went on. "The incident in the hotel shop triggered a similar reaction. And there too the man was all bundled up. There you saw only his back. You never did see his face, did you?"

"No, I didn't," replied the other, turning where she stood. "But, you're right. It was the same feeling on both occasions."

"You thought you recognized the man?"

"Yes. In the hotel, I thought it might be a colleague, since a number of people I know come to the convention every year. I didn't linger over it."

"But I very much doubt that the driver of the van was a colleague, yet he too had seemed familiar."

"Yes."

"The nagging sensation that you knew the man was the same, on both occasions?'

"I know it sounds strange, but . . . yes."

"And just now, what happened just now? You had that same feeling?"

"Yes, yes, it all came back to me!"

"What came back, Dr. Masterson?"

"The hat! The beaver hat! It's exactly like —" She turned, took a few steps toward the little group, stopped, glanced back at Markarian, all color drained from her face. She turned to Jenny. "It *is* Ellis's, isn't it! He wore it that first winter I knew him. Before you went abroad —"

"I thought I'd told you, Jill; I gave it to Hart right after the funeral . . . ."

Markarian now took off the hat and coat and returned them to the plastic bag. McCalley waited until his colleague was seated once again, before resuming.

"This morning, when I phoned — and I apologize again for the early hour, Mrs. Bantry, but things are moving fast and we have to cover a great deal of ground quickly — I asked if your husband had brought a hat with him on his trip to Los Angeles. You told me he had: a beaver hat, made expressly for him by —" here he broke off to glance at his notes and read off the name of a prestigious outfitter of men's outerwear. "We were able to confirm that the hat was one of a kind. They never made another hat like it."

Hartley Quinn pointed to the bag and said with a little laugh: "Is that your case, Inspector? You'll have to do better, I'm afraid. I may have worn that hat in Jill's presence somewhere, but I doubt it very much. This year the weather has been unseasonably warm, I've had no occasion to wear anything heavy, least of all a fur hat! I don't think I've touched the hat since Jenny gave it to me. And I don't think Dr. Masterson is ready to swear under oath that she saw me wearing it on the occasions she spoke of, or that the hat she saw was this very one." The expression on McCalley's face told Quinn he had hit the mark. He looked to Jill for confirmation, but the woman refused to meet his eyes. Jenny Bantry spoke up:

"All this is making me dizzy, Inspector! You seem to have reached some extraordinary conclusions. Hartley wasn't even close to Ottawa when Jill was there. He was skiing in Maine. Came back right after Christmas. Took me to dinner on the Sunday. The twenty-ninth, it was."

Quinn relaxed where he sat. "Would you like to know what we ordered, Inspector?" He watched McCalley write in his little book. No one spoke. When he was finished, McCalley looked up and met the lawyer's sarcastic smile.

"I would much rather know what you were doing in Ottawa between the twenty-second and twenty-seventh of December —"

"I strongly suggest none of you answer any more questions," Quinn went on calmly but no longer smiling. "I'm certainly not going to!"

"Dr. Masterson didn't see your face, Mr. Quinn, but others did. The hotel clerk has positively identified you. The clerk at the desk, the maid who let you into the room, the porter who brought your bags up, yours and Mr. Tasselbaum's, and the cashier in the gift shop saw and remember you, Mr. Quinn. The hat especially. They all seemed fascinated with the beaver hat. They all identified it at once. Two of the other people questioned expressly mentioned the unusual hat you were wearing. The hotel clerk said something to you about being surprised to see such an unusual hat twice, in a short span of time. He has positively identified both you and Ellis Bantry. Mr. Bantry had been there late in November; you, more recently, over the Christmas holidays. The maid and porter who took you to your rooms told us pretty much the same thing. They had never seen such a hat, the same hat twice, on different men within a month's time. Oh, did I mention the car rental clerk? Yes that one too recognized you both from photos we showed him; but he remembers the hat in particular."

Quinn laughed, not fazed in the least. "You're counting on photos for positive IDs?"

"For the time being, yes," replied the other.

Hartley Quinn said to Jenny Bantry: "Could we talk, privately?" He took her arm and started to lead her from the room, drawing her closer as they neared the entry hall. "Jenny, I'm asking you again to go away for a while. Leave them to do whatever has to be done. The story will be all over the TV, the papers. . . .You don't want to be here —"

Jenny Bantry stopped to face him. "But I do, Hart. I do want to be here. I have to know what happened." Quinn tried to ease her out of the room. McCalley moved swiftly to stand in front of them. "Mrs. Bantry!" She stopped, uncertain, but Quinn pulled her forward with him. Markarian rushed past and reached the door first. He stood squarely before it, his eyes fixed on Quinn, all the while. McCalley moved around him and opened the door wide.

Four police officers were standing outside. "There are more down the road," said Markarian, taking Mrs. Bantry's arm and pulling her away from Quinn. The others had all come into the hall and stood watching.

"Nowhere to go, Quinn," said the Inspector.

Quinn laughed. "Sorry, Jenny. Can't even have a chat with a friend, with these fellows hanging around."

"Hart, tell me it's not true, what they said back there."

"But of course, Jenny. You yourself gave me the hat."

"That you were in Ottawa. And that Ellis had gone there before you. I thought he went to Los Angeles."

Quinn said, almost flippantly: "Oh, well, "I'm sure the Inspector will fill you in."

"Was the ring stolen, Hart? Tell me that, at least!"

331

"Ask the Inspector, or the Lieutenant. They're dying to share their crazy theories!"

She shook off Markarian's restraining arm and faced Quinn. Incomprehension, expectancy, and wonder held her rooted to the spot. Quinn put on a clown face, spread his hands in a gesture of helplessness. "Sweet Jenny. You could have been spared all this . . . ."

Jenny Bantry put her hand to her mouth, her face drained of color, her eyes wide with shock. She turned, almost fell as she stumbled back into the room. Jill rushed after her. In the stillness that followed, no one moved. Markarian finally broke the silence. "We've got lots more questions for you, Counselor."

"What about *him*?" asked Quinn, gesturing toward Tasselbaum, who stood nearby.

"Oh, he's already told us a great deal. He was going to call his lawyer but then decided to talk with us, instead."

Quinn's eyes narrowed as he looked at the other man, as though assessing him for the first time. He recovered quickly. "Ah, you think I'm his lawyer? Even with all the money he's taken in, he couldn't afford me," he replied with a brazen smile.

"And all the money *you've* taken in was never enough for you!" Tasselbaum spat out angrily. "Always pushing for more, to put on a show you couldn't afford!"

"I admire your confidence, Paul, but it doesn't suit you. You're still the fool you've always been."

"Not as much a fool as you've turned out to be," was the smug reply. He was obviously enjoying his moment of triumph over the man who had always given the orders. "All your great investments, your gambling, those friends of yours who were always willing to help you out in return for your legal services. Raking it in and losing it the next minute. Living from day to day. All that show, your own law firm, ha! Using your friend's name all the time he was away, to transfer the goods here. You really thought no one could

332

touch you! All the while waiting for the big prize! All of this —" with a wide sweep that encompassed the entire house "— and the lovely lady herself! You were counting the days! But even without her, as Bantry's Executor, you suddenly became a millionaire several times over — what's the percentage you're entitled to? — and as his Trustee you would be drawing additional millions every year. It was worth killing Bantry just for that, wasn't it? The other business was peanuts, by comparison!"

A smug, self-satisfied expression lighted up his face. He seemed inordinately pleased with himself. Watching Quinn struggle with his demons seemed to give him immense pleasure.

"Well, my dear Hartley, Paul Tasselbaum has taken all that away. Didn't think it would happen, did you? No one could take it from you! Well, *I* have! That's right, I'm the one who has brought you down, Counselor!!" The man's face had turned ugly. "Oh, yes! They know all about the morning of the fifth, . . . all about the mob friends you enlisted to do your dirty work, the way you got everybody off, all that and much else!"

Quinn face had frozen in a tight smile. Suddenly the mask fell, revealing an almost feral expression. His eyes blazed with anger and frustration, his mouth twisted into an ugly sneer. Before anyone could restrain him, he had leaped forward with his arm already stretched out. His fist landed hard on Tasselbaum's nose. They all heard it crack.

Tasselbaum gave a yelp of pain.

"Bastard!" he shouted. "You weren't even going to represent me!"

Officers came forward and took hold of Quinn. He didn't resist; his eyes were fixed on Tasselbaum.

"You really trust them? It'll cost you, mark my words! And I'm not talking about money!" He turned to McCalley standing in the doorway. "Are you arresting me?"

"At the moment, just restraining you, Counselor.

We all saw you strike Mr. Tasselbaum. And I believe he wants to press charges?"

Tasselbaum nodded with exaggerated emphasis.

"I most certainly do!" he said, examining the blood-stained handkerchief in his hand. The nose and surrounding areas were already beginning to puff up.

The lawyer burst out laughing. His face assumed an air of arrogance as he turned to McCalley: "I like your style, Inspector, especially your sense of humor. . . . Are you really taking me in on an assault charge?"

"Not I," said the Inspector.

Markarian came forward, handcuffed the lawyer, recited the charges against him, and read him his rights. He and McCalley watched as detectives eased Quinn into one of the police cars that had driven up and were waiting in front of the house.

"I think he broke it," said Tasselbaum, nursing his nose.

"Could have been worse," said Markarian, as he led him out the door.

NOT QUITE THE END

After the initial shock of Inspector McCalley's startling resolution of the Canadian murders and Lieutenant Markarian's final closure of her husband's murder case, Jenny Bantry emerged with new energy and aspirations.

Since her recent ordeal, she and Jill Masterson had grown (if at all possible) closer, surer in their bond. With a decisiveness that surprised even her old friend, long before the trials were due to begin, Jenny had put the mansion on the market, had supervised an estate sale of most of what was in it, had bought an apartment in a new condominium near Lincoln Center and furnished it with simple essentials that dramatized the spectacular view from the floor-to-ceiling windows — lower Manhattan on the south and the Hudson on the west side. The kitchen was small but functional; the large living room uncluttered, with two small sofas, some chairs, and a dining table against an inside wall; the bedroom had only a Dux bed and two long chests of drawers across one entire wall. There were no curtains or drapes to obstruct the view. What wall space remained glowed with rich paintings, chosen carefully from what had graced the mansion. The apartment was high enough to be virtually isolated in the midst of other tall buildings. No one could look in. A wide balcony, extending along the south side was an added bonus. Jenny moved in as soon as the bedroom furniture was in place. She hooked up her computer in a small dressing room she had converted into a work space, and resumed her writing. "It's Jenny at her best," Jill had confided to Jack Glasner, after their first visit there. Jenny had prepared a simple meal for the three of them and they had toasted the occasion with champagne Jack had brought.

Jill and Gasner were now an "item," in spite of many heated discussions, which at times made Jenny nervous. Except for their constant bickering about renaissance history and literary criticism, they seemed to get along as though they had known one another for years and had learned to tolerate what each considered the other's flaws. Jill spoke her mind; Jack gave back in kind, often with a wry humor that thawed any resentments that might have been provoked. Their sparring was like fencing matches. They both seemed to thrive on it but respected the rules that prevented full-scale confrontations. Somehow their differences never got in the way of their personal feelings for one another.

Lieutenant Markarian not only received high commendations for solving the Bantry murder but, in the wake of Slattery's announcement that he would retire in the Fall, was promoted to Captain, in anticipation of the new job he would have, when Slattery left.

Back in Ottawa, Inspector McCalley was properly honored and also raised a notch in rank. To celebrate, he took Susan to Quebec, for a brief week-end break. The Tiffany pin was "ahhed" and "oooohed" many times; the box it came in, admired just as enthusiastically. McCalley was sorry at first that he hadn't bought her the larger, more expensive pin, but after a while he concluded, from Susan's evident delight in the one he had picked for her, that his choice had been the right one.

On McCalley's recommendation, Sergeant William Kenney received a substantial raise, promotion, and a framed citation, which his wife immediately hung in the small entrance foyer, where guests taking off or putting on coats could not possibly miss it. Bill himself was pleased by it all, but he didn't dare tell his wife that things could have been even better, had he agreed to move out of the section headed by McCalley to work in the district superintendent's office. He didn't hesitate for a minute over the choice. There would be plenty of other opportunities, he knew. Right now, he still had a lot to learn, and McCalley was the best teacher he could hope for. The Inspector had found out about the offer and knew that Bill had turned it down, but neither one of them spoke about it openly. It was, after all, Bill's decision; but McCalley was secretly pleased. The detailed report the Inspector had submitted would find its way into Kenney's file and would serve him well, later on. Kenney himself never regretted his choice.

To everyone's surprise. McCalley admitted, when it was all over, that they had had lots of lucky breaks. An even greater surprise was Kenney's defense of his boss for not giving in to idle speculation. "A cool head, that one," he'd say over a beer at the pub, when asked what it was like working with Inspector McCalley, "has a real knack." Those listening would nod in agreement. He was, after all, the expert on the man.

Besides, he had in hand the ultimate proof of the complexities of McCalley's mind, had recovered it from the wastepaper basket, where the Inspector had trashed the jottings that had survived the trip home. It was a single sheet of paper on which were drawn the most intricate lines, all flowing together into a central core, a rather attractive design. Kenney had not seen this one in the making — it had been done while McCalley was still in New York, when the cases finally came together in a dramatic climax, with a number of arrests, including those of a notorious mob boss, a prominent lawyer, and a well-known antiques dealer — nor did he try to figure out how it had helped to solve the case; but he knew instinctively that it was the Inspector's way of unraveling the knots, of finding a pattern in the disparate parts. When, back in Ottawa, McCalley had cleaned out his briefcase, Kenney had quickly retrieved the crumpled sheet from the wastepaper basket, smoothed out the wrinkles as best he could, and on the way home stopped at his friend Jimmy Nottingale's shop, to leave it for framing.

"What is this?" his friend had asked, holding at

arm's length the sheet of paper covered with wiggly lines.

"McCalley's doodles. That's how he solved the murders."

"Are you sure you want this framed?"

"Right."

Jimmy tried to dissuade him again when Kenney insisted on a top-of-the line silver frame, black matting, and non-glare glass.

"You want to spend that kind of money for this wrinkled sheet of paper?"

But Kenney was adamant. "Be sure to mount it on that special adhesive backing, so it doesn't slip down, once it's under the glass."

"You want I should iron it before mounting?" asked the other, sensing a good story for the pub.

"Can you do that?" said Kenney, without blinking an eye. "Here," he said, handing Jimmy a sticker he had carefully typed. "Put this at the top, in the center of the matting." Jimmy read the first two lines out loud:

"The Jenene-Dobie-Bantry Case
Solved by Inspector Luke McCalley."

Another sticker was for the bottom. It gave the dates of the trials and the convictions meted out to the major players: three consecutive life sentences without possibility of parole for Hartley Quinn, a short term in jail for Paul Tasselbaum, who had appeared as chief witness for the prosecution. Wisely, Kenney had decided not to detract from the two major defendants in the case and made no mention of certain mob figures, also found guilty and convicted on a number of assorted charges.

The framed memento was hung inside the tiny alcove that had been closed off to serve as his den, where Bill could sit at his desk and study the strange design at leisure. In time, he might even discover what it meant.

On the stand, Tasselbaum told how he had met Quinn through mutual friends, how they had gone skiing together a number of times, met for dinner occasionally; how Quinn often visited the shop, had even made some purchases; finally, how the lawyer had approached him with the idea of using top-of-the-line specimens to hide contraband and how they had pulled it off without incident for the three years Bantry was away. In all, they had brought sixteen specimens from Canada to New York, ostensibly on long-term museum loans. Bantry was listed as the importer for the specimens; Tasselbaum provided the point of delivery for the importer. Quinn, the mastermind, had cleverly covered his tracks all along the way: his name did not appear on any of the documents; arrangements for the trips to Canada — hotel accommodations, car rentals, plane reservations — were all in Paul Tasselbaum's name. Best of all, Bantry was abroad and would never get wind of what was going on; but should questions arise, he was the most likely suspect: a clever thief, who left others to accept specimens coming to him from Ottawa. But who would ever stumble on anything that might arouse suspicion? Still, in the unlikely event that anything went wrong, Bantry would emerge as the prime suspect. His death had further simplified matters: he could never be questioned. . . .

Neither he nor Quinn could ever have imagined that Jenene would make copies of the transfer documents. Some originals had to be left with Customs, each time; the rest of the papers had been burned, with the specimens, once Quinn was done with them.

Jenene's murder put a glitch in the works.

He had to be killed, of course; but his body wasn't meant to be discovered until much later, in his car, a victim of an accident caused by the blizzard.

No, Tasselbaum insisted, he knew nothing about Dobie's death, except that Quinn had told him that he too, like Jenene, had grown greedy and was now a threat.

They had served well, those two. Dobie had found them the best animals (for three or four times what any museum would pay for them); Jenene, for amounts in five figures, had processed them and provided the paperwork on museum stationery. Under Tasselbaum's watchful eye, he also worked the contraband inside the specimens.

No, Jenene never was told what went inside the specimens. He'd take the small sealed packets Tasselbaum brought him and (following instructions) would drill them into the metal rods. Tasselbaum was at his side, watching, until the job was done.

No, Quinn had never gone with Tasselbaum to pick up specimens and pay the two men. He'd always waited for Tasselbaum back at the hotel. Only this last time had he gone along — "to tie up loose ends," he'd said to Tasselbaum.

No, he didn't see Quinn strangle Jenene, nor had he any idea that Dobie had been shot or when, exactly.

The operation was to end with Bantry's return to the States: Quinn had been adamant about that. In fact, he had been working on an alternate plan long before Bantry got back. Things might have continued smoothly, if Bantry hadn't started asking questions. It soon became clear that somehow he had learned of their activities. The decision was made to kill him; and, "to play it safe," kill Jenene (and the trapper too, as it turned out), who had been asking for more money.

With the decision to kill Bantry, Tasselbaum went on to explain, Quinn lost interest in any alternate plan. He convinced his "friends" that it was impossible to continue. The real reason, Tasselbaum took obvious delight in telling the court, while trying to hide his envious resentment, was that Bantry's death would make Quinn, Bantry's Executor and Trustee, a multimillionaire for life. He could indulge his expensive life style without any more worries.

When asked, Tasselbaum admitted that it was Quinn's idea to send one of his "friends" to sign in for Tasselbaum at the ski lodge in Vermont. "To cover his own

340

tracks," the dealer had insisted, with obvious hostility.

He had also explained how the aquamarine ring was part of a carefully planned job that had netted a number of rare pieces of jewelry, worth several millions, the ring among them. The theft was unrelated to the smuggling, except that Quinn was brought into it, to serve, as usual, as "legal counsel" for his "friends," should he be needed. The "friends" had devised the ingenious plan of the bold entry after hours, deactivating the alarm systems, taking only those pieces destined for certain clients and "a few other items to pay for expenses," and enlisting the help of certain museum officials to insure that all went well. Among Quinn's share of the booty was a sum in cash and several pieces, including the ring. When things started to unravel, Quinn made arrangements for the ring to be delivered to Ellis Bantry in such a way as to raise suspicion. He made sure that it would also be recognized as one of the stolen pieces, briefing Tasselbaum as to what he should say. The untraceable ring delivered to Bantry's door, and his name on Jenene's documents should have made Bantry the obvious and only suspect. It could easily have ended that way; Bantry's visits to Tasselbaum's shop made to appear as efforts to locate the ring and thus strengthen the notion that Bantry was involved in illegal activities.

Yes, of course Tasselbaum knew what went inside the specimens. How could he not know? He was a partner.

Not drugs, no. One of Quinn's powerful "friends" had approached the lawyer with a proposition to smuggle out of Canada, from time to time, an extremely rare and important metal called palladium. His "friend" had plenty of clients ready to pay a fortune for any small amount they could get. There was big money in it for everybody.

Quinn had done research of his own and was convinced that it was the opportunity of a lifetime — the metal was so precious that it was weighed in ounces. Knowing he would need help in carrying out the plan, and realizing that Tasselbaum (and the antiques shop) would serve his purpose, Quinn recruited him (for a certain percentage).

He had shared with Tasselbaum the research he'd done on palladium. Sixty-seven percent of the world supply was found in Russia, twenty-four percent in South Africa, only eight percent in North America, Canada mostly — and the supply was fast declining. At a melting point of 1,554 degrees Celsius and for its other qualities, it was described as "the precious metal of the twenty-first century." It was used in manufacturing, electronics technology, dentistry, jewelry, photography, as a catalyst for exhaust emissions, but most important, for certain experiments in cold fusion energy. But what made palladium an excellent "investment" (Quinn had told him), were government controls. Rumor had it that the precious metal was being kept a closely guarded secret by those countries where it was found, that it impacted directly on national security. As a result, its export was carefully regulated. Those who found ways to acquire it, by whatever means, and who succeeded in smuggling it out of the country, could name their own price.

No, Tasselbaum had never risked asking how Quinn's "friend" was able to get the precious metal. Once in Ottawa, Quinn would receive instructions and drive alone to pick up the packets. Tasselbaum never was invited to accompany him.

When questioned, Tasselbaum admitted that their sources might indeed have dried up in time, but that it was Bantry's learning about the wolf that forced Quinn to end the operation abruptly.

High point of the trial was Tasselbaum's fingering Quinn as Jenene's murderer, his description of how Quinn went back, after chloroforming the taxidermist, to finish the job. He told them about Quinn's dreaming up the gang shootout, with the help of his "friends," how he helped to work out the legal angles ahead of time, the improbable

342

scenario that let all the teenagers off the hook.

The last set of prints in Dobie's Jeep were never identified, but other things found in the vehicle proved worthy evidence, especially traces of fibers that matched the beaver hat Quinn had worn and the empty coffee containers that yielded DNA samples placing Quinn inside the Jeep with Dobie. The gun used to kill the trapper, a Safari Browning Automatic found a short distance from where the Jeep was discovered, had been bought in Ottawa by Tasselbaum, on Quinn's instructions, right after they arrived; but the dealer had never seen it again after turning it over to the lawyer.

According to plan (following Quinn's instructions) Tasselbaum phoned Bantry on his return to New York and asked him to come to the shop that Thursday morning on the pretext of wanting to tell him about certain decisions with regard to the shipments. Not suspecting what was in store for him, Bantry agreed. The dealer insisted that Bantry never knew of Quinn's involvement, although at one point he may have begun to suspect it. . . .

In the end, everyone agreed that it would have been a much weaker case, if Tasselbaum had not testified. His detailed account insured Quinn's conviction on two counts of murder and smuggling charges, in Canada; in New York, he was found guilty of murder, grand larceny, illegal activities, consorting with known criminals, and other assorted charges. Tasselbaum, as prime witness for the prosecution, won a much-reduced sentence with the possibility of parole after a few years.

In spite of certain pressures from private and other interests, McCalley was able to keep the arctic wolf in careful custody all through the several trials. Its ultimate fate would be decided in the courts.

The ring was eventually returned to the museum from which it had been stolen. The other items were never found.

343

The source of the palladium was never discovered, but the most credible explanation focused on certain thefts from a number of government facilities, where the metal was kept. Canadian officials had started an investigation "under wraps," making sure no information leaked to the press. No government official was available for comment.

The "friend" who had first approached Quinn with the smuggling idea was not to be found for questioning.

Tasselbaum admitted to having stashed away large sums in the Caymans and in Geneva. Quinn's finances showed huge debts to maintain a life-style far beyond means that were constantly being depleted by an expensive gambling habit, a love of expensive things, and general reckless spending. He seemed to have survived the obvious consequences of his excesses by providing on-going expert legal services to certain mob figures and poker buddies.

The media had a great time reporting on wolves, the Bantry estate, museums, taxidermy, even academic conventions and, that constant favorite, "the mob."

Jenny Bantry was not present for the trials; her depositions were enough. The Renaissance art book was completed and in the publisher's hands by the time the trials ended. She and Jill Masterson were planning to celebrate with a river cruise through the French wine country in the Fall.

Jack Glasner was due for a six-month sabbatical. He and Jill were planning to visit San Francisco late in July, then Ashland and the Oregon Shakespeare Festival for about a week, followed by a short trip into the Yukon early in August to see where Robert Savage had lived and written his well-known ballads. They were even thinking of visiting Ottawa again, on their way back, to see McCalley and take the museum tour they had missed.

Jack was also considering postponing work on his new book in order to join the two young women on their cruise into the French wine country, early in September.

344